Miljenko Jergović

Mama Leone

Translated from the Croatian by David Williams

archipelago books

First published as *Mama Leone* by Zoro in 1999.

Archipelago Books
232 3rd Street #A111
Brooklyn, NY 11215
www.archipelagobooks.org

Library of Congress Cataloging-in-Publication Data
Jergovic, Miljenko, 1966–
[Mama Leone. English]
Mama Leone / Miljenko Jergovic ; translated from the Croatian by David Williams.
– 1st Archipelago Books ed.
p. cm.
ISBN 978-1-935744-32-0 (pbk.)
I. Title.
PG1620.2.E74A2 2012
891.82354—dc23   2012030029

Distributed by Consortium Book Sales and Distribution
www.cbsd.com

Cover art: Paul Klee

The publication of *Mama Leone* was made possible with support from Lannan
Foundation; the National Endowment for the Arts; the New York State Council on
the Arts, a state agency; and the New York City Department of Cultural Affairs.

The translator wishes to thank Marina Čižmešija for her peppy linguistic assistance.

Contents

When I Was Born a Dog Started Barking
in the Hall of the Maternity Ward

You're the angel

When I was born a dog started barking in the hall of the maternity ward. Dr. Srećko ripped the mask from his face, tore out of the delivery suite, and said *to hell with the country where kids are born at the pound!* I still didn't understand at that point, so I filled my lungs with a deep breath and for the first time in my life confronted a paradox: though I didn't have others to compare it to, the world where I'd appeared was terrifying, but something forced me to breathe, to bind myself to it in a way I never managed to bind myself to any woman. Recounting the event later, first to my mother, and then my father, and as soon as I grew up, to friends, they brushed me off, said I was making stuff up, that I couldn't have remembered anything, that there was no way I could've started drawing ontological conclusions the first time I cried.

At first I was pissed they thought me a liar, and I wasn't above spilling a few bitter tears, hitting myself in the head, and yelling *you'll be sorry when I'm dead!* With the passing of years I calmed down, having figured that this world, of which I already knew a little and could compare with my experience and my dreams, was predicated on mistrust and the peculiar human tendency to think you a total idiot whenever you told the truth and take you seriously the second you started lying. This aside, relatively early on, when I was about five or six, I came to the conclusion that everything connected with death was a downer and so decided to shelve my threats of dying, at least until I solved the problem of God's existence. God was important as a possible witness; he'd be there to confirm my final mortal experience and he could vouch for me that I hadn't lied about the one in the delivery suite.

Does God exist? I asked my grandma Olga Rejc, because of anyone I met in those first six years of my life, she seemed most trustworthy. *For some people he does, for others he doesn't,* she replied calmly, like it was no big deal, like it was something you only talked about all casual and indifferent. *Does he exist for us?* It was most diplomatic formulation I could manage. The thing was, I'd already noticed how my family placed exceptional value on my socialization efforts and loved me talking about stuff in the first-person plural: *when are we having lunch, when are we going out, when are we coming down with the flu . . .* at least at the outset I thought questions of faith would be best set in this context. *For me, God doesn't exist,* she said, *I can't speak for you though.* It was then

I learned about truths you only spoke for yourself and in your own name. I was pretty okay with all this, though less than thrilled I hadn't been able to resolve the God question off the bat.

Ten years later I still wasn't straight with God, but I'd figured the moment Grandma decided he didn't exist. It was early spring, everyone was out somewhere and I'd stayed back at home alone. As usual I started rummaging through their wardrobes. I never knew what I was looking for but always found something, something linked to the family, Mom and Dad, Grandma and Grandpa, something they'd tried to hide from me from some reason. Their private histories were so dark, or at least they thought them so, and my investigative spirit so very much alive, that after a few months' work on their biographies I knew way more from my secret sources than they ever told or admitted to me in the rest of my life put together. My starter's curiosity soon turned into an obsession, and then into a mania. I'd be disappointed if I didn't turn up something juicy or dirty. I wanted proof my father was a homosexual, my mother an ex-tram driver, Grandpa a spy or at least a gambler who'd lost half of Sarajevo in a game of Preference. I loved them all, you have to believe me, but even more I loved the little testimonies of things they'd wanted to hush up so they'd make it into heaven – if only in the eyes of their son and grandson.

But that was the day I discovered the false bottom in the big bedroom wardrobe. I lifted up the base and found a carved wooden box, a round glass container, and a green folder full of documents. I laid everything out on the rug, heaved a sigh, and opened the box. It was full of dirt. Regular brown dirt with little stones and blades of long-dried grass that disintegrated to the touch. *They won't be planting flowers in this dirt*, I thought, and then, not without some trepidation, sunk my fingers into the box to explore. But there was nothing there, just pebbles, grass, and all this dirt. You wouldn't believe the amount of dirt that can fit in a wooden box. Much more than you'd think. You want to picture what I'm talking about, then tomorrow grab a cardboard box – I mean, I doubt you've a wooden one at hand – go to the park, and fill it up with dirt. You won't believe your eyes!

I moved on to the glass container. It held a pocket watch, a ring (it was too big for my ring finger, I tried it on), this miniature metal figurine of some saint, a tie pin, and a little booklet by Anton Aškerc, printed in Slovenian, the pages the thinnest I've ever seen. The only other things were these two green army buttons with spread-winged eagles, which gave me the heebie-jeebies because I had the feeling I'd seen them somewhere before.

Before opening the folder I stopped to think of all the stuff you're not supposed to know about in life. I wondered about the secrets that have to stay secret so the world makes some kind of sense, but since I couldn't remember any, I decided to push on. The folder contained three bits of paper. A birth certificate in the name of M.R., a baptism certificate in the name of M.R., and a telegram that read: "We hereby inform you that private M.R. perished in battle against a Partisan band on September 10."

M.R. was my uncle. I knew he died in the war, and I knew he wasn't a Partisan, but I'd never dreamed that he was the enemy.

I put everything back in its place and closed the wardrobe. Closing it, I knew nothing in my life would ever be the same as before I discovered the false bottom. I also knew my investigations into the family were over. Now it was time for asking questions, but only of those who questions wouldn't hurt and who could answer them without leaving a bloody trail in their wake.

I waited for days for my chance, but it never came. Grandma almost never left the house, and when she did Mom wasn't there, and Mom was the only one I could ask. She didn't know her brother. She was born four months before he died, and although he never saw her, he gave her her name. Grandpa had wanted to call her Regina, but M. wanted his sister named after a tree native to Bosnia. The tree's native to other countries too, but we didn't care about other countries because they were just places Grandpa, Uncle, my father, and everyone else went to war.

I went to see Mom at work. *Can we have half an hour alone?* She frowned, and I could already tell what she was thinking: *he's going to admit he's a druggie, he's got some girl pregnant, he got his fourteenth F in math, he's a homosexual . . .* I wagged my index finger left-right, though we hadn't yet said a word. I sat down. *Everything's fine, just give me a second.* But Mom just got more wound up. I had to get it out before she jumped out the window and broke her leg. Me: *I opened the wardrobe.* Mom: *It had to happen sometime.* Me: *I found something.* Mom: *What?* Me:

Everything. Mom: *Even the dirt?* Me: *From the grave, right?* Mom: *Please, just one thing. Don't ever tell her.* Me: *I know. I came to you.*

The part of the story that follows I learned back then, from my mom, and it goes something like this. When he finished high school, the same one I'd attend fifty years later, my uncle got the draft. Because he spoke perfect German and had a German grandfather, they put him in a unit formally part of the Wehrmacht but made up of our people. They sent them to Slavonia in Croatia. My grandpa combed the city in a blind panic, badgering one acquaintance after another in one office after another, just trying to get his son out of the army. But of all his connections, only a Communist one proved any good. A friend, a manager in the railways and member of the resistance, told him how it could be arranged for M. to desert his unit and be taken in by Bosnian Partisans a couple of kilometers from his base. Grandpa was all for the idea, but when he relayed it to Grandma, she got scared. For a start she thought in his German uniform the Partisans would shoot her son on sight, and even if they didn't, he'd be sure to lose his head in a Partisan one. More to the point, she was of the view that he was safer being the enemy. Grandpa tried to persuade her, but it did no good. He hollered so loud the whole apartment shook, desperate because he himself wasn't sure what was best, but also because he was certain how it all might end, who had justice on their side, and who would win the war. Mom of course had no idea what all Grandpa's hollering was about, but I'm sure he hollered the exact same thing when I was just a boy and he told me the story of the Second World War: *Hitler's an idiot. That's what I said right back in 1939. Idiots lose wars, but they kill more people than you could ever imagine. And then that trash Pavelić came along. He sent our kids to Stalingrad and turned them into criminals. He created a shitty little state dangling out a big Kraut ass. That was Pavelić for you, and I knew that from the get-go, but that knowledge doesn't help you any, because it won't save your neck.* I think that was also about the gist of what he yelled at Grandma in the fall of 1971, when he again made the house shake and went as red in the face as the Party flag, and his lips went blue and Mom went up to him and shook him by the shoulders and said *Dad, calm down, calm down . . .* But he wouldn't calm down, he just went on, hollering about Maks Luburić, who cooked people in boiling water and in March 1945 skinned Grandpa's railwayman friend alive in the house of horror in Skenderija. Then Mom started crying, imploring *Daddy, sweetheart, please stop, for God's sake, I beg of you . . .* Suddenly he calmed down, not for God's sake, but because of her tears. He put a funny face on and said *let us alone you silly woman, can't you see we're talking about men's stuff.* Then he turned to me and whispered *politics isn't for women. They just start bawling. Golda Meir is the exception.* Back then I didn't know Grandpa had tricked me, that he'd actually told me another story, not the one I thought he was telling me. Mom didn't bawl like other women when politics came up. That I know from when I found the box.

Anyway, when Grandpa was done yelling at Grandma, having failed to convince her to go along with the Partisan plan, which she steadfastly rejected, Grandpa started living months of his own private hell. He'd wake at night, bathed in sweat, with a single recurring thought: that M. wasn't coming home, and that if he did, the sum of Pavelić's and Hitler's crimes would be on his conscience. Grandma was only worried about one thing: that her son stayed alive, the how was no matter. It was in those months she started praying to God.

How they took the news of Uncle's death, whether they cried, yelled, screamed, or just absorbed it in silence, I'll never know. A few months after the liberation of Sarajevo four young guys in Partisan uniforms showed up on their doorstep. Grandma cried, Grandpa held his face in his hands to keep it from crumbling like a ceramic mask. One of the young guys put his hand on Grandma's shoulder and said *don't cry, madam. You've got another child. Look at your little girl. M. talked about his baby sister every day.* My mom, a blond baroque angel, sat on her potty in the corner.

Seven days after my uncle's death, the unit in which he'd been stationed deserted in its entirety and went over to the Partisans. To that point M. had been their only casualty. At war's end three more lay dead. But they were no longer the enemy.

Grandpa and Grandma lived together for a full thirty years after the death of their son, never speaking of him. They held their silence in front of others and probably held it between themselves. Don't expect me to be so banal as to say I know Grandma blamed herself for her son's death. She never once set foot in a church again, she forgot Christmas and Easter, and only once a year did Grandpa put on his best suit and head to Sarajevo Cathedral for midnight mass. He didn't have much of an ear, but he liked singing the songs heralding the birth of the eternal child.

Grandma didn't decide that God doesn't exist, more that he just had nothing to do with her. She stopped believing in him even if he did exist. Grandpa died in 1972, and Grandma began her dying in the early spring of 1986. She had throat cancer and it got harder and harder for her to breathe. Sometimes she'd call me by M.'s name. They were little slips and I didn't call her on them. Or maybe they weren't little slips at all. By that time I was her only surviving son.

At the beginning of June, an ambulance came and took her to the hospital to die. They cut her throat open, but she still couldn't breathe. She fixed her gaze straight ahead and set her hands together. I smiled like it was all no big thing and that she'd be better tomorrow. But I knew exactly what was going down. Death came slyly and unfairly. It grabbed my grandma by the throat and shook everything left out of her. What was left was the memory of her son. She died during the night of the fifth of June.

Like all old folk, she'd talked about her funeral while still in good health. Under no circumstances whatsoever did she want her photograph to appear in her obituary, over her dead body. But she didn't mention anything about a priest. No one had asked of course. That would have been stupid.

Over her dead body, we got a priest and paid for a memorial service.

I can't explain why to you. Maybe so that God, if he exists, smartens up his act. That's how a friend of Grandma's put it.

I never even visited her grave come All Saints' Day. I can't tell you why. I just didn't ever feel like it. I was sorry she'd died, particularly in such a terrible way; I guess I thought visiting the grave would be to honor such a death. A few days before this most recent war, my friend Ahmed's father died. On my way back from the janazah, instead of heading for the exit gate I decided to take a walk over to the Catholic plots. On the tombstone under which my grandpa and grandma were buried, a huge black dog lay sprawled out in the sun. I sat down beside him, and he lifted his head lazily, looking at me with half-closed eyes. I'd long since stopped caring that no one had believed my first insight and first memory, the one of a dog barking in the hall of the maternity ward the moment before I let out my first scream. *You're the angel, aren't you?* He wagged his tail on the marble a couple of times and sunk back into sleep. My hand followed him.

How I started shouting in my sleep

Through the summer and fall Grandpa recited his last words and got ready to die. To Isak Sokolovski, his Preference partner, he said *I know every card and that's why I'm leaving.* He spun his hat on his index finger, cleared his throat for the last time in Isak's life, and left. To Grandma he said *you sleep, I'm fine. I've been fine for some time now.* She was sleepless until the day he died. To Mom he said *there's no one left. Just the two of us and the darkness.* And then he died. Mom closed his eyes and wrote the words down on a box of laxatives. I was at the seaside at the time, with my auntie Lola, Grandma's sister. I marked the date in the calendar with a little cross. So people would know my grandpa had died. Actually, no, I did it so they'd know I knew my grandpa was dead.

That day Auntie Lola baked some cakes, put a plateful in front of me, sat down across from me, and placing her elbows on the table said *eat up, little man*. I ate, scared she was going to tell me Grandpa had died. I didn't know how I was supposed to react. Was I supposed to stop eating cakes, burst into tears, ask how he died, shake my head, and say *tsk-tsk-tsk* like I saw Granny Matija from Punta doing the time I peeked out from the pantry, or was I supposed to do something else, something I didn't even know about. I'm only six years old and don't have any experience with the rituals of death. I ate a plateful of cakes and got a tummy ache. I climbed into bed, the blinds were down so it looked like it was dark. I flew a plane through the darkness. I didn't do the *brmm brmm brmm* because the plane was supersonic so you couldn't hear it, but eavesdropped on what Auntie Lola told the neighbors gathered in the kitchen with their gifts of coffee, bottles of rakia, and something else I couldn't see. *The good Signore Fran suffered so, may God rest his soul*, said Ante Pudin. *He's at peace now, but who knows what awaits the rest of us*, said Uncle Kruno, a retired admiral. *The little one might as well be an orphan now; parents today, God save us. Whatever he learned, he learned from his grandpa*, said Auntie Lola. My tummy still hurt. I shut my eyes tight, farted, and fell asleep.

Seven days later, Mom and Grandma arrived from Sarajevo, head to toe in black. I pretended this was normal. They pretended it was too. I was scared Mom was going to start talking about it so kept out of her way. I knew Grandma wouldn't say anything. She wasn't one for start- ing conversation; she'd leave it up to me and then join in. It was like she kept quiet about things I didn't want to talk or hear about. There was nothing to say about Grandpa's death, just as there's nothing to say about anyone's death. I had no idea death was a widespread occurrence, that grown-ups talked about it all the time.

Between thunderclaps of his rasping asthmatic cough, Grandpa would every morning repeat *sweet, sweet death* and Grandma would say *zip it Franjo, I'll go before you do*, and so it went every day. I thought other people didn't go on like this, just the two of them, that they were special people because they were my grandma and grandpa, and that everyone else was just a puppet in a puppet theater. When Grandpa died it turned out Grandma was a pretender. I thought she should be ashamed of herself because she'd done something bad. She'd said she would go before him, but now he was dead. You don't really die of your own choosing, but it does have something to do with you, so you shouldn't say you're going to die before someone else if you're not. Later on I forgot about Grandma's shame. Probably because it didn't seem like she was ashamed.

Once we went to visit Auntie Mina in Dubrovnik. Mom said *I don't know if the little fella knows.* I was playing with the garden gnomes and making like I didn't hear anything. Auntie Mina looked at me in silence. She would've loved to ask me if I knew about my grandpa's death, but didn't dare. You don't ask kids those kinds of questions. *The poor old boy peed his soul out,* Mom told Auntie Mina. *The hospital botched the treatment plan. They shouldn't have given him the laxatives. His heart turned into* a rag, into an old scrap of a rag for washing the floor. The gnome gave me the evil eye. I felt lost in this terrifying world. So it is, fairy tales don't lie after all: my grandpa died without a heart, in its place was a dirty, ugly, smelly square rag like the one we kept next to the toilet seat. I wanted to howl for the horror of it all, but couldn't.

From that day on, whenever I'd go pee, I was scared I was going to pee my soul out. I watched the jet stream, white or yellow, or really yellow when I was sick. I didn't know what a soul looked like, but I was sure I'd recognize it if it whizzed out. Days went by and it still didn't show. Then months. I asked Grandma what a soul looked like. She said a soul doesn't look like anything, that it was just a word for something you couldn't see. *Can you poop your soul out?* I asked, trying to find out what I wanted to know, but trying to hide where all this was coming from, to avoid admitting I knew Grandpa was dead and any opportunity for her to mention it. *What do you mean can you poop your soul out?* she asked, nonplussed. *I mean, when you poop your soul out and die, so you don't exist anymore,* I said like it was common knowledge and highly unusual that she didn't know anything about it. *You mean, can someone die on the toilet? I think you can, but people don't usually die there . . . Where do people usually die? . . . In bed or traffic accidents, or they die in war or earthquakes . . . And the soul, what happens to the soul? . . . Nothing, the soul disappears . . . How can something that exists disappear? . . . Just like jam, it gets used up and disappears . . . Does the soul disappear inside you or go outside and then disappear? . . . Where would it go, it doesn't have anywhere to go, it's not like a dog being let out. It disappears, ceases to exist, end of story . . . So all in all, you can't poop your soul out? . . . Not a chance, I don't know where you got that idea from.*

This set my mind at ease some. I peed fearlessly and didn't bother looking at the whiz anymore. If you can't poop your soul out then you can't pee it out either. Mom had been talking nonsense to Auntie Mina.

Six months after Grandpa's death, Grandma and Mom suddenly stopped wearing black. It was a Sunday, Uncle and Dad had come over. The table was set with a fancy white tablecloth, like it was someone's birthday or someone was getting married. *Today we remember Grandpa,* Uncle said. I pretended this was normal, like I didn't remember him every day. Maybe I lie when I play Ustashas and Partisans by myself because I'm not a Ustasha or a Partisan and because one person can't be two people at the same time, but they lie worse when they remember Grandpa today, getting out the special plates, cutlery, and glasses, walking around the house in their ties, not taking off their shoes when they come in, doing all the things they never otherwise do and lying that they don't remember him every day. How could they not remember him when he was here all the time, when it was just recently and they haven't forgotten anything, and his umbrella is still there by the coatrack. I was scared of their lies. The lie is alive, I thought. It swallows things up and makes everything different from what it is.

First we'll have a teeny-weeny bit of soup, said Mom. She always talked like that when she remembered I was there. When she forgot, then she'd cuss and talk all serious. *And then we'll have the suckling. I got it from Pale, it's not even five months old*, said Dad. I looked at Grandma. She sat there smoking quietly. Uncle was talking about dam-building in Siberia.

My heart started pounding like crazy. Everyone sat there polite as pie reminiscing about Grandpa and waiting for it to arrive – the thing Dad got from Pale. The suckling must have done something really bad, otherwise it wouldn't have ended up in the oven. I thought we were going to eat a baby and I was sure we weren't eating it because it was tasty or because it was customary for people to eat a baby in memory of a dead grandpa but because they were warning me what would happen if I were naughty.

I was sweating some as I ate my soup and couldn't hear what they were talking about anymore. I was completely alone, my heart beating inside my ears, wanting to get out. When Mom cleared the soup plates and said *now for the delicacy*, I shut my eyes. I tried to take deep breaths, but something caught, and it was like I was sobbing.

I looked up and saw a big round silver platter stacked with slices of roast meat. Dad grabbed a fork, dug it into the biggest bit, and put it on Uncle's plate. He gave a smaller piece to Grandma, then a bit to Mom, and then he fixed his eyes on me. *Gosh, you're pale. More blueberry juice, more beetroot, and more meat for you.* That's what he said putting a bit of the infant's flesh on my plate.

He didn't live with us. Mom and Dad were separated, but he'd come visit once a week or whenever I'd get the flu, bronchitis, a cold, measles, tonsillitis, angina, diarrhea, or rubella. He'd place his stethoscope on my back and say *deep breath, now hold it*, and I'd take a deep breath or not breathe at all. I assumed Mom and Dad didn't love each other, but I would have never figured Dad bringing dead babies over for Mom to roast. Today was actually a first, the day we were all supposed to remember my dead grandpa.

I ate the meat, but couldn't taste the flavor. When Grandma said *eat the salad*, I thought I was going to cry, but I didn't because I was too scared. That night I shouted in my sleep for the first time. When I woke up, Grandma was stroking my forehead. But it wasn't her anymore, it wasn't her hand, and it wasn't my forehead, and I was no longer me. Nothing in my life was ever the same after the day we ate that suckling. For a while I hoped Grandpa wouldn't have let us eat babies, but later I realized that it didn't have anything to do with him, that it was just a custom, that people scare naughty children with this one everywhere, because really naughty children end up in the oven.

I never mentioned Grandpa's death, not even after I accidentally found out that a suckling was the name for a little pig, and not a baby person. It didn't matter anymore because I'd already started shouting in my sleep, and the shouting continued, the reasons don't matter, and I don't even know what they were anymore.

Girl with a Pearl Earring

Words flowed in cascades, gushing over the edges of the world being born, making laughter, lots of laughter, echoing through all our rooms and the biggest of all, the room under the sky, the one where we're all still ourselves, and so speak words out of joy, words superfluous and with no connection to the world or to the pictures in which we live and which cause us pain. Only words cause no pain, in them there is no sorrow, they take nothing from us, and never leave us on our own in the darkness.

On my first birthday Mom went back to Sarajevo; I stayed behind in Drvenik between Grandma and Grandpa, between stone walls and below high ceilings with spiders crawling along them, hanging by the barest of threads, free as the air, and lying on the bed, completely still, as if bound to the earth, I understood that the difference between me and them, me and the spiders, was one of eternity, and that I would always remain down here, lying on my back gazing up at them, and that nothing, only words, could help me get closer. Someday I'll say that that's where I go, up there, that I hang by a thread like they do, that at night, when Grandpa and Grandma are sound asleep, I live among the spiders and that'll be the truth, they'll be words, everyone believes in words, and it'll be no matter that I'm stuck to the bed and that I'll never be able to jump high enough to stay up with the spiders. In words I could do anything, even before I knew how to say them.

I'm three years old crouching bare-bottomed in the sea shallows in front of our house. Old Uncle Kruno is coming down the street, calling to me *what are you up to Signore Miljenko?* I'm happy about being a *signore*, but I know he's only joking. *I'm catching crabs*, I reply, and Uncle Kruno laughs because he hears something else; he thinks I'm saying *I'm watching wabs*, because I can't say words beginning with *c* properly. He doesn't know I'm just saying that I'm catching crabs, because actually I really am just watching them, I'm scared of their claws, but what I'm saying is the truth. He goes away thinking I'm catching crabs.

Six months later I caught my first crab, his claws were weak and he was really mad and tried to get my finger, but his claws only tickled me. I pulled one off, then the other, but he kept thrashing his legs, not like he was hurt but like he was still really mad. Then I pulled his legs off; he had lots of legs, more than I knew how to count. I left him with just one and put him down on a rock. He wriggled across, but he couldn't walk. I didn't know if he was still mad. I looked for his eyes but couldn't find them, maybe a crab doesn't have eyes; they don't know how to talk, maybe they can't see anything either. I picked up a rock and banged him with it. He splattered everywhere, but he didn't have any blood in him, he was yellow inside. That one crab turned into lots of pieces, but none of them wriggled. Then the waves carried them off somewhere, washing from the rock any trace that a crab had ever been there.

The day Mom came back from Sarajevo I decided to show her the crabs. I'd already told her that I catch them, and she'd just nodded her head and said *yes, yes, that's my boy*, but for her words were something else. Everything she said you had to be able to be see, and she only believed in words when there was a picture to go with them. I didn't like that about her, but then I realized that everyone, really everyone was like Mom, and that only Uncle Kruno believed I was catching crabs if I just told him so. I got a plastic bag and went down to the shore where there were lots of crabs, I caught some and put them in the bag, Mom called me inside, *yeah, just a little bit longer*, but she didn't ask what I was doing, she thought I was playing, and when you play, for her that's like you're doing nothing, she never thought I'd ever catch crabs because she didn't know how to catch them.

I crept back in the house, opened the drawer where the knives and forks were kept, and tipped the crabs in. They were all alive and started crawling over the silverware. It'll be lunchtime soon, Mom will set the table because that's what she always does when she comes back from Sarajevo, here she is, opening the drawer, now Mom's screaming, Mom bursts out crying *Dad, look at this*, Grandpa puts the newspaper down, jumps up from his chair, looks in the drawer, and laughs *your boy was out catching crabs.* Mom looks at me, her eyes are big like the biggest blue Christmas tree decorations; she won't get mad at me, she can see how little I am, but I can do something she can't and that she'll never be able to do, I catch crabs for her, I catch them so she'll believe me and won't think my words are things that don't exist.

Then Mom goes back to Sarajevo again. It's winter, I'm scared of the dark, there's no power, but there are two lights in the room: the brown light of the gas lamp and the blue light of the gas stove. The blue light is like night snow, but actually it's hot. Grandpa lights a cigarette, he's all wrinkly; when he sweats, beads run down his wrinkles, and his face turns into rivers running through a gray-gold land. When he sweats, I can imagine a whole crowd of people building houses on his face, sitting in the dark and sweating like him; on Grandpa's face lives another little grandpa, who also sits in the dark, lights a cigarette, rivers run down his face too, and next to them live even smaller people and even smaller grandpas, and they too sit in the dark, in blue and brown light, next to their grandsons who on their grandpas' faces see crowds of even smaller people and even smaller grandpas. Only we don't live on somebody's face, we live in the big wide world, in which everything is real and terrifying.

The rooms of our house in Drvenik are full of pictures. Most of them were painted by Popa Lisse, my cousin Mladen's grandpa. They're of Drvenik, the same one where we live today, but lots smaller and somehow weird, like you're looking at it with eyes full of tears. The pictures are real, the houses in them are real and so are the people who live in the houses, but you can't see them because they're inside. I'm inside our house in Popa Lisse's paintings too, I'm just lots smaller, weird, and invisible. When I look at them before I go to bed, I always know that come the morning I'll be outside the pictures again and that I'll be looking at the real, big Drvenik. The paintings were only done so that at night we don't forget we're in Drvenik and don't get surprised when we go outside again.

Above the bed where I sleep there's a little picture with my mom in it. *Mama* was my first word, I said it looking up at her face above my head, and when Mama would go to Sarajevo, I'd point at the picture and say *Mama, Mama*, and then it was hard for Grandma because she didn't think it was Mom in the picture but couldn't tell me that because she thought I'd start crying. That's what she told me later, and I thought that was funny. Why would I cry when I know it's Mom in the picture and that nobody else in the whole world looks like that, nobody else's mom, just my mom. She looks down at me from the picture, she's far away and wants to tell me something, but she's so far away that not even a single word can be heard between us, and she'll keep looking at me until she comes back to Drvenik or we go to Sarajevo.

The picture isn't in Sarajevo, only in Drvenik, and I only look at it when Mom's not here. The picture is like a word you whisper in someone's ear, a word no one else in the whole world hears, it exists only between her and me, and others think it doesn't exist; others think it's someone else in the picture, because they don't see the picture with the eyes of the person it was meant for. I lived and grew up in Drvenik without Mom, but she was scared of the dark when I was scared of the dark, she dreamed of a boogeyman when I dreamed of one, she felt everything I felt because she was in the picture and only in the picture was she so pretty and so still.

The summer we went back to Sarajevo for good Grandma and I walked down Tito Street. In a shop window there was a big book with the same picture on it, Mom's picture. Under her head it said Vermeer. We stopped, Grandma didn't say anything, we just waited. I felt a great sorrow welling up inside me, one where tears don't flow from your eyes but jump out like fireflies. I knew what Grandma was thinking: she couldn't tell me when I was one, or three, or five, but here we go, now I'll see for myself. I was pretty blue because she didn't understand anything, for her time passed in a different way, and pictures and words were tied to each other in chains and she thought what I was now seeing would change the picture I'd looked at ever since I'd said the word *Mama* and pointed to her because I still thought there was no difference between what I saw and what those closest to me saw.

That was my mom, I said to Grandma. *Do you want us to buy the book?*

. . . What do we want the book for? . . . For the picture . . . I don't need it, I've got one, my mom's in it. The story about the picture ended that very moment. Nobody ever mentioned it again because it filled the adults around me with a pain I didn't even know about or ever myself feel. They felt guilty about me not having grown up with my mom every single day and they thought I was unhappy because of that, or that as a punishment they would be unhappy. And maybe they really were unhappy, it's just that their unhappiness was no big thing for me because it didn't have anything to do with me, or our lives, but with the fact that their eyes weren't right for the picture. I couldn't understand why at least Mom couldn't recognize herself in it; it was like she'd let some passing angels frame the face above my bed.

I was in my third year of elementary school when for the first time I opened a heavy thick book with *History of Visual Art* written on it. I saw the picture again on page 489, it was called *Girl with a Pearl Earring*, and it said that it was painted in the year 1665. I thought about how big and strange the world was: three hundred and two years before I pointed my finger at the picture and said *Mama*, someone had seen me lying on my back in a dark room watching spiders dawdle along the ceiling, dangling in the air, and they had painted my mom.

I didn't pull the claws off crabs anymore, and I didn't smash their bodies in the shallows; I resigned myself to not knowing anything about them and not being able to see their eyes, I knew they didn't have any blood and that they weren't like me, but another world had already closed shut above my head, one in which every word had an exact meaning and every one of them could frighten and hurt. I didn't see Mom in the picture anymore and I ached for all the dead crabs.

What will Allende's mom say

School began on the sixth of September, the teacher said *fall's here kids, pencils, paper out, down to work.* I looked out the window at the sunny summer day, why fall when it's not fall I thought and started lying: "Trees are stripped of their leaves, rain pours from the clouds, a sleepy dog shuffles at my feet." That was about it. I hadn't the foggiest what the teacher wanted to hear about the fall and what else I could peddle to her. I put my hand up. *Miss, did you bring an umbrella? . . . Excuse me? . . . I was wondering if you brought an umbrella . . . Why do you want to know? Write your essay, time's running out.* I wrote: "The teacher passed by. She didn't have an umbrella because she'd forgotten and left it at home. I said hi and asked: 'Miss, look's like fall's here, don't you think?'" I signed my work and handed it in. The teacher was surprised that I'd finished so soon; actually she didn't act that surprised, more like the

34

essay must be no good. I'm just a second grader and haven't yet figured out how things work at school – the shorter and less descriptive your essay, the lower your score. *Let your imagination run wild, show a little spark, don't just say "fall" – say the soft, sumptuous, auburn fall*, that's what she told me the next day after she gave me a D. *But in my imagination fall's not soft, sumptuous, and auburn, it's fall and that's it*, I protested. That afternoon the telephone rang, the teacher, wanting to speak to my mother and asking her to come to school the next day for a talk. *What've you done?* She frowned like she was going to throttle me, *I didn't do anything, I just said that for me fall wasn't sumptuous and the teacher gave me a D . . . If the teacher says it's sumptuous, then it's sumptuous*, my mother concluded pedagogically. I opened an encyclopedia called *The World Around Us* to the page where there was a picture of the circus: trapeze artists on the trapeze, a lion jumping through a flaming hoop, an elephant standing on its hind legs, and a man in a striped suit with a gigantic mustache holding big black weights above his head. I'd had a bellyful of the fall and the first day of school, I wanted to see a circus. Actually, I didn't want to see a circus, I wanted to join one and perform, as a lion, elephant, or giraffe, and felt so cruelly trapped in my human body. Unfortunately I hadn't read Sartre yet and didn't know anything about existential angst. I only found out what that was all about when I actually didn't have it anymore, because by then I myself had turned into a ball of existential angst, and the fall really was soft, sumptuous, and auburn. Fall for an A plus.

The television news starts at eight, quarter to eight is the cartoon, then the ads, then a watch hand circles the screen for a full three minutes, then a globe dances in rhythm to a symphony and cosmic rolls of thunder, continents float by, the world begins with giant Africa and little Europe, then come the two Americas, the vast silent ocean and Asia, by the symphony's end Africa and Europe are back, and then Mufid Memija's face, his tie in a bulky knot, a piece of paper in hand, the latest from Santiago de Chile, the presidential palace is still holding out, the military junta's forces are advancing, the truck drivers' strike continues, Salvador Allende has sent out a dramatic appeal to all Chileans and the international community . . . *Are we the international community too?* I ask Grandma. *On the one hand we are . . . On which hand aren't we? . . . On the hand you're waving in front of the screen so I can't see anything.*

I got an F in math and immediately decided to keep it quiet. Parent-teacher interviews aren't for another fifteen days. That's how long Mom won't know. I already felt like a prisoner on death row with only fifteen days left to live. Luckily I was only seven, and when you're seven fifteen days seems like fifteen years. A long and slow stretch lay ahead of me; the older I get, the faster the time will go by, it'll speed up like a big intercontinental, intergalactic truck, until it goes so fast I won't be able to catch up, so it'll get way out in front of me and it'll seem the biggest part of my life was back then, when I was seven years old. A quarter of a century later I'll have the experience of a seven-year-old who accidentally fell into a machine for premature aging. Having kept quiet about the first F, I'll keep quiet about all the next ones too, until I get tired and old, until I finish school and Mom ends up getting bored with worrying about my Fs.

I'd come home from school with a secret. I thought they might be able to read the secret F on my face. Mom couldn't, she didn't read what was written on my face, same goes for Dad, he didn't dare read it because he was only here to visit his son, but Grandma, she definitely could have read it, but she doesn't care about my Fs. She's already sitting in front of the television, it's almost eight, she's smoking anxiously, waiting for the news to start. *Chilean President Salvador Allende has been killed in the presidential palace of La Moneda*, says Mufid Memija, *bless his poor mother*, says Grandma. A man with a mustache and a helmet on his head enters the palace.

Augusto Pinochet, says Memija, *fascist pig*, says Grandma, *who's that, I ask, he killed Allende*, says Grandma, *why didn't we defend him? . . . How were we supposed to defend him from Sarajevo? . . . Well, didn't he ask us to? . . . What, who did he ask? . . . Us, on the one hand we're the international community . . . Well, on the hand that we're the international community, on that hand we did defend him, bless his poor mother . . . Who's Salvador Allende's mother? . . . I don't know, poor thing, she's probably not alive . . . Why wouldn't she be alive? . . . She's better off not alive if they killed her son . . . And what if they'd killed her, would it be better if he wasn't alive? . . . No, that's different. Sons should outlive their mothers.* I looked at my mom. She wasn't paying the news any mind. She was sitting at the kitchen table and eating beans. She's just got back from work, and when Mom comes home from work she usually eats beans or she has a migraine, and will skip the beans, go to her room, pull the blinds, and lie down and groan so we can all hear.

Why was Salvador Allende killed? I ask her. She puts the spoon in the bowl, leans her elbows on the table, and rests her head in her hands: *because fascists killed him.* It is, of course, all clear to me, when fascists kill, you don't ask why they kill; she looks at me, somehow full of pride, she's young, and in those years young mothers were happy when their sons asked about Salvador Allende. Death didn't give me the creeps then; death still had a certain allure, still just a scratch on the face of the earth. Fall was just a scratch too, soft, sumptuous, and auburn. I didn't know anything about beckoning death, and I wasn't superstitious either, so I didn't know you shouldn't mention death too often and invite it in, but in any case I still didn't ask Mom whether she was going to die before I did or if she'd watch pictures on television from La Moneda Palace, like Allende's mom. That's if Allende's mom was still alive of course, and I'm sure she must be when Grandma's been dreading it so much. Everything she ever dreaded always happened.

Saturday came around, Mom was vacuuming the house and I was playing with a plastic pistol. I don't know who I was playing war against, probably against Pinochet. Mom bent down and tried to vacuum the dust under the couch. I went up to her, pressed the pistol on her temple, and pulled the trigger. She dropped the vacuum cleaner hose, stood ramrod straight, her face in horror. I thought she was going to hit me, she didn't, tears were streaming down her face, she ran out of the living room yelling *Mom, Mom.* Grandma was sitting on the terrace reading the newspaper. I knew I'd done something terrible, but that I wasn't going to get a hiding. I slunk into the hallway, tiptoed to the terrace door, and peeked out. Mom was sobbing convulsively, her head in Grandma's lap, Grandma was caressing her and saying *it's all right, it'll be all right, calm down, it's nothing . . . How is it nothing, I gave birth to a monster.* I went back to the living room, opened the encyclopedia to the page with the circus, but I didn't see anything. It was hard for me to look at anything. If I'm a monster, something scary is going to happen.

Why did you do it? Grandma asked me. Mom was at work so we were alone. *Because of Allende's mom . . . What's Allende's mom got to do with your mother, why did you shoot her? . . . I was just playing . . . What were you playing? . . . Chile . . . You were playing Chile and shot your mother? . . . I was Allende . . . Allende didn't shoot his mother, for God's sake!* I'd never seen Grandma like this, she was deadly serious, but not angry, just really sad. *You said it would be better if Allende's mom weren't alive,* I was already messy with tears. *I said that, but Miljenko . . . Well if you said it, what did I do wrong, I was just playing Allende and just wanted his mom not to be alive.* I'd never been so inconsolable. *Don't cry, Allende was good and would never have killed his mom . . . Why not if it's better she weren't alive.* I didn't even notice that Grandma was getting more and more upset with every sentence. *Sons never kill their mothers, ever, not even when it's better, because it's never better when sons kill their mothers and now give Allende a rest, play something else, play Partisans and Germans, kill them if you want to kill someone, but don't you ever shoot your mother again.*

By the afternoon everything was fine. Mom had forgotten I'd shot her and was quietly eating her beans. I'd quit playing Allende and was waiting for the evening news on television, for news from Santiago de Chile. At some soccer stadium Pinochet had cut a guitarist's fingers off, a friend of Allende's, and it was then I swore I'd never play guitar.

On the fifteenth day, just before Mom was going to find out about my F in math, the teacher brought a new pupil into the classroom. *This is Ricardo*, she said, *he doesn't speak our language, but he'll learn.* Small and dark, Ricardo sat in the back row, his hair so dark you'd almost think it was blue. *Ricardo is from Chile*, the teacher filled us in when it was homeroom, *but now he's from Sarajevo too, and so I ask that you treat him like he's always been from Sarajevo.* I didn't understand what she meant, though I figured it must be something really serious. Before Ricardo learns our language I'm going to learn how to treat people who've always been from Sarajevo. It was very important to me. Because of Salvador Allende and because of his mom. I'm going to ask Ricardo if Allende's mom is still alive, if she is then we'll play La Moneda Palace, Pinochet will try and kill Allende again, but Ricardo and me will save him. The main thing is that I hear what Allende's mom says when they try to kill her son again.

No *schlafen*

In the mornings someone eats our dreams, gulping them down and swallowing up the little creature of darkness, the little creature of dawn, the hours that disappear in sleep or in preparation for death, a time sure to come and to leave nothing behind, neither an object nor a memory, not a single trace of a path on which I might light out like the brave prince who heads into the forest in search of something lost that might save the kingdom. In the moments before waking the little creature of darkness slips from the head, the heart, and the room, hurriedly departing this world, always sloppy and running a bit late, always forgetting something, leaving something behind, and this something is what I remember in the morning. I keep it as my dream stolen from the darkness, from the slinky creature just departed. Sometimes I see his little black foot slipping out my bedroom door, see him dragging a little suitcase covered in stickers saying Amsterdam, Berlin, Novosibirsk, and Sarajevo . . . Sarajevo, the precious Sarajevo of my dreams, a gigantic city, the most gigantic in the world because it's the only one I know, because I'm just four years old, and because last night's dreams are in that little suitcase, heading off into another world. But they'll be there to meet me one day, up in the sky, a sky that doesn't exist. They'll be there to meet me, a me who will no longer be, in a room like this one, furnished only with these dreams, the only trace of me.

I don't like sleeping. I fight sleep with all my might, but all my might isn't yet all that much. Grandma pulls me to her chest and says *c'mon, time for schlafen*, and I yell so that the whole house, the whole street, and the whole gigantic city can hear – *no schlafen, no schlafen.* She pays me no mind but carries me to my room and lies me down in bed, even though I'm still howling *no schlafen.* I can't hear what she's saying anymore, she's betrayed me, she doesn't get it. She thinks I don't know anything, that my tears are just a little boy's tears and that what I'm saying is just an overtired grizzle. Grandma doesn't know anything about the terror that sneaks out when she puts me under the covers. I'm asleep before she's even tucked me in, and then I'm alone, sinking down into a world not mine, where my loneliness is the biggest in the world. It won't mean a thing when one day you leave me; you can leave me now, whenever you like, I'll just shrug my shoulders, because nowhere will I be so alone, nor will any world be as distant as when I am alone in that strange world of dreams. I dream of things I know nothing about, I dream of horrors and terrifying ghosts, of fears that will some day run me down. I dream everything I'll ever live to see. One day I'll see a man lose his head in the middle of the street and then I'll say, hey, I dreamed that when *no schlafen, no schlafen, no schlafen* ricocheted all over this very city. I dream every night and in my dreams try to let out a scream, so that someone might hear me, so that someone might come get me and take me outside, but I don't let out a sound. I'm as quiet as the grave probably is, my grave or someone else's, it doesn't matter. I keep quiet and dream away until morning, until the moment I start to forget and wake up. Then Grandma looks at me, and I smile at her, as if it were nothing, as if nothing terrifying had happened. She says *blessed are the children, they forget everything, children don't remember a thing*, and she really believes it and thinks I've just forgotten my dreams and woken up all smiley.

Grandma's going to Russia. Why aren't I going? I'm not going because I'm still little. It's stupid to take little kids on such a long trip, it's not worth the effort. I'm not going because I'd just forget everything I saw. That's what Mom and Grandma say. I sit in the corner sulking, playing with my little model Volkswagen Bug and promising myself that I'm going to remember all this. One day I really will drive a gray Bug like this one, in the real world and on real streets, but I can't know this yet. I'm four years old and I don't know anything about my future because the future hasn't happened yet. One day when I'm on a real road driving a real Bug it'll be hard to figure what has actually happened. Have I grown up or just shrunk so much that now I can fit into the little car I was playing with the day Grandma was going to Russia and I was blue thinking *I have to remember, I have to remember, I have to remember* . . . Because if I don't remember, then she'll never take me anywhere with her, I'll never go to Russia and I'll never see myself in fancy photos from overseas.

Let's go to sleep, said Mom. I open my mouth, wanting to say something. I want to yell *no schlafen* but I can't because she didn't say it right, she didn't say *time for schlafen*, and that's the deal, they're the magic words that make me yell. Now I just button up, my mouth half open, a look of horror on my face, no longer registering a thing. She puts me to bed, kisses my cheek, says *good night*, and leaves. I can't close my eyes because I know that if I close them I'll stay this way forever, and I'll never again fight against sleep, I'll get weak and helpless and believe there are battles lost in advance and wars unworthy of tears.

When Grandma was in Russia my dreams weren't scary. They were just sad. Little wooden boats sailed through them, all the fishermen wearing straw hats like my grandpa. The tiny boats sailed and sank, and as they sank, the old men on board didn't lift a finger, they vanished from the surface as if there were no difference between the world above and the world below, as if nothing really mattered in the vast salty ocean of my dream, the water salty like the salt of my tears when I lick them from my hand, keeping an eye out that no one sees because if they see me licking my tears they'll know I'm done with my sulking.

When Grandma was away I woke up without a smile. Mom noticed and was downhearted. For her it was proof enough that I loved Grandma more than her because, you know, I smiled to Grandma in the morning. God, my mom was so immature and silly. One day she'll say to me *if only I were twenty-eight and knew what I know now*, but I won't say anything to her because I don't want to hurt her, but I could tell her what I'm now telling you: *Mom, you're stupid – stupid, stupid, stupid – you just needed to say c'mon, time for schlafen, time for schlafen, and I would've smiled to you in the morning too, and it would've never crossed your mind that I loved you any less.*

Grandma came back from Russia with a dead fox around her neck. The fox had glass eyes and a plastic snout. Poor little fox. The next time Grandma told me I wasn't allowed to kill ants because they're someone's children I asked her *is the fox someone's child too*, but she never replied. She was cooking lunch and couldn't answer absolutely every question, but the questions she didn't answer because she was cooking lunch were always the most interesting ones. *Russia is gigantic*, she said, *gigantic and cold*, and from her bag took a wooden doll inside which there was a smaller wooden doll, inside which there was a smaller doll, inside which there was a smaller doll, until a sixth wooden doll you couldn't open came out. But I was sure there must have been a wooden doll inside her too because I couldn't see any reason why there wouldn't be. Then one by one I had to put the dolls back inside each other, and when I was done Grandma put them on a bedside cabinet as an ornament so we could forget about them and one day put them in a cardboard box and store them in the attic. When people die, they're put in graves; when things die, they're put in the attic. One day things go from the attic to the city garbage dump, but that usually only happens after the people who put them in the attic are put in their graves. At four I only know about the start of this long journey. I know about people in graves and things in attics.

Grandma put me to bed again. She said *c'mon, time for schlafen, let's go,* and I yelled *no schlafen,* and she said *you haven't changed at all, I thought you'd be big boy when I came back from Russia.* She wanted to sound mad, my grandma, but she was actually just sad. I'll never be as big as she wants me to be and I'll never tell her what was going on back then, and I won't tell her everything I remember either, that I haven't forgotten a thing and that she should have taken me to Russia with her, I'll never get to any of that because Grandma will die and go in the grave, and when she goes we'll clean up the apartment, and the attic too.

I had terrifying dreams again that night, and I wanted to yell but couldn't, because as always the little creature of darkness popped up from somewhere and took my dreams away before I woke up, but this time he left something behind. It was a dream of a scary black man who in the distance, from the top of our street, was coming toward me with a big black dog. In my dream I thought *look, it's the boogey-man, he's going to hurt me or make me disappear, but look, a big black dog's coming and he's going to gobble up the big black man, but then an even bigger black man's going to show up with another big black dog and the dog's going to gobble up the bigger black man after he has hurt me or made me disappear.* I woke up smiling.

That day we went to Drvenik, where Grandpa was waiting for us. He gave Grandma a kiss. He didn't usually do that. He kissed her because she'd just got back from Russia. I learned that people kiss each other when they come back from a big trip or if they haven't seen each other in ages. While I was in Sarajevo and Grandma in Russia, Grandpa had made a new friend. He told us about him on the way home. The story went that Grandpa was walking to Zaostrog and wanted to sit down on a bench because he was tired, but his friend-to-be was already sitting on the bench. Grandpa asked politely if he could sit down, but his friend-to-be didn't understand. So Grandpa asked him the same thing in German, and his friend-to-be answered and that's how they met. His name is Ralph, an American who has a big German shepherd. Grandpa thinks Ralph is a spy, but Grandpa doesn't care. *We all have to work, all that matters is that we do our work well.* Ralph's in Makarska at the moment, but he's coming to visit this afternoon.

Around four o'clock a big black man arrives, leading a big black dog. He offers me his hand, shaking my hand seriously as if I were an adult and as if he knew I like it when people shake my hand like I'm an adult. Then I make for the dog, but Grandpa says *wait!* so I stop. Ralph goes up to the dog, whispers something in the dog's ear, and waves me over. The dog's name is Donna. I sit down in front of Donna, put my hand on her forehead, and say *Donna, you're an American boy . . . Donna's a girl*. Grandpa corrects me . . . *Donna, you're the first American girl I've ever met and I love you.* Everybody laughs. Grandma translates what I said into German for Ralph. Ralph laughs like a giant out of a fairy tale *ahahahaha . . . ahahahaha . . . ahahahaha.* Donna looks at me, her snout resting on the kitchen tiles, her eyes blinking, and I know she knows and understands why I love her. She remembers my dream because I remember it too. She was in my dream, but she hadn't been sleeping, so the little creature of darkness couldn't steal me from her memory. Donna gobbles up scary black men, that I know. But why would she gobble up Ralph, he's Grandpa's friend. He's black, but he's not scary. Then I was sure that Grandpa was right. Ralph isn't a scary black man. Ralph is a spy.

The next day we went with Ralph and Donna to Dubrovnik. We drove in his Cadillac, which if you saw it from a distance looked like it was made out of silver, but it wasn't, it was metal like all the other cars. *The Cadillac glides like a ship*, Grandma told Auntie Lola when we got to Dubrovnik. I was sitting under the dining table and Donna was lying in front of me. We kept quiet. She because dogs don't talk, and me because at that moment I was the prince from the beginning of the story, the master of an endless kingdom and there wasn't anything that wasn't mine. I sat and waited for Donna to do something, to creep into my dreams and make me their master. For a long time I thought Donna had cheated me that day, because she didn't do anything.

Ralph and Donna came the next year too, and then Ralph started sending postcards from all over the world, from distant cities and islands none of us had ever heard of. He sent his greetings to Grandpa and Grandma and never forgot to mention that Miljenko's American girlfriend says hi too.

When we hadn't received a postcard for more than six months Grandma asked *what's Ralph up to? He hasn't been in touch for ages.* Grandpa just shrugged and sighed. Another six months went by and again Grandma asked the same question. After four stretches of six months went by Grandpa said *who knows, maybe Ralph died. He was all alone in the world, he probably died in some hotel somewhere.* Then I wondered what had happened to Donna and for a long time I hoped she'd show up again somewhere, my American girlfriend, at least in my dreams. I think I'll always think that. When one day I see people losing their heads in the middle of the street, then I'll know that only Donna had saved me from these kinds of dreams.

The kid never panics

It's June already, my birthday was seven days ago, and yesterday I discovered the world of split shadows. It was like this. We arrived in Drvenik, Grandma and me, and as soon as we got there she said *go on, go and play*, and I knew why she so was quick to get rid of me. She wanted to pick up the phone, ring Dad in Sarajevo or my uncle, Mom's brother, or someone else she could have a serious talk with, someone as worried as we were, because the day after my birthday Mom had gone to Ljubljana for an operation. Dad said *it's nothing serious*, but two sharp lines creased Mom's face, two crevices between her eyes. She said *you never know, it could get bigger*. Dad said *and that's why you're going to Ljubljana, to be on the safe side and so that it doesn't get bigger*. Grandma asked *well, what is it exactly*, and Dad said *nothing, just a tiny bump on the cervix*. I sat under the table pretending I was building a Lego castle for Queen Forgetful, but I actually wasn't building anything, I was eavesdropping and trying to understand what was going on. But I didn't understand anything. Instead, a vast freezing emptiness swelled in my chest, right there under the bones where we breathe, where the heart beats. I didn't know what it was. It wasn't a space holding old fears or guilt at something I'd done, but something strange and new, something I couldn't figure out because there just wasn't anything there. But I felt it swell, pressing against my bones, this vast freezing emptiness, dissolving into dead air, into a shadow hovering over my heart and the grown-up hearts of Grandma, Mom, and Dad, my heart that now shares terrifying and serious things with others. Bump is a nice little word, like tummy and mommy, but it means something terrible. Words like this didn't exist before. Before this bump everything little was harmless and sweet, tiny to the eye and pretty to look at, but this had all changed. It changed the day after my birthday when I was eavesdropping on Grandma, Mom, and Dad. The time of little things and their goodness had come to an end. From now on the world would no longer hide in diminutives, no longer reside in their little lost paradises, in Lego cottages or on tiny ottomans upon which the dreams of secret princesses lay scattered.

Grandma's on the phone now. I thought it over as I traipsed past the stone Dalmatian houses. I wasn't just walking, I was stamping, really getting into it. I wanted to stamp right over the top of whatever was lodged in my head. Mom had gone far away, all the way to Ljubljana, and she was in the hospital, having an operation. *You go to the hospital to get well, not to get sick*, Dad said when they were going to take my tonsils out. But why do they take your tonsils out in Sarajevo and you have to go to Ljubljana because of a bump? Because a bump is so terrible that you have to go far away, like in a fairy tale where they cross seven mountains and seven seas to get well. But not all long journeys have fairy-tale endings. A fairy tale is a fairy tale because it's a story with a happy ending, it's just that happy endings don't happen very often and people don't usually live in them. There isn't enough room for everyone. In fairy tales there's only enough room for a couple of old kings, for their good, bad, and clever daughters, and for the queen and a few witches, but not for people, the millions of millions of people. There isn't enough room for my mom either, who isn't a queen or a princess but just a regular mom who works in accounts, suffers from migraines, and sings on Saturdays, enveloped in steam and water until her hands have finished doing the washing that isn't allowed to go in the machine. If Mom has gone far away, all the way to Ljubljana, she must be totally lost. She'll never come back because her life isn't a fairy tale, she gets two creases between her eyes and thinks bumps can get bigger. My mom isn't Snow White, Cinderella, or Queen Forgetful. She isn't coming back from Ljubljana, she's going to stay there forever and come back to us dead, just like the people who don't get well at the hospital come back dead, because you can easily lose good health in white corridors and green boiler rooms, in the smells of chloroform, ether, and medicinal alcohol, in places where the air reeks of worry.

That's what I was thinking as I started following my shadow. It was moving along the asphalt a little behind me. I could see it out of the corner of my eye but didn't want to turn my head toward it. I wanted to watch it sort of in passing, to not change anything, just to keep seeing it. When I moved along the white stone wall a little, half the shadow disappeared from the asphalt and climbed up the side of the house. Up to my stomach I floated along the asphalt, my chest, neck, and head making their way along the house. My shadow split in two, but I stayed as one. You see, a shadow isn't actually an image of a person that always follows him, tracing his every move and being just like him. A shadow splits in half. But I wouldn't have felt or noticed a thing if I hadn't been looking. It keeps following me; it's just that its life isn't mine anymore.

I turned around and marched back the other way. The shadow moved a little out in front of me. Heading home, I stayed close to the wall, my shadow still split in half, Grandma was probably done on the phone. *Mom's woken up from the anesthetic,* she said. *The bump's gone? . . . Yes, it's gone, but what do you know about that? Were you eavesdropping again? . . . No, I just overheard . . . You're not allowed to listen to your elders' conversations . . . Why? Because they're sneaky? . . . No, because you don't understand them . . . When will I understand them? . . . One day, when you grow up . . . Are they really that scary? . . . Who's that scary? . . . Are all grown-up conversations as scary as yours? . . . No, our conversations aren't*

scary, you don't understand them . . . A conversation about a bump isn't scary?
. . . No, it's just a conversation about an illness . . . Why am I allowed to listen
to conversations about my bronchitis but not about a bump? . . . Oh boy, no
more conversations about bronchitis for you, you little devil, look at the mess
you're in. Go wash your face and hands, and don't ever let me see you in such
a state again. Grandma grabbed the frames of her glasses, just like she
always did when she wanted to show me she was angry.

I lay tucked in up to my neck, staring at the ceiling, listening to
her voice. She was reading me *White Fang*. Ten pages every night. We
were already halfway through. White Fang is a wolf who thinks and
feels, and scary things happen to him just because he thinks and feels.
It's not a fairy tale and that's why I'm scared there won't be a happy
ending, but today I don't listen to Grandma's voice. I don't remember
sentences and I don't feel like I'm White Fang, because to listen to the
story of White Fang I need to feel like White Fang, because when you
don't do that the story doesn't work. In fairy tales you don't feel like a
prince, princess, old king, brave knight, or Queen Forgetful, just like in
fables you don't feel like a fox or a raven, but in true stories you need
to feel like White Fang to understand what happens to him. Fairy tales
and fables are made up, but true stories actually happen. If they haven't
happened, then they happen when we listen to them, or when we learn
to read one day and we read them. They happen to us when we're reading the story, and this means we have to have lots of courage because
stories don't always have happy endings, and because you have to kill

your fear so you can live in the story. Life in a story is more beautiful than life in real life because in a story only important things happen and because in stories there aren't any of those days when nothing happens and the world is as empty as the white dates in the wall calendar.

Will Mom be back from Ljubljana before we finish White Fang? I interrupted Grandma as she was reading. *I don't think so, we've got eighty pages left, and that's eight days. Mom will be back in about fifteen days . . . Are you allowed to know how a book ends before you've read it? . . . It's allowed, but then the book isn't very interesting . . . Have you read* White Fang *before? . . . Yes, at least five times . . . And you always forget the end? . . . Well, I don't actually forget it, but it's as if I don't know how it's going to end and the ending might change . . . I don't want anything bad to happen to White Fang before Mom comes back from Ljubljana . . . Why do you think something bad's going to happen to him? . . . Because good things only have to happen in fairy tales. Otherwise they don't . . . Who told you that? . . . No one told me. I just know . . . Well, I didn't know that . . . You're just pretending you didn't know . . . No, I really didn't know that. I've never thought about it . . . Well, have you ever thought about why shadows split in half so half of you is on the asphalt and half of you on the wall?* Grandma looked at me, closed the book, and said she was sleepy. That was weird. She had never been sleepy before I fell asleep. I didn't know about after because I'd already be asleep by the time she went to bed. That night it was different. Grandma was scared Mom was going to die, I knew it. I knew exactly what she was thinking. If Mom dies, we'll be left alone, her, Grandpa, and me, and they're old, and old people are scared of being alone with children because they think one day they'll close their eyes for an afternoon nap and never open them again, and then the children will be left alone, helplessly trying to phone someone, hollering to the neighbors, but always end up waiting there all alone next to their grandpas and grandmas. Children shouldn't be alone because loneliness is something grown-up; we grow up so that one day we can be completely alone and no one has to worry about it. That's what Grandma was thinking when she pretended to fall asleep before me.

In the end she really did fall asleep. In her sleep she wheezed like a big mouse. She breathed in through her nose, and then puffed out through her mouth. You could really hear a puff. Only she slept like this. I know because I'd already slept in the same room as all of them, lying awake as they slept. Mom was a quiet sleeper, but once she said a word in her sleep. I asked her *what did you say last night?* and she looked at me like she'd brought an F home from some school of hers. But even she didn't remember her dreams because the little creature of the darkness came to visit her too. Dad slept smacking his lips and grinding his teeth. His sleeping was funny. It was like he was trying to make someone laugh with his sleeping, or like someone wouldn't let him go to sleep unless he first made them laugh. Uncle snored horribly, and for a whole night I was seething.

But none of them slept puffing, not even Grandpa and he'd lived with Grandma for more than fifty years and he even said that in fifty years two people become very alike. But he coughed in his sleep because of his asthma.

I heard a last puff. A lot of time went by and I was waiting for a new puff, but it never came. I wasn't really scared, but I was starting to get a little bit worried. I mean, Grandma was still breathing and she was still alive, but I didn't think this was enough. I was worried something wasn't right. I sat on my bed and wanted to wake her up, but for some reason didn't dare. You need to be tough because only when you're tough does everything work out. You're not allowed to panic – *oh boy, she's not breathing, or maybe you just can't see it 'cause it's dark* – I don't know what's going on, but somehow she's not moving anymore. *That's it, here we go, I'm going to scream*, but I'm not allowed to scream. If I scream, Mom won't come back from Ljubljana, and I'll be left on my own before I grow up, but that's not allowed because children aren't allowed to be left alone, just like they're not allowed to kill ants, and they're not allowed to cross the street without looking left and right. They're not allowed to scream, that's panicking, and I don't get panicky, *the kid never panics*, my mom tells her work colleagues, and when she says it, she's all aglow, my mom who's in Ljubljana at the moment. *The kid never panics* is the nicest thing she ever says about me and if I scream now she'll never say it again, and I'll just be a regular kid, a kid you can't say anything about, and I'll spoil that story from Dubrovnik from when I was two and a half when Nano lost me at the Pile Gate and I calmly made my way to Auntie Lola's place, the length of the

Corso and around behind St. Blaise's. I'd knocked on the door and Grandpa had opened it and asked *where's Nano?* And I said *Nano got lost* and quickly got it in that it wasn't my fault he got lost. They were all proud of me then, and Mom said *the kid never panics* for the first time, and when we got back from Sarajevo she told Dad how Nano got lost, and then Dad said *my big boy* and that's how the legend began, the one they still tell to this very night when I'd rather howl, but I'm not allowed, or this whole world made up of Mom in Ljubljana and Grandma who's not breathing in the dark will be destroyed, just like I destroy Queen Forgetful's castle when I'm bored.

That time in Dubrovnik I did something bad. I didn't burst out crying in the middle of the Pile Gate like other children, and I didn't because I was scared of crying in front of so many strangers and I was ashamed about being left alone. Others would have cried and they wouldn't have been scared or ashamed. Being scared and ashamed is no good and it's better to burst out crying. It's definitely braver. I couldn't because I'm a coward and that's why I went to Auntie Lola's and gave it my all to remember the way, even though I'd always walked it with someone else. But I remembered. It was the longest journey I ever made in my life. When I'm a thousand years old like an old king, even then I'll never go on such a long journey because when you're two and a half there isn't a longer journey than the one from the Pile Gate to St. Blaise's.

You know, I'd never even thought about it before. I liked them thinking I was a kid who never panics, but the truth is I really am a scaredy pants and I get ashamed, and when this happens I make journeys that kids who cry in front of a crowd of strangers would never make. But my mom doesn't cry either and she isn't that big. She's smaller than Grandma, Grandpa, and Dad, and she gets ashamed and is always scared of this or that. She takes her fears out on all of us, on me most of all, and we all love her when she's ashamed. Shame is something worse than fear, but it's nice to watch. Mom would have found her way home like me if Nano had lost her at the Pile Gate, she would have found her way back no matter how far it was, I know that for sure because you can spot fear and shame really easily, much more easily than courage, and that's why I know Mom better than anyone else and that's why I always know what she's capable of. So anyway, if she knows how to get back from the Pile Gate on her own, she'll find her way back from Ljubljana. Ljubljana is much closer because Mom is much older than me and she'll make it back easily. She's scared and ashamed and that's why she can't stay in Ljubljana, she can't die, the bump can't hurt her, the rules for big people don't apply to her. Fairy tales exist for the scared and ashamed because in them people cross seven mountains and seven seas just so they won't be scared and ashamed.

I breathed a sigh of relief. My face is wet, my back and stomach too. If I've cried, I didn't cry down my back, everyone has to believe I'm telling the truth there. Grandma has to believe me too. Is she breathing? I can't see anything, but if she's breathing I'll tell her in the morning that everything is fine with Mom. Actually, I won't tell her anything because

I don't think she'll understand, just like she didn't understand the thing about split shadows. But I'll show her that tomorrow, and she'll just have to wait for Mom, she'll have to worry for the whole fifteen days until Mom comes back from Ljubljana, and then I'll tell her I knew the whole time. I'll tell them all, Dad and Uncle and all those worriers on the phone who call when I'm not around, and I'll tell Grandma, and Mom, I'll tell them that only I knew, only I knew she had to come back. Tomorrow we'll keep reading *White Fang*. I'm brave enough for any sad ending.

If only Grandma would let out a little puff, then I'd fall asleep, my first time after her.

That nothing would ever happen

We lived from one special occasion to the next in a happy and ordered world, sometimes sick with feverish kids' sicknesses and sometimes with serious grown-up ones, in a world in which everything had its place and moment in time. *Don't run before you can walk*, Grandma used to say. We didn't know what she meant, or maybe some did, but they weren't saying, so I kept running because time passed by so slowly. I couldn't wait for it, I had to hurry, get out ahead, skip the good-for-nothing days because they weren't special occasions.

You couldn't buy ice cream in the winter back then. It disappeared from the confectionaries in the first thick November fog and only showed up again in April. Why don't people eat ice cream in winter too? Because ice cream gives you a sore throat. They were looking out for us, making sure we didn't get sick for no reason, and that every day had its place in the calendar and time in the seasons, that we would never think that we were alone and abandoned, forsaken like the far-away countries we heard about on the radio. Young slant-eyed soldiers were dying in those countries, a little machine gun in one hand and a tiny baby in the other. That's how they died, leaving behind little slant-eyed wives to hold their heads in their hands and grieve in their funny incomprehensible language.

I laugh whenever I see little slant-eyed mothers next to their little dead husbands on the TV. Saigon and Hanoi are the names of the first comedies in my life. I spell them out loud, letter by letter, laughing my head off. Those people don't look like us, and I don't believe they're in pain or that they're really sad. Words of sadness have to sound sad, and tears have to be like raindrops, small and brilliant. Their words aren't sad, and the tears on their faces are too big and look funny, like the fake tears of the clowns I saw at the circus. I'm just waiting for Mom and Grandma to leave the room so I can watch Saigon and Hanoi and have a laugh. When they're there I'm not allowed to laugh because Mom will think I'm crazy, and Grandma that I'm malicious. Craziness and malice are strictly forbidden in our house. Great unhappiness is born from malice; malicious children put their parents in old folks' homes, never thinking that they themselves will one day get old and that their children might bundle them off to old folks' homes too; Grandma and Mom were scared of malice and craziness because they were born old and with fears I don't understand, but I knew one day I'd have my turn; it'll happen the day they say I'm a grown-up, the day I run when I first meet someone who's crazy, because craziness is infectious, just like all the sicknesses and misfortune in this city. *When you grow up and have your own house and your own children, then you can do whatever you like. But in my house you won't.* Grandma loved the little slant-eyed mothers and pretended she understood them.

I get really careful in the run-up to special occasions like New Year's Eve and my birthday. I don't even laugh when I'm on my own; I keep my mouth shut like the angels on Grandma's postcards, and I squint to see if I've already grown wings or if I still need to wait a bit. I never know what those two are going to get me for my birthday or New Year's, only that Grandma's presents are always better. She buys me books – encyclopedias and picture books – and Mom always gets me practical stuff. Practical stuff is stuff that they were going to have to buy anyway, but instead of just getting on with it without all the pomp, they wait for special occasions and give them to you all wrapped up in shiny wrapping and expect you to get excited. But who can get excited about socks, undies, undershirts, and winter slippers? Mom expects me to get excited about her presents. If I don't, it means I'm malicious. There's no such thing as everyday stuff for her, not even socks, everything's a special treat, you have to earn everything in life, you have to bust your gut. If you listened to her you'd think humanity would go naked and barefoot if everyone told their mother that undershirts and slippers don't cut it as birthday presents. But I pretend to be excited about her presents because if I don't she gets angry and starts with the nurturing stuff. When she cranks up the nurture rant it's much worse than when she gets a migraine. Mom's kind of nurturing is out of books called *You and Your Child* and *Your Child Is a Personality*. She bought them from a traveling salesman, spent a month reading them, and then decided to put her foot down about my nurturing. Luckily she doesn't have time to stick at it, so unless I remind her, she totally forgets the whole thing. Nurturing amounts to Mom screwing up her face and repeating the same sentence ten times, wanting something from me without ever actually saying what it is. The less I understand, the happier she is because then she thinks she's being strict, and no strictness means no nurture. For me strict nurturing involves keeping your mouth shut, saying *yes*, nodding your head and not asking any questions because there's nothing to ask because you don't understand anything.

For special occasions Dad gives me model railway, motorway, city, and chemistry sets, all with thousands of little pieces. Then we sit down on the living-room floor and open the box. Dad puts his serious face on and starts scratching behind his ear, spreading the thousands of little pieces out on the rug. I watch him and he's as funny as the little slant-eyed mothers, and he gives me a nod that says *trust me* and starts putting the thousands of little railway pieces together. He knows what he's doing, and I like watching him put it together much more than I like the railway itself. Mom thinks he likes this stuff so much because when he was a boy they didn't buy him toys, so he never got a chance to play his little heart out and now he's making up for it. I don't think she's right. If that's how it was, he'd buy toys for himself.

Nano gives the best presents. He's not actually Nano, his name is Rudolf Stubler, but nobody calls him that. Nano is Grandma's older brother and once, a long time ago, he studied math in Vienna. Today he spends his time exploring far-off cities, going hiking, beekeeping, and playing the violin. We see him in photographs: Nano in London, Nano in Paris, Nano in Berlin, Nano in Moscow, Amsterdam, Kiev, Prague, Rome, Florence, Madrid, and Lisbon. They know Nano in all these cities because their buildings and bridges, cathedrals and skyscrapers have their photos taken with him. They don't have any pictures of their own without him, without him these cities are just postcards, and postcards aren't real cities, they're just letters with photos where nothing is real. Nano stands waving in front of the Trevi Fountain, a coin in his hand and a wish in the coin. We don't believe the wish, Grandma says wishes don't come true in water, but that doesn't matter because the Trevi Fountain believes in wishes, and so Nano tosses a coin in and has his picture taken, so we'll know what Rome looks like. Nano comes over before every special occasion, puts a pen and paper down on the table, and says *come on, tell me what you'd like for New Year's, doesn't matter if it's a sewing needle or a locomotive, leave it up to me to see if my financial means stretch.* Only Nano uses phrases like *financial means*, because he talks to me like I'm a grown-up, so I talk to him like he's a grown-up too: *For a start I need to say that I don't want a sewing needle or a locomotive. I can borrow a sewing needle from Grandma, and I'd need a driver's license for a locomotive . . . Very well, let's see, how do you feel about musical instruments? . . . I think I'm tone-deaf and that it'd be a complete waste of money. I'd prefer something that might stimulate my intellectual development . . . What do you think would be most appropriate? . . . I'm not sure, perhaps a volume on world history, an encyclopedia of sports or of the animal kingdom . . . Got it, I've made a note. And where do you stand in regard to sporting activities? . . . I've already got a bike, and I don't need a ball because somebody might steal it. Don't get me roller skates because only girls go skating, and I could fall and break my neck . . . How about a chess set? . . . Well, perhaps, but a wooden one. I think I've outgrown plastic.*

And that's how it went. Nano would neatly jot everything down, and then when the occasion rolled around he'd be there with two presents, one I'd chosen and a second one that he liked. The second was usually better, better because it was a surprise and there's no such thing as a bad surprise. A bad surprise is called a disappointment, and a special occasion is not a time for disappointment. I'm not even disappointed with Mom's practical presents because that's what I expect from her, and when you expect something it can't be a disappointment.

The day before a special occasion Mom bakes a cake. When Mom bakes a cake we all have to put our serious faces on and cross our fingers, just like we did when Neil Armstrong landed on the moon. Baking cakes is an unpredictable business: Mom mixes the dough, or actually it's more like she gets a mountain of flour and makes a deep hole in the middle so the flour mountain looks like a snow volcano or a heap of sand and cement to make concrete, and then she breaks the eggs and puts them in the hole. When she's broken all the eggs, she knocks the mountain over, mixes the flour with the eggs, and starts with her *oh boy, what if the dough doesn't rise*, and I laugh at her, but she doesn't get angry, she just says *and that's the thanks I get*. She's happy because she's enjoying her anxiety.

The dough kneaded and ready for baking, she covers it with a cloth and waits. Smoking one cigarette after the other, every five minutes she peeks under the cloth and calls Grandma over to say how the dough's going. Grandma says *no, not yet, just a little longer*, and then she says *ready*, and then Mom almost flips out and I'm not allowed to laugh at her anymore. With trembling hands she covers the cake dish in oil and keeps repeating *God save me, what if the dough sticks*.

As soon as she's put the cake in to bake Mom starts cussing out our oven. First the upper heating bars are no good, then the bottom ones aren't working, and then she starts cussing out the company in Čačak that made the oven and looks up at the ceiling, as if she's looking up at the sky where the whiteware bosses of the world are in a meeting to decide who deserves an oven that might bake a decent cake this New Year's. Grandma just listens and nods her head. Mom gets on Grandma's nerves sometimes. *She'll give me a nervous breakdown one day*, and later she'll complain to Auntie Doležal, *her and her cakes*, and

Auntie Doležal clasps her hands and says *oh, the young ones, my dear Olga, those young ones, they'll make a science out of baking a cake yet, and to think I once made five cakes for my Jucika's habitation and it didn't faze me none.* Jucika was Auntie Doležal's husband, they killed him in Jasenovac, but she always talked about him as if he were alive, as if he was going to appear on the doorstep in about half an hour, so I felt like I knew Jucika too, and wouldn't have been in the least surprised if he had actually shown up and said *I'm home* and Auntie Doležal had again baked him five cakes for this habitation thing.

It riled Grandma most of all that Mom wouldn't let her bake cakes for New Year's or my birthday. Other times were fine, but for New Year's or my birthday, no way. I'm her son, and it was her job to bake her son a cake on special occasions. *Okay, you bake them for him then, but quit dragging me up to see whether the dough has risen,* Grandma said once, and that made Mom really wild and she yelled back *You've been hounding me my whole life,* burst into tears, and immediately got a migraine. Grandma never again complained about being called over to see whether the dough had risen. *Just let it be,* said Auntie Doležal.

The most exciting part was when the cake came out of the oven, because then nobody, not even Grandma, knew whether a catastrophe was in the cards. A catastrophe was when the middle of the cake caved in or shrank, so the cake didn't look like a cake anymore but like something else, it's hard to say what, but something awfully funny that you weren't allowed to laugh at, because Mom and Grandma would be there hovering over whatever that something was. Mom would bury her face in her hands like those little slant-eyed mothers when their husbands were killed, and Grandma would start cussing. She never cussed otherwise, just when a cake flopped. And if the cake flopped a replacement had to be made. Then we'd have two cakes for the special occasion: a normal one to serve to guests and a second that tasted normal but looked so bad nobody was allowed to see it except us. We ate that one on the sly before the guests showed up.

Before the New Year of 1977 Nano came over, got his pen and paper out, and again I told him I didn't need a sewing needle or a locomotive and that we could get straight down to business on the present list. I told him that my relationship to time and its passing had fundamentally changed and that as such, I needed a wristwatch. He wrote it down, went home, and three days later died.

He was in my dad's ward, in a deep coma, and at the time it was all everyone talked about. I didn't actually know what a deep coma was, but it meant this New Year's wasn't going to be a special occasion and that there'd be no one to take the blame for unfulfilled promises. Up until this point promises had been disregarded or broken because someone had forgotten them; grown-ups were promise-killers, all you could do was look at them, shake your head, and think: But why? Why one more little graveyard, full of unfulfilled wishes and forgotten words strewn on balmy city streets like summer hail that melts in the blink of an eye, leaving nothing but an image behind, a single, tiny, inconsequential image at the bottom of the gaze of all for whom it has fallen like a promise?

Nano couldn't keep his promise because he was in a deep coma. Mom sat at his bedside for two nights saying things like *Nano, sweetie, it's just started snowing, it'll be New Year's soon, it's already scrunchy underfoot, and soon we'll be eating this year's apples.* She said all kinds of things to him, watching for an eyelash to flicker or a quiver in the corners of his mouth, because Dad had told her that you never know with a deep coma, that you can't be sure whether Nano could hear anything, feel her hand, or sense the slipstream of words through the world and the cosmos, along the nerves that lead to the brain, like unstamped letters dropped in a distant post-office box, letters in which we all tell him that we love him.

Dad stopped by every half hour, listened to what Mom was saying to Nano, putting his hand on her shoulder and gently stroking her hair. He was in his white doctor's coat, a silver fountain pen peering out from a small pocket. In his doctor's coat my dad wasn't the same dad as the one without a doctor's coat. Regular Dad lied, didn't keep his promises, and was often weak and downhearted. He looked like someone liable to be hit by a car on a pedestrian crossing or prone to spilling plates of soup in his lap. This dad, Dad the Doctor, he was God, Comfort, and James Bond. For him there was no such thing as an incurable illness, nor a life bearing any resemblance to death, not even a life in a deep coma. Every moment was worthy of celebration, and there wasn't a single moment when you pulled the shutters down on life and said *fine, that was that, now I'm dead and I'm leaving.* My dad didn't let people leave, and he was sure Nano's eyelashes would give the world a signal, that humanity would shudder the moment a lone hair on any one man moved, having stolen itself away from the world of darkness. *There are medical truths that serve the healing process and medical truths that confirm that healing is not possible, gravediggers can worry about the latter because I won't.* That's what he once yelled at drunk Dr. Jakšić, who when we were on a trip to Mount Trebević said that even in the coffins buried in Bare Cemetery, Dobro – my dad – could find a couple of people to declare alive and try bringing back to life.

On the morning of the third day Nano heaved two deep sighs and stopped breathing. Life ends with a sigh, that's no surprise at all. When I sigh I say to myself *okay, fine, let's start again from the beginning.* Sighs are like sleeping, they separate life into a thousand thousand pieces, and before going to bed you put them together and that's how memories are made. There's no sighing or sleeping in memories; in memory life is whole again. When death came Nano sighed, told the deep coma *well that's that,* and left without saying goodbye. The deep coma waved to him, but Nano didn't see it, so it was left there with its hand in the air. Nobody ever says goodbye to deep comas when they leave.

Dad hugged Mom and whispered *we lost him.* Mom cried a little on his white coat, then Dad called Dr. Smajlović over and said *exitus,* and Dr. Smajlović looked at his watch, took out his fountain pen, and entered the exact time of death in Nano's hospital notes. Even though they straight-out forget it, don't have to tell anyone, and nobody ever inquires about the hours and minutes in question, the exact time of death is very important to doctors. In a filing cabinet somewhere there's a file with the time of death written down, just in case it becomes important one day as some details in life do. Auntie Doležal is of the view that one day God is going to assemble all souls and assign them grades. The time of death in one's hospital notes is just waiting for that day, even though we live in communism and none of the doctors believes God exists. But like our own, this belief is a little shaky. So, who knows, maybe Nano will appear before God and maybe God'll say *so often you used to say I didn't exist, and now you're not in the least surprised to see me.*

Dad and Mom went outside. He took out a packet of cigarettes, and Mom said *look how much snow there is already.* The snow was as thick as the pillows in the rooms of gentle giants, falling without pause on Mom's black jacket and Dad's white doctor's coat. By the time they'd each finished their cigarette their shoulders were covered in snow, and if a bird had chanced overhead, they would have looked as white as each other, my mom and dad, and the bird would've thought them two creatures of winter, in love.

Mom said *go, you'll catch cold*, and he said *no*; I think in that instant he was ready to remain in the snow forever, just to hear her say that *go, you'll catch cold* a few more times. A love sometimes returns like a word you believe to be true, then it flies away and never comes back; but in its wake it leaves a brilliant trail, which gives a winter morning a certain meaning, and so even after a farewell a little hope remains – let's say the hope of stumbling upon the magic word, even if it comes after a death and the sacrifice of a Nano.

A taxi arrived and Dad asked *do you want to see him again?* They went back inside, the taxi driver opened his newspaper and switched the meter on. Nano's pillow was gone, Mom looked at him but didn't cry, she just stood there silently, not moving, at a loss. She'd seen her uncle for the last time and knew that from now on she'd only be able to imagine his face or look at him in photographs. He was dead, and she'd seen him for the last time in her life. When she leaves this room, something in her will be forever, just as death is forever. My mom felt a little dead, something she'd later repeat quite often. There was no sadness in the story, just astonishment in the face of how little it takes for one to bid farewell to the world, just a single glance, how much one sees each day for the last time in one's life, unaware, not thinking, goodbyes the furthest thing from one's mind.

Dad went up to Nano, placed his hand on his forehead, and said *the last gentleman.* Every summer he'd play Preference with Nano in the gardens in Ilidža, and Nano would tell him stories about Vienna and the beautiful Jewesses who in the fall of 1917, as the dual monarchy crumbled, would open their ladies' umbrellas, their ankles so slender and angular, so fragile you had to approach them on tiptoes in case they would break. Dad didn't know anything about Vienna or Viennese women. He grew up in a harsh, hard world in which you had to guard your refinement and sensitivity, and for him Nano was someone from another world, one where things of beauty seemed inherent and certain, where now forgotten words still existed, a world where such things could be preserved. That morning my dad only managed to remember the word gentleman.

So in the end I missed out on the wristwatch. Nano was buried the day after Christmas, Mom baked her cakes, and everything was ready in time for a strange celebration at which nobody celebrated anything, but because of me, she and Grandma decided we couldn't just skip New Year's. They went around the house all in black, the mood not festive in the least. I don't understand this! I never understood how they didn't know how to celebrate and grieve at the same time: celebrate the special occasion and grieve because of Nano's death. With them it was always one or the other, as if they were scared someone was secretly watching them, testing the depth of their grief and the height of their celebration. When Nano died they wouldn't have paid any mind if I laughed at little slant-eyed mothers, but they weren't on the news anymore. The war in Vietnam was over, and other wars didn't make the news in the lead-up to New Year's. What a shame! If I'd laughed Mom wouldn't have started with the nurturing stuff. That was a sure bet.

Dad came over on New Year's Eve, bringing something with a thousand pieces. He sat down in the middle of the room and began putting it together. I sat down next to him, my hands on my knees, waiting to see what it would be. I wanted his building to go on and on, that we would stay here forever, in this room, on this rug, that the whole world would wait until we were finished, that nothing would happen before Dad had built whatever he was building, that time would stand still too, that everyone would look at their watches believing everything comes to an end, that eventually they'd see what he'd built, that it would be and stay like this forever and that nothing would ever happen anymore.

My dummy dear

Dad brought the kitten home. It'd been meowing in a doorway up on Koševo in the late-November rain, a little black kitten the size of a child's hand, one eye open, the other closed. Kittens are born with their eyes closed; sight only comes when they've sniffed and licked the world around them, once they know what they're going to see. Dad had it in his pocket, *I had to*, he said, *it's okay*, said Mom. Grandma fetched a saucer of milk and an eyedropper. Placing the kitten in her lap, she turned it on its back and fed it, drop by drop, while Mom and Dad discussed its chances of survival. Grandma didn't say anything, not then, and not in the days to follow. I'd head off to school and she'd be there with the dropper in her right hand and the kitten's head in her left, and when I came back she'd be doing the same. And so it went for days. It was three weeks before the kitten began to drink milk on its own, to explore the house and to purr. When her other eye opened we knew she would live.

In those years the seasons marked the comings and goings in our house just like in children's books. Spring: Mom takes the rug out into the yard, throws it over a clothesline wire, beating it with a wicker paddle. The blows of my tennis-playing mom resound and the dust flies everywhere, every blow a thunderclap. Other moms are out beating their rugs too and the whole city reverberates, the air dusty like the heart of an old watch, every ray of sun visible. The sun circles the earth to the rhythm of a thousand blows, the city a heavenly disco. In the broad light of day all the angels and all the saints gaze down to see what's up as moms beat their rugs in the early spring. Or the summer: Footprint traces in the fresh asphalt, I become famous with every step, each imprinted forever. Sweaty I enter the cool of our house, so good in the summertime, its coolness a contrast to the heat of the whole steaming world outside. I'll be off to the seaside soon and already miss the house. I'm going away, that I'll be coming back is no relief because there's no coming back worth such a leaving. Autumn: The house is fragrant, the rain falling outside our steamy windows. Paprikas, tomatoes, cabbages, and floury apples jostle about the floor, we're making winter preserves, warming ourselves with their scents and colors, warming ourselves on the feeling of immortality among all this food to see us through the winter. Now we can sleep like bears and dream big long bear dreams, until with the first days of spring, warmed, we wake from our slumber.

With the cat the first fateful month entered our house: February. She was already a year and a half, her coat shone in the light, a cat ready for the catwalk at a world expo of miniature beauty. She was asleep on top of the television, but occasionally opened her eyes, eyeballing us huddled there in front of the screen with our hands in our laps, as if she didn't like what she saw, as if bestowing a magnificent contempt upon us all. And then she just disappeared, leaving the house and not coming back for three days. On her return she was matted and muddied, one ear bitten. She went straight for her feeding tray, meowed her way around the house, and then curled up under the table to sleep. *Been out whoring have we?* said Grandma. The cat opened one eye, but under the eyelid was another she didn't deign worthy of opening. She was smug; February had come.

Two months later Mom was in a flap, *we're going to have kittens.* Grandma scowled in Dad's direction, and he scratched his head, the guilty party. I was peeing myself with joy. What are we going to do with so many kittens? It doesn't matter, kittens don't eat much, they'll live with us, but next year when February comes there'll be more kittens, and that's okay too, even that many kittens don't eat much. A thousand kittens don't eat as much as Grandma, Mom, and me, let alone Dad when he comes to visit; he eats more than a hundred cats put together.

At the beginning of May the cat tried to sneak into the linen cupboard, *get out!* Grandma trailed her, then she slunk under the bed, *get out!* Then she tried my toy box, *get out!* Grandma shunted her from one hiding place to the next, and I didn't get it. She picked up the cat and set her down in a box of rags in the broom closet. *That's that,* she said. *What?* . . . *Doesn't matter what.* We sat there watching TV, Mom was flicking through the newspaper, and I forgot about the cat until I heard this weird meowing. *It's started!* . . . *What's started?* I jumped up. *Come take a look,* said Grandma knowingly. *Don't want to,* I was a little bit scared. *Come on, nothing's going bite you* . . . *Do I have to?* . . . *Oh to hell with you if you don't want to!* But I did sidle up, peering out from behind Grandma and Mom. The cat was meowing, looking Grandma straight in the eye, but this time she wasn't sneering, just inquisitively staring *what's this, what's happening to me, I haven't a clue, why didn't anyone teach me about all this, why didn't you tell me?* But Grandma just nodded her head and whispered *everything's okay, it's okay, everything's going to be okay.*

Look, the first one! Mom yelled. A little lump that really didn't look much like a kitten popped out of the cat. Then she remembered what to do. She licked the lump until it became a furry something. The tiny kitty was as big as a key ring. *Look, there's the second one!* It'd been ten minutes. *Look, the third!* . . . *the fourth!* . . . *the fifth!* . . . *Look, the sixth!* Mom was hollering as if she were the courtier at a royal feline court and it was her job to announce the number of neonates the queen had borne to city and state.

Now she needs peace and quiet, Grandma commanded, and Mom exited the broom closet obediently. I was proud of Grandma; it was like she had this infinite feline or maternal experience. But my pride was short-lived, because three days later something happened that I've never told anyone and which I spent years trying to forget. The season of great deaths had to come, so I could start processing it and add my offering up to the time when the seasons and February disappeared, and all victims became something we could speak freely of until we made someone cry or fly into a rage.

Where are the kitties? I asked. *They're gone*, she said. *How come they're gone, where are they? . . . I don't know, they're gone . . . The cat's looking for them, where are they? . . . I don't know, they're gone . . . You do know!* I screamed, *you know where they are, go get them! . . . I can't go get them, they're gone*, Grandma had turned pale and was trying to get away from me. *Bring the kitties back, shame on you! . . . I can't bring them back . . . Bring them back, stupid!* I was crying now, *bring them back you bitch, bring them back or you deserve to die . . .* Grandma clammed shut, looked away, and tried to disappear every time I'd come near. Something terrible had happened, but I didn't know what. Something so terrible that I wanted to say the most vile things to her, but luckily I didn't know how to say them; if I'd known I would have, I would have killed my grandma with words.

When Mom came home from work she found me whimpering under the writing desk, doubled up like a fetus. The cat roamed the house, meowing in search of her children. But her children weren't there. Grandma sat in the living room staring at the wall. She didn't make lunch that day. Mom crouched down beside me repeating my name, but I didn't respond. I didn't want to say anything, or I couldn't, I don't remember anything else. She wanted to run her fingers through my hair, but I moved my head and hit the wall. My forehead bled; tears mixed with blood. The blood was sweeter than the tears, but it burned my eyes. Mom was crouched there trembling. Grandma stayed where she was. Grandma wasn't there. *I hope she never comes back*, I thought.

She'd drowned the cat's children in the washbasin and tossed them in the garbage. *I'll never do that again!* she said to Mom, *never again, those kittens have cost me half my life.* I made like I didn't hear them and that I'd forgotten everything. That's the best thing to do if you can't forget anything. I couldn't forget those kittens.

Grandma had fed the kitten with an eyedropper, had given her a life already lost and taught her things only grandmothers can teach people and cats, had helped her give birth, and then she killed her children. I couldn't understand that; I'll never understand it, even though one day, along with a world and a city that had lost the seasons of the year, I'd get used to living with death and with exile from a life without death.

Ten years later Dad brought a puppy to the house, black and less than a month old. *We'll call him Nero*, said Grandma. For the first few weeks Nero stayed in the house with us, until Schulz, the super, built him a wooden kennel in the yard. By the time he'd grown up Nero had a split personality: one minute he was a guard dog on a chain in the yard, the next he was a household pet sprawled out on our living-room floor. He was a good dog and a stupid one. Though he liked everyone he'd still bark his head off; he even liked cats, but they didn't like him. The only thing Nero hated was the hedgehog that lived in our garden. He'd go wild when the hedgehog trundled the yard at night, pricking his snout on its quills, his muzzle frothing. Grandma used to say *myohmy, my dummy dear*, and he'd yelp and whine at a world where there were hedgehogs and a dog couldn't live without constant stress. That's what my mother so wisely observed.

The three of us felt pretty guilty the days and nights we left Nero in his kennel, down in the yard. We were actually fine with it when he slept up with us, but for some reason it was unacceptable he switch from being a guard dog to a household pet. I don't know why we didn't want him as a pet, but I fear we gave him a kennel and chain because we thought he was dumb, that it was beneath us to live with an idiot. Or maybe we thought we'd be less tied to Nero if he was farther away. I don't know what it was all about, why we banished him from our daily lives.

Grandma passed away in early June, out in front of his kennel Nero howled the whole night long. At dawn I went down to the yard, it was a full moon, everything lit up. I sat down to give him a hug; faithful, four-legged Nero. My grandma was dead, but I couldn't howl like him; it was as if the dog was sadder than me. Though he lived on a chain, he'd lost something I could never be conscious of, something I obviously didn't even have, so my loss could never be like his. I took him in my arms, trying to make the sadness mutual, to take on a little of his grief, a little of his goodness, so that I too might be ennobled by this late-night grief and for a moment enter a better heaven, a dog's heaven, where there's no place for people, because such a heaven doesn't have anything to do with God but with friends who die in dogs' eyes.

Six months later, on the coldest day of the year, worried about Nero I hurried home from university. He was still in his kennel because I hadn't let him in to warm himself by the coal stove. No one had looked after the animals or plants since Grandma died.

Nero wasn't out in front of his kennel. He wasn't inside either, nor was his chain. I found him dead, hanging over the neighbor's fence. He was stiff, eyes half open. I lifted him up, a cold, furry object. I tried to close his eyes, but it didn't work. They stayed open. I saw the empty and vacant eyes of death, nothing there, nothing of the world or hope; everything that had once lived there gone, never to return. This is what the eyes of all the dead look like. I didn't ever need to see them again, because every man or woman who had ever lived and now lived no more had Nero's eyes.

It took me three hours to dig a grave in the frozen earth and bury my dog along with his chain. *Why with his chain, like he was a galley slave!* said Mom. She wasn't wrong actually. Nero really was our slave; he appeared at the wrong time, to people who didn't deserve him and who he couldn't save. Sometimes there really is no hope for us until we've strangled the very last thing we have left, that which will haunt us more than any horror or suffering to come.

If you can see it's a car, tell me

That there in the picture, that's a toy box, but when I want it to, it stops being a toy box and turns into a car. I wake up early when all the others are still asleep, wrap a sandwich in a checkered napkin, and write a letter, even though they haven't taught me to write yet. The letter's for them, but they don't have to read it. I'm leaving one because it's the thing to do, because everyone who suddenly goes off somewhere leaves a letter behind. I write how I've had enough of them, that I'm never coming back and that I'm going to a place where there aren't any other people, and I'm going to stay there forever, and be rich, with a real car and a real train, a real pistol and real cowboys and Indians, and Partisans and Germans, who I'll play war against and beat whenever I want, and when something needs rescuing, like when Sava Kovačević saved the high command or when Chief Big Bear sent smoke signals to the world so that stars might fall to the earth, but the Gold River would never fall to the white man. I'm going because they tricked me again, I don't know how, but they tricked me, just like they do every time they know I don't want to go somewhere, and I'm going to cling to the table leg with all my might and scream my head off, and no one's going be able to tear me loose, because I know that wherever they're taking me something's going to hurt like hell, or something else is going happen to make me sorry I ever let go of that table leg. I leave the letter behind for them and on top of it the big key to the cellar. That's my key and they can give it to whoever comes to take my place.

I sit down in the box, there's not much room with all the toys, but I'll manage because I'm big and by myself. I turn the car on and drive off. *Brrmmm, brmmm, mmmmmmmm*, I drive far away, and my lips vibrate and go dry. I can't even lick my lips because then the *brrmmm, brmmm, mmm-mmmmmm* will stop and the car too, and then they might catch up with me and take me home or turn the car back into a box. Once I'm off and driving I don't stop until lunchtime when Grandma comes to get me and says *c'mon you little moppet, you'll wreck your throat screeching away in that box.* Then my car vanishes, and all the kilometers I've driven too, France, Germany, and America vanish, all the countries I've traveled, the cowboys and Indians vanish, and so does Sava Kovačević and the high command and the Sutjeska canyon, which smells of darkness, menthol candies, and explosives. I'm back in the yard from which I set off into the world, in the toy box I turned into a car, a car that vanishes the moment someone who can't see it comes along, like Grandma or Mom, because for them a box is always just a box, and nothing ever turns into something else.

What've you been doing? Mom gives me that look moms give their little boys when they're a bit peculiar but aren't allowed to know they're a bit peculiar. Maybe the look's got a different name, I don't know what it is, but I know when I answer I've got to really be smart to make it go away. *I was playing driving . . . That's nice, and how does playing driving work? . . . You just sit in the car and drive . . . And what's this? . . . It's a letter, I left it for you so you wouldn't get worried . . . And what does it say?* She was looking at the wavy inked lines that looked like the ocean or a doctor's scribble. *How can you ask me that, you're the one who knows how to read, not me. You should know what it says . . . It looks to me like it doesn't say anything, there aren't any words . . . There aren't any words because I was playing. When I'm playing nothing's for real, because I don't have a real car and I don't know how to write . . . Why don't you play with other children? . . . Because they don't know how to play driving.*

Mom gives Grandma a dirty look and I know that tonight, when they think I'm asleep, they're going to spend hours whispering and stinking up the cellar with cigarettes, arguing about whose fault it is and why I spend every morning in a cardboard box, snorting and spluttering like – *ohmygodsorry* – a dimwit. I'm not exactly sure what the word means, but I figure it's really bad to be a dimwit because I've noticed they only say it when they have that look reserved for little boys who are a bit peculiar.

The photo where I'm in a cardboard box, I mean, in my car, driving to America, was taken by a German guy last summer. Back then I was afraid of having my picture taken. Actually, that wasn't what I was afraid of; I was afraid of injections, and every week they'd trick me into having an injection, so I started pretending I was scared of having my picture taken too. As soon as I spotted someone with a camera I'd burst into tears and run for my life. Put a camera in front of me and I was even prepared to jump into the sea, and I was only three and a half and didn't know how to swim, that's how much I pretended about being scared of having my picture taken. I kept it up for months, and they all tried, Mom, Dad, even Grandpa, until one day this German showed up, because Grandpa used to translate tourist stuff for them, and the German crept into the bushes and hid there until I got into the car, and just as I was about to turn the ignition he jumped out and snapped. I let out a howl but it was already too late.

The German sent the photo from Germany, and Grandma put it in an album to show guests. Some aunties from Sarajevo who I didn't know, but were important and had gray hair as blue as the sea – I didn't get it how something could be gray and blue at the same time – said *uuuu, what a sweet little boy, he could be in a fashion magazine*, and I was so embarrassed that I'd lower my head, shrug my shoulders, and hide my eyes. So they'd see I was a dimwit and leave me in peace. When they gave me a hug I'd go all floppy like a chicken just come from the butcher's, and let them pinch my cheeks with their thumbs and fore-fingers, all the while their gray heads blue like the sea smelling of pickled paprika, roses, and high fever.

It was hard for me to hit the road after the photo, because it got tougher and tougher to turn the box into a car, because that photo, where it was clear as day that I wasn't in a car but an ordinary cardboard box that used to have little packets of cookies in it, was always in front of me. Photos are like grown-ups because they show everything in a way that can only make you get all worried; in photos everything looks like it'll never change, like it'll never turn into anything else. Nothing is as you imagined and it never will be, the only thing you can be sure of is that in the picture you'll look confused, confused smiley or confused angry, because your eyes see everything differently to how the camera sees it, and now they're there in the photo without all the stuff you've imagined, and the whole world appears exactly as it would if there were no one who played and no one who made anything up, there's just the eyes that once saw other stuff and now are confused because that stuff's not in the photo.

I lie in the dark and can't stop my breathing, I can't sleep, and I can't be here when morning comes. Tomorrow I'm going a long way away and I won't be back. I'm never coming back, and I'll never again look them in the eyes, nobody who knows, not Grandma or Grandpa, not Mom or Dad. It's all finished with them. I said to myself *if only they were dead*, but I know they won't die and that they'll grab my head and force me to look them in the eyes, and in my eyes they'll look for me, their child, the one they can do anything to if they think it best for him. I don't like them doing what's best for me because everything that's best for me makes me cry and turn into something I don't know the name of, but it looks like a box that turns into a car and then back into a box; I'm that box when they do what's best for me.

In the morning I'll hop into the car and go far away. I'm going to screw my eyes shut tight and then open them and take a good hard look. If it's still a box and not a car I'll set off on foot, taking only the essentials, just the stuff I won't be able to do without when I get where I'm going: my little yellow spade, my teddy bunny, and my winter sweater. Everything else I'm leaving behind for them, for the child they get to take my place and who won't be called Miljenko, because from tomorrow on they're going to cry whenever anybody says Miljenko. I know they're going to cry; they're going to cry like they do when someone dies, but I'm not going to die, I'm simply going to leave. But I'm going forever, and when you go forever it's like you're dead for those who remain.

It all started on a Saturday. Mom and Dad arrived from Sarajevo, and Grandma said *the kid hasn't been on the potty for three days.* Dad raised an eyebrow – *three days?* – and I was already scared, but I pretended I couldn't hear anything and continued building a castle for Queen Forgetful, my heart pounding hard. I thought they were going to grab me by my hands and legs and cart me off to the hospital or some other place, some big toilet where nurses, paddles in hand, scare little boys into pooping. But nothing happened. Dad gave me a hug and said *my little man*, and Mom said *you're not having any more chocolate 'cause chocolate blocks you up*, giving Grandma another dirty look like she was about to scream at her for stuffing me with chocolate, but Grandma hadn't, and we all well knew that. Grandma says that bananas and chocolate are luxuries and that we should eat spinach and carrots because spinach is good for the blood and carrots for the eyes, but best of all, they're not luxuries. A luxury is something you should be ashamed of because Mom and Dad work from morning until night and we can't indulge in luxuries and eat bananas and chocolate, because Mom and Dad could lose their jobs because of bananas and chocolate, and then we'd die of hunger like those black people because we'd all have to live off Grandpa's pension.

On Sunday Dad went to Makarska but came back before lunch. *They were really good at the medical center. Not a problem, what are colleagues for, how about a cup of coffee, how are things in Sarajevo, just a minute, the nurse will bring it out to you. And they didn't charge me a thing*, he said. I slunk under the table thinking: if he calls me to come out in that wouldn't-hurt-a-fly voice I'm gonna yell and get ready for a fight because that wouldn't-hurt-a-fly voice always means one thing – an injection's coming my way. If he calls me to say I've got to take a pill, then I'll come out because it's beneath his dignity as a doctor to lie to a patient and be there waiting with an injection instead of a pill. That's what he once said and I took him on his word.

I waited anxiously, not letting out a peep. And they knew I was waiting and were all silent too. Dad got up from the table, took a glass, and filled it with water. He crouched down next to the table, but I was already pressed up against the wall. *Here you go, this is a pill for constipation, you gotta take it, you gotta drink up*, he said as if he were scared of me. Actually, I think he was a little scared that I was going to start howling, and I was sure he'd spent ages dreaming up that word constipation, which didn't even exist, he just dreamed it up so I'd believe he was talking to me like I was a grown-up.

Anyway, I took the pill and drank up. Grandma asked when it should start working and Dad said *if nothing's happened after twenty-four hours and six pills, then . . .* I froze, because he didn't say what would happen then, and I already knew it was going to be something terrible and that's why he interrupted himself, so I wouldn't hear. They're going to take me to the hospital to see the surgeon and he's going to cut my tummy open and take all the poop out.

Grandma asked *you want to go potty?* But I didn't. A bit later she brought the potty over, *c'mon, sit down, maybe you'll go poopoo*, so I sat down, but nothing happened. *C'mon, squeeze a little*, she said. Mom rolled her eyes, and Dad said *it'll all be fine*, and Grandpa sat there the whole time chuckling to himself, trying to keep it down so no one would hear him and Grandma wouldn't call him an old hillbilly. The thing is, for Grandpa everything to do with farting, the toilet, and going to the shittery, which is what he used to say when someone – usually me – needed to go poop, was the funniest thing ever, and he'd laugh like he was retarded because he thought nature invented these things to give people something to smirk about and make women get embarrassed.

I spent all day yesterday sitting on the potty, and the whole day again today, right there in the middle of the room, trying to make the impossible possible. I didn't feel like going poop because I just didn't feel like pooping, and it didn't help any that I was so scared of what would happen if the pills didn't work and I wouldn't be able to poop even if I wanted to.

Things went downhill after the TV news when Dad got his doctor's bag out. As soon as I saw it I was on my way under the table but ran straight into Mom's lap. Her skirt didn't smell like lavender anymore but fear. Mom was as strong as a villain and I fought her, kicking and screaming, but someone lifted me up in the air. I didn't see who because my eyes were shut and I was screaming. First I howled *let me go, let me go*, then I tried *I need to poo, I need to poo, where's the potty*, but they didn't believe me or say anything. I kept howling, but they went quietly about a business they'd agreed on in advance and there was no change of plan, not even if my bones started breaking and all the color ran from my face and everything broke into the tiniest little pieces, into Lego blocks you could build a whole new person out of, someone who could go poop every day and who you didn't have to catch in the air like a butterfly and get that colored stuff all over your fingers. They got me down on the bed, Dad said *what's the matter, there's nothing to worry about, it's not going to hurt* and I was sure that something terrible was going to happen. As soon as they say it's not going to hurt, it only means one thing: it's going to hurt like hell, because whenever he or some other doctor says that something's not going to hurt, it always does.

They took my undies off and flipped me on my tummy. Mom was holding me so tight I couldn't move. I turned my head to look at the injection, but then I saw that Dad didn't have an injection in his hand, there wasn't a needle in sight; he was holding something red, which looked like a pear, a rubber pear, and instead of a stalk it had a little thin see-through tube. It looked way scarier than an injection, so I screamed my lungs out. Mom turned my head back the other way, and I felt someone holding my bum, pulling it apart and sticking something up there inside me. Though there were no bombs, cities silently crumbled in my pounding heart, *they're sticking something up there, but why? Stuff's only supposed to come out of there, don't they want me to poop? Why are they putting more stuff up there?* And then the stuff they were squirting up my bum expanded, hot, wet, and strange. It burned and stung and kept expanding, and I was full of this strange stuff, and there was more and more of it, and I thought it was never going to stop and that I'd just keep getting fuller and fuller with that stuff until I burst or admitted something they hadn't even asked me yet.

Grandma came over and said *now be a good boy and sit on the potty. If you get up on the potty we won't ever have to do this again.* But this wasn't my grandma, it was a German telling a member of the resistance that he'll quit the torture if he betrays his comrades. I spat at her, but she didn't hit me. I sat on the potty and looked at the floor. Something gushed from me onto the tin pan below, gushing out of me against my will, the same way it went in. *Are you done?* someone asked. I bit my lip and looked at the floor. *He's done,* someone said. I kept staring at the floor. Someone lifted me off the potty and wiped my bum. I didn't say anything, just looked at the floor, and when the floor wasn't there to look at anymore I shut my eyes. They sat me down on a chair. I looked at the floor. *Go play,* someone said. *Put him to bed. Everything will be fine tomorrow,* said someone else. I just sat there looking at the floor.

Now I'm lying in bed and waiting for the morning so I can finally get going. You can't leave at night because it's dark, which means you can't see where you're going, and my car doesn't have any headlights. I'm going to have another good look at that photo and see if I can see me sitting in a real car and not a cardboard box that used to have packets of cookies in it. If you can see it's a car, tell me. If you can't, I'm going to have to take my spade, my teddy bunny, and my winter sweater and set out on foot. If I stay, I'll have to look at the floor for the rest of my life, never say anything, not telling apart the voices talking to me.

When someone gets really scared

Donkeys sleep at Profunda, that's what we whisper so the old folk don't hear, because if they heard, then we'd be in for it. Profunda is out of bounds, because that's where little Vjeko went and fell and broke his neck and there was a big funeral, the procession went from one end of Drvenik to the other, from Punta to Puntin, and then it went up on Biokovo, where the cemetery is, and everyone cried because the body was a little one, and when the body is a little one, really everyone cries. When it's a big one, the only people who cry are those who loved the dead person or those who love those who loved the dead person. No one had been to Profunda since then, no one even knows what's there anymore, but by the time three years had passed since Vjeko's funeral, the wonders of Profunda had gotten bigger and bigger. Then the biggest rumor of all started going around, the one about the donkeys sleeping there at night.

Profunda used to be Mate Terin's house, but then the war started and the Italians came and they set Mate's house on fire. No one knew why they did it, why his house, and why they spared everyone else's. Maybe they just wanted to make an example of someone, show how tough they were, and they picked Mate's house by chance. Mate hung himself when he saw the remains of his house, and because he didn't have a wife or children, or any relatives except a brother who lived in New Zealand who never wrote to him, there was no one to grieve for Mate or to repair his house when the war finished. All that remained were big rough walls, white as snow, all traces of fire washed clean by the rain. The burned stone had gone white, much whiter than it was when it was a house.

You get to Profunda from the hillside above because the house is dug into the earth and cut into the rock. You can jump onto the ruins from the rock above and walk the walls on which the roof once stood. Actually, you could only do that until little Vjeko fell and broke his neck.

We're gonna do it on Saturday, said Nikša, *but we gotta wait 'til it's dark.* There were five of us, four locals and me, who wanted to be a local, but to them I was an outsider, the Sarajever. This meant I always had to prove myself more, just like I had to prove myself more when I was in Sarajevo because I was an outsider there too, a Dalmatian outsider. For half the year I spoke Dalmatian and the other half Sarajevan, but no one trusted me because they all knew that I'd always be going back to where I wasn't a Sarajevan or a Dalmatian, where I'd speak like I wasn't one or the other.

On Saturday it's Fishermen's Night, that's a village festival, and they don't make anyone go home, mothers, babies, or grandpas, and so we're going to make the most of it and go to Profunda, to see where the donkeys sleep and walk on the walls and check the whole place out, but only the brave among us of course. Scaredy-cats don't have to walk the walls, but I've got to use my chance, because if I miss it I'll always be the outsider from Sarajevo and no one will ever believe me when I speak like a Dalmatian.

Grandpa was reading the paper, Grandma cleaning the fish. *Dearie, listen to this*, said Grandpa looking at Grandma through his glasses. *In research undertaken in 1923, the noted scientist von Hentig concluded that earthquakes had an effect on the internal secretion of fish and their behavior, and that artificial convulsions could in no way explain the phenomenon. Animals obviously react to a unique geophysical phenomenon preceding the earthquake, one that culminates in the quake itself.* He read really slowly, word by word, to make it sound more serious, but I knew Grandpa was just playing serious, only reading it out loud to get Grandma going, but not too much, just a little bit, just enough for her to start bickering. He'd always needle Grandma into a little bicker when he was in a good mood.

She raised her eyebrows and curled her lips, as if surprised to hear about the fish and the earthquakes, but she continued preparing the fish for lunch all the same. I knew she knew what he was up to, that he just wanted her to say *fine Franjo, I'm preparing the fish, and you're reading about earthquakes*. Then he told her about the importance of knowing when there's going to be an earthquake because you have to be prepared and that it would be good if she could check the internal secretion of those sardines she was fixing. That's how it was supposed to go, but it doesn't because Grandma just raises her eyebrows and acts all surprised.

He keeps looking at her for a while, like a rascal; sometimes she says to him *what are you giving me that rascal look for*, and that always makes me laugh because my grandpa is seventy-five years old, and there's no way he can look at her like a rascal, but ever since Grandma started calling it the rascal look I call it that too. Grandpa goes back to his paper, heaves a deep sigh, and forgets about the rascal look because his needling didn't work out.

It's Fishermen's Night on Saturday, I say. Grandpa doesn't bat an eyelid, and Grandma keeps cleaning the fish. *Are we going to celebrate? . . . We don't have anything to celebrate, we're not fishermen, but if it's fish you're after, you'll be eating fish in about half an hour . . . But there's free fish from the grill on Saturday . . . You were going to pay for these ones, right? . . . It's not the same, those ones are from the skillet, on Saturday they'll be from the grill . . . All right, you go celebrate . . . Can I stay until after dark? . . . We'll see. If the other kids do, you will too.*

Grandpa read the paper through lunch; he'd grab a sardine with his fingers and eat it all in one go, from head to tail, the fish bones making a crunching sound between his teeth, *they're good for you, think of the calcium!* He'd leave the tails to the side so he knew how many he'd eaten. Grandma looked at him unimpressed, and I thought about what would happen if I ate a whole sardine, just like that, without picking the bones out and said I was thinking of all the calcium. I swear that when I'm big I'm going to read the paper and eat sardines whole, and no one will be able to say or do a thing about it. I don't care what I'm going to be when I grow up, I couldn't care less if I'm going to be a pilot, a butcher, or a forestry expert like Uncle Postnikov, all I care about is that time goes by really fast so I can be like Grandpa and eat sardines head, bones and all, put my glasses on the end of my nose, and read the paper. That's the important thing, to learn to read the paper, see what's going on in the world, particularly on a day like today when it's been really boring here and we ate sardines from the skillet, not from the grill. The world is so big that there are always people who weren't bored, so the papers write about those people, and the people who are bored read the papers, like us for example, like Grandpa who'd love to bicker with Grandma, and Grandma who can't be bothered bickering, and especially me, because I have to wait until Saturday to go to Profunda, to see the donkeys while they're sleeping, to walk a circle on the edge of the abyss around the burned out house of Mate Terin and be done with being an outsider from Sarajevo.

You set a fine example for the boy, says Grandma to Grandpa as he drops a sardine on the paper. He picks it up between his thumb and forefinger and puts it in his mouth, the fine bones crackling like dry pine needles under the wheels of a truck, a greasy splodge in the shape of a sardine imprinted on the paper. Like a photo! Grandpa has snaffled the sardine, but its outline stays on the newsprint. You can see its length and width, the kind of head it had, and the kind of tail. The piece of newspaper looks like a tombstone with a picture of the deceased, the deceased one in Grandpa's tummy.

It was dead when Grandma was cleaning it. That sardine was dead even when it was in the fish shop. It was dead as soon as they hauled it out of the sea. *What do sardines die from?* I asked. *They die from air, just like we'd die if someone held us under water,* said Grandpa. *That means fishermen throw out their nets to drag fish into the open air so they die? . . . No, they catch fish so we've got something to eat, and we eat only what is dead . . . What about chard, is that dead too? . . . I think it is, but no one really knows because chard doesn't have eyes. At least as far as we know, dead things are things that once upon a time moved their eyes . . . There should be fish that cast out nets for people and drag them into the sea and fry them and eat them . . . Where'd you come up with that nonsense? . . . Then we wouldn't be sorry about eating fish because we'd know fish eat us too. Get it . . . No, I don't. Why would we feel sorry for fish? . . . Because they were alive, and then fishermen caught them in their nets. If the fishermen hadn't caught them, they'd still be alive . . . You can't feel sorry for fish, if you felt sorry for fish, then you'd also have to*

feel sorry for chickens, and pigs, and calves, in the end you'd die of hunger . . .
I don't care, I'm going to feel sorry for them . . . Suit yourself, feel sorry for them,
but you'll soon see you've got nothing to eat. Grandpa was angry now, so I
decided to shut up and eat my sardines. He didn't understand fish, and
he wasn't sad when he saw a greasy splodge on the newspaper, a photo
of the sardine he'd just eaten. It was because he'd been to war, and in
war people learn what it's like to be dead and as long as they themselves
don't die, death becomes normal to them. He fought on the Soča front
as an Austrian soldier, and then the Italians took him prisoner in 1916,
and he says he had a great time back then. He was imprisoned for a full
three years, he learned Italian and kept a diary about everything that
happened, things he wanted to tell someone but didn't have anyone
to tell. He wrote the diary in Italian, but using the Cyrillic alphabet
because the Italians didn't know Cyrillic and the other prisoners didn't
know Italian, so no one could take a peek at his diary and laugh at his
secret longings. The diary is kept in Grandpa's drawer and the first of
his descendants to know both Cyrillic and Italian will be the first to read
it. Grandpa's son, my uncle, and Grandpa's daughter, my mother, don't
know Italian, so that means that one day, if I learn Cyrillic and Italian,
it could be me. Maybe then I'll find out how soldiers stop caring about
fishes' deaths and why they don't care about fish even when they're old
and not soldiers anymore, but pensioners who no army in the world
would ever send to war.

Tomorrow was Friday. There was only one more day until Saturday.

C'mon, I'll show you something you've never seen before, said Nikša. We set off for the old camp ground, to the little wooden hut where they used to keep the sun umbrellas, and sat down on old beer crates. Nikša dropped his pants. He didn't have any undies on; he was older than us and everything on him was bigger, the thing he wanted to show us too. *Check this out!* he said and pulled the skin up. I'd never done that, but I was sure it had to hurt. He put the skin back down and pulled it up again; my throat tightened like it did when they used to take me for my vaccinations. He repeated the up-down thing with the skin a few more times, *that's gotta hurt*, I thought. Everyone was silent, waiting to see what might happen next. Nikša said *look, it's getting bigger!* And it really had gotten bigger, but it was big before too.

I was scared and looked over at Zoran and Miro, but they were dead still, staring at the action between Nikša's legs. Nikša breathed faster and faster, and everything on show got redder and redder. I was scared what was going to happen next, actually most of all I was scared because Zoran and Miro were just sitting there watching not worried about a thing. Then I remembered I was an outsider from Sarajevo. I jumped up off the crate and took off outside.

I don't know whether they burst out laughing or yelled that I was a scaredy-cat, I don't know anything, because I just ran and ran and ran and didn't stop until I got home. *What's wrong, speedy, you're covered in sweat*, said Grandma. *I was doing athletics!* I gasped convincingly. She saw me and she saw Dane Korica on his way home from the Munich

Olympics. I was dying of happiness because I'd made it home and had managed to lie like a champion. I lie best when I'm happy.

On Saturday I woke up dead set that I wasn't going to leave the house. I'm not going outside until we go back to Sarajevo. Grandpa had gone to Zaostrog, I'd said I wasn't going with him, Grandma asked *are you sick?* I said *I think I'm sick*, and she said *well, you're not going to Fishermen's Night then*, I said I didn't want to *well, well, you really are sick*, she said, and fetched the thermometer. *You don't have a temperature. Where does it hurt? . . . I don't hurt. I'm just feeling a bit sick and I don't want to go outside . . . Did you get into a fight with someone yesterday? . . . No. Nothing happened yesterday, I just don't want to go outside today, and not tomorrow either . . . Why? Are you going to be sick tomorrow too? . . . If I have to go outside I will be . . . You've decided to never leave the house ever again? . . . I'll go outside as soon as we're back in Sarajevo . . . Did someone say something mean to you? . . . No, but I'm a little bit scared . . . Of what? . . . Of the donkeys that sleep at Profunda . . . Have you been to Profunda?* Grandma shot out. *No, I haven't, and I'm not going to go either, because I'm not leaving the house. Do donkeys really sleep at Profunda? . . . What donkeys? You know there isn't a donkey left in Drvenik . . . Last year there were three, Mijo's, Dušan's, and Stipe Alača's, that must be them . . . God, where'd you get that from, those donkeys are long gone! . . . Where are they then? . . . They were taken to Makarska . . . What are they doing in Makarska?* Grandma sighed and looked at the ceiling, mumbling something like *ohjesuschristsaveme* and then said *fine then, I'll tell you, but don't you dare start bawling! There's nothing there at*

Profunda, it's just a ruin like any other, full of brambles. The donkeys were sent to the slaughterhouse because nobody wanted them anymore.

I closed my eyes, my heart was really pounding; fine, I'll suck this one up too. *No more questions?* I shook my head. *But I'm not going out until we're in Sarajevo.* Grandma didn't say anything else, but I knew she was thinking that tomorrow I'd change my mind and tear off out of the house. That was what I was most afraid of because I knew there was no way I could tell her that the real reason I can't go out is because something I saw had made me really scared, something others could watch, but I couldn't, and that's why I can't go outside.

Am I a Sarajever? I followed her into the kitchen. *No, you're a Sarajevan. People from Sarajevo are called Sarajevans . . . Is that good, to be a Sarajevan? . . . It's good to be whatever, it's good to be from wherever . . . Then why do they say I'm a Sarajever? . . . Who says that? . . . Zoran and Nikša . . . They say that because they don't know anything about it and they've never been out of Drvenik . . . And why do they call me a Dalmatian in Sarajevo? . . . For the same reason. Because they've never been out of Sarajevo . . . And why do we always move? . . . Because Grandpa has asthma and has to spend lots of time at the seaside. Besides, it's good to move around because then you're in lots of places at once, the place where you really are and the place where you've come from, and if you don't like it, you could always spend the whole year with your mom in Sarajevo . . . Promise me you won't force me to go outside until we get back to Sarajevo . . . Fine, I promise, but only if you tell me why you don't want to go outside all of a sudden . . . I don't want to because they keep calling me a Sarajever*, I lied and went to my room. I always leave like that when something is really important, because as soon as I go, Grandma takes everything I've told her more seriously. I threw myself on the bed too, just in case, burying my head in the pillow and waiting to see if she'd come. When she came in, I pretended to be asleep. She pulled the covers over me and crept out.

I slept through Fishermen's Night and the mission to Profunda. Actually I slept right through everything that happened after that, everything I didn't want to see. I spent the whole seven days before we went back to Sarajevo in the house or the yard, playing by myself. One night I ran across the road, to Uncle Postnikov. He got his sketch pad and felt-tip pens out and drew snow, snowy villages and snowy cities. Uncle Postnikov is eighty years old, a Russian who once, a long time ago, fled the revolution. *Why?* I asked him. *Because I was scared*, he said, calmly sketching a reindeer-drawn sleigh with a girl on it wearing a big brown hood, her long blond hair peeking out from underneath. *When you're really scared, you have to run . . . And never go back? . . . I don't know, I couldn't go back . . . Why? . . . Because of those who weren't scared, the ones who stayed . . . I'm never going back either . . . Where are you never going back to?* he asked, surprised. *I'm never going back to the old campground*, I said to Uncle Postnikov. *If it's because you're scared, then we're the same*, he answered, and turned to a new page where the whole of Moscow was to be drawn.

The sky is beautiful when you're upside down

The world is beautiful when it's turned upside down. The sky beneath me means I could walk on it, and the top of our house in Drvenik is pinned to the sky and it's like our house is going to topple over on its side because it's resting on a single tip where the two sides of the roof meet, but the house doesn't topple over, nothing happens, there's just my laughter and wishing it would stay this way forever, that the sky stays forever under the soles of my feet, that I'm tickled by clouds of sheep, that I can walk across the sun like I do across the steamiest August asphalt, that when night falls the stars will prickle me like the sand on the island of Brač, like the shingle where Ismet Brkić is building his weekend house. I want it to stay like this forever. Squealing in delight I scream *no, no, don't let me down*, but Uncle Momčilo isn't listening, and the world spins around me a couple more times and then everything is back to normal. The concrete yard is beneath my feet, the sky high above, and our house is sitting like all the other houses, the walls rising up to the roof. There, high in the air, everything gets thinner and smaller, because in this world everything on the ground is wide and everything up high narrow, and that's how it'll stay if I can't get Uncle Momčilo to grab me by the ankles and hold me upside down, to give me a little joggle so I can see what it's like when sky and earth quake, but nothing collapses, when everything stays anchored and beautiful, and there's no pain that might kill the miracle in your eyes.

Uncle Momčilo used to be a colonel, but he's been retired from the military twenty years or something. When he retired he was younger than my mom is now. Grandma says it was *because of Đilas*, and saying it in her hush-hush voice means there's no way I'm to ask what *because of Đilas* means, because then something might happen to me *because of Đilas*, or Grandma will get mad because I've put her in a sticky situation. *Because of Đilas* is my name for a sticky situation, and that's the way it's going to be when I grow up too. When something bad happens, and all I can do is shrug my shoulders in the face of a mountain of trouble and wait to see how things play out, I'll think: Here we go again, it's all *because of Đilas*. And that'll calm my nerves some, because I'll remember Uncle Momčilo who was the first to show me how beautiful the sky is when you find yourself upside down.

Uncle Momčilo built the house next door to ours. His house isn't an old Dalmatian house, just a regular tourist one. *Zero aesthetics*, says Grandma, *a whiff of the barracks and that's how they build their weekend houses.* I don't understand what she's talking about, and what I don't understand is hard for me to remember. I sit on the floor building a castle for Queen Forgetful and repeat after Grandma *a whiff of the bawacks and that's how they build their weekend houses . . . Oh shut it you, little devil, and don't you go around saying that to people because if I hear you, you'll never set foot in my house again. And it's barracks, not bawacks.* She often does that: says something, and the second I repeat it after her or ask her a question she's already threatening me that I'll never set foot in the house again or that she's going to skin me alive.

Uncle Momčilo has a wife called Auntie Mirjana. He's got a son called Boban too, but I've only ever seen him once in my life. Boban is short and fat, and he's got a squeaky voice and doesn't look like a grown-up even though he goes to work and drives a green Fiat 1300. Auntie Mirjana bakes bread rolls and cooks baked beans. Bread rolls and baked beans are the two best things to eat in the whole world. Auntie Mirjana loves it when I ask her *when are you going to bake bread rolls again?* And she always brings me some the next day, and Grandma gets mad and says *you little scallywag, the woman'll think you're a little bread piggy,* and then I tell that it's not bread I like but bread rolls. You buy bread at the supermarket, and you bake bread rolls in the oven. Grandma says that bread rolls are actually just bread. Grandma isn't lying, I know that for sure, but I don't believe the meaning of some words, because any word can mean what I want it to mean, just like it could to her if only she weren't so grown-up and worried someone might punish her if a word means something to her that it doesn't to them. I hear the words bread roll and I'm flat-out hungry, I hear the word bread, I couldn't care less.

Auntie Mirjana taught me how to walk. I was nine months old and it was my first time in Drvenik. Grandma was cooking lunch, Mom had gone to the bank in Makarska, and I was with Auntie Mirjana in their yard. She held my hand and said *c'mon, left leg, c'mon, right leg, now left leg, now right leg*, and then she yelled *Olga, Olga, Miljenko's walking*. Grandma ran out holding a knife for gutting fish, *oh no, not now when Javorka's in Makarska . . . Maybe we shouldn't tell her*, Auntie Mirjana worried. *Out of the question, you can't keep such things from the mother*, said Grandma.

Mom came back on the afternoon bus, Auntie Mirjana said *watch this*, lifted me up by my fingertips, and I was away. Mom burst out crying and scooped me up in her arms, *my boy, my big boy*, and then I started to cry. She was supposed to be crying out of happiness, why I was crying I don't know because I don't remember a thing.

Today everyone says that Auntie Mirjana taught me to walk and it's a really big deal for them, but bread rolls are a really big deal for me, and so is Uncle Momčilo teaching me how to look at the world from upside down.

It's a shame when people only see each other once a year, aging so quickly in each other's eyes, Grandpa said. *Franjo, believe me, you haven't aged a bit*, said Uncle Momčilo. *Get off with you, the old fossil's mummified like Tutankhamen*, said Grandma. *And you, Miss Olga, you just get more beautiful with age . . . Oh please, Momčilo, mocking old ladies doesn't become you. I wear every wrinkle as a memory, and you know, I remember a lot. That's why I don't go senile, because every single one reminds me of something.*

They repeat the same story year after year; one year the old fossil is mummified like Tutankhamen, the next he's as shriveled as a dry plum, and the one after that he's embalmed like Lenin, everything else stays the same. They lie and they're happy when they're lying, and I'm happy when I lie too, it's just that everyone gets mad at me but there's no one to get mad at them. I don't get mad because I can see that they're somehow sad. Grandma's sadness is in the corners of her mouth, Uncle Momčilo's in his eyes, Grandpa's in his nose. Each of them is sad where you can see the sadness best, and they're sad because they really can see each other getting older. For grown-ups, old age is reason enough for sad mouths, eyes, and noses, because they think it's better to be a child, and no one can convince them otherwise.

We didn't come by ourselves, said Uncle Momčilo. *Momir is with us*, Auntie Mirjana folded her arms. *Who's Momir?* I asked. They'd thought I wasn't there again because I was building a castle for Queen Forgetful. They looked at one another, startled. Grandpa shrugged his shoulders, Auntie Mirjana raised her eyebrows, and Grandma said *you know, Auntie Mirjana and Uncle Momčilo have a grandson now . . . Good for them,*

I answered coldly and returned to the castle, which had been under heavy snow for right about three seconds now.

I don't want to see him . . . But why not? He's a baby, baby Momir . . . What do I care? You go, I'm not . . . But Auntie Mirjana has baked bread rolls . . . Good for her, I'm not hungry, I don't care. So Grandma and Grandpa went to see baby Momir, and I stayed with my castle and everything suddenly went quiet. I'd never heard such silence. All you could hear was a big summer fly and my breathing. I stared at the wall and listened. Inhale, exhale, inhale, exhale, just like that, but then it was more choppy inhale, long exhale, choppy inhale, long exhale, and then came the flood. I thought about Auntie Mirjana's bread rolls and how I'd never eat them again. I was all alone, but my loneliness wasn't mixed with fear, it was loneliness mixed with sadness; mouth, eyes, and ears, all sad. I didn't have anyone anymore, they were all with baby Momir.

When Grandpa and Grandma came back I was already sitting in the broom closet, there behind the heavy curtain where Uncle kept the oars and motor for the dinghy. *Here you go, Auntie Mirjana sent this along for you,* said Grandma and held out a bread roll wrapped in a white cloth. I took the bread roll, hot and heavy, and put it in my lap. But I didn't want to eat it. I can't eat on such sad occasions. I can just stare at the tips of my toes, listen to my breathing, shake my head at every question I'm asked, a rusty old buoy no one's ever going to tie their boat to.

How about a walk in the clouds, Uncle Momčilo came over as soon as I woke up. I looked him straight in the eye and didn't say a thing. *I know you want to. It's our thing, just between you and me. No one else knows how beautiful it is . . . I will if you promise me something . . . If I can do it, I can promise you, shoot, just don't forget that I'm not Il Grande Blek or Commandante Mark . . . Promise me you'll never show Momir how to walk in the clouds.* Uncle Momčilo went quiet and put his finger to his bottom lip, like he always does when he's thinking. *You know, this is a complicated business. I mean, you've caught me on the wrong foot, on my left foot. You see, the thing is, I wanted to ask you something about that, and now I don't know how to begin . . . You mean, you won't promise me . . . Wait a second, that's got nothing to do with it. It's something else. I need your help, but I don't know how to explain it to you . . . Promise me you'll never show Momir how to walk in the clouds,* I repeated, word by word, slowly because my inhale had gotten choppy, and Uncle Momčilo's face had shattered into a thousand pieces, flashing in brilliant strips of light, the rays with which tears begin on a sunny day. *Of course I promise you, but I also want to ask you to promise me something . . . Promise you what? . . . You know, I'm already an old man, and when Momir grows up a little bit, I'll be even older and weaker, my strength will have gone, you understand, so if I may, I'd like to ask you something, if it's not going to be too big a problem for you . . . C'mon, just tell me what I need to promise you.* I wanted to be serious because Uncle Momčilo was really jumpy and it seemed like I was his only hope. *I'd like you to promise me that you'll show Momir how to walk in the clouds. You'll be big and strong by then, and you'll be able to show him, and because I taught you how to walk in the clouds, I can't ask anyone else. That's it, that's what I'd like to ask you, if it isn't too big a problem.*

That night, my promise to Uncle Momčilo went to the top of my list of priorities in life. I needed to be strong, to be really, really strong, to be so strong that when baby Momir isn't a baby anymore I'd be able to teach him how to walk in the clouds because his grandpa can't teach him. And he can't for two reasons: The first is that he promised me he would never teach him, and the second is that people get older and in old age they lose their strength, so one day they become children who need someone to show them how to walk in the clouds, but no one shows them because it's impolite to grab old people by the ankles and hang them upside down. There are lots of impolite things that could make the whole world happy. I don't mean burping, because burping has never made anyone happy, and you only burp because you're asking for trouble and risking a box on the snout. I was more thinking of all the beautiful things forbidden to old people. My grandpa would definitely be happy if someone picked him up by his ankles and flipped him upside down, so one last time he could see how beautiful the sky is beneath our feet.

I decided that first thing in the morning I'd go over to Auntie Mirjana and Uncle Momčilo's, take a look at baby Momir, and expertly assess how much time I had before I'd teach him to walk in the clouds.

You're funny, be funny for us again

It's hard to believe there are Germans who catch colds. Take Hans for example: He pulls into Drvenik every February, parks his camp trailer, doesn't bother unpacking but just strips to his swimming trunks, throws his clothes on the backseat and a towel over his shoulder, and dashes off to the beach. Grandma says Hans is as ugly as a bulldog with his stubby legs and shoulders as broad as three non-German men. I like Hans because he's funny, and he's funniest when he runs through Drvenik in his trunks on the first day of February, wheezing like a locomotive, tearing down the pier, and plopping into the water – really, he just plops. Hans doesn't jump in feet- or headfirst; he throws the length and breadth of himself into the water, the same way other people happily flounce onto a soft bed that's been waiting for them a good long while.

The Drvenik kids all gather on the pier, cheering Hans on as he battles the waves and the wild, unfazed whether it's blowing a southerly or a northeaster – and there's always something blowing in February. Hans doesn't care about the cold either, whether the peaks of the Biokovo range are dusted in snow or crabs have frozen in the shallows. Hans just swims, yelling *ah fucking son of a bitch* as he goes, and the whole of Drvenik, from Ćmilj to Lučica, knows the crazy Kraut has arrived and opened the goose-bumps and winter swimming season. When Hans swims, everyone who spots him out there in the sea gets goose bumps too.

The first few years people thought Hans was going to drown, it was just a matter of time before his heart stopped or the waves carried him off, but in time they got used to his ways. People figured that the world was full of all sorts but that only Germans were this sort; the miracle was that they had cold blood, as if they were fish and not people. Whenever someone caught a winter cold they'd think of Hans, because Hans never caught cold, because Hans didn't care about the cold and he'd plop into any February sea.

Every winter Grandma fretted about our bougainvillea. That's a flower that once lived in the ancient forests of the Amazon and was brought to Europe by a Frenchman. Europe is dry and cold for a bougainvillea, so it always needs protecting from drought or the chill, at least until it shoots up into a big rambling vine with pink-and-violet flowers. Someone should actually take it back to the jungle, but since no one knows where that is or how much a ticket costs, my grandma is in charge of protecting it from cold and drought; in February she wraps it in netting and plastic bags, and in August she gives it plenty to drink.

She'd just finished wrapping it when Hans ran past. *You poor wee thing, where on earth has the wind blown you*, she said to the bougainvillea. She doesn't think the flower understands but knows plants don't really die because a seed or root always remains, but Grandma wants to save this bougainvillea's life all the same and carps on about how it's going to flower beautifully and be such a pretty sight. This is a lie: She's not thinking about beauty or pretty sights, she's just afraid that one morning she'll find a dead frozen plant in front of the house, and that this will give her the feeling you feel for everything that's dead but was once alive. She'd like our bougainvillea to be like Hans, and she'd like Hans to be like our bougainvillea. A flower shouldn't have to suffer cold and drought, and a German wouldn't make a fool of himself if he were a little more sensitive to the cold and didn't go swimming in the wild winter sea.

Franjo, the Kraut's back, she said coming inside. Grandpa puts the paper down and asks if there's any beer without waiting for the answer because he already knows there isn't any because there's never any if Hans isn't here, so he takes his wallet and heads for the store. Hans and Staka will be over before the hour's up. That's how long Hans needs to plunk in and dry off and Staka to sort out the camp trailer. Grandma calls them Krauts even though Staka is from Smederevo and isn't a

Kraut at all, but Grandma's in the habit of giving joint names to everyone who comes to visit: our relatives from Zenica are Zeničanians, Auntie Mirjana and Uncle Momčilo are the Nikolićs, Uncle Ismet and Auntie Minka the Brkićs, Uncle Postnikov and Auntie Borka the Postnikovs, and Rajka and Božica *the rubes*, so it never takes much to know who's over. Hans and Staka's family name is Kirchmayer, so it's easier to call them the Krauts than the Kirchmayers.

Hans comes in hollering *Hey Franjo, what's up, what's down*, and gives Grandpa a hug, backslapping him so hard I always notice how full of dust Grandpa's back was before Hans beat it out of him. *Madame Olga, you just get more beautiful, like Greta Garbo in* Ninotchka, Hans bows and kisses Grandma's hand. Only Hans and actors in black-and-white films kiss women's hands, I mean, maybe there are other people who kiss them too, but not in my life. Then he comes up to me: *you've still got blond hair, if you're blond the next time I see you I'll teach you German so you can hit on a Berlin girl.* He takes me in his arms, throws me in the air, and catches me. Every time I'm scared I'll get stuck up on the ceiling and stay there like the saints in Sarajevo Cathedral.

Staka stands to the side smiling, just waiting with a bag full of presents. She always gives me a bar of Braco chocolate because she thinks I'm the little boy on the cover, and I always tell her that I'm not, but it never helps. That's Staka for you: She believes what she believes and that's the end of it. Grandma says she couldn't be with Hans if she were any different, but I don't get what that is supposed to mean.

Why couldn't she be with Hans otherwise? I don't know, probably she couldn't be his wife or couldn't travel to Drvenik with him unless she was sure that I was really the boy on the chocolate packet.

The only time Hans stops shouting is when he talks to Grandma and Grandpa in German. Then he's quiet like everyone else. He says he didn't learn to speak our language but to shout it, and that if he had to speak it, he wouldn't know a single word. Nobody believes him when he shouts that, but everyone laughs. Staka laughs along too, and I think that it's real love when you can laugh along with someone even though you see them every day and you've lived with them your whole life or maybe a bit less.

Hans became a German soldier when he turned eighteen and he came to fight in Yugoslavia. When I was little, two, three, four, I'd always look out for Hans in Partisan films because no one ever told me they were all actors and that in a film nothing's real, but even then I knew none of them were Hans because they all died and Hans was still alive. *Hans, were you at Sutjeska*, I ask him. *I was, I was*, Hans yells, *twice, with Staka and without Staka . . . And did you kill Sava Kovačević? . . . I didn't, I shot up into the treetops, you know, into the pines. I was afraid of killing . . . So who killed Sava Kovačević? . . . I don't know, there were lots of Germans, and when there are lots of people, it's hard to know who's killing whom.*

When the war finished, Hans got taken prisoner. He worked building a factory in Smederevo, Partisan Staka keeping watch on him through the crosshairs. Back then he didn't know how to shout in our language, but there, from a distance and staring down the barrel of a machine gun, he told Staka he loved her, and when she somehow understood what he was saying she loaded the gun and sought permission from Commandant Joža Beraus to execute the prisoner. He said there had been enough killing, confiscated her rifle, and decreed that henceforth she had to keep guard unarmed. Staka bridled and burst into tears, and Commandant Joža gave her a hug and said *lassie, you're fifteen years old, and you've got no idea what that weapon'll do to your sweet little finger, the one that wants to pull the trigger. You're angry with me now, but one day you'll say thank you, Uncle Joža.*

So it went, Partisan Staka guarded the prisoners, and every morning Hans clutched at the air in front of his chest, made the shape of a heart with his fingers, and blew the heart to Staka. She got mad and reported him to the commandant and got a chiding for her trouble: *you should be ashamed of yourself, are you a Skojevka or are you not? You're there to guard the prisoners, not to worry about their flirting.* Things went on like this a whole six months, until one day Hans wasn't a prisoner anymore and showed up at the construction site in an ugly gray suit and with an army satchel on his back. He stood before Partisan Staka, took a piece of paper from his pocket, and read aloud: *I apologize if I offended you, but I loved you and loved it most when you were on guard to stop me escaping. I will always remember you.*

Staka spat at his feet, but not hard: just hard enough for him to get the message that she was a Partisan, and that he'd been an occupying soldier. Come the next day she was desolate without him. *My heart has gone*, she said, and someone reported her. *Enough's enough*, said Commandant Joža, *I've had it up to here with bloody kids who want to kill one minute and fall in love the next.* He sent Staka packing, her Partisan days were over.

Hans left for his city, but when he got there his street, his parents, his sisters, none of them were there anymore; everything lay in ruins, and what wasn't in ruins was dead. Without a single living relative, Hans was left all alone. *Back then I could have been a German or a China-man, it was all the same, you're nothing without your kin.* Staka was the only one Hans had, so he swung his step back to Yugoslavia. They put him straight in jail. Hans told them he wanted to be a Communist. They asked him why he wanted to be a Communist, and he said it was because of the working class and because he'd been left all alone in the world, and as a good Communist he wouldn't be alone anymore. They said *very well then, you can stay in Yugoslavia, but don't let us catch you spying.* Hans said he wouldn't spy and headed for Smederevo to look for Staka.

I don't know what happened next, just that in the end they got mar-ried, and that Commandant Joža Beraus was their best man. At the wedding they sang "All men will be brothers" and began the life that came after the one where Hans had been a fascist and Staka a Partisan who wanted to write his death sentence. I don't quite know how all this came to pass and neither do Grandpa and Grandma. Grandma says *they're both crazy*, and Grandpa says *they're not crazy, it's the times.* They philosophize like this after Hans has drunk all the beer, given us our hugs and kisses, and gone off with Staka to sleep in their camp trailer.

It's not actually a camp trailer because Hans has concreted around it and built a little hut alongside. In front of the house Staka has planted a lemon tree and an oleander tree and roses and marigolds. It's such a motley mix that Grandma says it's as ugly as Hans himself and I say it's as funny as Hans himself. Their weekend house is the strangest place in Drvenik and the building inspectorate has twice come from Makarska to demolish it because they think it's an eyesore scaring off tourists, but they didn't demolish it because Hans has a building permit. They said *signore, don't yell at us*, and then they left. Grandpa says they're just looking for a loophole in the law and that in the end they'll demolish Hans and Staka's little hut, and Hans says that much worse things could happen, and it would just mean he and Staka would have to start a new life. Hans thinks there's only one thing for every misfortune or unpleasantness suffered: to begin a new life. Grandpa says this is brave, and Grandma says that it's dumb.

It's such sorrow we don't have children, says Hans, *everything is peachy, but that's so sad.* Then it's like the cat's got Grandma's and Grandpa's tongues, and they look at their hands laid out on the table as if they're somehow guilty or have done a number on someone because they've had three children. *There's joy without children too*, says Grandpa. *Of course, of course there's joy, but there's so much sorrow without children,*

Hans howls back. *You know, children grow up, get married, and leave, you end up on your own again,* Grandpa tries to get Hans to quit it. *You can be happy on your own too, but without children, without children, there's such sorrow,* Hans nods his head. *You get older and forget you brought them into the world,* Grandpa sticks to his tune. *Whether you forget or not, there's still joy, but Franjo, buddy, there's such sorrow without children,* Hans howls back, and I know that all hell's going to break loose any minute. Grandpa's getting edgy – his asthma, according to Grandma – and boy does he go for it when he finally blows his top.

He bangs his fist on the table knocking over Hans's beer. Grandpa's bellowing in German, Hans grabs his hand, I'm crying, God what's wrong with me, why am I crying. I'm crying because I'm scared, I'm scared because Grandpa's knocked Hans's beer over, and Hans is cute and funny, he's Grandpa's friend, and now Grandpa's yelling at him, Grandma's hugging Staka, Staka is smiling like someone who's misplaced their smile, no one notices me, and Grandpa just keeps yelling, Hans grabs his other hand, saying something to him softly in German in a voice much quieter than Grandpa's now hoarse one, and I don't understand anything, not a thing.

Grandpa's breathing heavily and I've hidden myself under the table from where I'm sneakily looking at Hans. Hans has his head in his hands and his elbows on the table in the puddle of beer. His face is serene like he was dead, just his droopy bottom lip quivering sometimes, like a tamarisk leaf in the wind. Grandma's gone into the yard with Staka. Nothing happens for a while: It's just the two of them, one who's breathing, the other with a lip quivering in the wind. I want to slip outside, but they'd see me. They must think I'm not here. And it's better I'm not here. Sometimes it's so good you're not here that you really wish you weren't there until everyone starts to smile again.

A tear runs down Hans's face, turns at the nose, and descends on his plumpy tamarisk lip. Then there's a second drop on the other side of his face, again turning at the nose and falling on his lip. Then a third and a fourth. Hans is funny even when he's not making a joke, like something sweet and dear that makes you smile. *I'm sorry, Franjo, I didn't know, I just wanted to say how sad it is without children, I didn't know I'd upset you.* It seems Hans can actually speak our language quietly. *You didn't upset me, it's just the southerly, and that I can damn hardly breathe*, said Grandpa, *and you, little man, out from under the table, scram. Eavesdropping on your elders' conversations, you're a bloody disgrace.*

I ran into the yard. Grandma was showing Staka our bougainvillea. Staka was stroking a leaf with her index finger, the same finger she'd wanted to kill Hans with. *I'm going to play*, I said, and ran out onto the road. Grandma whispers *lucky the little one doesn't understand German*. I heard that because I always hear her when she's whispering. She doesn't know how to whisper so I don't hear. However quiet or far away she is, I can always hear her whispering, and when you whisper it's because there's a secret to be kept, it's just that this time I don't know what the secret's about, what I wasn't supposed to hear, why it's lucky I don't understand German, what Grandpa yelled at Hans and why he got so mad at him just because Hans said how sad it was without children. I can't make head or tail of any of this, but one day I'll find out and then I'll tell everyone.

The next year the building inspectorate demolished Hans's weekend house. I mean, they demolished the hut, the camp trailer they hauled up on a big truck and carted off to Makarska. The concrete foundation, mangled roses, and uprooted oleander and lemon trees were all that was left. Grandpa phoned Hans and Staka in Smederevo. He said *don't cry, my dear*, and then switched back to German. I only understood two words, *Kamerad* and *Freunde*. The first he said coldly, the second warmly, so I thought the second word sounded lovely and meant something like *see you soon*, and the first word sounded cold and meant something like *they found a loophole in the law and demolished your house*. But Hans wasn't afraid of cold words, just like he wasn't afraid of the cold sea. Hans is never cold. He's not even cold when crabs freeze in the February shallows.

Hans and Staka never came to Drvenik again. *Idiot Kraut, he says you can never go back where they demolished your house*, said Grandpa, sitting down to write Hans a letter. *What do you want to say to Hans, dictate it to me*, and it was then I had to compose my first letter: *Dear Hans, thank you for not killing Sava Kovačević, it's cold here like the cold when you sit with your bare bottom in an empty bath. We've all caught colds without you. You're funny, be funny for us again.*

When I die, you'll see how many better people there are

The almond trees bloomed in February and Grandpa said *here we go again, spring in midwinter.* He said that every February, never getting used to winters finishing so early at the seaside, the rules of nature of a lifetime no longer applied. The rules didn't apply because he wasn't in Travnik, where in February the snows fall on Mount Vlašić, and he wasn't in Sarajevo, where they cover Trebević, Igman, and Tolmin, the whole world a whiteout. He was in Drvenik now and the only things to go white were the blossoming almond flowers, which he called the buds of spring. He'd sing *snow falls on the buds of spring* and we'd all think nostalgia had got the better of old Franjo, and that he was summoning his native soil to leap the Biokovo range and cover the sea in snow. *Do*

you think the sea will ever freeze over? I ask. *I don't think so, but it's possible
. . . Does something that's possible ever happen? . . . Of course such things
happen. That's why we say it's possible . . . So the sea will freeze over? . . . I
don't think so, but let's say it does. What's it to you? . . . Well, then we could
walk across the sea to Sućuraj. You could buy a newspaper and then we'd come
back . . . We can buy a newspaper here . . . Yeah, but it's not the same. We've
never walked to Sućuraj, but if the sea froze over we could . . . That wouldn't
be a good thing. The fish wouldn't have any air . . . But they don't need air.
What do they need air for when they don't breathe? . . . They need air. You'll
learn this stuff at school. If the sea froze over the mackerel would die, and then
what would happen to the dolphins, it's not worth thinking about. Dolphins
are like humans, they come out of the water to breathe . . . Where do they get
out, on the beach? . . . No, they jump up above the surface, breathe, and then
dive back down again. They're very practical . . . Why don't they come right
out, wouldn't that be better than all that jumping? . . . They'd die if they were
always out in the air. Their skin needs the sea, their lungs the air. They don't
live in the sea or out of it, they live somewhere in between . . . Like we do? . . .
What do you mean, like we do? . . . You know, we don't live in Sarajevo or in
Drvenik, but somewhere in between, because you'd die of asthma if we were
always in Sarajevo . . . You could put it like that. I'd die because I'd be breathing fog and smog . . . And do dolphins feel sorry they're not always out in the
air? . . . Why would they feel sorry about that? . . . Because you're always
sorry about not being in Sarajevo and that you don't get to see the snow fall
or the whiteness of the mountains anymore . . . I'm not sorry about that . . .*

Then why do you start singing about snow falling on the buds of spring the minute the almond flowers blossom? . . . Because that's my song and I've got every right to sing it, even if it doesn't snow and the sea never freezes over.

Grandpa tells everyone he doesn't fear death. When he's coughing away in the morning thinking he's never going to catch his breath again, he murmurs *oh death, sweet death*, as if he were wooing it because he's fallen in love with it, but death's not interested. *Does death hurt?* I ask. *I don't care if it hurts, just as long as it doesn't suffocate.* Grandpa doesn't believe in pain and so nothing ever hurts him. Any kind of pain is something strange, like it's got nothing to do with him. When he had a tooth out he told Leitner the dentist, our neighbor, *take it out, but no injections*, and Leitner said to him *but Mr. Rejc, it's not the Middle Ages.* Grandpa ignored him and said *I don't care what age we're in*, so Leitner took his tooth out just like that and Grandpa didn't even clench his fist in pain. *My Franjo's no hero*, said Grandma, *he's just scared of the anesthetic . . . I'm not scared of anesthetic, I just want to know what's happening to me.*

But Nikola, who's from Ćmilj, he's afraid of pain and dying and anesthetic. He comes over to see Grandpa and says *Signore Franjo, I'm a dead dog am I*, and Grandpa replies *Nikola, buddy, get yourself off to the doctor*, and Nikola mopes: *I can't, I don't know if I'm more scared or more ashamed.* After that Grandpa doesn't say anything, just pours him a rakia and they just stare at each other until Nikola drinks up and leaves. Nikola comes over to our place so someone actually looks at him because in the village people have been looking straight through him for years. They go by him looking at the tips of their toes or out to sea, giving Nikola and his fears and his shame the widest berth. Some people say hi and look away at the same time, but most just make like he's not even there, like he's committed some terrible crime and you can't forgive his just being alive.

Nikola's got tuberculosis, and in Drvenik tuberculosis is a disgrace. He doesn't go to the doctor because he's ashamed and because his family won't let him out of the house in any case. Everyone knows what he's got, but it's still better the doctors in Split don't find out, that way at least the story doesn't spread all the way there. When someone has tuberculosis in Sarajevo or in other cities, they aren't ashamed and neither are their families, they just go to the doctor, stay in the hospital for a while, and go back home happy and healthy. A disgrace in the city is different from a disgrace in the countryside. In Drvenik it's a disgrace Nikola's got tuberculosis, but in Sarajevo it's a disgrace when someone pees in the building hallway and they catch him.

There will be heavy rains this spring, that's what Grandpa reads in the newspaper. That's not good news for people with sick lungs. He and Nikola have both got sick lungs, but Nikola's problem is infectious and Grandpa's isn't. His asthma is his business and he can't give it to anyone else – except I could inherit it because he's my grandpa – but Nikola could give his tuberculosis to anyone, especially if they blew their nose with his handkerchief. Once Nikola took his hankie out of his pocket and I got shivers up and down my spine. I wanted to grab it and blow my nose so bad. I'm scared of pain and the doctor and I don't like being sick, but I wanted that hankie, and if Nikola had accidentally dropped it I would have grabbed it and got sick. It's like when I'm standing on a really high balcony. I always want to jump, even though I wouldn't like to be dead. Putting your nose into Nikola's hankie is an adventure, but I know that I won't because we're not daredevils, we're people quietly and politely getting on with our lives, and we don't go looking for the real devil; he shows up on his own account. Daredevils spend all their time daring the devil, trying to catch him by the tail, but he gets away, and they just laugh and that's why they burn bright and die young and are always a burden to everyone.

It's really been raining a month now. Grandpa's finding it hard to breathe and he's always real pissed. Grandma says it won't be his heart, asthma, or kidneys that kill him, but his impishness. Only Grandpa and I have impishness, but everyone yells at me because of mine and I have to scram so I don't get it on the snout, but they never say anything to him when he's being impish, they just stay out of his way, everyone except for Dad when he comes from Sarajevo. He's always testing Grandpa for something, holding his hand and checking his pulse, tapping him with his finger, looking him up and down, and even though Grandpa answers all his questions he's even more pissed when Dad goes. He's pissed because he's kept something to himself and now he feels guilty about it. Asthma is for Grandpa what a cake-baking disaster is for Grandma: It's something that chanced upon him one day and made him sick, but it didn't just happen to him all willy-nilly but because he'd done something wrong and because in life in general he didn't know the ratio of flour to milk to eggs or something else you make life with, so that's why he got asthma, to torture and suffocate him and it would always be his own fault. It's always worse when it's your own fault because then you're even more pissed with everyone else. And there's something more besides: Grandma can hide her baking from guests and no one ever knows about it, but Grandpa can't hide his asthma from anyone because we all hear him wheeze when he breathes. There was a time when roosters woke people in the morning in Metjaš and Drvenik, but now my grandpa's cough does the job. He coughs away and all the while fathers are tying their ties, mothers are getting ready for the office, and fishermen are returning to shore.

It looks like Nikola died, said Grandma when she came back from the store. *What do you mean – it looks like he died*, Grandpa asked. *That's what it looks like, nobody wants to say anything but they've all gone to Lučica, the whole village is there. The road to Zaostrog has probably collapsed . . . Can we go to Lučica too*, I asked. *No, we can't, looking at a dead man isn't like going to the circus*. It's always like that, the minute something interesting happens in Drvenik I'm not allowed to see it and they always tell me it's not a circus, that it's not for my eyes and it would be better if I put a sock in it and quit asking my questions. I'm going to miss all the important stuff, so when I'm in Sarajevo and they ask me what's up in

Drvenik I'll only be able to say I don't know because my grandma and grandpa didn't let me see if there was anything up.

The next day I found out what happened to Nikola. All the kids were talking about it so I just made like I knew it all already and hung on their every word. He took ill where the highway makes a sharp bend and sat down on a rock even though it was raining. He felt so bad he preferred getting wet to walking. Then he started to cough up blood. There was more and more blood and it rained harder and harder. In the end he coughed up all the blood inside him, but the rain was so hard it washed the blood away and half the highway turned pink like someone had melted the Pink Panther and poured him all over the road. Blood goes from red to pink in the rain and that's why it's better to bleed in the rain because then you don't scare anyone. Nikola wouldn't have been scared, or at least less scared than if he'd bled on a sunny day when all the colors would have been brighter and there would have been nothing to make the red blood go Pink Panther pink.

He was dead when they found him. He sat on the stone, his face as white as lime and smiling like an angel. I don't know how angels smile, but that's what Granny Tere said Nikola's smile was like and she always goes to church so she knows how angels smile. Nikola was smiling because he was dead and wasn't scared or ashamed anymore, so he could finally smile again, like back when he didn't have tuberculosis. People smile when they think something's funny but it's nicest to smile when it's nothing to you. Something was up, you were in pain, suffocating and worrying, and then it's nothing and it's funny because it's nothing and you think there was nothing there to start with, you just got a bit anxious and thought you were in pain, suffocating and worrying.

The next day they took Nikola up into the mountain and buried him in the cemetery on Biokovo, out from which you can see the whole vastness of the sea; the sea beyond Hvar and Pelješac, beyond Korčula, beyond Vis, all the way to Italy. In the end, beyond everything there is still the ocean, but out there it gets round. When you're up on Biokovo, when you're at the cemetery, you understand why once upon a time people thought the earth stretched out flat: that's because they'd never climbed Biokovo and couldn't see the ocean is round, and if the ocean is round, then the earth is round too. I think the cemetery is built so high, right up there on Biokovo, so when the living bury the dead they can take comfort that they know what the dead didn't. When someone in Drvenik dies, you learn that the earth is round.

Grandpa and Grandpa went to the funeral and came back all red. After the rain a fiery sun had beat down; Grandpa was furious and breathing heavily and cussing Nikola out for not dying some other day, like some sunny day so that when they buried him it would be raining, so the funeral procession wouldn't have fried climbing up Biokovo and baked all the way down. *No one cried*, said Grandma. *They've washed the shame from their hands*, said Grandpa, disgusted not by the shame that was no more – by Nikola – but by the living, now all relieved there was no one in Drvenik with tuberculosis anymore.

Fine, I'll take you to see where he died, said Grandpa and reached for his umbrella. There had been five days of rain and I couldn't wait for it to stop. I wanted to see the place of death and was worried the highway wouldn't be pink anymore like a melted Pink Panther. And my worry was well-placed: The asphalt was black, like any other highway. I looked around and everything looked rainy and normal, no trace of a special place for dying, no sign of anything Nikola must have left for us so we'd know where he died.

That's where he sat down, Grandpa pointed to a white rock where the number 480 was written under a red line. *It means he died on the four hundred and eightieth kilometer of the highway, but that doesn't matter. Nikola's gone, no story, straight to bed. You happy? We can go home now.* Actually I wasn't that happy. I was confused. I thought there would be a mark at the spot where he died; maybe the highway wouldn't be pink but at least there'd be something giving away that someone had been there and then suddenly wasn't there. If there isn't something like that, then there's also no reason for someone to die and when there's no reason for someone to die, then the sadness is much bigger than a little cry and bye-bye. Then you would never stop crying when someone you loved died.

Why do people die? . . . They die because they get old and because if people just kept being born and didn't die there wouldn't be enough room on earth . . . It would be better if no more people were born and people didn't die . . . Why would that be better? . . . Well, because then only people we know would be alive, who were good, and new people who we don't know wouldn't come along and make old people die . . . How do you know those new people wouldn't be better than the old ones? . . . No one is better than you . . . Nonsense, of course there are people better than me. There are lots of people better than me, you just haven't met them yet. You'll see when you grow up . . . I'll see when you die? . . . Yes, you could put it that way. When I die, you'll see how many better people than me there are. Your friends will be better, the woman you marry will be better, and your children will be better. They'll all be better than me and one day you won't be sad about my death anymore . . . You'll die for those better people? . . . Yes, and you'll die for those better people too. The important thing is we die in the right order and children don't die before their parents.

He'd never spoken for so long and so quietly and calmly. He let the umbrella down and shook it out. The drops splashed all over the kitchen tiles and all over Grandma's hair. He did it deliberately and smiled. *You old fool*, said Grandma without even looking at him. She doesn't have to look at him to know why he shook the umbrella out on the tiles and all over her hair, and he doesn't have to see her eyes to know she's not mad. Even when he doesn't shake the umbrella out, he knows she thinks the same thing – *old fool* – it's just there's no reason to say it aloud. They're happy because in the rainy season when it's tough for people with sick lungs so some people have to die, that it was Nikola who died, who no one said *old fool* to, and who didn't have anyone to shake the umbrella out on. There are big crowds in places where people die; it's like at the bus station with everyone pushing and shoving, so when you look from afar, it seems everyone wants to get on, but actually they're pushing and shoving to not get on, to hang around until the last bus comes along, which you climb aboard because the crowd's gone, because you've got a ticket in your hand and there's no one left to say excuse me to if you stay alive.

I beg you, don't let her jump

It was summer, wildfires burned red beneath the Biokovo range, fire-brigade sirens wailed, people ran with containers full of water, the sea smelled of Coppertone and glimmered in the colors of a petroleum rainbow, and we packed our things in the Duck, our Citroën, and got ready for the journey to Sarajevo. Grandpa had died eight months ago, I'd finished first grade in Drvenik, and now we could head happily home. Sarajevo would be home now, the time of a little Sarajevo, a little Drvenik was over. It was all over with Grandpa's asthma too, and from now on we'd only go to the seaside as tourists. Drvenik wasn't our home, which is what I'd thought; it was the home of Grandpa's illness, like a hospital where you go to get well but everyone knows you're going to die there in the end.

We're leaving forever. I have the feeling we're leaving forever because that's the only explanation for why we've packed our winter sweaters and shoes in the trunk and we're not leaving anything behind except the feeling we're never coming back. If we do come back it'll be as folks on vacation, folk just passing through, all nervy because they're dead set on making the best out of their vacation, so they yell at each other and drag other people's children along by the ears. I feel sick thinking that next year we'll be tourists too, and already feel like a little German who'll run screaming out of the water when he sees a crab among the rocks and gets marched off to the medical center in Makarska if he stands on a sea urchin. There are three tiny black dots on my big toe, three sea urchin spikes from three years ago. I didn't tell Grandma and Grandpa I'd stepped on a sea urchin because then they would've heated a needle in a flame, which is a terrifying sight. It would've hurt like hell if they took the spikes out with that, so I tried myself with my fingernails, but they wouldn't come out, so now I'm taking the three spikes to Sarajevo with me as a memento and proof that I'll never be just a regular tourist.

We drive slowly through the village and we pass people with inflatable mattresses and a girl wearing a rubber ring with a duck's head around her waist, half girl, half duck. People we know line the roadside, Auntie Senka, Uncle Tomislav, Granny Tere, they wave to us because they know we're not leaving like we do every year but we're leaving forever. Grandma waves back and I lower my head because I'm ashamed. I'm ashamed because something important in our lives is happening and everyone knows about it. Important things are supposed to happen in secret. We should have slipped away in the night while everyone was still asleep, so that no one saw or heard us or knew we'd gone. They might've thought we'd never been there in the first place. In actual fact, we should have made our exit as if we had died too.

Uncle Naci is driving us, my uncle from Ilidža. He's got whiskers, glasses with black frames, and size thirty-nine shoes, and he looks to me like a French table-tennis player who's always going to lose to a Chinaman in the end. He turns around and asks *are you sad*, I say *no, I'm not sad*, and stare out at the tiny heads of bathers in the glistening sea, two yachts far from shore and Hvar still farther off, right out there on the horizon where earth and sky meet, where Hvarians live, who, before they took me to the island for the first time, I thought were half human, half Martian.

I don't know if I'm sad, I just know that I'm scared, but I'm not admitting to one or the other. One shouldn't ask such questions, and when I grow up, the first chance I get I'm going to say *one shouldn't ask such questions*, because there's only one answer, there's only *no, no, no*, there's always only *no, I'm not sad, I'm not scared, I'm not anything*, and now everyone can smile themselves to death and jump for joy and have everything fall out of their pockets and jingle on the asphalt because for the zillionth time someone said they're not sad and not scared, but everyone well knows that that's exactly what you say when you're sad and scared but don't dare tell.

Down there in the pines, poor little Fićo's down there, I tap Uncle Naci on the shoulder. *Fićo, who's that? . . . He's not a person, he's a car. He flew off the highway last summer and nobody's come to get him yet . . . Maybe that's because he's just a wreck and he's no use to anyone now . . . No, that's not the reason. It's because Fićo doesn't have any family anymore because they all died, the driver and the two passengers . . . Poor things . . . No, last summer they were poor things, but now Fićo is the only poor thing. They took them to Bjelovar and buried them there because they were from Bjelovar, but Fićo stayed down in the pines, even though he's from Bjelovar too. I saw his license plates . . . Doesn't matter where a wreck's buried. A wreck is just a heap of junk . . . Fićo isn't a heap of junk, he's a poor little Fićo and he was their car. Someone loved him once.* Uncle Naci shrugged and the Duck shrugged with him – there you go, now let him say the Duck might be a heap of junk one day too – just like grown-ups always shrug when they don't understand something and you have to explain it to them. *Nothing is forever, so what if someone used to love him. Now he's a heap of junk, end of story,* he said. *Are dead people a heap of junk too?* I asked, and I knew what he was going to say in reply, just like I knew that *dead people* actually meant my grandpa. *Quit your babbling,* Grandma cut in, and Uncle Naci just drove and kept his mouth shut all the way to Sarajevo.

The city was steaming and empty. The river stunk like a million people had forgotten to flush a million toilets. I came to the conclusion that someone had to be responsible for all of this, or that I was being punished for something I hadn't done but for which I'm being punished anyway, and everyone knows about it and now treats me like I'm a jailbird or a prisoner of war on some Pacific island, in a film where Japanese people scream and shout, women write letters, and Lee Marvin lies tied up in the sand, the sun burning his eyes. *Poooo!* I said as we passed the National Library. *You little brat!* Mom tried to hit me, but I moved out of the way in time. She's been pissed since we arrived. *Don't think she doesn't love you*, Grandma whispered. I made like I didn't hear her; I moved farther away, dead set I wasn't going to say anything else. That I was never going to say anything else ever again. I don't care if the Miljacka stinks, she can yell all she likes, anything can happen, but I'm never saying anything ever again.

The whole problem is that my mom is scared of me. She's not scared of me per se, she's scared because she's got a kid. She wasn't scared before because Grandpa was alive, because we were apart a lot and then she could see how I was growing up. When someone's always there with you, you don't notice how much they're changing, they're always the same to you and you only see their bad sides. Since we came to Sarajevo forever, Mom and I have discovered each other's bad sides. I don't know all the bad things she's discovered about me and I don't want to think about all the bad things I've discovered about her, but it's like we're really disappointed in each other, and that most of all, we're disappointed because we're scared. In the fall I'll be going to Silvije Strahimir Kranjčević elementary school; I don't know anyone there and I don't want to get to know anyone. I want to be invisible and only show up every now and then, show my face to my dead grandpa for example, who is nice because he keeps quiet and doesn't get angry, he doesn't do anything, but he still exists somewhere, in my head, in Mom and Grandma when they avoid opening the wardrobe where his ties are still hanging, still crumpled in the spot where he tied the knot.

Dad arrives like the guy from the ads on TV. He takes something out of his pocket or briefcase, says something important, and for the rest of the day this sets the tone for all of us. This is possible because Dad only comes over once a week so he has six days to think something important up. *Today we're going to take a good look around our local environs and we're going to drink miracle water from a special spring, just for us men*, he said, packing us into the Renault 4. I felt a little like puking but tightened my tummy to stop it slipping out, and when a bit slipped out I'd swallow it. *You need to puke?* Mom asked on the approach to Olovo. *No!* I said. That was a mistake. I shouldn't have opened my mouth: The second I opened it I puked right down Dad's neck while he was driving. He just sunk his head down a little bit between his shoulders, his neck getting shorter somehow, and kept driving until we got to the first roadhouse. He stripped off his shirt and went over to wash it at the hose. He was wearing an undershirt that looked like a fishing net, his gray hair poking out everywhere from underneath. From behind my dad looked like a monkey someone had dressed in a human undershirt for a laugh. *Don't worry about it*, said Mom, *but for chrissakes, next time don't lie, if you need to puke say you need to puke, it's fine.* I was real surprised neither Mom nor Dad was mad at me. Normally they get mad about much smaller stuff. When you say you're fine, act tough and make like there's no way you're going to puke, no one holds it against you even if you do. I don't know why it's like that, but the next time I need to puke I won't let out a peep either.

Let's hit the road, said Dad. The shirt was on a hanger hanging out the window to dry. Mom kept looking back to see how I was doing, and Dad drove in his undershirt, from behind looking like those truck drivers you see in American films. A stranger who caught a glimpse of us at that particular moment would've thought we were a happy family who did everything in life together. In actual fact, maybe back then we were a happy family, and maybe our life consisted of two parts that alternated back and forth, on and off, something like that. In the first part they were divorced and lived their totally separate lives. She was sore because he was how he was and because fate had had her meet him, and he was sore because he hadn't known how to hold on to her and had done everything wrong, and grown men aren't allowed to do everything wrong. Only Mom and Dad knew the truth about that first part, nobody else, and if they did tell other people anything about themselves and their dead marriage, then – and this I'm sure of – they only told lies or said things to shift the blame. In the other part of their life, which occurred once a week or twice a year, the two of them were a happy family, bound to me like horses tied to a waterwheel plodding one behind the tail of the other, never touching the whole day through.

We arrived in Kladanj. The hotel was empty; the receptionist stood at the counter, head resting on the guest book, asleep on his feet. The waiter was whistling one of those songs where there's a couple who love each other, but one is sick and the other gloomy. He carried a big silver tray, his face contorted in a grimace, and it appeared a distinct possibility that when the song was finished, he was going to slam the tray against the wall, rip his waiter's jacket off, and throw himself in the river, heartbroken that whatever had happened in the song had happened. I don't understand why people sing and whistle those kinds of songs if afterward they're going to feel so bad they want to smash stuff.

What can I get you? the waiter said, having forgotten to change the expression on his face. *Two coffees and a Coca-Cola*, said Dad. *We're out of Coke!* the waiter shot back. *Fine, a cloudy juice then*, Dad quickly recovered. *Coffee, coffee, and a cloudy*, the waiter translated the order into waiters' language, and showed up a couple of minutes later with his tray balanced like a circus act. The coffee cups and juice glass slid from one end of his tray to the other, but they never collided, and he didn't spill a drop either. Pleased with himself, he completely forgot the song with the sick and gloomy lovers.

There's a pool behind the hotel, shall we take a look? Dad knew this place well. Mom didn't care either way. *C'mon, c'mon*, I jumped up. The pool was big and blue, that blue color you only see in swimming pools, but there was no one in the water and no one just hanging out. Full to the brim with water, a totally deserted pool stretched out before us. Up above there was a diving board as high as a skyscraper. *Shame we don't have our swimming gear*, I said. *It wouldn't be allowed*, Dad hurried, and Mom gave him the look you give people when you've caught them lying like a dog. Dad was sorry he ever mentioned the pool, because even though it was impossible, he now thought we were going to strip off and jump in, and that he'd have to stand there on the edge and simper, and that we'd try and get him to jump in too and then he'd have to dream up an explanation and excuse why he can't. The thing is, my dad can't swim, and he thinks I don't know that. Mom told me ages ago that he never learned to swim and that he's ashamed about it. She told me that he's even more ashamed because he suspects that I can, but he's too embarrassed to say or ask anything. He's made such a fine art of not swimming I never notice what I already know, so we can be in Drvenik for fifteen days and the whole time it seems perfectly natural he never goes in the water.

Nice diving board, said Mom, and then went and climbed right up to the top. Fully clothed, one step at a time, she walked slowly out along the board, which was trembling and wobbling under her weight. When she got to the end she looked down and spread her arms wide as if she was going to fly away, but then slowly let them fall. Dad looked up at her, beads of sweat lining his forehead, he opened his mouth as if he wanted to say something, and he did want to say something, but he didn't know how, or whether to say it to me or to her. Mom spread her arms wide again, the board trembled beneath her, she laughed at the depths below, and then let her arms fall, happy, like someone who has scaled a great height and now really feels they're on top of everything in their life and that nothing bad can happen anymore, because people are tiny as ants, houses are small like they're made out of Lego blocks, and there isn't a single problem or fear that doesn't shrink from such a height.

Is she going to jump? I asked, not caring that she was still in her clothes, high up there, and that water is hard when you hit it from that high. I didn't care that my mom could smash like a glass object or come out of the pool dripping wet, in her bright skirt and her shoes, her hairdo all messed up, even though when that happens Mom gets depressed, takes Lexilium, and says she's old and already halfway gone, her best years behind her and that nothing beautiful will ever happen to her again. I wanted her to jump so bad, just as she was, so that in the pool she'd turn into something else and then climb out, or that the sleepy receptionist and desperate waiter would drag her out, that we'd call an ambulance, that she'd lie on the edge of the pool, that Dad would check her pupils and take her pulse, happy and relieved to have her back on dry land, and that on dry land you don't need to know how to swim.

Is she going to jump? I asked louder so he couldn't say he didn't hear me. *I don't know, she shouldn't,* his voice sounded like he'd been hauled in front of a firing squad and he'd wanted to die bravely, but what can you do, he'd shit his pants. *Why shouldn't she, of course she should, why did she climb up there if she's not going to jump? . . . It's awfully high, and she's still got her clothes on . . . So what, her clothes will dry out, why doesn't she just jump?* I was impatient and enjoying his fear; I wanted it to go on and on, that she would stand up there and spread her arms wide, that we would torment him until he burst out crying. She was tormenting him for her own reasons, probably because of a truth she'll never tell anyone, and I was tormenting him because I was enjoying it. I was tormenting my dad like I torment ants, removing their little legs and wings, watching how they thrash around trying to walk with a missing leg as though it were still there, because they're ashamed someone might notice, that other ants might notice they're missing something, and that in the ant world they're never going to be what they once were. *I beg you, don't let her jump,* Dad stammered, begging me for the first time, the first time in my life, that is – it had never happened before because he was big, and I was a kid. I had already known that this day would come, the day when fathers beg their children, I knew it from the story of my grandpa's dying, the one I wasn't supposed to know but did because they didn't know how to keep anything secret, because they'd always mess up thinking I was asleep or that I couldn't hear what they were saying behind closed doors. Grandpa lay on the bed where I'd slept since we came back from Drvenik, they brought him from the hospital because he wanted to die at home. Maybe he thought he wouldn't die if they brought him home; you can't die among things that remember you being alive. Mom sat at his feet, sometimes he brought his middle and index finger to his lips, *I beg you, give me a cigarette*, he said, *no Dad, you're not allowed to smoke*, she replied, though she knew it didn't matter because when someone's going to die, nothing can damage their health anymore. They stayed there in silence for half an hour, he'd bring his fingers to his lips, the only sound the rustling of starched bed linen. No one knew why Grandma starched the linen, maybe so our every movement, including our very last one – before sleep and before death – left a rustle behind. Then he repeated *I beg you, give me a cigarette*, and she yelled all stroppy *don't be crazy, Dad, you're not allowed to smoke*, because she thought she had to hide death from him. Grandpa looked at her with his blue eyes, our blue eyes. There aren't many people in the world with blue eyes, but our whole family has them. *Don't you be crazy, I know it all already and beg you to the high heavens, give me a cigarette*, he said. Mom says he said it with a melancholic inflection in his voice, but I don't believe her because I know Grandpa yelled with all the might of the dying, and that there was no melancholic inflection because one thing he couldn't stand was horseshitting. She lit a cigarette, took a drag, and gave it to him, his last cigarette, the cigarette for which he as a father had had to beg his child. One day I saw a young guy and his girlfriend in front of the Hotel Europa, first they kissed and then she lit a cigarette, took a drag, and held it out to him. One day when I'm grown up, if I ever see a guy and girl do that again, I'll tell them that you're not supposed to do that and that they should wait until they're on death's door before they start that stuff.

So that's how it was then, in my eighth year of life my dad had already begged me for something. Instead of feeling grown up, fear took hold. *What do you mean – I beg you, don't let her jump. If she wants to jump, she'll jump, what's it got to do with me, leave me out of it, I didn't talk her into climbing up there*, I was furious with him because he was scared and so weak, and because he'd begged me in that voice I beg with when I'm scared and weak and they're going to do something terrifying to me. But that begging never works, and no one ever pays it any mind, not even he who now expects me to make amends for the fact he never learned to swim, or me to make amends for something else, something I can't grasp, just like he can't grasp a single one of my fears.

Why don't you climb up there and beg her not to jump, I suggested to him like it was perfectly normal and pretty weird he hadn't already thought of it. Dad didn't reply, he just stared up in the air at Mom every now and then waving her arms, her smile so broad you'd think she was going burst out laughing like she did watching Charlie Chaplin films, and that she'd fall off the board. *Get up there and tell her not to jump, she'll get soaked, and maybe she'll smash to pieces if she jumps*, I tugged at his sleeve. He bit his bottom lip and yelled Mom's name. She made like she didn't hear him, or maybe she really didn't hear him, and then he headed toward the diving board, his legs shaking and knees knocking like kids' knees when they try and jump from the fourth step. He climbed up the board itself, slowly he climbed, my terrified, non-swimming dad, the dad who was scared of heights, scared of his ex-wife at heights, she who had become so strong she was taking her revenge on him and probably didn't know why. He's climbing up there because I told him to and because he hadn't managed to come up with a reason to wriggle out of it. He'd lost his mind, which until that point had got him out of ever going in the sea without me thinking it weird, always having an excuse for every attempt to get him in the water, the kind of answer only big, serious fathers were capable of.

Hey, wait, what are you doing, I'm coming down now, yelled Mom when she saw him halfway up the metal stairs. She turned around on the board as if she did it every day, like there wasn't a great height below her. A moment later the three of us were standing next to the pool and everything began to fall back into its old familiar rhythm, one in which every fear lay sleeping at the bottom of our hearts, at the bottom of a big black cave, not coming out unless a devilish someone prodded one out.

We went back to our waiter. *Are you drinking and driving?* Mom was confused. The waiter brought a double grappa for Dad and cloudy juices for Mom and me. That went: *cloudy, cloudy, double grappa.* Dad said *I don't usually drink, but today I need one*, and Mom didn't ask *why do you need one today.* She just said *there probably won't be any cops.*

After that we went to the spring and drank our fill of the special men's water. *Are you going to become a man now?* Mom laughed, *it's a bit late for me . . . But for me it's not*, I said and drank another glass. Dad didn't say anything, he drank in big grown-up gulps, gulps that could have swallowed the ocean if it wasn't so salty. I remembered the sea and Drvenik, and that I'd never live there again. This life, this Sarajevo-and-nowhere-else life was very serious, and I already didn't like it because in this life lived fears no one understood. Everyone had their own fears and loaded with these fears they collided with others for whom they meant nothing, were just a plaything. I had the feeling I knew what it meant to be a grown-up.

We went back to the car, the shirt was already dry. Dad put it on, *you're not going to puke, are you?* he laughed, and I looked at the ground and didn't say anything because I knew I was sure to puke, that's how it had to be, and they'd be happy because of it. I couldn't escape, there's never anywhere to escape anyway, you can only lie a little, and just never in hell open your mouth when they ask you if you need to puke, or if you're scared, or if you're sad. Yes, and you don't need to explain to anyone why a poor little Fićo is a poor little Fićo and why fathers aren't allowed to beg their children.

Mom sighed like Marija in the village of Prkosi

On the last day of fall we're going to Pioneer Valley. That's what we agreed, doesn't matter if it's raining cats and dogs and the heavens themselves open, a deal's a deal, that's what Dad says. The three of us are going to Pioneer Valley, and we're going to look at the lions, monkeys, and other animals. They'll be brought indoors on the first day of winter and put in secret sleeping cages, where they'll stay until the first day of spring. Until then only the zookeepers will see them because animals don't like being watched while they're sleeping. Their wanting to sleep alone needs to be respected. We'll see them at the very end, on Sunday afternoon, and when we go, the zookeepers are going to lead them into the secret sleeping cages, Pioneer Valley will be locked up and the keys given to the mayor, who'll look after them until spring comes. Then we'll come back, the animals and us, and see the changes the winter has brought. I'll never see the lions as a five-year-old again, because in the spring I'll be six.

It's so foggy you can't see your finger in front of your nose, said Grandma coming back from the market. *I made it there and back from memory because I couldn't see where I was and would've thought I was nowhere if I hadn't remembered the way. Now let them say I'm senile.* She put her shopping bag on the floor, a head of lettuce and a leek that looked like a palm poked out, but there was nothing in there for me, and if she'd bought spinach too it was going to be a really yucky Sunday. Luckily we're off to Pioneer Valley, and besides, it doesn't pay to prematurely get anxious about lunch.

C'mon, wakey wakey! Grandma searched the bed for Mom. Mom always pulled the covers up over her head, hiding under the duvet so you really needed to search the bed for her if you wanted to wake her. Mom murmured something, and Grandma beat the white linen with her hand, like a blind person looking for their wallet in the snow. *C'mon, wakey wakey, why am I always the youngest here,* yelled Grandma, *get up, it's foggy outside, I made it back by memory, so try putting that one about my sclerosis on me now.* Mom poked her nose out, as tousled as Mowgli when he was growing up among the animals, *who's been telling you you're sclerotic? . . . I don't remember right now, I've forgotten.* Then they started joshing, no harm intended and not really wanting a proper fight, just a little Sunday-morning bicker, because we're all at home on Sunday mornings and that's when everyone gets to play their games.

Grandma's game is called *I'm not senile* and what happens is that she walks around the house talking about all the things she remembers and has caught Mom forgetting because then she can say *and they say I'm senile.* Grandma's other game is called *I'm not deaf* and is often played at the same time as *I'm not senile.* Mom invented both games because she's freaking out that Grandma might stop remembering stuff and go kooky like old people often do, waking up one morning and asking things like *who are you and what am I doing here.* So Mom checks her sclerosis every day and gets blue and a bit pissed when she notices Grandma has forgotten something. Grandma's the only one who's not allowed to forget anything, because then Mom will think her sick and old, and then Mom will walk tall like a national hero, beat her fists on her chest like King Kong, and swear to her colleagues, Uncle, Dad, Grandpa, and other relatives that she's ready to care for her mother to the death, to bathe and clean her if need be, and that she couldn't care less if her own mother, having gone totally senile, doesn't remember her. These stories get on Grandma's nerves, mainly because she's the one who looks after Mom and me, makes us lunch, cleans, and irons, while Mom just prepares herself for a heroic age Grandma thinks will come, God willing, the day little green creatures land on earth. Grandma wins the *I'm not senile* game because she really doesn't forget anything, or at least she doesn't forget more than Mom and I forget, but she always loses the *I'm not deaf* game. It goes like this: Mom says something, and Grandma doesn't reply; then Mom says the same thing over, and Grandma says *sorry?* – at which point Mom screeches at the top of her lungs, a screech so loud hikers up on Mount Trebević could hear it, to which Grandma replies *quit your bawling, I'm not deaf!* Then Mom says *why can't you bloody hear me then?* At which point Grandma mutters something and it's clear to all she's lost the game. Of course, to make the game work Mom has to screech at the top of her lungs, because if she just raises her voice a little she won't be able to tell Grandma she's deaf and can't hear a thing.

Mom's Sunday games are *I've got a migraine* or *look at the state of the place, we're cleaning under the rugs today.* I like the first game better because then Mom spends the whole day lying in bed whining, sighing, and grasping for the barf bowl. As long as she keeps it up, I can go about my business building a castle for Queen Forgetful and flicking through the encyclopedia, I'm just not allowed to shout, but that's it, everything else is okay. In our family migraines are passed from generation to generation, from head to head in actual fact, so we can't remember an ancestor who didn't get migraines. Mom says our ancestors who didn't get migraines were actually monkeys, and that their heads started hurting the moment they became human. Grandma says that if she got a migraine, she'd lock herself in the bedroom, put earplugs in, draw the shades, and let the kids smash the place up, just so long as they leave her in peace. I can't figure why I'm not allowed to smash stuff up when my mom has a migraine. *You'll see what it's like*, Mom would say, *the joke isn't going to pass you by, and after you've had your first migraine you'll understand everything your mother has suffered in life.*

Mom's other game *look at the state of the place, we're cleaning under the rugs today* is a pure catastrophe. The game involves shunting wardrobes around the house, taking the rugs out into the yard, cleaning floors and windows, Radojka the cleaning lady coming over and my mom playing Alija Sirotanović until Radojka goes home and Mom gets tired – which is when the game is called off. But this doesn't mean the rugs are put back on the floor and wardrobes shunted back in place. No way! The mess lasts at least another ten days, and then we live in a state of emergency, sleeping in our beds in the middle of the room, not watching television because we don't have anything to sit on and because the screen is covered in curtains taken down to be cleaned. Mom gets really uptight when we play this game and no one's allowed to say anything to her because then she just starts screaming and crying and talking about the past. In the past everyone maltreated Mom. I don't know a single member of our close or extended family who hasn't maltreated Mom and who she doesn't rail about because of that. Only I never maltreated her in the past because in the past I wasn't even born, but apparently I'm making up for that now.

Today isn't a day for Mom's migraines. Today we're going to Pioneer Valley. Dad's coming for us around noon, lunch has been put back to four, which means we'll have a whole three and a half hours for looking at the animals. *God, father, look at the fog*, Mom said, almost pressing her nose up against the windowpane trying to see out. But there was nothing out there, just fog and milk and the boughs of the cherry tree beneath the window disappearing into the milk rather than growing from the trunk. *What did I tell you?* Grandma replied. *What did you tell me? . . . That it's foggy out . . . I don't know, I don't remember, I was still asleep . . . Fine, play the smarty-pants then . . . I'm not playing the smarty-pants, I was asleep and didn't hear you,* Mom was getting snippy, and that was always dangerous because her snippiness could finish with us not going to Pioneer Valley. But luckily Grandma bit her lip. Grandma always bites her lip when a ring girl starts strolling around the apartment with a sign saying "Fight Time, Round One," because she doesn't have the strength for a fight of fifteen rounds. She's mature and experienced, but Mom is young and up-and-coming and would knock her out by the third round.

Maybe you should give Pioneer Valley a miss after all, Grandma stared at the foggy whiteout outside the window. *I don't know, I really don't know,* Mom drank her coffee and lit her first cigarette. *Here we go, you're going to back out on me again,* I put the last block on the top of the tower where Queen Forgetful was holding her parents prisoner. *No one's backing out on you, be reasonable, take a look at the weather,* Grandma wasn't falling for it. *What do you care, you're not going to Pioneer Valley, it's all the same to you what the weather's like . . . Yes, yes, it'll be all quite the same to me when you come down with bronchitis and I have to look after you.*

Dad arrived fifteen minutes before noon. *We're going to Pioneer Valley, right,* I got it in before Mom and Grandpa could open their mouths. *If that was the deal, let's go,* he replied. The two of them looked at each other. Mom sighed like our national hero Marija Bursać when she was injured in the village of Prkosi and headed off to play the martyr. Outside there was either a light rain falling or it was the fog turning into drops of water, I don't know, but the whole thing looked like a ginormous cloud had come down on the city, covering the roofs of the houses and the streets as if we'd ordered a giant duvet for Sarajevo so we wouldn't have to climb out of bed.

There was no one at Pioneer Valley. The ticket seller in the entrance kiosk was dozing, and some young guy puttered by on a two-wheeled cart loaded to the brim with bluish-looking meat, singing *seaman sons are always so late ashore, and poor mothers weep forever more.* As he passed by he said *good day, folks, make yourselves at home.* Dad turned after him like he was about to cuss, and Mom gripped her handbag and said *Christ, do they have to hassle me when I'm at the zoo too.* Then they both shut up, and I shut up too because I already felt a little guilty.

The monkeys were surprised to see us. They scratched their heads and looked at Dad as if seeing him for the first time. *Looks like they're into you,* Mom teased. *And why wouldn't they be?* Dad made like he was lost in thought. The guy on the cart came by again: *it's strictly forbidden to feed the animals,* he shouted, and then continued on with his singing. *Oh get lost, bully boy!* Dad yelled after him. *He's just doing his job,* said Mom. The guy turned his cart around and came back. *Who are you telling to get lost, huh?* His light-blue eyes looked like they'd been found at the bottom of an Olympic swimming pool and he seemed really dangerous. *Who do you think you are, talking to me like that?* Dad took Mom and me by the hand and led us off toward the lion cage, but the guy caught up to us, cutting us off with his cart. *I can throw you out of here, you know, I could punch your lights out too*, he shouted. *Get out of my way or I'll call your boss! . . . You know what, old fella, the boss can kiss my ass.* His eyes were popping out of his head at Dad like he'd seen a heap of shit. Then not waiting for a reply he took off.

Mom sighed and shook her head, Dad breathed through his nose, snorting mad. We stopped next to each cage, but I didn't feel much like looking at animals anymore. It occurred to me that none of us knew why we were here. Mom and Dad didn't even look at the animals. Dad just stood in front of the cages, stared at the bars, and shut and squeezed his eyes together like he was going to fire a bullet from each, or maybe a thunderbolt, and Mom just looked up in the air, high above the lions and tigers, all in the hope someone might finally notice her sacrifice, or someone would attack her so she'd at last be able to defend herself. The fact was, she was itching for a fight. I wanted to say I felt like going home but didn't know how to begin. I'd spent seven days laying the groundwork for our visit to Pioneer Valley, how was I now supposed to say I didn't want to look at the animals anymore?

As we crossed the bridge, a little stream flowing underneath where ducks swim in the summer, Mom tried to take Dad's hand, but he made a quick long stride and got away from her. That was the sum of his courage. She wasn't his wife and he had every right to let her fall into the stream, and he wasn't her husband and she had every right to hate him for bringing her to Pioneer Valley in such fog. I didn't want to get mixed up in their relationship; as a matter of fact I wasn't interested in their relationship, though it felt a little weird when I thought about the fact that I was the child of two people at opposite ends of the earth who are completely different and total strangers to each other. If we each have our own star like it says in "Cinderella," then their stars are so many light-years from each other that no one could even be bothered counting them.

Dobro, she said quietly, taking me by the hand. He turned around unsure what she meant, whether that *dobro* meant *fine* or whether she meant his name, which was also *Dobro*. The accents had gotten lost in the fog, so you only heard how estranged they'd become from each other, and I knew they'd rather go home, each their own way, if only I wasn't there between them, silent, prolonging their horror. But they have to stick one beside the other until the very end, until we've been around all the cages and done all the things that this Sunday, the last day of fall, has in store. Even if they don't have anything in common anymore, they still can't run away from each other because I'm here as a memento of a time when they still had things in common. I won't let them forget this because I'm here, in this fog, in Pioneer Valley, as a guarantee the two of them will never go senile and never forget what they meant to each other, why they separated, and how estranged they seem to everyone who sees them together.

We got to the cage with the llama, my favorite animal and the main reason I wanted to go to Pioneer Valley. I love the llama because he spits at his visitors. Running away from his spit is the best time you can have in the whole zoo. After he spat at me for the first time in my life, I wanted to be a llama. Instead of growing up and becoming a doctor like Dad or an accountant like Mom, I wanted to turn into a llama and spit on people I didn't know from morning to night, and for this to make them laugh and make them happy.

The llama stood in mud to his knees and stared at us. *Hey, llama*, I shouted. *Hey, llama, spit! Spit, llama, spit!* He didn't move, didn't gather a ball of spit in his mouth, he looked like someone who'd never spat at anyone because tears were running down his snout, real big tears, like the tears of a grown-up kid. *The llama's crying . . . He's probably crying because of the mud*, Mom said. Dad didn't say anything.

We headed for the exit. I turned to look back at the llama, hoping he'd be watching us. He wasn't watching; he was just staring at the spot where we'd been standing and was crying. You could see his tears from ten meters away. You could see them for as long as you could see the llama. I didn't know whether to believe the llama was crying because he was standing in the mud. Maybe he was crying because of something else. I don't know why, but I'm pretty sure I wouldn't know something like that even if I saw my mom or dad crying. People are alone when they cry and no one knows anything about them. Only when I cry everyone knows why I'm crying because I always tell them. When I grow up, I'm not telling them anymore. That's the rules.

My shift starts soon, Dad said and headed off toward the hospital.

Mom nodded, and that's how it ended. We got home and there was a plate too many set at the table. *Dobro didn't come*, said Grandma, even though she could see Dad wasn't there. Maybe that's what being senile is: saying things that are obvious but which you should keep to yourself. *He had to go to work*, Mom made a martyr of herself for our senile Grandma. *How was it at Pioneer Valley? . . . It was nice. The llama didn't spit, he just cried, but we still tried to have a nice time.*

Would you care for some rose jelly?

A big bone lay between me and my other grandma, my dad's mother. Under other circumstances it would have just been a regular beef bone, gnawed clean, yet no one who heard the story ever forgot it, they took the memory to their graves. Though it was no big thing for me, I remember the bone too. I got it when I was turning three, and at that stage in life you don't really care about the kind of bones people give you.

That grandma of mine, I won't mention her name, wasn't happy when Dad married Mom. She wouldn't have been any happier had he married some other woman; she wanted Dad to stay on his own, that she, his mother, be the only woman in his life. She despised happy and joyous women, women's frivolity she just couldn't take, she spent her days pressed up against the window of her room watching them flitting about in the breeze, unharried women who would live and die happy. For her, happiness wasn't a woman's word. But the other kind of women, ugly mousy little women, the ones who hid their every curve and would never catch a single male eye, these women were saints, condemned to suffer until death as a consequence. On Judgment Day they will win God's mercy, be blessed with forgiveness for their sins and those of their drunken roughneck husbands. She thought herself a saint because her husband had abandoned her with a newborn child, my father, for whom she would care a lifetime long, and for his brother and sisters too. They all lived in Nemanja Street in a tiny one-room apartment, half of which was taken up by a piano, the other half by beds. The piano served no practical purpose because no one knew how to play, it was just a symbol that they had once been wealthy, though no one remembered when that was – probably so long ago that every key had long since forgotten its tone. It was an apartment bare of beauty or generosity of spirit. Under the piano was a repository for winter provisions, jars of pickled paprikas, sacks of potatoes, cabbage, all the things other people kept in pantries and cellars.

There's no way my mom could have ever been a saint for her. My mom smiled, had blond hair, and looked like a woman out of a Socialist film magazine, full of intolerable and irresponsible optimism. Even worse, she was young and pretty, rich in the way you are rich before figuring out that your poverty is eternal. Her very appearance was an insult to my other grandma, and no doubt nothing ever violated the innocence of her room and the sanctity of the gold-plated Christ hanging above the front door more than the moment on a January day in 1965 when my mom walked in, a thousand snow crystals in her hair, filled with a hope that today no one knows the name of. Dad had probably had to beg his mother for hours and days, all the family secrets had to tumble from the high ceilings, he had to pay like never before for her to finally allow the she-devil incarnate to cross her threshold. Grandma was deeply religious, but she was also tone-deaf to the fluttering of the wings of angels; she saw only the devil in a thousand shapes and guises, above all in beauty, in the feminine beauty come to kidnap her beloved one, the apple of her eye, her son.

She sat in her armchair, offered Mom rose jelly, and simpered until her heart turned to ice and her belief in God's goodness grew, believing the Almighty would protect her and her son, that my mother would disappear just as every temptation God had placed before her in life, testing her heart and its contents, had in the end disappeared. For an hour they sat there across from each other. Dad tried to get a conversation going, which was more a plea for his mother's mercy, mercy she wouldn't grant him. She believed in God and everything she did was born of this belief, yet Dad believed in her, tried to break her resistance, not knowing that she would break him, that his love wouldn't endure long enough for him to understand that life has two beginnings: one at birth, with our first memories, and one that begins with love. What set Dad apart was that he had to kill the first in order to win the right to the second, but it all proved beyond him.

It couldn't be said he didn't try though. He left with my mother, leaving his own mother to hold him in her prayers and pray to God he not be led into temptation and that he be untouched by every evil. Some time later, in the Hotel Panorama in Pale, on a beautiful sunny Sunday, he begat me and believed I would save him, most of all from his weakness of character, his lack of steel and resolve, that I would free him from his need to make a decision because with the birth of a child his mother would finally understand that the devil hadn't entered his life, because you can't conceive a child with the devil.

Are you sure the boy's yours? she asked. He'd barely set foot in the room. *Yes*, he replied, and turned and left. In that instant he believed in himself and not in her, but it was a tepid self-belief, not fiery or cold, and it dissipated before he understood that you don't give anyone an answer to those kinds of questions, not even your own mother, because the question isn't about anything to do with you – your child – the question is about you yourself. In any case, he went to see my mom, kissed her, and smiled, giving her a hug much too firm, one meant to conceal doubt, a doubt not easily concealed. Mom looked at him, shaken and speechless, she began to age, her love turning to hate.

I was a big tubby baby on white crocheted pillows, a raspberry mark on my left temple. The neighborhood women said *you must've had cravings for raspberries or strawberries while you were pregnant.* Astonished,

Mom conceded *yes, I did, I've always loved strawberries*, and the women nodded their heads and wanted her to feel guilty. In time the raspberry began to grow, and the doctors said it would cover my whole face unless removed, so for six months when I was two they injected saline solution in my temple. That pain remains the clearest memory in my life.

You think this isn't your son? she yelled at Dad. My real grandpa and grandma were frozen in the next room. *I don't think that, God help me, I don't think that*, he replied and went again to his mother's. He came back with a year-old potted plant and said *this is for our apartment*, knowing full well that nothing would ever come of the apartment or the plant. My evil grandma had succeeded in seeing her will be done, but in hearing her prayers, God allowed himself a little joke: He didn't drive the she-devil from her son's life, but from the she-devil's life she drove her son, who, in but a fleeting second, had proven himself unworthy of fatherhood.

This is how it was to be: A God-fearing mother kept hold of her son, yet was forever punished by an unusual twist of fate. By the time I was just a year old my face was well defined – and I looked like my dad. The same head shape and forehead, the same chin, nose, and eyes, even my fingernails were the same shape; other children resemble their parents too but not to this extent, they don't just resemble one parent. Instead of my dad not being my dad, it was like my mom wasn't my mom, my face containing none of her beauty, not a single smile or gift. Back then I took completely after him, and when Dad showed his mother my photos, she pursed her lips and fell into an even greater despair at fate's cruelty. She saw the resemblance in the child's photos, just as for a lifetime she'd recognized with horror who her son resembled: We were doubles of Grandpa Đorđe, the man who had ruined her life. His image would now live on until her death and much longer besides, which only went to show that suffering is eternal, enduring even when those who would suffer are no longer around.

And what is it you want from me now? she asked, handing him back the photos. *I would like you to see my son,* Dad replied. *I've seen him, and now what? . . . I want you to see him in real life, in this room.* She didn't say a thing, just looked at him hoping her silence spoke for itself, that he would get the message and know there were things you simply didn't say in God's presence, things requiring caution, which you were to only approach the way you would someone you loved. For her only a mother's love for her son was greater than God, and from her son she expected nothing less than that his love for her be greater than God.

You have to do this for me, Dad tried to convince Mom. She lit her third cigarette even though two already burned in the ashtray. *You have to, after this everything will be different.* She didn't believe him, but at the same time she knew she'd have to accede, the strength of her resistance having no bearing on a decision made long ago. Yes, of course, she'll bathe her son, get him scrubbed up, make him the most beautiful little boy in the world, and take him to that woman who happens to be his grandmother, as unbelievable as it seemed and regardless of it having been long clear there was no place for grandmothers and grandchildren in this story because it was a story that had ended long ago, in a time that had nothing to do with Mom, a time when the notes from that piano perhaps still resounded.

You're coming with us, right? Dad turned to my grandma and grandpa. In her black Sunday best Grandma sighed like you sigh before starting a big job. Grandpa just shook his head: *I'm not going. If you ask me why I'm not going, I'd have to say I don't know, but I think I'm old enough to not do anything I don't want to. You're young, attend to it yourselves.* Although he probably didn't understand what old Franjo was telling him, Dad didn't insist, nor did he respond. In actual fact, he was probably a bit relieved. Better not to have witnesses like Grandpa in life if you're not prepared to man up, because they can destroy your entire world with a single wave of their hand. Grandpa could be gruff, and though everyone attributed it to his asthma, Dad suspected his gruffness was of a different kind, the gruffness of a man who didn't forgive others things he hadn't forgiven himself. Whatever went down in the room with the piano, it was better it happened without old Franjo.

I sat on my dad's knee. On their knees my grandma and my mom held little coffee cups with flowery saucers, the other grandma smiling from her armchair. The silence was much bigger than the room, bigger than the piano, and bigger than every silence the living are capable of keeping among themselves. Words came out without order or purpose.

I'm very glad to finally meet you, said my grandma, *would you care for some rose jelly?* replied the other grandma, and then an age passed before anything else was said. *You have a beautiful grandson*, my grandma finally managed, *and why didn't your good husband come*, the one in the armchair volleyed back. No one knew how long this went on, but it went on all right. I eventually fell asleep looking at the cross above the doorway and the man pierced with nails, frightened because I didn't know who he was. In memory he became a symbol for that room, where only a piano, a cross, and a crone lived, my wrong grandma, who had never gotten up out of that armchair in all my life, so I didn't even know if she could walk.

I woke up in the car. Mom had me in her arms, Dad was driving, and my grandma was holding the handgrip, beating her big nose in the air to the rhythm of the road. Thinking I was asleep, they didn't talk. Mom tried to peek into a plastic bag holding something wrapped in white gift paper. The next fifteen minutes were the last hope for saving her marriage. When we'd left, my other grandma had jumped out of her armchair and said *I've got something for the little one, he's growing up now*, and taken a plastic bag from the fridge and given it to Mom. She looked like someone who had almost forgotten something really important. For Mom it was a small but endlessly important detail, a sign maybe all was not lost, that her mother-in-law's love had, in spite of herself, found a way to creep from the darkness and free itself from the chains in which it had been bound since the time the piano was still young.

In that fifteen minutes Mom forgave her everything, chiding herself her lack of compassion for the woman's misfortune, for having only thought of herself and the child who lay dozing in her lap, for never thinking how that woman had once, long ago, held such a child in her arms, totally devoid of hope in the man whom she loved.

Grandpa was waiting for us at the dining-room table. Old train time-tables, beekeeping manuals, and a Hungarian dictionary lay strewn out before him, all to help pass the time quicker, so he wouldn't think so much about us or fall to his fears for the mission on which his wife and daughter had set out. *How was it?* he took his glasses off the moment we came in. *Let us catch our breath*, said Mom. *Now we'll see how it was*, said Grandma and reached for the plastic bag. *Wait!* Mom grabbed her hand. *Fine, I'm waiting*, said Grandma and put the bag down. Grandpa raised his eyebrows and went with the flow. This was unusual for him, but this was an unusual situation; everyone except me knew a life was splitting in two here, my mom's life for sure, but maybe another life was involved too, my life, which, truth be told, had just begun, so hadn't yet gotten that far.

Mom took the package out of the bag and unwrapped the paper. There, in the middle of our dining-room table, lay an enormous beef bone, picked perfectly clean. It was whiter than white, no traces of meat or blood, as if someone, the Almighty for example, had created it exactly that way and sent eternity out a message: "You shall be a bone and nothing else, you shall have no purpose nor meaning, you shall not procreate, nor shall you be either dead or alive." Mom held her face in her hands so it wouldn't shatter, and Grandma sat down. Grandpa said *right then*, and they all stared motionless at the bone.

Let me see, let me see, I ran around the table yelling. I couldn't know something bad was happening because nothing had actually happened, nor did I sense their anger or sorrow because they weren't angry or sad. Maybe they were white and cold, maybe they, at least now in retrospect, resembled that white bone on the fancy black veneer of the table. Useless and beautiful in equal measure, the bone was a final evil after which no good could ever come. For my mom the bone was the abyss at the end of the road; a sign she should turn around and start out on a new path, if there was indeed one she could ever envisage, sure from the very start that a bone for her son wouldn't be waiting at its end.

Give it to me, give it to me, I howled, but they wouldn't give me the bone. Grandpa picked it up, stood for a moment in front of the trash can – either the bone was too big, or he realized such things weren't for the trash – then headed outside with it. I can imagine him walking through Metjaš with this ginormous beef bone, people scrambling out of his way, seeing in his eyes and from what was in his hand that he was mad. He carried it off somewhere, I'll never know where, and returned half an hour later. I cried because they hadn't given me the object of my affection.

The next day Dad asked Mom what his mother had given me because she hadn't wanted to tell him, but Mom didn't say anything. She didn't know what to say. It wasn't something you could put into words, and had left us more confused than all the dead pianos in the world.

I never went to that room again, nor did I ever see that other grandma of mine. I don't even know how she died or where she's buried, or whether Dad ever showed her my pictures again. If he did, she must have been a bit relieved. As I got older I looked less like him and she would have been able to believe God had quit testing her and answered all her prayers.

The violet fig

for Nada Stilinović

When the frost bites hard and the teeth chatter and thick snows fall and no one can come to us and we can't go to anyone, Grandma says this winter is nothing like the winter of 1943, the thought of which makes me freeze and my heart pound wild because I love the years before my time. That's when miracles happened, and everything was huge and terrifying. *It was a Friday in Zenica that winter when the Old Devil got dead drunk and headed for home. The snow was two meters high and blue in the moonlight, so he thought it was his bed or a duvet. God knows what goes through the head of an eighty-five-year-old who's spent a minimum seventy-five of them dead drunk, maybe even eighty of them. But he saw that much snow and he just lay down and made himself comfortable, covering himself in it, and with his hands under his head started snoring away. Heaven knows how long he'd been lying there when the miners coming back from the second shift dug him out and got him to the hospital. Alive! Alive, I tell you, and he'd lain in the snow that winter of 1943, and that wasn't like this winter, bit of frost, bit of snow, nothing much, but a real winter like you don't get anymore, one I'll never see in my lifetime again. They took the old coot to the hospital; luckily they didn't take him home because the next day he got pneumonia, eighty-five years old and a temperature of 104 degrees, but you think that knocked the wind out of his sails? Fat chance! He shuffled to the window and tossed kids some money to get him medicinal alcohol from the drugstore, that hundred-proof stuff, but kids being kids they took the money and scampered. I think that killed the Old Devil and not the pneumonia. Only rakia could kill him, or truth be told, him not having it. He didn't have the taste for anything else. He might've been a drinker, but the alcohol didn't do him in, it got everyone around him: a first wife, then a second, both younger, then a daughter, another daughter, his sons scattering to the four winds. God knows who and what else that rakia killed, but it didn't get him. He woke up drunk, went to bed drunk, forged the horseshoes in his workshop drunk, and drunk he laid waste to everything in his path and everything that let itself be laid to waste, all until that winter, the 1943 mother of all winters got him. Sometimes I think it got so cold just to knock the Old Devil off,* said Grandma when the temperature fell, shaking with rage and anger, but not cold, because she wasn't afraid of the cold. The Old Devil was the only person she hated in the entire world, and of all perversions, vices, and weapons, of all human depravities and evils, it was alcohol and alcoholism she had no truck with.

The Old Devil was my great-grandpa and his name was Josip, but Grandma never called him that, he was always the Old Devil, and no one, not even Grandpa whose father he was, ever got angry with her or corrected her or told her how swell it would be if she could call her deceased father-in-law by some other name, the one he was christened with for example, or the one by which everyone in Zenica knew him: Blacksmith Joža the Slovenian. At the mention of his father my grandpa would bow his head and bite his lip, just like his brothers, our uncles Karlo and Rudo, who never forgave him the rakia, nor themselves for having been children not able to save their older sisters from their deaths at my great-grandpa's careless hand. Whenever the Old Devil came up, you saw the same disposition in Grandma, Grandpa, and Mom's eyes, a familial mark of Cain, a color that differentiated the Rejcs from other people, a light-gray anti-rakia hue. It marked their lives in different ways, and boy did it mark my life with them. Grandpa would drink two short ones of rakia and even under threat of medieval torture you couldn't make him have a third, dead sure that if he did he'd turn into the Old Devil. Mom would drink half a beer and already have the fear of God inside her that she was dead drunk and that the Old Devil was there smiling at her from just around the corner. Grandma didn't drink at all. Not at New Year's, not at birthdays, never! That was the Rejc family for you, and then I came along.

Takes after his father's side, said Mom. *God, father, the kid doesn't have any Rejc in him,* said Grandpa. So it was no surprise I didn't share the Rejc anti-rakia disposition, I wasn't even scared of the Old Devil. Actually, I didn't know anything about rakia, except that it stunk real bad and that the stink reminded me of the hospital, vaccinations, and having your tonsils out. But my great-grandpa, he loomed large all right.

I don't pay Grandpa's dead sisters any mind because I can't, because I don't know anything about them, just that they're dead and that they died very young. That's the only thing anyone ever says about them, and that's not enough for me to love them and blame the Old Devil for their dying young. He's the main character and the only character in a story that's been going on for a hundred years and continues to this day even though he's long dead, and in this story Blacksmith Joža the Slovenian is like Flash Gordon: Everyone's afraid of him, but no one can hurt him. This great-grandpa of mine is the strongest and the biggest, so strong and so big that the winter of 1943 had to come along to do him in so he could make a brief exit from the story, but he's sure to make a comeback one day. I know this because these kind of stories can't end before I make my entrance, doesn't matter if I'm five, seven, or eleven years old, one day when I dream of the Old Devil I'll offer him my hand and say *you were terrifying, but I'm not scared of you, and everyone was scared of you except me.* I don't know what he'll say to that, but I have the feeling he might burp in my face. My great-grandpa, Blacksmith Joža the Slovenian, that's him for you.

We learned proverbs at school and on the blackboard the teacher wrote: "Everyone forges his own good fortune." We were supposed to write an explanation of what it meant in our notebooks, so I wrote a story about how my great-grandpa forged his own good fortune and about how forgers of their own good fortune were usually forgers of others' misfortune because they find their good fortune at the bottom of a bottle of rakia. The teacher called Mom into school for another visit, but Mom didn't tell me anything, not why she was called in or what the teacher told her, but I saw the red in her eyes and that she was all upset and desperate because of me. The next day the school psychologist turned up in class, stood next to the teacher's desk, hands behind his back, and the teacher said *this is comrade Mutevelić, he's a psychologist and he's going to sit in on our class today and see how you're doing,* and after five minutes I could see his eyes were all on me, staring at my head and glancing away when I caught him, and the teacher kept asking me stuff, all smiley and kind like she never was, like I was really sick or something, all kinds of weird questions about things we hadn't even studied and I'm sure aren't even in the teacher's book, like *are people good or evil,* or *who's smarter, the raven or the fox,* or *is Videk happy they sewed him a shirt.* This Videk is a kid in a lame story, he's supposed to have walked around naked until some nice folks sewed him a shirt. I replied that good people are good, and that evil people are evil, that the raven is smart because he found the cheese, and that the fox is smarter because she took it from him, but that maybe the fox was dumb because she couldn't find the cheese herself and that the raven was stupid because he let himself get played by the fox, but that I had no opinion about Videk because I just couldn't imagine a kid walking around naked and someone sewing him a shirt. When I said the bit about "having no opinion," I shot comrade Mutevelić a look because I knew he'd be shocked. I know exactly which words are going to shock people as soon as they come out of my mouth, and I know why they're shocked. When I say "in my opinion," or when I say "taken in general," or when I say "characteristically," everyone acts like I've put a suit, tie, and hat on, all fancy. That's how it is now: Comrade Mutevelić raises an eyebrow in surprise, takes his pad from his pocket, and scribbles something down.

The boy is very clever for his age and has a rich vocabulary, but his emotions are completely childlike and along with his undoubted intelligence they're an explosive little cocktail. That's what comrade Mutevelić told Mom, and amazingly that's what she told me, word for word, probably because she'd just read something in her book *You and Your Child* about the value of periodically shocking me with psychoanalytic findings or what grown-ups think of me. *I'm not that smart, it's just they expect me to be dumb . . . Who expects that of you? . . . The teacher and comrade Mutevelić. They asked me whether Videk is happy someone sewed him a shirt. You only ask that kind of thing when you want to make someone look like a retard . . . Why did you write that everyone forges their own good fortune and others' misfortune? . . . I didn't write that, I wrote that Great-grandpa was a blacksmith and everyone around him misfortunate. That's what I wrote, I didn't write anything about anyone else because I didn't have time and because I don't know anything about any other blacksmiths . . . Do you really have to write down what you hear at home? You could make something up . . . You mean, I could lie about something? . . . Not lie, make up . . . And what in your opinion is the difference between making up and lying? . . . Liars lie and writers make things up . . . So who writes and talks about stuff that really happened then? . . . For chrissakes, I don't know, historians probably, but that's not the point right now, try outdoing yourself and biting your tongue every now and then.*

That's how my first encounter with a psychologist played out: A very unpleasant experience and one I'd very much like to avoid in the future, although my reputation in class skyrocketed afterward because everyone figured that comrade Mutevelić was there because of me and figured it was because I was either really crazy or really smart, but no one was able to solve that particular dilemma, apart from Šandor, the class bonehead, who was repeating the grade and gave me a hiding every day after Mutevelić's visit, presumably having decided that crazy or smart, I deserved a thrashing either way.

Given that the Old Devil and the family fear of rakia and alcoholism was at the root of everything, I decided to carefully monitor my family's relationship to alcohol, make a few notes from time to time, it being obvious that inebriety was key and that I had to act with caution in the face of their fears. As soon as Grandma or Grandpa got scared about something, I'd get bawled out for not sharing their fears. Then I'd have to be scared of all the things I wasn't scared of, and given I couldn't stop being scared of the stuff I really was scared of myself, I had to carry around my own fears and their fears besides, which, I'm sure you'll agree, is a rather unpleasant state of affairs when you're five, seven, or however many years old.

I noticed that our pantry was full of alcohol: homemade slivovitz and grappa; dozens of bottles of brandy and cognac; two liters of whiskey; vodka, gin; bottles of white, red, and rosé wine; menthol and chocolate liqueurs; Macedonian mastic and Greek metaxa . . . The bottles were neatly arranged and unopened, apart from the grappa and the whiskey, at the ready for when guests came. The bottles belonged to long-forgotten wakes and birthday parties, or were New Year's presents from the time before I was born. When someone dies, the neighborhood comes to say how sorry they are and people bring bottles of alcohol, which then get stored in the pantry forever. Everyone knows we're pretty much a nondrinking household, but tradition is tradition, and people cling to funeral rites most faithfully of all because even if they make no sense they're still not for messing with because death is a time when the living have to be good to each other, and you're best when you do something of no use to anyone, which makes it all the more moving.

The menthol and chocolate liqueurs were presents for Mom when she was really young and before I was even born. On one of the bottles there was a tempera heart and arrow with Mom's name and the name of some guy in it. This is a happy memory for her, which I don't get at all. How can a bottle of liqueur be a happy memory when she's terrified of alcohol? Do you think that heart is the happy memory? Nice: a memory written on a bottle full of fear.

If someone in our house dies, or someone else falls in love with Mom, there won't be any room in our pantry for anything but bottles of alcohol, and soon there'll be so many we'll have to keep them under the bed or in the coat cupboard. It's all because of the Old Devil. He's the ghost in the pantry and it's no matter he died in 1943 and everyone's always thought he was buried forever in Zenica Cemetery. But he wasn't going to be banished from the pantry until someone else turned to the drink. Me, for example! *What if I became an alcoholic?* I asked Grandma. *At six years old?* She was shocked. *Not right now, a bit later . . . How much later? Oh, to hell with you, become whatever you like, just wait 'til I'm dead . . . I didn't say I will become an alcoholic, but what if I did? . . . And why, pray tell, would you be an alcoholic? . . . Well, how about so someone empties all those bottles from out of the pantry.*

That weekend my uncle from Zenica came and took all our alcohol away. He parked his Volvo station wagon in front of the house and spent an hour loading it with bottles. Everyone was in a crappy mood, Mom and Grandma most of all, so I wasn't allowed to ask anything, not even what he was going to do with all those bottles of brandy, cognac, vodka, and wine, and the menthol and chocolate liqueurs. He took

Mom's happy memory away too, her heart and the guy's name written inside it. Grandma wiped the shelves down and covered them with bright paper. *There, now there's much more room for ajvar and paprikas*, she said, but I was sorry about the bottles. Maybe because I felt that one day I really could've drunk them all up, and maybe I was sorry because the ghost of Blacksmith Joža the Slovenian – my great-grandpa, the Old Devil – had been so violently tossed from our pantry.

This year we're going to put a rum pot on, Grandma solemnly announced and put an enormous five-liter ceramic pot on the table. It had funny Gothic letters on it, words written above drawings of pears, apples, cherries, figs, and grapes that weren't yellow or red but green like grass or the cover on our couch. Rum pot is fruit for wintery days, that's what they told me, and I'll only get to eat it if I'm good and I display maturity in all possible situations. I don't have the foggiest idea what maturity in all possible situations is supposed to mean, but I solemnly promised that I'd give it my all because I was really into this rum-pot thing because you made it with rum, and rum is alcohol, and that seems to have slipped Mom's and Grandma's mind. Or something else was going down; I didn't know what, but I'd find out in the fall, at the beginning of November when the rum pot was opened.

At the end of May, right around my birthday, Grandma filled the pot with rum and tossed half a kilo of strawberries in. She spread her arms, said *all done*, and threw me out of the pantry. Fifteen days later we were in the pantry again, she opened the pot, tossed two handfuls of cherries in, spread her arms, and again said *all done*. She also said *all done* when the figs, apples, cantaloupes, watermelons, pears, and grapes were ripe and ready. If you really want to know, I think spreading her arms and saying *all done* were part of the recipe and that for the rum pot they're just as important as the fruit and rum. I'm not sure if everyone can say those words and spread their arms in that particular way, but if your rum pot doesn't work out, you can more or less be sure the recipe is lost for all time because I've obviously forgotten some tiny detail or secret ingredient, and by the time you read this my grandma will already be dead, so you won't be able to ask her.

On the eve of the twenty-ninth of November a big snow fell, and on our Independence Day the temperature fell to minus twenty. *The hare's been looking for his mom tonight*, my mom declared, *today's the day for rum pot*, my grandma concluded; my heart beat like crazy. I could smell the rum before Mom had even opened the pot. There's no greater surprise than a first time, this I know well, because everything that has ever happened to me for the first time was great, and luckily the world was still full of first times and you just had to be a little patient and another first time would roll around. Flags had frozen on the flagpoles outside, the red of the Party and the red of the republic, between them the state tricolor. All was quiet, icy, and calm, not a breath of wind, and the flags, well they hung there as if made of steel or like someone had frozen them at the height of their flapping so they had to wait along with me, eyes wide open, nostrils flared, and fists clenched for the rum pot to be set on the table, in midwinter, on this coldest of all days, which also happens to be our Independence Day, the fruit of last summer, the fruit of boiling-hot days when everything burst with life, now preserved in rum, in that terrifying alcohol, so that another first time would come to pass.

I got one fig, two cherries, a slice of apple, and three strawberries. *That's too much for you*, said Grandma, *you're not going to get drunk on us*, said Mom, but I looked at the fruit in my bowl, a little disappointed. The fruit had lost all its color: the figs and strawberries were brown, the cherries black, the apples almost gray. Instead of fruit, what I saw looked like the corpses of fruit; dead fruits that hadn't been eaten when it was their time, fruits that didn't continue life in our tummies and veins, in hearts remembering them and palates tasting their sweetness. Someone had left them to die, to see in Independence Day dead and soaked in rum.

I held the end of the table with my fingers and stared at the bowl. I didn't know what to do, from which side or fruit to start. *What's wrong? . . . They look like eyes to me . . . What kind of eyes? . . . Like the eyes in formalin at the medical faculty.* Mom shot Grandma an angry look: *See what Dobro's done . . . Oh Jesus Christ*, said Grandma. *I'm telling you, he's got a screw loose . . . What can I do about it? . . . You let him take him there . . . What could I do, ban him? I'm not his mother and his father.*

So you see, there were problems before I'd even tried the rum pot for the first time, and it was all Dad's fault because he'd taken me to see

185

the organs in formalin. He thought I should see that stuff and there was absolutely no reason why kids shouldn't see parts of former people, and maybe he thought I'd get interested in medicine and follow, as Auntie Doležal liked to say, in his footsteps. Instead, everything dead and fake started to remind me of organs in formalin, from my cousin Regina's plastic dolls, which looked like spleen in formalin, to pickled paprikas filled with cabbage, which in see-through jars looked like brain tumors in formalin, to fruit from the rum pot, which looked like eyes in formalin. I didn't get what the problem was and why something wasn't allowed to remind me of something in formalin, but it was obvious that asking was out of the question, that I was just supposed to smile and act dumber than I really am.

Grandma grabbed my bowl and scraped the fruit back into the pot. *It doesn't remind me, it doesn't remind me!* I howled, but it was already too late. *You're not getting drunk on me,* said Grandma. *Go do some math,* said Mom. I lost it and started braying. Afterward I always tell myself that I'm not allowed to do this, but it's no good, I start bawling at the critical moment, I just squawk louder and louder, and my nerves go floppy like slithery noodles in beef soup and it's blindingly obvious I'm not going to achieve anything because they don't care about my tears, it's like I'm a fascist in a Partisan film, but what other option do I have when they do this sort of stuff to me, especially on our Independence Day when we're supposed to love each other more than on other days because it's a public holiday and everything is supposed to be flashy like it is on TV.

I kept the squawking up for hours, but they didn't want to listen, they just quietly went about their business. I stopped when Mom started doing the vacuuming. The insult was bad enough as it was, and the vacuum cleaner sounded like it was mocking me, almost perfectly imitating my voice. Anyone would have thought the vacuum cleaner and I were performing a traditional song from the Far East, from the Siberian wastes or the Mongolian desert or somewhere.

I shut up and went on an anger strike. I didn't look at them the whole day, answering questions briskly and coldly and only those of an official character, for example, how many classes we had at school tomorrow and whether my PE gear needed washing, Mom said *little bastard, look at him sulking*, and I sucked that insult up too. She tried being all cuddly before I went to sleep, but I pulled the duvet over my head in a huff and waited for her to leave.

I was angry the next day too. After lunch Grandma asked *would you like some rum pot?* And I could hardly wait to tell her *no, it's disgusting! . . . Excuse me, how is it disgusting? . . . It's not food, it's al-co-hol – al-co-hol. I'm not a boozer and I don't need al-co-hol.* I broke it up into syllables and looked her straight in the eye. She can't do anything to me because whatever she wants to say, the Old Devil is going to dance before her eyes, my great-grandpa Blacksmith Joža the Slovenian is going to wake from his grave, my great ally for the day.

Fine, you don't have to have any, more for us. I snortled out my nose and tried to smile cynically. I practice that smile all the time, for situations when I don't know what to say or need to shut my mouth so

I don't get it on the snout, but I always get the impression that I don't do it that well, that to them it looks like I'm going to burst out crying instead of into a smile.

I didn't try the rum pot that year. I refused it even when I'd quit being angry, even when guests came, even when Nano was here for New Year's and said *c'mon, try a little of mine.* I couldn't break now, even though I wanted to try that dead fruit and the alcohol in it and find out why the fruit died and what my great-grandpa had enjoyed his whole life and what Grandma, Mom, and Grandpa were so desperately afraid of.

Grandma made the rum pot the next year too, she spread her arms, said *all done,* the whole routine repeated right down to the grapes, the last fruit to go in, and the first icy days of fall when the pot was opened. Grandma said *try this fig, for my sake.* It was then I gave in because it was a fig and figs are a special fruit for my grandma. Everything to do with figs was tender, quiet, and distant, buried in some long-lost time, and if she went back to that time, she'd become unsteady and unsure of herself, a little girl, my grandma the little girl, because for her all the figs in the world were from Dubrovnik, from the Dubrovnik where she grew up going to an Italian school and looking out to sea from Boninovo. The sea was without end, and life itself had no end, and so at the ends of life and the sea, the only thing in which she was still a child was those figs, in the most beautiful of them all, the violet *Ficus indiana,* the fruit in which my grandma lives without a single disappointment in life, without a single great pain of adulthood where things stop being child-like and nothing ever happens for the first time. Grandma bore children and buried the first of them, Grandma loved Greta Garbo, her silence and her blue eyes, Grandma delivered grandchildren and buried the first of them, Grandma loved Grandpa and buried him too, Grandma hated the Old Devil because the Old Devil had brought Grandpa only suffering in life and Grandma couldn't allow it that someone she loved suffered. This is what I was thinking when she said *try this fig, for my sake*, or that's what I thought much later when I was growing up fast and more and more things were for the last time and fewer and fewer for the first time. That fig is lodged in my brain from a different time and it belongs only to her and it will stay that way forever.

The dead fig from the rum pot was my first alcohol in life. I don't know what it tasted like, I don't remember or I don't want to remember because with these kinds of memories you risk a comrade Mutevelić showing up and crapping on about how intelligent you are and how you're going to explode like a bomb one day because you cry for no reason, even though you know your tears are silly, do no good, and that no one understands them. I don't mean tears of rage but the other kind, the kind that made me eat that fig. But for me the snow didn't seem like a deep blue duvet under the icy moonlight, the duvet under which Blacksmith Joža the Slovenian lies sleeping.

A castle for Queen Forgetful

Auntie Doležal told me the story about Queen Forgetful. It was Friday and it was summer, and we'd come over to her place for coffee. I mean, Grandma had come over for coffee, I was just going along for Sombrero candies and petit beurre biscuits, which at Auntie Doležal's place were all soft, not a single crunch left in them. Mom said it's because Auntie Doležal's biscuits are stale and they're stale because no one eats them except me, because she doesn't have anyone come visit her and eat biscuits and she only buys them because everyone has to have biscuits for when guests come over, but the less guests come, the softer and soggier the biscuits, like someone's been crying on them.

As soon as we arrived I got stuck into the biscuits, trying to snaffle them all up so Auntie Doležal would have to go the store and buy some new ones, muttering to herself the whole way *God help me, guests on the doorstep and not a biscuit in the house*, which is what my grandma always says. But better this *God help me* than Auntie Doležal's biscuits get even soggier because she doesn't have any family left and we're the only ones who come visit her.

My Micika, I can hardly walk, Grandma bellyached, a brown coffee spot on the tip of her nose. Auntie Doležal pretended not to notice it because it's impolite to notice such things, even when the person is your best friend. *You don't need to tell me, when I walk it's like someone's banging nails in my feet*, Auntie Doležal brushed her off and stepped out of her slippers, *take a look, it's not even two weeks since I went to the podiatrist . . . I never find the time to go, it's always look at this, look at that, move this, move that, go there, come here, and days and months go by, and I've got corns like – Godforgiveme – I fell from the tree yesterday.* Grandma was rambling and a new coffee spot had formed next to the last one. *Olga, why don't you nip to the podiatrist now, the little one can stay here, it won't be boring here with me, will it now?* Auntie Doležal turned to me. *No, no,* I hurried, hoping like hell Grandma wouldn't remember that it's impolite to leave kids with other people. There was no way I wanted to go to the podiatrist with her, because I went once and it was a terrible thing. I was sitting in the waiting room and a mother came in with a little girl a bit smaller than me, and then some guy in a white coat showed up, like he was a doctor, but he wasn't, and the girl started to bawl, and he put some metal thing up against her ear and it popped and the girl screamed, and then he put it up against her other ear and there was another pop, and then the girl and her mother left, the girl holding her hands over her ears screaming her head off, and I was scared stiff thinking the guy in the white coat might come for me next to do the same thing. Then Grandma came out. *What was that?* I asked. *Nothing, ear piercing . . . Ear peeing?* I blanched. *Not peeing, piercing.* Peeing, piercing, it was all the same, let your guard down for a second and you're in for it. The girl had come in all smiley and went out howling in pain. The bottom line is that I'm not going to the podiatrist with Grandma again unless I really have to.

Auntie Doležal was uncomfortable the moment we were on our own. I was sitting on the couch, and every little thing, every chair and cupboard grew before my eyes, all so immense, dead, and dusty. It was as if we were in a museum where no one had lived for thousands of hundreds of years and that Auntie Doležal was the guardian of a secret bounty and framed yellowed photographs of serious-looking people in funny uniforms. In one picture there was a man with long twirly whiskers and something funny on his head, something like an iron hat with a spike on the top. *Who's that? . . . That's my dad,* Auntie Doležal brightened up, because I wasn't scared of all her dusty stuff anymore. *He was a soldier and fought for Czar Franz . . . And he wore that thing on his head when he fought? . . . He did, I think he did, it was actually part of the uniform . . . Did Czar Franz's other soldiers wear that thing on their heads too? . . . I don't know, probably . . . They really wore those same iron hats on their heads?* I really was surprised because I couldn't imagine someone running around with that sort of thing on their head. *Well, I'm not at all surprised they lost all those wars.*

Auntie Doležal smiled thinking me pretty witty and smart for my age, and me, I was just uncomfortable because she was uncomfortable, so I searched the place for something similar for us to talk about, just not something belonging to her dead husband. They'd killed him in Jasenovac and you weren't allowed to talk about him with Auntie Doležal. Actually, it was allowed, just no one wanted to, just like Auntie Doležal didn't want to talk to Grandma about the little brown spot on the tip of her nose. The polite thing to do was to shut your mouth and hope Auntie wasn't thinking about her Jucika, even though almost everything in her apartment reminded you of Jucika, and all his stuff was exactly where it was when they came for him.

I had the impression everything was Jucika's so we weren't allowed to talk about anything. Auntie Doležal held her hands in her lap and waited, I had to say something but didn't know what. *Auntie, how about telling me a story?* I remembered that grown-ups expect these sorts of requests from children and made a face like I wanted to hear a story more than anything else in the world and I'd be heartbroken if she didn't tell me one.

Auntie Doležal fidgeted a bit, but the discomfort was gone. She just needed to remember a story and then everything would be all right and it wouldn't matter that there weren't any toys or picture books in her apartment and that sitting here like this was as strange and new to her as it was to me. *I don't know many stories, I've forgotten them, but here's one about a girl called Forgetful.* Auntie Doležal folded her arms on her chest and felt herself very important, the kind of importance grown-ups feel when they tell stories, which is why children beg them to tell stories in the first place. It'd been a long time since Auntie Doležal had told anyone a story so she felt even more important. *Forgetful forgot everything. When her mom sent her to the store, she couldn't remember what she was supposed to buy, when she went to school, she forgot her books, when she went to visit her grandma in the village, she forgot to bring her knitting wool. Forgetful forgot everything you could possibly forget, but she never forgot her forgetting and this made her very unhappy. She knew that others always remembered or would go back for what they had forgotten, but she was lost and all on her own because absolutely no one forgot so badly that they couldn't remember what they'd forgotten. So Forgetful decided to write down everything she might forget. She wrote down what she was supposed to buy at the store, that she had to bring her books to school, and that she needed to take her knitting wool to her grandma's. But the more Forgetful wrote down, the more things she had to forget. For every single thing she wrote down and remembered there were another ten she had to write down, and another hundred for those ten. The world was so big and forgettable that in the end Forgetful came to the conclusion that there was nothing else in the whole world except the things she forgot. This made her even unhappier and she spent all day waiting for good fairies, but they never came, so she waited for angels, but they never came either. Actually there was no one else around but her mom and dad who'd look in on her every now and then and say, Oh, Forgetful, Forgetful, you've forgotten everything again.*

Auntie Doležal clapped her hands. I was surprised: In the end nothing happened in her story. There was nothing about what happened to Forgetful, whether she was alive today or whether she grew up and stopped her forgetting. There was no end to the story because it just got bigger and bigger like the circles around a stone thrown into the sea; there's always another circle around the other circle, and inside one thing forgotten there was always another and no one can count all these forgotten things because forgotten things can't be counted. It's like they don't exist and they never existed, but if you're Forgetful and everyone knows that you of all people are the forgetful one, then you start to count and write all the forgotten stuff down.

I looked at the wall, Auntie Doležal asked *did you like the story?* but I couldn't answer because I was trying to remember something that I knew yesterday but had forgotten today. I didn't know what it was, but I'm sure there was something and that I had forgotten it. *Did you like the story?* Auntie Doležal repeated. *Wait a second, Auntie*, and again I tried to remember. *Okay, I'm waiting*, she said.

You forget things because they're all different. If they were the same, you wouldn't be able to forget them. If her mom had sent Forgetful to the store to buy the same things every day, if Forgetful had to take the same books to school every day and take the same wool to her grandma's, then she wouldn't have forgotten anything. *I'll build a castle for Forgetful! . . . So, you liked it then? . . . No, I didn't like it, but I'll build a castle where she'll live by herself and it's all going to be the same and she won't be able to forget anything in it and no one will remind her of her forgetting.*

There was a ding-dang-dong. Grandma was back from the podiatrist. *Uff, my Micika, that's a relief. You have no idea how much of a relief that is,* she said, and Auntie Doležal made another coffee, I wolfed down the last biscuit, and then we went home. I don't remember how Grandma and Auntie Doležal parted, I don't remember if it was sunny when we left and I don't remember if Auntie Doležal watched us from her window and if we waved to her from the tram stop. I'm sorry I don't remember because we never saw her again.

The ambulance came for Auntie Doležal on a Monday. That morning the neighbors had found her on the ground floor, a bag of groceries in her hand – bread, milk, biscuits, and lettuce – just standing there. They said hi, and every time she'd startle but not say hi back. Then she climbed the stairwell, going from door to door and then back down to the ground floor. It was afternoon by the time she rang the Kneževićs' bell and said to Snježana, the girl who was my father's intern at the hospital, *I've lost my way!* Snježana was confused and asked *where did you lose your way, Auntie?* Auntie just smiled and said *I don't know,* and then Snježana called the ambulance.

First the doctors thought Auntie Doležal had had a stroke and that's why she had forgotten everything, and then they figured out she was perfectly healthy and that there was nothing wrong with her. So they thought Auntie Doležal had suddenly gone senile, but you can't go senile overnight; yesterday you remember everything and today you can't even remember where you live. Then they made some inquiries about whether Auntie had any relatives and discovered that Jucika was dead and that Auntie's daughter, Vera, was also dead and that Auntie's brothers and sisters were also dead, and in the end it turned out that we were all Auntie Doležal had left.

Mom went to the hospital and Dr. Muratbegović said to her *madam, I'm afraid we don't have any reason to keep her in, and given she doesn't have any family the only thing we can do is put her in Jagomir.* Mom bawled Dr. Muratbegović out because Jagomir was a nuthouse, and Auntie Doležal wasn't nuts, she'd just forgotten everything. *Forget it, I'll take care of her,* she said and took Auntie Doležal back to her apartment.

Auntie, do you remember me? Mom asked when they were in the tram. *I won't lie to you. I don't remember . . . And do you remember Olga, Auntie? Olga's your best friend.* Auntie just shrugged her shoulders and turned away. She looked out the window, rain was falling, and her eyes became moist and she was ashamed about being so impolite that she couldn't remember her best friend.

From that Monday on Mom visited Auntie Doležal morning and night. Auntie sat in her armchair the whole day through, reading the newspaper and doing the crossword. No one could ever figure out how she'd forgotten absolutely everything about her life but hadn't forgotten anything she needed to know to solve the crossword. She'd forgotten her Jucika but in crossword clues she knew that a bay was a horse.

Do you want to come to Auntie's with me? she asked Grandma just the one time, and Grandma said she didn't because all that mattered was that Auntie Doležal wasn't hungry and that she's clean, and that everything else was last year's snow and would never come back. She wasn't sad about it, but she would have been sad if she'd gone to Auntie's and Auntie didn't recognize her. That's my grandma for you, she lets things take their course, but she remembers everything Auntie Doležal has forgotten. Every time Mom comes back from Auntie's, Grandma talks about her Micika; she talks about lots of stuff Mom and me never knew. For example, right after the Second World War, when Grandma and Grandpa lived in Yugoslav People's Army Street next door to Auntie Doležal, there was an earthquake in Sarajevo, not a big one, only the black chandeliers swayed a bit, and Grandpa was taking a shower. When he felt everything shaking around him, he ran out of the bathroom, and with everything still shaking he ran out of our apartment soaped up and birth naked, hopping down the landing yelling *what's going on, what's going on.* Auntie Doležal stood in the doorway of her apartment and clasped her hands together, because to her Franjo was stranger than the earthquake. It was days before he could look her in the eye, and days before she could look my grandma in the eye. When the shame had passed and the earthquake was just a funny memory, Auntie Doležal said to Grandma *goodness gracious your Franjo's hung like a horse!*

Or when our cat Marko disappeared, also a few years after the war, and Grandpa paced the yard in front of our building for days calling him home, Auntie Doležal said she felt like crying when she saw him from her window so distraught because he knew the cat was never coming back, but that he needed to call him because you can't let one of your own vanish just like that and admit to yourself that they're gone and never coming back. Marko was the smartest cat in the world. He'd sit on the linoleum at the top of the hallway and wait for Grandpa to come home from work, and Grandpa would give him a shunt with his leg and Marko would slide all the way to the bathroom. For years after Marko's disappearance, Grandpa, on his way in from work, would wave his leg in the air and mutter *Ej Marko, Marko*, but this didn't get anybody down as much as Auntie Doležal. *Micika was terribly sensitive to Franjo*, says Grandma, and Mom puts her finger to her lips, *psssst!*, so Grandpa doesn't hear.

Every day when Mom came back from Auntie Doležal's Grandma would tell a new story about her friend, and in two months we'd heard her whole life story, and then one day the stories stopped. Mom stayed longer and longer over at Auntie Doležal's because she'd started forgetting that she needed to pee, she'd forgotten how to wash her face and hands, and she'd even stopped speaking. She just sat there with the same crossword on her knees, pencil in hand, staring at the empty wall. Mom had to bathe and dress her, and Auntie Doležal completely surrendered as if she were a little kid and didn't know what was being done to her.

In the end she didn't even remember how to sit up, so one morning she just lay there in bed and never got up again. Mom tried to get help from the hospital, but the nurse could only come twice a week, so she had to take care of Auntie Doležal all by herself. Auntie Doležal's life was over, and she was just waiting to die. Grandma didn't smile anymore, and she didn't talk about Auntie Doležal either, and Mom took sick leave because she had to be with her the whole day through. Auntie Doležal was like a little baby who had to have her diapers changed every so often, but unlike a baby she was never going to be a grown-up again. *How is she related to you*, the doctor who gave Mom the sick leave asked, and Mom told him Auntie Doležal wasn't a relative, but that everyone needs someone beside them so that they die like a human being.

She died just before the New Year, Mom, Grandma, and the neighbors went to the funeral. We bought Auntie Doležal a little wreath, the cheapest one. It was the only wreath on her grave, and all the other graves were covered in them. Luckily Auntie Doležal couldn't see this because if she had it would've definitely made her sad. The lone wreath would have reminded her that she had been left all alone in the world and didn't have anyone except us. In actual fact, there was nothing for her to forget, because all she'd now forgotten was already long gone: her father with the iron cap on his head, Jucika, the Sarajevo Partisan, and Vera, who twenty years ago had fallen asleep on the beach at Opatija and never woke up.

I think that on that Monday, on the way home from the store, Auntie

Doležal forgot all of us on purpose, the living and the dead. She even forgot where her apartment was on purpose and who all the people in the pictures were and whose fountain pen had been lying on the writing desk for the last thirty years, even the guests she'd bought the petit beurre biscuits for. She turned into Forgetful, and everything she once remembered she left to us to look after.

That day I started building a Lego castle for Queen Forgetful. The castle is the same from all sides and there won't be anything in it that you can forget. There's one hundred rooms all the same, just for her to live in, Forgetful, who in the meantime has become a queen because she forgot the most in the whole world and her kingdom has grown so much that there isn't one that can match it. The kingdom is so big it is the envy of all the kings in the world, and you just wait and see how they're going to envy it when my castle is finished.

That we all have one more picture together

If they were cherries shining red beneath the window when I shut my eyes, or if they were something else – maybe I'd caught a fever – I don't know anymore. But if they were cherries, then it was June, the second half of June, when the tree in our yard bore fruit, always a month later than the trees in the heat of Herzegovina. Our cherry tree had survived a cold winter and that made the month delay seem almost heroic. Even if they weren't cherries and it wasn't June, the gist of the story remains the same, clear as day in the photos themselves. There we were standing and crouching on the terrace in our short-sleeved shirts and T-shirts: my auntie and uncle, my cousin Vesna and her husband, Perti, my mom, Grandma, and me. In some pictures there's only Uncle and Grandma, in others Vesna and Grandma, or Mom and

Grandma, Grandma and me . . . If I showed you the pictures now and hadn't told you anything about them in advance, you'd think we were some hippie-dippie family who'd picked Grandma as our household chief or guru who had to be in every photo, and that the only thing the rest of us cared about was having our presence with her recorded for eternity. Maybe there's some truth in that, but I don't want to talk about it because I love my grandma too much and if I admitted you were right I'd spoil the rest of the story.

It was a Sunday, that I'm sure of, because in our house guests always came over on Sundays. This was probably how things were before I was born, so my family just kept it that way even after everything changed. I'm not actually sure, but it doesn't matter in any case. The fact is that the guests had come from all over: Uncle and Auntie had come from Moscow where Uncle was a rep for the Zenica steelworks, and Vesna had come from Helsinki where she lived with Perti, but he hadn't come from Helsinki, he'd come from Vladivostok. I don't know what he did in Vladivostok, but I remember Grandma saying *poor fellow, he's been at the end of the world*. For some reason she thought the end of the world was terrible.

We ate lunch, talked over the top of each other, and Auntie called me *Miki*, dead set that every child had to have a nickname, and I remember feeling somehow privileged that in addition to my real name I'd gotten another one besides. Grandma looked at me reproachfully every time Auntie said *Miki*. She didn't like the nickname, but I'm not sure how that made it my fault. Uncle poured himself a whiskey he'd brought from Moscow, *it's from Beryoshka, only foreigners buy stuff from Beryoshka*, and then he slapped himself on the forehead: *uh shit, I forgot the camera.* We weren't too bothered though, fine, he'd forgotten the camera, we kept talking over the top of each other and he did too, but every fifth sentence he'd throw something in about the camera, like *what a bloody donkey leaving it behind like that* or *my brain obviously checked out when we left.* Soon everyone was upset about the camera, so I made like I was upset too and tried to tell the story of how I once forgot my sneakers for PE, but no one wanted to listen.

We'll call Dobro, he's got a camera, said Mom. She picked up the phone and fifteen minutes later my dad arrived with a camera already loaded with film. Uncle quit his anxiety act, which let everyone else relax too, he poured Dad a whiskey, told the Beryoshka story again, and then he said *now, everyone on the terrace, light's best there.* We took our marching orders, probably scared his anxiety might come back if we jerked around. Dad was photographer for the day. He took pictures of us in all combinations, but no one took a picture of him. He's the only one who doesn't have a picture with Grandma. I wanted to ask why someone didn't take his picture too, but shut up in time. When your parents are divorced you've always got to shut up in time because what you'd like to ask might make your elders stutter and blush or make them want to say or do something to please you, and then you feel like a whipped-cream pie that's been standing in the sun all day and they all say *oh, what a lovely cake.* Actually, I know what would've happened if I'd asked. Dad would've had his photo taken with Grandma but either the laboratory wouldn't have developed it or no one would have wanted to have it.

The next week the guests went back to Moscow and Helsinki, leaving us with three complete sets of pictures, one each for Mom, Grandma, and me. In other circumstances one complete set would have been fine because we all lived together and didn't fight over photos. Mom got some albums, put the photos in, and by the next day we'd forgotten we'd even had our pictures taken.

On the thirteenth of December of the same year, the phone rang at half past two in the morning. I woke with the first ring and waited with closed eyes for what was going to happen next; there was a second ring, then a third, fourth, and fifth, then Mom's sleepy voice said *hello* and then a suddenly awake *yes.* She'd never gone from being asleep to completely awake so fast. *Yes . . . I can hear you . . . Yes . . . Yes . . . When . . . How is he . . . Is she there . . . Oh my God . . . Fine . . . All right.* She put the receiver down without saying goodbye. She flicked the light on in my room, I opened my eyes, the light straining them, her face was gray and somehow taut, she spoke like she'd been wandering the desert for days without water: *pull yourself together, Vesna's dead.* I was hurt by what she said, that *pull yourself together.* It was the first death in the family directly communicated to me. I was eleven years old.

I don't know how she told Grandma that her granddaughter was dead, but later Mom said she'd feared for Grandma's heart. We all thought Grandma had a weak heart. That's actually what the doctors had told us, but it turned out they had it wrong. Her heart could withstand what the strongest in the world couldn't. It swallowed the sadness like a big snake swallows a rabbit, and kept beating, and we never saw anything on her face, just sometimes a tear would fall when she was watching television. But she didn't cry.

The next day the three of us went to Zenica. The wake was at Uncle's apartment and all the mirrors were covered in black shawls. I didn't know any of the guests. Mom sunk into her brother's embrace. Grandma held my hand tight. I was big enough for this sort of stuff, but still too small to offer Uncle my hand and say a few of those weird sentences people say in these situations. I felt really awkward, the angst in Uncle's apartment smacking me around and eating me up. I sat in an armchair with my head down, just wanting it to all be over as soon as possible. People took turns crying. Uncle was beside himself, but there was always someone ringing the doorbell, offering Uncle their hand, and he'd just cry again and again and again. The terrifying flood of grown-up tears made me fear life for the first time, not life, just the growing up. I didn't cry for years because of his tears. Actually, I didn't cry until the war, but ever since then I can almost cry on demand. I mean, if you were to say to me now cry for five seconds, I'd cry for five seconds. I can do that sort of thing like a party trick. You need tears, I'm your man. I'm not telling you how I make them come, it's my secret, a little trick of the trade. Just like fakirs and their secrets when they lie on a bed of nails, I've got mine when it comes to crying. But that's all a different business, at the time of this story I sat dead still in a giant armchair trying not to look at Uncle's crying because I couldn't imagine him without tears anymore.

I didn't get around to thinking of Vesna, although I should have, and I should have because I loved her. She was fifteen years older than me, but because I didn't have any brothers or sisters, she was my sister; we said *my sister on my uncle's side.* Anyhow, that's who she was to me and how I felt when she was alive. When she died, I was an only child again.

It was already night when people stopped coming and when everyone who didn't belong to the inner circle of grief left. I was still sitting there in the armchair. Uncle was flushed red, veins cursing in his forehead, next to him sat Auntie, but she wasn't crying, across the way sat my mom and she wasn't crying either. She said to Grandma *Mom, go lie down.* With neither words nor tears Grandma left the room in complete silence. It was the only time in my life Grandma left a room and didn't look at me.

Uncle was crying again. He started to say *my darling child's gone, and this summer I forgot the camera, I thought we could all have one more picture together, that she could have one more picture with her grandma before Grandma dies, my child, my darling, darling child . . .* He hid his face in his trembling hands. Auntie hugged him like you hug a little kid or how every man would want the woman who loved him to hug him. It should have been a distressing sight, but in that instant I couldn't grieve and I couldn't love him; he, my uncle, had just explained something that in the world of grown-ups was probably normal but in mine wasn't. He wanted to take a picture of Grandma with us all because he thought she was going to die. As soon as he could think that, it was like he killed her, and like he wanted to take our picture with someone dear who was already dead, who appears like a hologram, beamed into our hearts, forever captured on tape, and then she goes and disappears like dreams disappear in the morning when you wake up or later when you don't remember them anymore.

The night we grieved for Vesna the world of grown-ups was but another world of horror. Of course I forgave Uncle his betrayal, but I never liked those photos. When I look at them today, I only notice Grandma, her dancing face blind to the deception, as we were all smiling next to her, unknowingly participating in her funeral, burying her alive, just so we could have our picture taken with her. No one spared a thought that Grandma was scared of dying and that for her it would be forever.

I see Vesna's hand on Grandma's shoulder. It's a young hand, as young as I'll never be again. Today I am five years older than that hand. And this is a kind of deception and betrayal too. How can I be older than my cousin if she was born fifteen years before me? I'm scared, I'm so scared that one day I'll also do what my uncle did that summer, when something turned red, cherries or not cherries. Or maybe my betrayal was under way the moment I became older than Vesna.

Where dead Peruvians live

Auntie Lola used to live in Peru. It was before I was born and Uncle
Andrija was still alive. They got their passports in Belgrade, they bought
ship passage and plane tickets in Split, and that's where Uncle Andrija
bought a newspaper – as a memento, because they thought they were
never coming back and needed to remember the day they left. On the
front page there was a bold headline: COMRADE NIKITA SERGEYEVICH
KHRUSHCHEV'S SECRET PAPER. They came back two years later.

The altitude was tttterrible, sputtered Auntie Lola. *Higher than Jahorina?* I asked. *Ttttwice as high!... And were there big snows and was it twice
as cold as on Jahorina?... No, there was almost no snow and it wasn't very
cold... Why did you come back then?... Because the altitude was tttterrible
... And did everything look really small from up there?... No, everything was*

big, but at such a tttterrible altitude there's no air . . . Is there a lot of smoke and clouds? . . . No, there isn't a lot of anything. There's just no air and it's all empty there. And you, you little dork, quit jerking me around. If I ssssay that the altitude was tttterrible, then that's that, end of sssstory.

You couldn't hold a conversation with Auntie Lola for very long. As soon a conversation started getting interesting she'd start a fight. That was just her nature: cantankerous. And when someone's cantankerous, you have to be mindful of this because they can't do anything about it. Cantankerousness – at least how Granny Almasa from Ulomljenica used to explain it – is a sign that someone's from a better home and that not even life itself can change them. Auntie Lola was the only cantankerous one in the family and generally speaking she'd fought with everyone except Grandma because we, to my regret, had never worried too much about who was cantankerous and who wasn't.

Auntie Lola and Uncle Andrija had a son called Željko. He was a pilot. He graduated from the Royal Air Force Academy in Belgrade, and when the war started he became a Home Guard pilot in Rajlovac. It was never hushed up in our house; we didn't even bother with hushed voices, because Željko was our only family hero. One day he'd defected to the English in his plane. We've got photos of him in his RAF uniform next to Big Ben, and Tower Bridge, and playing golf on some meadow with men dressed in white.

But we shut up about Željko when Auntie Lola came over. I was under strict instructions to not ask anything about him, but as soon as she left Grandma started her stories. When the Allies bombed Sarajevo near the end of the war, Željko had been in one of the planes. Afterward he said *Auntie, I was really careful not to hit your house*. Grandma always repeated the line and then added *little sop, how was he going to be careful, he well knew you can't be careful about anything from that height.*

In the spring of 1945, Željko flew over Europe and saw everything. He saw Berlin, which was no more, Warsaw, which was no more, Dresden, which was no more, Auschwitz, which was also no more; come to think of it, how did he see everything when everything was no more? It would be better to say that he didn't see anything or that he saw nothing, but Grandma didn't think like that. Half-closed eyes, her gaze gently raised like she was talking about angels and birds, she'd tell of everything Željko saw from above, it was as if back then he'd taken care of some really important job for the whole family and now the rest of us had inherited that picture of Europe from May 1945 and we all had to follow Grandma's lead and repeat sentence by sentence, city by city, camp by camp everything Željko saw. Today when I hear the word Europe, everything Grandma said Željko saw assembles before my eyes, and it can't be helped; from a great height I dream a Europe frail and real, through the eye of an old aircraft, a Europe scorched and devastated, beautiful and small, enveloped in barbed wire, telegraph poles ripped out, a Europe of a thousand tiny cities, little boys digging through the ruins, little girls hugging exhausted soldiers and giving them flowers, a ruin of Europe without the dead and wounded because you don't see them from such a height, they're buried in the ground, hidden in hospitals.

Željko brought peace to Europe and Željko bombarded Sarajevo, but he never wounded or killed anyone. That's what we believed because we need belief like soldiers need bouquets of flowers. Having brought peace, in August 1945 Željko got drunk with some pilot friends, and was drunk when he took off from Zagreb Airport. Airborne a short time, he died in Zagreb Hospital. The son of Auntie Lola died an ally, not the enemy, so you could talk about his death. We talked about it often, it was as if his death had offered someone salvation, it was as if Željko had to die so that my uncle M.R. could find peace beneath the earth even if he never managed to find it in his parents' hearts.

Željko is buried at the Boninovo Cemetery in Dubrovnik, in a tomb full of old skeletons for which no one grieved anymore, only the very eldest among us remember who they once belonged to. Auntie Lola and Uncle Andrija seldom visited the grave of their only son; in actual fact they only went on All Saints' Day because you had to go that day, it was the custom. I didn't know why that day, but I know both of them went, and that probably they didn't want to, and that they probably wanted to put as much distance as they could between themselves and that grave, so they moved to Peru.

They didn't write or get in touch with anyone, one day they just came back. It was pretty high over there and there wasn't enough air, *the living can't survive without air*, Grandma said, as if to justify Auntie

Lola's coming back, and it was then I thought there were only dead people in Peru, and that Lima was a city of the dead where Auntie Lola and Uncle Andrija had got lost by mistake, and that they had to come back because the living can't live with the dead, so they justify themselves and their coming back and explain it away by saying that there's no air. I dreamed of Lima and Peru and the dead, but in my dream they were calm, friendly, and smiling; I flew above them and then I began to fall, I fell a long time, children grow when they fall in their sleep, I was growing and happy in my dream among the Peruvian dead and the condors, dead birds in a land of dead people who my Auntie Lola and Uncle Andrija had seen with their living eyes. *A condor's wingspan is as wide as this room*, Auntie Lola spread her arms in the living room, the biggest room in her Dubrovnik apartment, and I believed her.

I believed everything and from this grew the world I have in my head and today it resembles what I believed it to be back then. In vain I imagine a Europe without detonated cities, barbed wire, and the expanse of a charred Auschwitz, but there is no such Europe in my head, there's no room in it, because I'd first need to get rid of this old one, but it doesn't work, just like I can't get rid of Peru, the land of dead people and condors with no need for air, whom the living visit only sometimes and only by accident – Auntie Lola and Uncle Andrija – and the living me, in my dream. Željko is sometimes alive, the Allied pilot who belongs to our whole family, he soars above us, looking at us as we are now and how we might be in our thoughts and dreams. If only he'd let us know what we look like from such a great height and whether we've changed in any way, or whether we are as beautiful and sad as Europe in May 1945.

When I try and hunt him down in the sky and the ground beneath my feet moves, the same way my cities and homelands move and disappear, and my native soil becomes a Europe without the soldiers little girls greet with flowers, when I search the sky for the living Željko, I feel how easy it is to be someone else; it's like going into a changing room in some big department store and after two minutes leaving as one of the thousands of faces I can imagine because I know they exist and that they live someplace far away; just not in Peru, because only dead Peruvians live there, and the parents of dead sons who need air.

Mama Leone

You have to remember this! I said. *What do I have to remember?* Mom asked. *I'm not talking to you, I'm talking to myself.* She held me by the hand, deeply frustrated that she isn't a mother like other mothers, and her son isn't a son like other sons, because he mostly talks precocious garbage. *You're not allowed to talk to yourself. Thinking's okay, but not talking, you'll be nuts before you know it.* She's obviously wound up, so I just nodded my head. When she's wound up I nod my head so she doesn't start yelling, doesn't start her ranting and raving and I end up getting it on the snout. For me the word snout is yuckier than any box on the ear. Mom just had to say *snout* and it was message received loud and clear. *You'll get it on the snout* grossed me out so much I would just shut my trap.

We walked along the seashore, almost to Zaostrog. She held my hand, never letting go. She thought I'd disappear if she let me walk on my own. Mom was like moms aren't allowed to be. She didn't feel enough like a mom, so out of fear, she put it on. Actually, she was most scared that maybe I was more of a grown-up than she was, a kind of mini-forbear who'd popped out of her uterus by mistake, just wanting to check up on her and how she was doing in life, put her through an exam she was bound to fail. So she played at being a grown-up and put me in my place with stuff about me going nuts if I talked to myself.

I noticed she was holding back, expecting me to say something, something for her to pounce on. I bolted my tongue to the roof of my mouth, silent as the grave, breathing real quiet so she couldn't make words out of my breathing. But she couldn't help herself. *What do you have to remember?*

I had to choose a strategy fast: either to pretend I didn't understand the question, or to make her think that the whole time I'd been thinking about what it was I had to remember. *I have to remember a precise moment in time, the moment three scents came rushing to me: the scent of the sea, the scent of the pines, and the scent of olive oil.*

She stood there, let go of my hand, a look of shock on her face but a harmless one. She smiled and said *you're my son!* She hugged me tight and asked *who's your mom, who do you love most?*

This was already way past stupid and I don't remember what happened next. I don't remember if we went to Zaostrog. Maybe we went to the confectionary for cake or to the diner for an *ora*, an orange lemonade that I called *oratalismaribor*, like in the ads. I don't know if we sat inside because Mom couldn't smoke in the open air, or if we sat outside because she wasn't so anxious and jumpy that she needed a cigarette, or if we went back the same way by the sea, or if we took the main road . . . I don't remember any of this, nothing at all. I've forgotten everything after *who's your mom, who do you love most*, and I'll never remember. That part of my life is dead. My mom killed it.

Fifteen years later, I was twenty-two, and I'd had a terrible fight with Nataša at a campground. *You're so awful when you talk to me!* she said, her face turning into revulsion itself. No one before or after her could do that, turn their whole face, ears and everything, into an expression of revulsion. The horror cut my legs out from under me, my sweetheart turned monster. But she wasn't gross or disgusting, it's not like she transformed into a festering boil that would have made me leave any sweetheart in the world. Just her face turned into revulsion, like a kid turns into a rat in a horror film. Normally I'd put my hand on her shoulder and pull her toward me; she'd try and break free and in the breaking free she'd go back to her old self. She had to smile and come back, because the old Nataša always came back.

But I was shitty that day on Korčula. I turned around and stormed off. By the fifth stride I didn't know where I was going. I wanted to stop but couldn't, there was no point in going any farther, yet no point in stopping either, so I just kept going and going and going . . . Of course it hurt that Nataša didn't come after me. She stayed put in front of the tent or wherever she was at that moment. She didn't put her hand on my shoulder. She never did that, nor would she ever. I wanted to hate her for it. When you're on an island it doesn't matter how shitty you are, or if you don't actually know where you're going, you hit the sea eventually. I stopped at some jagged rocks, as cutting as a final decision, the waves lapping stroppily as a big boat passed the island. You could see little people on the boat waving to someone. I was lonesome because they weren't waving to me. Or maybe there was some other reason I felt lonesome, however things were I remember that that's exactly how I felt, and it was then I became aware of the three scents: the scent of the sea, the scent of the pines, and the scent of olive oil.

My God, why do I do it to myself! I said aloud – or maybe I just thought it, I don't know – but by then I was already running back, across the rocks, through a stand of pines, through the camp, trampling on people's towels and getting caught on guy ropes. Nataša wasn't there in front of the tent. She wasn't inside either. I ran for the water fountain and spotted them both from ten meters away, Nataša and the fountain. Nataša was cleaning a big round tomato, and a few people were waiting in line behind her. I didn't have time to stop. I couldn't change anything. I had really run, it'd been a good long run and it seemed like I'd been running for hours. Yet those ten meters were the longest. I remember every split-second, every drop of water on the smeared surface of the tomato, every drop that fell at her feet. Like at every campground on

218

the Adriatic, there was mud in front of the water fountain. But I didn't even slow down through the mud, splattering myself, the people in line, and her, who'd started to turn around. This splattering and turning around went on and on, but she didn't quite make it around in time, she couldn't see who was coming, she didn't know it was me, that I was throwing myself at her. Then it was us falling in the mud, the tomato falling from her hand, her letting out a short, sharp cry, me lying above her, me lying on top of her and holding her tight.

Get off me already! she said, careful that not a single word, not a single sound rang harshly, and in that moment itself everything, her body, hair, muddy clothes, breathing, gave her away as wanting me to stay. I couldn't let her go because I thought she'd disappear, just like everything had disappeared from Zaostrog so long ago. I wanted her to stay silent, for her to stay here, immortal in this moment and never again, in the mud next to a water fountain, in a campground on Korčula, half a meter from an abandoned tomato no one will ever slice. The tomato dead the instant it fell from her hand.

Five years passed in the blink of an eye. Nataša was in Belgrade, and I was in Sarajevo. The war was raging. The war of my life, the only one I remember and the only one in which it seems that I'll die, yet remain alive, undamaged and whole, like some kind of Achilles who didn't even get hit in the heel. The phone lines were down. I was in the Jewish Community Center at the Drvenija Bridge. All around there were people waiting for a connection, in front of me a ham radio operator with a funny machine like something out of the Second World War. From the machine you could hear the hum of all the world's oceans, the cracking and creaking of every shipwreck, all at once. A voice surfaced from between and beneath the waves. The voice said *she's asking how are you?*

I turn to the operator: *I'm good, how are you?* He almost swallows the microphone: *he's good, how is she?, I repeat, he's good how is she?, receiving you.* And then again the cracking of ancient ships, the roar of the waves, the terror of the seamen: *she's good, what should she send him?* I'm not too cool with about fifty people listening in on my conversation. I lean down and say to the operator *send me newspapers and bacon!* He quivers invisibly from the breath in his ear and continues *have her send newspapers and bacon, I repeat, newspapers and bacon!* The whole room bursts out laughing, probably about the newspapers, and the voice from the other side crackles *she's thinking of him and wants him to be careful!* The time had come for the conversation to end. People were waiting in line, and I had one more sentence to say, one worth more than every silence, one that had to do the same thing as the hug in the Korčula mud. I was frozen in terror confronted by words, words, words that I could say, ones I didn't have to say, words that seeped like sand from a smashed hourglass, like mercury on the wooden floor of a chemistry lab, like a little death growing inside me, the death of a tomato next to a water fountain. It was then I remembered it, the tomato, I'd thought it had died, but it hadn't; it appeared one last time, falling from her hand, it came back to me, right here now as I sent my cry in the stormy night, because on the other side there's no one anymore, there's no me, no campground, no Korčula, no fight, no face turned to revulsion, a beautiful precious revulsion that is no more . . . I didn't move my lips down to the manly ear, nor did I whisper. I said in a loud voice, like we were really there, in her living room, alone because the general and his wife had gone to the seaside: *I love you more than anything in the world!* The operator turned to me. He saw my face for the first time ever. I'd always been at his back. He'll probably never see me again. *That you'll say yourself,* he whispered, taking the headphones off, me sitting down in his place. The hum was much louder in the headphones. I didn't know where my words were going nor who was listening, the kind of waves they were being lost on or whether there was a momentary lull from which they might be clearly heard, as clearly as they would, just this once, be spoken: *Nataša, I love you more than anything in the world!*

The Jewish Community Center cried like people do after a good theater performance. Everyone cried, men and women. A single sentence made so many people cry. That sentence had a weight to it, but only for he who had said it and she who had heard it. At that very moment everyone else could've snoozed away or picked their noses, fired their machine guns, prayed to God, or spoken some common-place truth, words to save the world, but instead they cried, probably because at that very moment they too were bidding farewell to their lives, another little death already eating at them. Today I don't remember a single one of those crying faces.

I don't remember the important moments, I forget them the second I say *you have to remember this.* Life would be long if I remembered more. I've forgotten almost everything. Except when I was running from the shoreline to the campground or being careful that Mom not say *snout.* Everything else is gone. Things that are gone divide into those I've managed to preserve in memory and those that have become a series of my little deaths. These deaths are like gray marks on an old map. Unless it's another India, nobody actually knows what's really there. I managed to preserve in memory the sentence *I love you more than anything in the world,* but I didn't know how to love someone more than anything in the world, and I didn't want to know that fear wasn't the best ally to have in life. Nataša stayed in Belgrade for a time, then she went to Canada because I never got in touch again. I tried that *I love you more than anything in the world* at different times and it felt as banal as a ham radio operator translating words across waters and oceans, every *I* becoming *he*, every *you* becoming *she*. Or something like that. Whatever, no one ever cried again.

I turned on the radio a little while ago, God only knows the station, but it was playing "Mama Leone" so it definitely wasn't one of ours. The scent of the sea, the scent of the pines, and the scent of olive oil rushed to me once more, all at the same time, as did everything those scents gave off. I don't know what the song's got to do with all this, but there's definitely some connection, it's from something I've forgotten, from one of those little deaths. I need to find a place for "Mama Leone" somewhere here, but I don't know where or how because there's no room left in the story I'm telling. There never was. In the meantime my mom has become a real grown-up mom, and I've become her son. Not some forbear. She doesn't say *snout* anymore, but sometimes things sound like that.

That Day a Childhood Story Ended

Here where squirrels die

That day a childhood story ended. His cough woke him up, his nose blocked, his cheeks and forehead on fire. He should have stayed in bed, just lain there and slept it off, but the devil wouldn't let him be. He got dressed and went outside. It was raining, cold drops on hot skin, the bus taking forever to come. He thought about pneumonia and meningitis. He remembered every sickness he knew by name, and a few others he didn't know anything about or his imagination had maybe dreamed up for the occasion. He was astonished to discover that he no longer feared a single disease in the world.

The bus was half empty. Where did all those people go, he thought, his head resting on the glass, banging against it the whole journey. He was reconciled to his fate for the day. Nobody was waiting for him, he wasn't expecting anyone, and everything was like the first day, repeated for the thousandth time, just now he was more indifferent, sanguine even, the way a man should be who has never made any attempt to hold on to the things around him, never tried for any great happiness. To this very day he has been waiting on fortune's call, which like the magnificent end of a war, with confetti, fireworks, and the dumbfounded embraces of lost loves, would return his life to its old rhythm, return to him these past six years spent in despair. This was how long Deda had lived in Ljubljana, a city he hadn't actually chosen but had simply been the farthest he dared go, when at the beginning of April 1992, sensing the onset of war, he had left home. He'd packed a single suitcase, a handful of shirts, a few pairs of underwear, and a Walkman. He said his goodbyes to his mother, telling her that he'd be back in about two weeks, by which time he thought mobilization in the city would be over. At the station he bought a return ticket, sat down in the bus, opened a book, and started reading, never looking back. Two weeks later he was watching pictures of the city in flames on television. Mojca wiped her tears, he hugged her and told her *Mocja, it's nothing, it'll all pass*, and she collapsed in his arms, the inconsolable viewer of a cinematic melodrama. That summer Deda found a job in a planning office, and a few months after that he got Slovenian citizenship, but the whole time he lived in the belief that he'd be going home and that this transitional period would come and go like an annual vacation. Setting off to America, Canada, and Australia, friends passed through Ljubljana, he'd spend an evening with them and they'd all ask *you planning on getting out of here?* and Deda always answered *no, I'll go back.* On parting he'd leave them his address and telephone number, and a letter or phone call would follow, but friends would inevitably disappear, some because Deda didn't reply, others because they had gone forever and didn't need anyone reminding them of what they had lost or left behind. Six years later Ljubljana wasn't on the way to anywhere for anyone: those who had wanted to leave had left, those who had wanted to stay had stayed, and Deda was as distant to them as if he himself had gone to the ends of the earth. But he hadn't gone anywhere or stayed anywhere; he wasn't at home or abroad.

He exited the bus and headed for the duty pharmacy. He was fourth in line; his head spun a little, the fever holding him in a daze, shielding him from thoughts too serious; he smiled at the pharmacist, handing her colorful banknotes and taking the bag with his prescription, *five drops three times daily*, he repeated after her, the girl nodding confirmation, the corners of her mouth rising as if she were having a little laugh on Deda's account, or as if once, in a former life, there had been something between them.

He was standing there on the sidewalk, his eyes peeled for a taxi, when a white Golf pulled up. *Deda, what's going on, what're you doing here? . . . I had to go to the pharmacy, now I'm off home . . . You're the right age for the pharmacy, bro . . . Bite me, dude, it's just a little cold . . . Get in, bit of fresh air will do you good.* Deda didn't say yes or no, in fact he didn't say anything, he just got in the car, not knowing where they were heading. He'd only wanted to sit down, even if it was crammed on the backseat next to Alma and Nuša, this fat Slovenian chick who was trying to tell Esad where to go, where he should turn and stuff, but you could see she suffered from that disease where no matter if you go left or right you've gone wrong, and so they kept ending up on one-way streets, Nuša waving her hand *left, left, I said, that's right, no, that's left, right.* Esad's girlfriend Mirna, who was from Tuzla, clenched the handgrip in furious silence. She couldn't stand Nuša and didn't know why Alma always invited her when they headed out on Sundays, and this time the situation was even worse: They were going to Nuša's cabin, so she'd have to be especially deferential.

I'll catch pneumonia, Deda sneezed after half an hour of driving. *It's about time, bro,* said Esad, tapping happily on the steering wheel. *What an asshole,* Mirna finally spoke up, *only an asshole would get off on saying something like that,* added Nuša in Slovenian. Mirna would get pissed when Nuša spoke in Slovenian, even when it was in jest, because she thought Nuša was rubbing it in that they were in Slovenia. *Well, we are actually in Slovenia,* Esad had just shrugged his shoulders when she'd once tried to explain this, only one of the hundred ways Nuša got on her nerves. Mirna didn't reply, just let her mind wander; since they'd arrived in Ljubljana it really hadn't occurred to her that they were in Slovenia and that in this Slovenia place they were supposed to live among Slovenes, not just any random people, people from Tuzla, for example, who Mirna felt were her own. *If we'd gone to America we'd have already met a hundred Americans, and in two years we've only met Deda, and he's a Bosnian too,* she told Esad. He clammed shut and made like he was lost in thought. Like Deda, he hadn't dared venture farther than Ljubljana.

I'll make you some tea, said Nuša as soon as they arrived. Deda sat down in a dusty green armchair. The log cabin was something out of a second-rate American horror film. They just needed to get cozy, a couple start kissing, the hostess light the fire, and the next minute some jittery pubescent would be there with a chain saw cutting them all to pieces. *Deda, you not feeling well?* Alma blathered, putting her hand to his forehead. She was sweet on Deda, in fact you could say that she was secretly in love with him, but she blew hot and cold. Mirna had tried to explain to her that you can't be like that with men, that you have to know what you want, and Alma would look at her all demure and say *but Mirna, I'm not sure,* and keep flitting about Deda, tugging at his beard, pinching his stomach, but the second he made a move, she vanished in the air. In the end it became clear to all that there would never be anything between the two, but in ten or fifteen years, when someday they met again, Alma was sure to confess, *Deda, I was sweet on you.*

They sat at a hard oak table and drank tea. Mirna was whispering a fight with Esad, Nuša and Alma took turns asking Deda how he was feeling, checking his temperature with their palms, smacking their lips worryingly, and then bursting out laughing. Deda mostly just sighed, fixed them with a stare, setting a stony expression on his face, which amused Nuša and Alma no end. *You two'd die of boredom without a patient*, Deda tried to sound sore but was actually reveling in being the center of attention and the girls laughing at him. He didn't have to think about what he thought about every day, what was on his mind today when he woke up and hadn't given him any peace until the white Golf pulled up. At long last he didn't feel like he was in the wrong place or hanging out in some kind of waiting room before a long trip home. There was nothing much in his hands, his heart, or his head; not even in the log cabin. He didn't feel any real closeness to these people, they certainly weren't on the list of friends in whose hands he'd put his life, but maybe that was the very reason he felt such release from everything he had done over the past six years, every wrong step he'd made from the moment he said goodbye to his mother.

Esad pinched a wad of hashish out with a pair of tweezers, softening it above the flame of his lighter. The three of them almost religiously followed his every move; he took out a bag of tobacco, laid a paper on the table, plumping the tobacco between his thumb and index finger, every now and then licking invisible intoxicating granules from them. Their lungs were soon full of laughter, *I died of a lung infection*, whooped Deda, while Nuša snorted like a steam engine, fat scrubby Nuša. Mirna hugged her, how easy it is when you're laughing, nothing's a turn-off when you're laughing. *Deda, I think I've got something to say to you now*, warbled Alma, *no, no, then I'll have to hunt you down in the forest*, howled Esad. Nuša got up to put on some more water to boil for tea.

And so it went for hours: hashish, tea, hashish, tea, Deda slowly forgetting he was supposed to be sick. At some point Alma got up from the table and went to the toilet. Exhausted from laughing they just watched her go, Esad was about to say something but changed his mind and sighed, which was reason enough for another huzzah. Alma burst back in: *there's something in the toilet! . . . What the fuck? . . . I don't know, there's something in the bowl . . . Someone forget to flush, huh? . . . No, it's not that, it's something else, it's alive, actually I don't know if it's alive, but it definitely was alive.* Esad got up, *stop*, Deda raised his hand, *you just sit down, bro.*

There, lift the seat up, Alma peered from behind the door. In the bowl, down in the little pool of water, there really was something, something dead and furry; a rat, no, not a rat, something else, rats don't look like that, this one's got a pretty head and pointy ears; Deda looked down at the tiny head, prodding it with a pencil, not having the foggiest what was in the toilet bowl and where it had come from. The hashish happy buzz lingered on, fuzzying his thoughts and movements; he just stared at the head, repeating *I don't get it, I don't get it,* the three of them jostling above Deda's head and waiting – maybe the creature would wake up, or Deda was about to reach his verdict. He's the most serious here, he had a beard, and although he'd just turned thirty-two it was almost completely gray, he's going to have to come up with something soon. *Esad, get me something . . . What? . . . I don't know, something to get this thing out with.*

Nuša went into the kitchen and came back with a big spoon, *this okay?* There was a clang of metal and ceramic and then Deda finally got hold of the creature, *it's a squirrel folks.* Alma covered her mouth with her hand, *it's not a squirrel, it can't be a squirrel, where would a squirrel've come from . . . I'm really sorry, but it's a squirrel, I know a squirrel when I see one,* Deda stood there holding the dead animal out on the spoon as if offering it to Alma, Mirna, Nuša, and Esad, but they didn't want it, they just kept moving away, *no, it's not a squirrel . . . listen to me, it is,* as if their lives depended on something else being there on Deda's spoon, something vile and worthless, a big black rat, anything, just not a squirrel.

Deda headed outside with the spoon, it was dark and there was a chill in the air, a wind blowing down from the snowy peaks, they didn't follow him, just stayed there in the doorway, watching his back disappear between the trunks of the pines. He headed on not knowing what he was looking for or how to get rid of the dead animal, if only there were a river nearby, or a ravine, anyplace where you could make a squirrel disappear.

He'd already gone too far, he turned around and couldn't see the light of the cabin, he couldn't see anything, just the full moon shrouding the world in gray. Deda knelt down, placed the spoon on the dead pine needles, and started digging. He dug with his fingers, thousands of needles from this year and all the years gone by, thousands of thousands of dry, damp, and rotten needles, until he touched earth, a soft black earth that got up under his fingernails. He dug down, piling the

234

dirt left and right until the hole was deep enough to fit the spoon and the squirrel. The end of its tail was still poking out a little, so he folded it over with his hand, touching the little creature for the first time, the dead fur comforting, as if it had never been alive. He then gathered a pile of dirt with his hands, first extending them as if before a hug, and then closing them as if in prayer, this ten times over, until all the dirt and needles were again in place.

He headed back to the cabin. The squirrel had drowned in the toilet bowl, but how it got there, how it made it under the seat and what it was after, Deda had no idea. He thought about lying to them, saying it wasn't a squirrel at all, yeah, that's the one, everything would then be okay again. But what was the point in lying; the squirrel wasn't going to disappear if he just said it hadn't been a squirrel, everything wasn't going to be okay if he simply told them it'd been a rat after all. No, he wasn't going to lie about anything. Deda's not a kid, it was a squirrel, and now let's try to forget it.

Away, I'd rather sail away

It was like it was the last day of summer; the sea calm and dark, the seafront almost deserted, barely ten people waiting for the ferry: a grandma with her grandchild, the kiosk lady waiting for today's newspapers from the mainland, three fishermen with their bottles of beer, a handful of nondescript men and women – and Boris. He was leaning on the ticket booth, smoking, gazing out toward the edge of the bay around which the ferry would soon circle. It was fifteen minutes late, enough time to smoke two cigarettes, but no one was worried about the delay. The passengers didn't appear in any hurry, the woman from the kiosk less than desperate to get back to work; the fishermen hadn't even finished their beers. Boris was in a funk about the ferry's arrival, and every delay gave him that much more time to pull himself together, to melt the ice cube in his stomach that had been there since he'd woken up and realized that today he was going to attend to what he had left undone for the past six years, something that might have changed his life had he, like a submissive Polish inmate in a concentration camp, said his farewells in an orderly and timely fashion.

He was thirty-three, and as his editor liked to say, already a few months older than Christ. He'd only come to the island to meet the ferry. He hadn't been to the seaside in years, but something in that telephone conversation had drawn him into a lie: the desire to portray his life as being as normal as possible, which meant telling her that he'd be on Korčula on the thirty-first of August, to which she had replied *hey, that's great, what a coincidence, as fate would have it I'll be showing my husband around the Adriatic then*, and naturally it was an opportunity not to be missed, and why would they; after so many years they were to see each other again, to put to rest what had remained unsaid, what in the staging of a life no one can escape, not even those masterfully adept at hiding, those who always – even when it's completely uncalled for – lie.

Boris had arrived from Sarajevo the night before and had rented a room for a couple of nights, planning to return the following day. He wore sandals on his feet and a straw hat on his head, disguising himself as a man on summer vacation – and oh boy, wasn't he just resting up. He hadn't tanned like people on summer vacation do, but that didn't bother him. She knows, she remembers that he always stays in the shade or under the canopy of a café. His hair isn't salty, he hasn't gone in the water and has no intention of doing so, but this didn't matter either, she wouldn't be probing the saltiness of his skin.

He stubbed out his cigarette and licked his forearm. It seemed like the thing to do. In the midst of a real panic attack it's best to have a completely imaginary one, something to heal you like those trusty childhood lies that return from time to time; they never harbored any ill intent, you never even told them to anyone. When you lie to your-self, it's not actually a lie but a way to repair the irreparable, to create space for a new life, for a joy only otherwise possible by exhausting encounters with reality and a Tarzan-like flight from one dunghill of whatever gets you down to another. So it's easier to lie, and in the end the result is the same, just so long as others never find out about it.

The ferry revealed its dull bow from behind the bay and began slowly gaining in size. Boris lit a new cigarette, hoping to ward off his fears, he ran his hand through his hair, and almost mechanically sucked in his stomach. The ferry needed ten minutes to reach the shore; it would be another two minutes for them to lower the gangplank, meaning he had another twelve minutes. It was like he had that long to live. He thought about the scandal with the American president, about his busted fridge, about the chair in his newsroom office that was too low for him and the computer he'd spilled Coke over so now it didn't work; the only thing he didn't think about was what was about to come.

A few people stood on deck. They started waving. The fishermen with their beers waved back. *Not every boat's the* Titanic, he thought. He would protect himself by playing out of character, by smiling a smile that wasn't his. He'd even bought a cigar, the first he would smoke in his life; he wouldn't say anything that might allow her a way in. He'd sense it if she was on his trail, and that would make him vulnerable.

As soon as the passengers began disembarking he felt incredibly exposed. He should have waited somewhere out of the way. He recognized Maja as soon as she stepped on the footbridge, but from that distance she didn't see him. Twice she accidentally glanced in his direction, her gaze then sliding on. This was good because it gave him more time. A tall, strong-looking man carried the bags; at that moment his height and strength were the only things Boris noticed, nothing else. Maja held a kid by the hand, a little kid probably no taller than the bollard to which the ferry was tied. *Funny she didn't mention the kid*, he thought, coughed, put a smile on and fixed it there, walking the assured walk of a man who in that moment feared shame more than anything else.

Boriiiiiiiiiis! she called to him, nonchalantly passing the kid's hand to Mr. Big.

They kissed in greeting; he felt the right corner of Maja's lips, *a bit too close*, he thought, holding her in his embrace and waiting for hers to recede. He didn't want the hug lasting too long – it wasn't actually a real one – there, in full view of her man. Mr. Big smiled a smile of happiness and sympathy, that's probably the best way to put it. He must have been happy to see his wife happy, while the sympathy might be accounted for by the fact she was visiting her homeland for the first time in six years, or actually her former homeland – because we are what is written in our passports – a country that had seen war come and go, and now she was meeting up with a dear *friend*.

Boris, let me introduce you! Mr. Big had a firm handshake, the kind of firmness you learn at a good preparatory school, where hands never tremble, show neither weakness nor excess familiarity – let alone your feelings, which just evaporate, as much a waste of time as this same lack of feeling. The kid was named after some pirate or avant-garde artist, a name definitely not pronounced the way it was written. *We'll skip the cynicism today*, he thought, although in other circumstances and with other people he'd have asked them to spell it for him.

So, how are you? her whole face beaming a smile, *I'm well*, he had relaxed a little, and out of the corner of his eye caught Mr. Big nodding politely, though he didn't understand a thing. Anyone watching the scene from the shadows would have thought Mr. Big was holding the kid like he was the nanny and not the father. The kid himself was silent and embarrassed.

Boris wasn't sure about where to go. He didn't even know how long the visit was going to last. The next ferry for Ploče was at five, when they were heading off for Dubrovnik; God, Dubrovnik – everyone who comes from abroad goes to Dubrovnik – but what to do until five, where to take them, what on earth she expected, he had no idea.

Are you hungry? he asked, though it wasn't yet noon. She turned to Mr. Big, talking fast, Boris trying not to hear or understand anything, particularly whatever it was Mr. Big had to say, but he couldn't avoid hearing a single word repeated three times over: *dear, dear, my dear.* Like in those films where it's repeated over and over by couples that start fighting the second they're left on their own. *Nothing's like it is in a film*, he thought and now nodded his head. They'd grab something to eat after all. Mr. Big has to try Adriatic fish. You don't get that stuff in the north. They only eat those gigantic Japanese monsters, tuna and herring, their whole lives they never see anything fish-shaped on their plates.

The restaurant was called The Long Line. There were three chairs on each side of the table. Boris sat down, Maja, the kid, and Mr. Big across from him. It was just like at the theater, only you didn't know which side the audience was on. Boris gave his all in making conversation, and she, not noticing anything or noticing everything – that's not for the telling here – babbled on and on, one minute about what they did yesterday, the next remembering her time with Boris, everything always shot through with laughter and happiness. There was no sadness for her, and you could see she was happy about their reunion. Mr. Big spoke softly to the kid, raising his head and silently smiling every now and then, not a trace of unease. He was one of those people you could spend twenty years with, head off to war with, travel and live with, without ever catching him off-balance, or wanting to tell you where it hurt. When this sort of guy asks you how you are, you've got to tell him you're great because if you say anything else, you start bullshitting or admitting you're not well or something, he'll think you a lower being or just plain rude, horrified at the thought he might have to help you out.

Maja hadn't aged. *You'd never guess you've had a kid!* he said and already knew he should have said something else. For a flicker of a second she seemed sad and afraid. She knew him well enough to know he never said things like that, and that if he did, there was a kind of darkness there, a darkness from which she'd escaped in the nick of time, so maybe the fear and sorrow never actually reached her, maybe her nerves didn't transmit the message to her brain, it had all just hung there on her face. *No, really, you look great*, he healed the damage, and she kicked off about childbirth there in the north, about their exercises and routines (*like we don't have that stuff*), the psychologists to relieve every fear, their pain-free delivery methods (*God, like she lived here in the last century*) that sent a woman home brand new. *It was a completely new and miraculous experience for me . . . We're not thinking about repeating it for the time being . . . But who knows what time might bring . . .* Boris took a cigar out and lit up. He wanted to delete everything he'd heard. The content didn't matter, that was all extraneous and easily forgettable. It was the syntax that got him, it wasn't her own; it wasn't even the syntax of their mother tongue. Hers were translated English sentences, where everything that should have been in the middle had unerringly been pushed to the end. He didn't actually know whom he was talking to: Maja, with whom he had spent three years, whose murmurs, intonation, faulty accents, and syntax he knew and loved, or a person resembling her, actually, a replica who had stolen Maja's life experience and appearance, translating her words from a foreign tongue, a language in which everything important came at the end, after every sentence and every story was over.

The waiter brought the fish, a giant oval silver platter laden with whole fried fish. *Whooaaaaaa!!!* Mr. Big rumbled like a hurricane. The kid looked on in fear at food he had never seen in his life, probably thinking that someone had hurt the fish terribly and that it was wrong they now eat them. Maja clasped her hands together and mouthed the kind of pathetic sentence typical of people on their first brief visit home in years, seeing in dead fried fish their homeland incarnate. This sort of shit made Boris sick and for the first time he felt like a man who hadn't gotten over a woman. He didn't care about Mr. Big or the kid, but that messed-up syntax was like watching his girl making love to another man and her going to town on it.

He just wanted Maja to shut up, to speak in their language, to eat the fish, take the bones out, feed the kid, smile at Mr. Big, smile at him, smile at whoever she wanted, anything but those insufferable sentences. His love, somehow, had finished up as language instruction.

What kind of fish is it? she asked. It was *orada*, but how do you say *orada* in English, because she wants to translate it for Mr. Big. But does she really think *orada* exists in English? Maybe Latin would help, but who knows how you say *orada* in Latin, we're not ichthyologists, no one here's an ichthyologist, just let it be *orada*, a nameless fish hidden in a lost language. It's not that important, you don't have to know everything, some things can be forgotten, and language, well, today it's a faithful reflection of experience, what doesn't exist in life doesn't exist in experience, you don't get *orada* in the north, so it doesn't have to exist in words.

Boris ordered a bottle of wine, they don't want any, but he does. He's dying for a drink. He empties a glass, stretching his bottom lip over his top one, smiling at Mr. Big who was frowning for the first time, pricked by a fish bone, ha, what do you expect from a savage country and language. Maja was feeding the kid, murmuring strange words, all of them finishing with an *o*. She didn't pay the men any mind. She was a mother now, fully concentrated on a role that had absolutely no connection with Boris's life. The scene was one free of pain, so foreign that had it occurred at some other time, he could have even tried to enjoy it.

He made no attempt at conversation with Mr. Big, and he, who knows why, didn't ask any questions. *God knows who she told him I was,* thought Boris, *if I'm just a good friend it's weird he's not asking me anything, and if I'm what I am or once was, what's with the dumb grinning innocent act?* Actually, Boris couldn't care less. Nothing life-changing was going to happen, and any awkwardness had been avoided. He watched Mr. Big, the pinkish hairy fingers struggling with the fish skeleton, the hair on his fingers blond at the base and brown at the tips, God, how did she get used to that, to skin devoid of pigment, which no matter the weather could only go red, a red-white color combo its only possibility, like the Red Star Belgrade flag, like scampi, like beetroot. Had she gotten used to this stuff before she started messing up her syntax, or was it the other way around, so she didn't need to get used to it, love had just blossomed overnight, one love for each life, one after every war, one in every peace, because then you could say you had been completely faithful, like you had lived in some old catechism, like in a fairy tale, until death, language, or fate did you part. The hairy fingers were fish-clumsy, mashing its skeleton, pulverizing it until all that remained were tiny piles of dead bones you would never guess had once been a fish. It could have been something else, tiny icicles, the twigs of an arctic tree, something Boris didn't recognize was born beneath those fingers. The imagined tendernesses with the body he once knew now belonged to those fingers, and even they seemed like Chinese symbols, outside any experience. If he'd seen those fingers on video, touching Maja's body, he wouldn't have recognized the scene, wouldn't have known what he was watching, what those fingers did with the fish so impossibly foreign.

Boris and Maja lost touch when the war started. He had stayed in Sarajevo, and she'd gone north. The last time they saw each other, they'd been a couple, their love beyond question. However pathetic it might sound, they parted because the war was men's business and women were better off out of it. Boris had Maja's phone number but never dialed it. Maja sent Boris a letter through the Red Cross asking him why he hadn't been in touch. Boris never sent a reply. There was no real explaining his silence, maybe it was because he feared for his life, maybe he didn't think he'd survive the war, and maybe he was jealous of her life or it was because Mr. Big had begun appearing to him even before he appeared for real in her life. A few more months passed and Maja moved farther north, Boris no longer knew her address or telephone number. Three years later he bumped into a friend of hers who wrote Maja's number on the back of a business card, without him having asked or her having said anything. One night he lay in bed, and when sleep wouldn't come he dialed the number. The voice at the other end burst with joy, breathlessly telling him she was married and expecting. Boris called again a month after the birth. And then again three months after that, until the seventh time they spoke she told him she would soon be visiting the Adriatic.

He got up from the table, gave Maja and Mr. Big the need-to-pee grin, and headed for the bathroom. The urinal was filthy, the tiles chipped, his stream of urine washing away the blue traces of a long-crusted detergent, the whole thing reeking like an abandoned barrack latrine where a whole company had pissed before heading off to the front. He tried to remember whether Mr. Big had gone to the bathroom and seen this, our local disgrace, but maybe it didn't bother him. The north is too far away for our tourist specialities to offend anyone way up there. In any case, for a second it comforted him to think he was the host and Mr. Big the tourist.

He stopped by the bar, *the bill thanks*, the waiter smiled, *I'll be over in a second*, expecting Boris to return to the table, *no, I'd like to settle up here*, the waiter made like he understood and smiled consolingly in total accord with the cardinal rule of his profession: accept the weirdest things as normal lest they disturb the general ambience.

He sat back down, rubbing his hands and looking at his watch. It was already past four. *This has been a long lunch!* Maja said. The kid was sleeping in his father's lap. There was no more disturbing the fish bones' peace. *I've loved it, I've loved it*, she repeated, *me too, me too*, he worried that he might sound cynical so said it twice, making it sound funny. Mr. Big already had that ready-to-go look on his face, the one he had arrived with.

Now they only needed to perform the farewell act, which was certainly less an emotional problem than one of convention. Saying your goodbyes to a person you haven't seen for six years and maybe won't ever see again isn't easy. Maja didn't have any experience with this sort of thing, such farewells obviously at odds with the philosophy of her new life. There were no dramatic farewells in the north nor could there be, there people's goodbyes are temporary, or death or hate parts them. *Of course we'll catch up again in the next few days*, she said, *it's not far for you to pop over to Dubrovnik, and we can always come back*. Boris opened his arms like this so completely went without saying that nothing more needed to be said. So they didn't say anything. Mr. Big held the kid to his chest.

They stood on the ferry gateway. *We're in Hotel Argentina*, she said, not quite yet free of the unease of their parting. *Great, I've got the number!* The lie was a transparent one, but Boris wasn't aware of it and Maja didn't notice. Why would he have the number for Hotel Argentina, doesn't matter, the ferry drew nearer. An elderly ensemble was playing on deck, dressed for a ball from the end of the last century, the singer on the podium not much younger than this century, his black tails looking from a distance like moths had celebrated the sinking of the *Titanic* on them. The singer had the gestures of old photographs, as if posing for someone or something at his death, the merry apocalypse that might just emerge as the bridge lowered toward the shore. In a soft voice, as gentle as if wiping a dust cloth over a piano, he sang *away, I'd rather sail away, like a swan that's here and gone, a man gets tied up to the ground, he gives the world its saddest sound, its saddest sound.*

Mr. Big jumped in excitedly: *whoa, El condor passa.* Maja and Boris laughed simultaneously, their pupils catching a chance square glance. Their pupils stilled, they shared a moment of intimacy free of any other thoughts or feelings, one they would never share again. They kissed and hugged, no mention of seeing each other again, in a few days, in Dubrovnik, or on Hvar. Maja and entourage crossed the footbridge, the bridge was drawn up, the ferry set off, Maja waved from the deck, the kid waved, Mr. Big waved, his waves like signals sent to illegal aviators high in the sky. Boris held his arm in the air, moving it to the rhythm of the farewell song, left and right, *away, I'd rather sail away, like a swan that's here and gone.* The ferry became smaller, Maja and her waving hand too, until she was as tiny as the brown tips of pine needles. Just before the boat disappeared behind the bay, Boris saw she had lowered her arm and turned around, or maybe that's just what he thought he saw. He punched his hand in the air, extending his arm as far as he could. He liked that. It looked ridiculous and cooled his sweating skin.

Ho freddo, ho molto freddo

The commotion in the train on the Trieste–Mestre line lasted half an hour. First the conductor came down the corridor, then immediately scuttled back, then a pair of carabinieri turned up, and then the conductor flew past again, returning from the dining car with a girl holding a glass of water. In Monfalcone a plump bald man with a doctor's bag got on and was followed down the corridor by the taller of the two carabinieri, and then all was quiet. When the train pulled into Mestre an ambulance was waiting on the platform. Two paramedics entered the nonsmoking car in second class and remained there until the train was empty. Then they went back to fetch a stretcher. On the stretcher lay a black plastic bag. They exited the train ten minutes later. The bag on the stretcher was no longer empty.

At that moment a full three hours had passed since Barbara Veronesse, a retired piano teacher from the music school in Sarajevo; her seven-year-old granddaughter, Azra; and Gianni, Aldo, and Marco, senior-high students from Trieste heading to Venice for a Black Uhuru concert, had all entered the compartment. Nana Barbara sat next to the window, across from her sat Azra, *look here*, Nana said, *this is where my grandma and grandpa were born*, and Azra looked and saw nothing but grass and stone houses, *look here*, Nana pointed, *your grandpa fought here*, and Azra looked and saw nothing but grass and the odd pine tree. She watched Gianni, Aldo, and Marco out of the corner of her eye, shouting, laughing, and clapping in a completely incomprehensible language. Azra knew the whole world didn't speak the same language, didn't even speak English, but she had never imagined that laughter and clapping in a foreign language might sound so strange.

Nana sighed and closed her eyes. Azra watched a lock of hair fall on her forehead, the wheels of the train banging away, *taram-taramtaram*, the lock falling lower and lower, now just above the eyebrow, with the next *taram-taramtaram* it'll be almost in her eye, no it won't, it'll take one more *taram-taramtaram*, there we go, it's fallen. Nana's asleep and doesn't notice, the foreign boys holler away, what's wrong with them, can't they see Nana's asleep? Azra closed her eyes, if they see she's sleeping too maybe they'll quiet down.

Barbara Veronesse had lived with her granddaughter in Poreč for two years. They had made it out of Sarajevo in the fall of 1992, a month after Azra's father was killed. Her mother, Eva Veronesse-Teskeredžić, had been dead for exactly how long Azra had been alive. She died two days after giving birth, eaten up by a tumor that had grown inside her for nine months, maybe a little longer; the doctors had told her she must abort to save her own life, a childless one for sure but a life all the same; she didn't want to, the doctor, Srećko, asked her whether she believed in God, and not waiting for her answer said *even Christ would forgive you, don't kill yourself, please*, to which Eva looked at him sadly and said *but doctor, I don't believe in him and I know there is no God.* Azra's mother only saw her once in her life. She was given her first dose of morphine shortly after, and the next day she was already dead.

Nana Barbara had wanted to show Azra Venice, believing the child would remember her by the city for the rest of her life. In seven days she was to see Azra off on an airplane that would take her to Boston, where her uncle Mehmed, a computer scientist, lived, with whom Azra would live too, with him and his wife, Nevzeta, in a big house with a yard full of cats and dogs. The truth was that Nana had only heard about the one dog, but she had told Azra there were at least ten to make the leaving easier on the child, and so she wouldn't cry because Barbara Veronesse couldn't stand tears. Tears were all that remained of her own daughter and she wanted to avoid them, even if she had to make up all the cats and dogs in the world. With her granddaughter leaving, she would return to Sarajevo, and then what would be, would be; if we have to die, let us die where we belong, where we've lived our whole lives.

Aldo tapped the old woman on the shoulder, who opened her eyes to see Azra bent over the seat throwing up. *My child*, she searched her handbag for a tissue, the Italians had squashed into their corner, palely looking on, Azra was crying, the conductor came in and asked Grandma something, she replied, and Azra choked *Grandma, don't leave me*, she squeezed her hand, *I won't, sweetheart, I'd never leave you, just relax*, Azra threw up again, *it's nothing sweetheart, you just had a bad dream*, the girl with the water came, trying to catch Azra's eye and make her smile, yet the child didn't see her, *but Grandma, I don't want cats and dogs*, Barbara Veronesse struggled to breathe, the child threw up again, who knows where she's getting it all from, the doctor came in mumbling something in a foreign language and pinched Azra's cheek, *Grandma, don't let me go*, Barbara Veronesse started to get dizzy, *God, just not now, don't kill me now*, she closed her eyes, she just had to close her eyes a little, Azra cried, the doctor murmured, someone held Barbara's hand, someone held both of Azra's hands, Azra screamed and lost her voice, *let's go home, please Grandma, let's go home to Bistrik*, Barbara Veronesse remembered her piano, the brothers would open the monastery windows when she played, when Brother Ivan died she had played *Eine kleine Nachtmusik* the whole night through. *Don't cease God's work*, a young seminarian had told her, and she had played until five in the morning when Brother Ivan's soul expired; she felt someone trying to take her pulse, she couldn't hear Azra anymore, the child must have stopped crying, must have calmed down, a silence grew from all sides, as big as Trebević and as wide as Sarajevo, she tried to open her eyes but couldn't, Barbara Veronesse's eyelids were as heavy as the big red curtains at the National Theater and didn't want to rise. *Mi aiuti, per favore*, his voice was shaking, she felt someone grab her feet, someone grab her shoulders, she was lying down, *signora, signora*, somebody had undone the buttons on her blouse, someone was slapping her face, someone's hands were pressing violently on Barbara's chest, they must have taken the child out of the compartment, *signora, signora*, there was a humming in her ears, she remembered the Bistrik stream and how it flowed when she was a little girl, she could tell apart every stone at its bottom, the hands pressed her chest in the same rhythm as the Bistrik's flow, and with each press the stones would jump from the bottom, just look how light they are, like they aren't stones at all but full of air, before sinking again, the water so deep you could drown in there in the fall, who had drowned? Barbara Veronesse was afraid, she was so terribly afraid that she opened her eyes and saw a big sweaty forehead with glasses. Azra wasn't beside the window anymore and the water was gone. That calmed her, it calmed her so much she no longer even needed to sigh. *Signora, signora, come sta, come va, signora,* the bald face shouted. Barbara opened her mouth, smiled, and said *ho freddo, ho molto freddo* and closed her eyes. The doctor took Marco's coat and covered her with it. For some time he held the wrist of Barbara Veronesse, the retired piano teacher from Sarajevo, and then he slowly laid her hand on her chest and with his fingertips, as if he was scared of waking her, placed the coat over her face. His eyes were full of tears. At that moment all the doctors in the world detested him, him, the doctor who cried.

In the next compartment Aldo and Marco tried to laugh, Gianni performed a pantomime for Azra. He played a man building a house, but the bricks kept falling down, then a man trying to change a light-bulb, then a man doing something else, he tried everything, but Azra just watched him, the nausea had passed and she didn't want to cry, she was in wonder at this mute world, seemingly at peace with it. In this mute world there was no Nana and no Bistrik, but neither were there people who lived their whole lives in foreign languages.

Like a little girl and an old dog

The sky above Surčin is low and heavy. Drunken angels have installed themselves on the clouds somewhere high above and are now celebrating, oblivious that they're sinking lower and lower, that they're about to hit the ground, among the plowed fields, where the Vojvodina plain begins and forgotten pumpkins freeze. The plane has just broken through the clouds, and here it is, growing, bigger and more real than when the story began. In a few seconds it'll touch down, the landing gear has long been extended, and the captain just needs to say those few words of signing off, of welcome and the weather, the hoping we'll see you again.

Marina is sitting in a fourteenth-row window seat looking out. Her gaze is empty; she can't see what she was wanting to see, nor can she even remember what it was she'd wanted. Marina is on her way home for the first time in three years. Actually it's not home, it's just where her parents live and where her things are, things she doesn't need anymore or perhaps never needed, things not for junking because wherever they are means you're home. She's never lived in Belgrade apart from the several months between their leaving Sarajevo and her leaving for Canada. But still she tries to recognize the ground beneath her, the runway expanding like it might swallow the plane, the screech of the wheels as they touch ground; she searches for the code to a former world, to which, as the story goes, she belongs.

It's cold outside, she inhales, catching on the air the faint scent of petrol and a hint of frozen winter grass, but this is all. Nothing she knows, nothing that after so much time would make you say *hello again, I'm back, take me in again for a little while.*

They don't know her time of arrival. She couldn't bring herself to tell them; who could have handled a meeting in the airport terminal, voices echoing to eternity, thousands of eyes rubbernecking at scenes that are none of their business, a situation where you have to stand, hug, wave your arms, wipe away tears, swallow pounding hearts, no sitting or lying down, no way, no cushioning your head, because it's an airport, people spit on the floor, you can't sit or lie down, crying's no good in a place like this, what would everyone think, each with his own opinion and explanation of the spectacle. When in the hour of greatest weakness and vulnerability, in the midst of sorrowful joy, people find themselves under a stranger's gaze, in a stranger's imagination, they risk spilling like water, their fates draining down into whatever strangers have dreamed up for them.

On the bus she closed her eyes, wanting to sleep the exact duration of the journey. She opened her eyes every few minutes, in fear of a stranger's touch or that someone might think her unwell and want to help her the way people do here when you're unwell – with a series of kindnesses and offers of assistance that make you feel even more unwell. Every time she opened her eyes she'd see something different. Apartment towers at the city's edge, women at an improvised market, one of them holding a box of matches and smiling, yellowed buildings and a poplar, young guys smoking in front of a movie theater, a house with a sign saying "Kolobara." It wasn't necessarily a single city. It could have been ten different cities, one for each opening of her eyes. Each was equally unfamiliar and unknown and only a queasy childhood premonition told you that in some way, distant but real, you belong to this scene; this same premonition reminded Marina of her anxiety when she used to go into a supermarket where a bitchy check-out woman, without asking, would give her a piece of bubble gum in place of her small change, at least until Marina was old enough to fire back *lady, what do you think, is this appropriate behavior*, but the premonition might have easily reminded her of something else, not that it mattered; Marina just didn't want anyone touching her or talking to her. Ideally your entrance into such worlds would be invisible, and you would stay that way, not uttering a word until you had established possible connections to your past. Spoken in such places, words disappear into dark spaces where you've never been in your life, or where you were once but have since departed, and then those words return when you want them least, to a world where you really are, and wound you.

She got off the bus and still hadn't said a word, but she would have to speak to the taxi driver. He's a little guy, stumpy and greasy-haired. Marina said *Senjak* and showed him a piece of paper with the name of the street written on it. She coughed, surprised by the tone of her own voice. The taxi driver was silent, a city full of people passed by, strangely making their way through the dust clouds, as if they were the clouds upon which those drunken angels sat perched over Surčin. In the coming days Marina will watch the dust, turbid and impenetrable, and when they speak on the phone, she'll tell Him that covered in dust Belgrade looked like Macondo in the final chapter.

Before the taxi gets to Senjak, it's probably a good time to explain who He is. She hasn't seen Him since leaving Sarajevo, and at the time, He was her boyfriend. Today she doesn't know what He is to her, but they are in touch from time to time, presumably because they never said their goodbyes and so have endured like baffling chronic illnesses endure, the ones that don't kill you or cause you pain but hang around until you're dead all the same. They could meet, but probably won't – although they want to – they'll probably never see each other again. If they passed each other in the street they wouldn't recognize each other. Marina doesn't know why things are the way they are, perhaps because sometimes people can become destroyed cities to each other.

Her father's name was written on the door. She raised her finger to the bell and then paused. Between her finger and the round red button was a space barely wide enough for a piece of paper, but she didn't press down. *How does this go,* she used to say aloud when she had an unsolvable math exercise, *easy as pie,* said a voice she was no longer sure was her father's. She heard footsteps inside, and what she thought was the clattering of plates, she could have been standing there for hours, her index finger pointing at something, if only that would have been the end of the matter, if only something painful or deathly hadn't clattered from the other side of the door, beckoning her back into a life she had sloughed off.

The bell didn't sound like a bell. It squealed like a little computer with an empty battery, the doors burst open; her mother, wrinkles, wrinkles, wrinkles, a face that had fallen like a sail at half-mast, the voice still the same, her words ones that once annoyed Marina, arms enfolding, arms holding tight, Marina says *wait* and smiles, her smile broad and painful, her father white and gray, her father huge like the tallest tower of cards, his face firm like the face of a father should be, always firm, that's how he thought he should be. Just don't talk about yourself, just ask stuff, smother and drown them in questions, admit nothing because anything you say will hurt them. They'll talk, they talk in stops and starts, they don't know how to talk to a daughter after three years, you don't learn that sort of thing anywhere, who would've thought they'd need to know something like that, if they'd known they would have learned, there must be a way to do it, there must be a manual somewhere, people know about this stuff, they have to, *why are you so skinny*, her mother'll ask her, there she goes, *leave her alone*, her father says, he's proud of his young daughter as if she were a son, because he doesn't have a son, hence the *leave her alone*.

Where's Astor? she asked, heading to the living room. A black cocker spaniel lay in an armchair, already a fourteen-year-old, watching this strange woman on her approach with her grimace ever shriller, who is she and what does she want, strangers never grimace at him like this, he took a long look at Marina, she looked at him and knew he didn't recognize her. At that moment she wasn't hurt Astor didn't recognize her, nor was she when she was telling Him about it later, but she couldn't be sure it wouldn't one day hurt, so she tried not to give it much thought, just said her dog hadn't recognized her, not a hint of sadness in her voice, but it brought a sadness out in Him.

She had been fourteen when Astor came into her life. Today she is twice as old, making her as old as a little girl plus an old dog. That's about how she had felt in Belgrade at her parents' side, in a different life, one neither frenetic nor euphoric, but gentle and slow, so you felt the pain all the more acutely the second it drew near. Astor had been the end result of the deepest grief, perhaps still the deepest she keeps. The grief's name was Hefest, a brown cocker spaniel that had been hit by a car in Grbavica and had spent the night dying in her room, in her lap. It was then she made a wish that she would never again get close to death, that she might run from everything precious and dear before it disappeared. Her father buried Hefest in the yard of the Viktor Bubanj barracks, and it was then for the first and only time in her life she saw her father cry.

I'm going to take him for a walk today, she said, grabbing Astor's collar and leash, noticing they were new, and leading him out in front of their building. It was something she'd done a thousand times in her life, and now she had to do it again, to feel like it was no big deal and that she could live without it, that it was something she didn't need to remember, something she had to forget, and the only way she could do so was to again, after so much time, take a dog that no longer recognizes her, because it's already much older than her life, for a walk in the park, which isn't actually the same park, but that doesn't matter. The park too was so full of dust you had to sneeze it out, to give yourself a good shake before boarding the plane, shake loose all excess; dust, walking the dog, whatever. *Astor*, she shouted, the dog didn't turn around, *Astor*, he waddled on like an old man, one leg in front of the other, but still fast enough that she had to break into a jog to catch him. *Astor*, Marina screamed, fuming mid-park that not only did the dog not recognize her, he held her in contempt. It was a sudden strange reflex from a former time, Astor was again her business, again her dog, and he shouldn't behave like this because what good is a dog like this, what's the point taking such a dog for a walk if this is how it's all going to end. In that instant Astor shot a random glance back, saw Marina's scowl and furious waving, turned around, and again, slowly, step by step, like a good little doggie, returned to her knee.

Uff, I forgot to tell you he's stone-deaf, it's been more than a year now, said her mother, busy fixing a lunch that would today nourish Marina's skinny limbs, and together with the next five to come would be a message to the world where her daughter was returning. Astor was again in his armchair, his head resting on his paws, looking at Marina with that senile sadness, one full of miscomprehension of those who would so constantly and so animatedly explain something. She could still feel traces of rage; in fact it seemed that this time her anger was moving slower than its source. She needed to change something urgently but didn't know what. It would be best to go now, to get on a plane today and disappear. But of course she won't. It's only right to stay another five days, and then take off among the angels and onward to a world where she wasn't beholden to anything, anything good or anything evil, where not a single one of her deaths existed.

Marina lived in Vancouver. She had gotten her Canadian passport a month ago and could now travel wherever she wanted. The process of becoming a Canadian citizen had lasted three years. As the Canadian authorities see it, that's how long you need to forget everything you might call home and accept that home no longer exists or at least that home isn't where you were born.

She worked in a shoe shop and once a month had an appointment with the caseworker responsible for her resettlement and integration, a Vietnamese woman who repeated over and over how she knew life under communism was tough, offering only a handful of rice a day. Marina would nod her head, smile in confirmation, *yes, a handful of rice and nothing more besides.* The Vietnamese woman was quickly convinced that Marina's integration and socialization would be perfect, and that soon she wouldn't even remember the many a horror of a system that forced everyone to wear the same uniforms.

She lived alone, she tried falling in love three times, every time she said *I love you, I love you, I love you,* it was like she was saying *oh, that's so great* at a dozy rest-home tea party. Not obliging her to anything, that's about what it sounded like. Then she would take off with barely an explanation, leaving behind confused young men lifting pairs of foggy glasses with their index fingers as if it were a rainy day.

In the free world you can live completely alone and never feel like something's missing. And so Marina ended up alone in Vancouver, surrounded by a mountain of shoes, like a Cinderella who after midnight had realized that not even a prince was much of a win in life, at least not in this country.

A few nights before the trip to Belgrade she'd had a dream in which someone was missing; one of the three, Astor, her mother, or her father, was absent, but in her dream she couldn't work out who. One moment Astor and her father were there, the next her mother and

Astor, the next her father and mother, the next Astor, her father and mother, but as a pair, not as a threesome. She desperately tried to account for all household members, but there was always someone missing. She phoned her sister in Los Angeles and tried to tell her about the dream; she didn't understand it, she said *my kid has a cold and I gotta go to work.* Marina put the receiver down guiltily and looked at the clock, in Zagreb it's four in the morning, she wanted to call Him, but how do you call someone in Zagreb at that hour to tell them about a dream from Vancouver.

Since arriving she'd heard her parents' breathing, seen the age spots on her father's hands and his choking at lunch. Her mother's face had an unhealthy complexion, or that's just how it seemed to her; *do you have any prescriptions,* she asked, *sweetheart, what's with that, we're not sick,* her father replied, surprised. Astor was still lying there, his head again resting on his paws, looking sadly ahead, his eyes only flickering when someone made a sudden movement.

That morning they had breakfast together. Her father brought three soft-boiled eggs in porcelain eggcups. It was snowing outside. They sat at the table, covered with a cheery and colorful tablecloth decorated with motifs of harvest scenes. They lifted their spoons almost simultaneously, tapping the tips of their eggs. Three taps was enough to break the shell. Nine taps in a gentle morning snow that would blanket all the dust. They remained there in silence like people who from here on in would always, every morning, sit in silence together around the same table. All three were relieved to have quit their thinking, each for his own reason. Saying their goodbyes at the airport in Surčin, they will remember this breakfast. Maybe they should have talked after all. When the plane finally takes off, her father will hug her mother, wiping her tears away with his left arm, waving to Marina, who won't see a thing, with his right. He'll be waving to the plane that is Marina. In that instant Marina will think how Astor was missing from the breakfast scene, a sign and an explanation of the dream. She knew she'd never see him again.

That's how it will be when she goes. Now she's still here, looking at the veins popping out of her father's neck as he tries to slurp up the contents of the egg. Only living creatures, precious creatures, could endure such torture while doing the ostensibly simplest things. He could smash the egg, be done with it, and eat in peace, a spoonful at a time, all the white and yellow. Later he would have forgotten all about it, but this way he'll definitely remember, he definitely won't forget slurping at the egg and the egg not wanting to come out. It could have all been so much simpler, done with so much less humor for those looking on. Marina wanted to laugh but didn't want to break the silence of the morning. Both sky and clouds are gone now. Outside everything is snow-white like under the wing of a drunken angel.

Bethlehem isn't far

Nana Erika is sleeping poorly. It's almost Christmas, their first since coming to Zagreb, but she can't go out to the market to buy butter for the cake, codfish, baking chocolate, a three-month-old suckling, dates, almonds, walnuts, tinsel, rose oil, that transparent plastic wrapping, and all the things she used to buy that meant winter was upon us, the snow quieting every voice, and a celebration was in order because we were still alive, we and all our loved ones, in the house in Bistrik, in Sarajevo, and all over the world wherever Potkubovšeks and their children might be. Nana can't remember exactly when that time ended; the festivities and preparations, the fingers freezing under the weight of shopping bags, but it seemed to her long past, maybe a few lifetimes ago, because in this life, one she still remembers well, the war continued apace, and there was no market, no Christmas, no festivities, nor would there have been any today had they not moved to Zagreb, to this apartment from which Nana has never ventured out because her legs can no longer carry her, even the journey to the bathroom she can't make alone.

It's a big world out there and there are many Christians in it, too many for one to ever meet them all. Nana Erika had always known this, but how could a regular three-room apartment be so big that she doesn't even know all the Christians within its walls? A strange girl brings her coffee and asks *do you need anything, Nana?* Then a kid, probably a high-school junior, pinches her cheek, puts his cold nose to her forehead, and says *I'm frozen, Nana, it's a thousand degrees below zero outside.* Nana Erika just smiles, giving them the ready answer she gives everyone: *yes, yes, my child, it's all misery and woe.* And then the girl, playing angry, says *I didn't ask you for the state of the nation, but if you needed anything.*

Uncivilized are these young folk: You don't who they are, let alone what they are, yet they pinch and tease you, talk to you when the mood strikes them, not even introducing themselves. It wasn't like this in Nana Erika's day. You knew the rules and your place. The first rule was that strangers – young, old, doesn't matter – weren't welcome in her house, and if you came knocking, you had to introduce yourself, announce your purpose, say whether you were a guest, the postman, or after a particular number or street. And now look; her Zagreb apartment is full of them. Maybe that's the custom, the done thing here, she won't protest if it is, but then they should tell her so, not leave her to linger alone among so many strangers.

Only Lujo's her own. Sometimes late at night he comes to her, takes her hand and caresses it, like back when they locked eyes as kids at the source of the Bosna's waters, and at such times Nana Erika discreetly, so no one hears, asks *Lujo, for the life of me, who are all these people, all these young folk?* Instead of telling her the truth, Lujo's eyes well with tears and he grips her hand and starts fumbling. Nana Erika knows Lujo's fumbling, they've been sixty years together, and she doesn't miss a beat, but she doesn't interrupt. She lets him go, every sentence leading him ever further into a lie: *Rika dear, they're our children and grandchildren, your Tvrtko and Katarina, and Klara and Josip. Don't you remember: a big snow had fallen when Klara was born, and you and I had been in Teslić and were on our way home. The train was stuck the whole night and the telegram just said "Katarina's given birth," so we didn't even know if it was a boy or girl. Do you remember us waiting the whole night through and the conductor bringing us tea and saying, "Fear not, madam, every train arrives sometime, and so shall this one too."*

Her Lujo is dear to her, but even so she can no longer forgive his not telling her the truth (what kind of truth might she dare not be told?), and as he moves to kiss her good night, she turns her cheek to him, like she has never done before, and he knows something's not right with his Rika, he knows Rika doesn't like it when they fumble their lies, least

269

of all when they're Lujo's lies. What children, what grandchildren, who knows who they belong to and what they're doing in her apartment, if this is indeed her apartment, and if you are allowed to have two apartments in your old age: one torched in the war, and a second here in Zagreb, a city she's never even seen, yet where she now has an apartment. She would need to plumb the depths of her brain, not to mention her morality, to figure out whether this might be possible or allowed, or whether it's something else. Maybe this isn't her apartment, maybe she and Lujo are just staying with these young folk and their parents until the war is over, until they go home, draw down a loan, and roll up their sleeves to rebuild what is given to be rebuilt, starting life over from the beginning. But then why didn't he just tell her this, that they were among strangers, she could deal with that, she's dealt with worse things in life, but she can't stand a lie.

All shall be revealed on Christmas Day, and that's the day after tomorrow. Everyone will gather around the tree, it's already decorated, when Nana Erika will ask them who they are and whose are they, and if she's in their apartment or they're in hers. They won't be able to lie, there'll be too many of them, and people don't know how to all suddenly lie the same lie, and how would they dare lie beside a tree so decorated, on this a holy day when every dishonesty and hypocrisy, every dirty look and vile thought count a hundred times more and are entered somewhere in heaven's ledger.

Nana Erika is sitting in the armchair in front of the television, her legs covered with a big Russian shawl. The shawl is black, scattered with whopping red roses, as whopping as her Lujo's lies. She runs her hand slowly over the roses, caressing them, imagining they are the night sky above Treskavica light-years ago, the flowers in place of stars, the sky reflected in two mountain lakes as if in two eyes in which everything might drown. Nana Erika hasn't forgotten anything; she remembers the roses instead of stars and the lakes on Treskavica, and if she thought of Lujo's words now, she'd burst into tears. You've forgotten this, you've forgotten that – she hasn't forgotten anything under the sun, nothing worth remembering, not even those things it would have been better had never happened.

A boy stands in the doorway looking over at Nana Erika. She doesn't let herself be thrown, though she knows the look he's giving her, she just strokes her roses. *Nana, let's go have dinner, everyone's at the table.* Nana Erika lifts her head; her glasses on the tip of her nose, a whippet of anger would be enough for them to fall into her lap. But Nana Erika doesn't get riled, she lets the boy take her hand and help her from the armchair; her legs feel the weight of her body, every bone bending, every muscle trembling, every vein trying to hold it all together. She had never been conscious of her body, hadn't been aware of it carrying or moving her, but now she knows it well; Nana Erika and her body have finally become one, and she's happy, because life's not easy with your soul on one side and your flesh and bones on the other, always out of kilter. The boy led her step by step to the dining room; her shawl had slid to the floor, left lying in front of the armchair; how careless and sloppy, he's not going to pick it up, that's all right, someone will take care of it, someone will teach these children how to behave, even this one walking at her side; she's not one for worrying the worries of others.

A grand long table covered with a white tablecloth. At its head sit Nana Erika and her Lujo, around the sides the strangers. There are more of them than usual. All look to the two of them; Lujo has rested his hand on hers, as if afraid of something, perhaps all these unfamiliar faces. *It's okay, Lujo, it's okay, it's our turn now*, she whispers to him, and he squeezes her hand.

How far is it to Bethlehem? Not very far, sang Nana Erika. They should listen; they need to learn the song and how to sing. Tonight there shall be no lies, tonight, after the song it shall be known, who is father to whom, who son to whom, and what she and Lujo are doing there in Zagreb with this crowd. They all close their eyes and start singing, but they don't know the words, and some of them don't even know how to sing. Nana Erika picks up on that immediately; she's got an ear for these sorts of things, for thirty years she sang in the Sarajevo Opera choir and from a hundred harmonic voices she knows who's messing things up.

The song at an end, Nana Erika gently laid her head to her chest. Lujo shook her arm, but she didn't wake. *She hasn't had enough sleep*, he whispered as if apologizing. Everyone began nodding their heads to an invisible rhythm, staring at Nana with the same look she used to stare at her roses. It's a shame Nana Erika couldn't see this, because if she had, she would have recognized their eyes and maybe come around to the idea that Lujo hadn't been lying after all, that everyone here really was a child or grandchild.

Merry Christmas, Nana, the girl was sitting on her bed offering her her hand. *Christmas? What do you mean Christmas? We haven't even had Christmas Eve.* The girl laughed aloud: *we have, we have, but you slept through it . . . Slept through it? Child, you don't know me. Erika Potkubovšek never sleeps through Christmas Eve and don't you be cheeky with me. We haven't had Christmas Eve, and there's no Christmas without Christmas Eve.* The girl looked sheepish – and so she should have, caught lying like that – and left the room.

Rika, Merry Christmas, Lujo came over to her, the devil peeking out from behind his every word. *Have you no shame, man?* Nana Erika turned her back to him. She looked at the wall and waited for him to go. He said something else, but she wasn't listening. Sometimes you have to forgive people the unforgivable. But they're not just any old folk, they're Rika and Lujo. In the thirties all Sarajevo turned its head when they walked the riverbank, there had never been such a couple, or so people said, and that's no small thing; when you're with someone for sixty years, there's no suffering you haven't endured together, no sin you haven't forgiven them. In a marriage like this people become similar to God: mercy and forgiveness embodied and only thus can they be happy. Nana will forgive Lujo this lie too. How could she not forgive him his lies when he's so certain he's protecting her from what she is to discover on Christmas Day inquiring of everyone who and what they are.

That day and the entire night, and then the whole of the next day, Nana Erika kept her back turned to the world. She looked at the wall, sometimes she would fall asleep and doze for an hour or two until someone came by, but she wouldn't listen, wouldn't say a word. She was punishing Lujo and knew well how long the punishment must last. Long enough for Lujo to think she would never look at him again and he would forever see only her back.

Promise me something, Lujo, she finally spoke, having checked that they were alone. *Promise me that tomorrow we'll celebrate Christmas Eve, and that the day after tomorrow we'll celebrate Christmas, and that all these people won't addle our minds and muddle our feast days . . . Rika, all this I promise you, just don't ever switch off again, and don't ever turn your back to me. What a wretch I'd be without you,* he said, framing her face in his hands and kissing her lips.

Nana Erika slept poorly because she spent the whole night worrying about butter for the cake, chocolate, codfish, decorating paper, and the suckling; who knows if there'll still be young sucklings at the market or whether they'll already be sold out, she thought, tossing and turning. And who'll fetch everything when she can't stand on her own two feet, and Lujo, well you know Lujo, he can't even buy mincemeat at the butcher's, let alone a suckling. She finally dozed a little in the dawn, but a girl woke her: *Nana, it's Christmas Eve today, isn't it?* Nana Erika caught a glimpse of mischief in her eyes. As if she were making sure that Nana knew about Christmas Eve and Christmas.

Nana Erika sits in her armchair in front of the television caressing the roses in their black sky. It's a summer night above Treskavica, Lujo's asleep in the cabin, but she can't sleep because he kissed her for the first time today. Roses had appeared in the sky in place of stars and no one would ever see them except her. Warm, soft, and tender roses on a black sky blanketing her legs, warming them like it never had before.

The boy leads her step by step to the dining room. At the head of the table sit Nana Erika and Lujo, around the table the strangers. *Lujo dear, do you know how many Christmas Eves this makes for us?* But he just shrugs his shoulders, turns the ring on her finger with his thumb and index finger, and lets his gaze wander as if afraid the strangers might notice something; that they might see that even after so many years the two of them are still in love, and try and destroy or trample what they have. Nana Erika won't let them though. She'll ask them whose they are and who they are, and on Christmas Day they'll have to tell her the truth because whoever dares lie on Christmas Day will burn in the eternal fires of hell.

How far is it to Bethlehem? Nana Erika begins the song, just Lujo accompanies her, the strangers remaining silent. They're probably ashamed when they hear the song and it's better they shut up and try to feel God's voice in their hearts, a voice to kill every lie, cleanse them of every doubt and hatred and return to them the hope that not a single truth is ever spoken in vain, not even the truth they shall soon speak of themselves and their intentions toward Nana Erika and her Lujo.

The last verses of the song disappeared in that first phase of deep sleep. When her chin touched her chest, Lujo shouted *Rika, wake up, Rika, it's Christmas Eve*, but sound asleep she didn't hear him. She slept the sleep of the just, the sleep of children and those who have endured great suffering but haven't done others the least harm.

Today is Christmas Day, isn't that right, Rika? Lujo sounded lost; his voice was pleading, but Nana Erika couldn't understand why, unless he'd forgotten you couldn't have Christmas Day without Christmas Eve. People forget all kinds of things, but how could he forget Christmas Eve; it doesn't matter, she's here to remind him and protect him from wild thoughts and those who would take advantage of him; naïve is her Lujo, that's how he's been all these years and if it weren't for her, who knows what would have become of him and what they, these people whose names she doesn't know, might have done to him. The world is full of Christians; she'll think that every Christmas, but you don't know their names.

No, Lujo dear, it's Christmas Eve today, it's not Christmas Day until tomorrow. Have you forgotten that they go in that order? said Nana Erika. Lujo lowered his head and let tears fall. *What's wrong old fella?* she worried. *It's nothing. I just want to know if this is ever going to end . . . It will, it'll end when we go back home, to our house,* she smiled, putting her hand on his chest. Strong is her Lujo, he's always been strong, so strong he could move a mountain if he wanted. *It can't end before then? Can't it just end before then? . . . Of course it can't, but you know what they say: sabur efendi, sabur, patience, good sir, patience, have patience and God shall have it too. We'll go home . . . And if we don't? . . . It can't be that we don't go home. Haven't you noticed how they look at us here? How could we stay among these people, their names unknown to us. Yes, I know, you're going to start saying they're our children and grandchildren. I know why you say that. You say it to make it easier on me, that my heart endure and not break from the waiting, but your Rika's heart won't break before we go back to Sarajevo. Don't you be afraid of a thing. With hope of home, the heart is strong and endures all. And quit that rubbish about our children and grandchildren. We don't have any, we never had any. Really, who would have children in such times, who would live in fear of their son being killed by someone else's son or having to pick him up off the sidewalk like you pick up tomatoes at the market because the plastic bag broke. We don't have children or grandchildren and that's a good thing too, because our suffering would be a hundred times greater if we did, and this way our only concern is going home and starting over, from the beginning. Fine, I know we won't be starting over, we're already old, but at least we'll die in our own home,* said Nana Erika, the tears frozen on Lujo's face. He must know life isn't easy, but that's no reason for us to lie to each other and invent some other world where nothing is difficult. It's

277

a fine world, Nana Erika doesn't think it's not, but such a world has only one failing, a lone error, a single downside; it simply doesn't exist. We can imagine one, but that doesn't make it real.

But why won't you accept these children as your own, as your kin, at least you could do that, Lujo tried. I like them, the same as I like anyone, but they can't be my children because they're not like me. Do you hear how they speak? Do think your children would speak like that, in that language? That, Lujo, is not our language, and they are not our words, just as this is not our home, but it is theirs. That's how it is. I can't accept others' children as my own because these children are staying here, here on their wooden floors, in their country, and we'll be going back to our home. What would I want with such children when I got home? And what do I want with these children if I never go home? Be reasonable, they're no replacement for one's home.

Lujo clasped his hands together as if about to beg her for something important, and then he slowly opened his fingers, one by one falling away and into the abyss. They intertwined under Lujo's chin, and Nana Erika was sure he would never again ask her for something she couldn't do for him, nor would he ever lie to her again. *Lujo, promise me something, please. We're already old, and I can barely walk and who knows what else awaits us. So promise me that every year we'll celebrate Christmas and that you'll never trick me and pretend you've forgotten.*

That evening at the head of table sat Nana Erika and her Lujo. Around them were strangers. Nana Erika looked at her Lujo, and the strangers looked at their full plates. Nothing was forgotten and nothing was missing. Not even the tinsel. She knew her Lujo would be there to support her when she asked them who and what they were and why they keep saying they're her children and grandchildren when they well know that Erika and Lujo don't have any children because who would bring children into the world in such times. She was so happy, singing in full voice *How far is it to Bethlehem? Not that far,* filling with holiness the festive hour.

It was then I longed for Babylonian women

A black car pulled up in front of Mary Kentucky's house. A man in a bellboy uniform got out of the car, glanced around nervously, whispered something to the driver, who we can't see from here, and ran across the lawn. He skipped along on his tiptoes, as if a lover were chasing him across a meadow or the ground beneath his feet were a minefield. He pressed the buzzer, holding his finger there until Mary Kentucky appeared at the door, and then almost slid under her armpit and scampered inside. He sat down on a small three-legged stool, took a hankie from his pocket, wiped his forehead, and let out a sigh of relief. Mary Kentucky rolled her eyes, clicked her tongue twice, and walked her walk into the kitchen.

A guy came out in a vest and boxer shorts decorated with little blue saxophones, hundreds of little blue saxophones. *Omer!* he was surprised, *what are you doing here, you'll lose your job.* Omer raised his hand like he was stopping a train: *wait!* . . . *Wait what, I busted my balls getting you that job!* Omer looked up, and calmly, as if in slow motion, got up from the stool, straightened, the whole time looking the guy in his boxers straight in the eye: *Osman, I have to inform you that our father is dying.* Osman leaned on the doorjamb like someone choosing between apathy and surprise: *where's he dying, bro?* . . . *What do you mean where's he dying, in the hospital in Crkvice* . . . *In Crkvice,* Osman repeated, although he knew well where it was, they had grown up a hundred meters from the hospital, but it had been so long since he had thought of either Crkvice or the local hospital that it was as if something precious and personal had surfaced from a great depth, bathing him in light, leaving the story about his father completely to the side. Later he would come to believe that his father had sent him the word, Crkvice, as his last bequest.

Omer skipped back over the lawn the same way he came, climbed into the car, and left Osman to try and convince Mary Kentucky that their father really was dying and that he needed a thousand dollars to fly to Bosnia and see him for the last time, to bury him and lay chrysanthemums on his grave. The chrysanthemums were the critical detail because they might just soften Mary up; they'll seem more real to her than the death of a man she didn't know existed, and she'll hand over the money, the last thousand dollars of her savings, which had practically melted since Osman appeared in her life two years ago. Mary Kentucky was a checkout girl at the supermarket and all her life had dreamed of becoming a country singer. She'd scraped the money together to record her first album, written her own songs, and dreamed of getting out of that small Alabama town for someplace better, someplace where she would forget her past life and finally become someone who only shops at the supermarket.

Osman gave Mary a hug, they were standing there on the lawn and she was crying, he tried to comfort her, at his feet two suitcases, in his pocket a round-trip plane ticket for Europe. *A month at the most,* he told her, but she wasn't sure whether to believe him. Somewhere deep inside, Mary Kentucky sensed that Osman didn't actually love her and was only with her because of her money and her house, and that some day he simply wouldn't come home. He'd vanish without saying goodbye, he'd return to his Europe, because sooner or later the war would be over, or he'd find some other girl who'll also have money and a house, but the house will be bigger and she'll have more money, or, as opposed to Mary, he'll actually be in love with her. The mere thought of all this made Mary Kentucky weep. While Osman slept, she'd clean his white socks, his precious white socks that he wore when he went to play soccer with other Europeans, and afterward they'd be so dirty you couldn't put them in the washing machine, so she'd scour them forever with a brush and she'd weep, because one day these socks wouldn't be here, and neither would Osman. Afterward she'd kiss his sleeping forehead, and he'd frown, smack his sleeping lips, and turn over. Standing there on the lawn, all this raced through the heart and mind of Mary Kentucky, and she couldn't stop her weeping. Osman was anxious; he was in a hurry and still had to stop by the hotel and say goodbye to his brother, but he can't go until she's stopped her crying. He can't leave her like this.

Omer looked at his watch for the third time. His brother had said he was on his way forty minutes ago, and he still hadn't arrived. Whenever Osman was late or vanished for a few hours or days, Omer would nearly have a panic attack. If it hadn't been for his brother, he would have never made it to America. He would have probably stayed on in Sarajevo until he got killed or some great force had lifted him from where he stood, but he would never have gone this far, never all the way to Alabama. *You have the heart of a hawk, he the heart of a pigeon. You're twins, but it's as if you're not brothers*, that's what his father had said back when they were fifteen-year-olds off to school in Sarajevo, and ever since, Omer had been an eternal burden for Osman, a precious piece of cargo borne on the road to happiness, a reason for everyone to forgive his stronger brother his idiocies and incivility, because to have Omer in your life was like having four hands instead of two and two heads instead of one, and all the while two hands twiddled their thumbs and only a single head did the thinking. Osman's every trait was reflected in Omer like in a mirror, a copied image, but turned the other way around. Osman was decisive about succeeding in life, Omer eternally scared that nothing would roll his way; Osman believed everyone had their uses, Omer scared that everyone had it in for him; when they went to the movies, scenes Osman found funny would bring Omer to tears; Osman loved women, Omer preferred men . . . And of course, Osman had found Mary Kentucky, and Mary Kentucky had got Omer the job at the hotel.

Osman left his things in the taxi and ran inside the hotel. Omer opened the doors of the elevator and Osman stepped in, the hotel had six floors, a minute to the top and the same back down to the bottom, they hugged, *everything okay?* Osman nodded, *I'll miss you,* Omer looked at him angrily, *say hi to father for me if you see him alive,* and the elevator was again on the ground floor.

His brother was at the exit when Omer broke hotel rules and hollered: *bring me back something from Zenica.* The reception clerk roused himself as if pricked by a needle, the gentleman reading the paper in a leather armchair glanced up at the bellboy, the little boy playing with a model Volkswagen Bug froze . . . The sounds they heard from the liveried young man formed words they would never be capable of repeating or recognizing, not even on a quiz show for the million-dollar question. Osman pretended he didn't hear anything and got into the taxi, the gentleman in the armchair returned to his paper, the little boy to his car, only the reception clerk kept his eyes pinned on Omer whose own eyes shone like glycerin, as if angels with cameras were clicking away with their flashes right in front of him.

The plane flew to Chicago, then Osman changed for Paris, then again for Zagreb. He sat in the empty airport hall, looking out through the glass at airplanes in the rain and tiny blond stewardesses, their umbrellas plastered in advertising slogans. He had no need for words of comfort, but had he sought them, he wouldn't have found words more consoling than those written on the yellow, blue, and red umbrellas: a little white birdie boasted – *it's quiet and warm under her wings, Colibri Airlines*. Osman was sleepy but afraid of closing his eyes in an empty hall that could suddenly fill with people whose every eye would be on him. He thought about his brother and about Mary Kentucky. The two of them would be lost if he didn't come back. It's weird to be so important to someone in life, yet not feel the slightest responsibility, not be in the least proud that you're their first and last hope. Omer was Osman's twin brother, but you couldn't say the same in the other direction. The stronger brother had been born so the eldest would have someone to guide him in life, just as the war had only erupted so Osman would go to America and save Mary Kentucky, who if it hadn't been for the war would have remained a lost soul, even if she had realized her dream and become a singer. Her singing was damn awful, but in the whole of Alabama there wasn't a soul who would tell her that because there wasn't anyone willing to listen to her until Osman came along and became her shoulder to cry on and ear to burn. He bitterly regretted being the one who could fill hearts and guarantee a peaceful sleep, and wished that at least sometime he might get to be a Mary or an Omer to someone, to be loved, powerless, and pathetic, someone who is helped because he knows how help is sought.

Two hours passed before the first passengers for Sarajevo started arriving. Osman didn't want to look at them. He didn't want to recognize anyone, or anyone to recognize him. It pays to remain anonymous when you're on an unwanted journey; it's not a return home anyway, and he's not going to Sarajevo to establish just how much he isn't from there anymore, he's going because his father is dying, sick and old, and you can't let yourself get too cut up, but he is dying and a son should see his father one last time, bury him as God commands, and then leave again, the same way he'd arrived, as a foreigner. He reached into his jacket pocket for his passport, a compact American passport in which not even his family name was written how he had written it his whole life, from the time he had gone to school. This family name was proof he didn't have to recognize anyone here and that no one should recognize him. The Croatian customs officer bowed to him courteously, and it was then he remembered how once, long ago, at the entrance to Maksimir Stadium before a Dinamo–Čelik game, a cop had sucker punched him just because he had a Čelik scarf on. That couldn't happen now. They don't beat up Americans around here, thought Osman, and he doesn't even have that Čelik scarf anymore. He can hardly remember what it looked like, just that it was black and red.

On the seat across from him there was a girl with a Walkman on, next to her a bright green carry-on with Benetton written on it. She closed her eyes, rocking discreetly to the rhythm of the invisible music. The music wasn't inaudible though, a distant melody made its way to Osman's ears, but apart from what you could see on her face it definitely was invisible. She had short red hair and one of those noses you would say was ugly if you looked at it in isolation from the whole, too wide and totally masculine, by no stretch the nose of a beauty. Her lips were also a bit big, and her auricles uneven, but Osman thought he was looking at the most beautiful woman he had ever seen. He stared at her, trying to catch every movement on her face, like a man who had made a long journey north wanting to see a deer, though a deer hadn't appeared for years, and he'd set up camp there in the north, and one day a deer appeared, but by that time he had already headed south, reconciled to the fact he was never going to see one.

The loudspeaker announced a half-hour delay on the flight to Sarajevo and Osman heaved a sigh of relief because the redhead didn't open her eyes. If she'd opened them he'd have had to stop staring. The corners of her mouth twitched, invisible muscles in her cheeks playing with her, and she frowned in rhythm, God only knows what rhythm, but it definitely wasn't country. Osman again remembered Mary Kentucky, good old Mary, who was sure to be sitting at the kitchen table weeping. She would never see this because she doesn't have the right eyes, doesn't matter that she's a woman, she doesn't have eyes that could see a redhead about to set off for Sarajevo, a woman who would today be the most beautiful in the city, and tomorrow and every other day too, maybe forever, the redhead in Sarajevo, beneath the white roofs of a city that was in flames the last time he saw it, and beneath which he, Osman, would never again set foot, not even today because he'd take a bus straight to Zenica, or ever again because that's the way he wanted it, such was his fate and his passport, American, and he needed to act accordingly, his loyalties clear when the government recommended American citizens not travel someplace because of a war. He was already sure the redhead was from Sarajevo and was going home. The beautiful and irregular face isn't one for other cities, that's how it seemed to Osman; such a face can only be Sarajevan.

The voice from the loudspeaker announced the flight and Osman thought: *time to go, beautiful.* The redhead opened her eyes, catching his glance with her green eyes and reaching for her little suitcase. If she'd only known what he was thinking she'd have said something reproving, but she didn't say anything, she just left. Though he didn't need it anymore Osman took out his passport, and then his plane ticket; the most important stage in his journey was over. Everything that happened from now on would be just the orderly closure of duties life had set down for him.

His dead father was waiting for him in Zenica. He was laid out on the red floor of the house, surrounded by women with their heads covered, all kneeling, quietly speaking the words of a prayer. Osman stopped and immediately wanted to take a step backward, but he thought: *hey, c'mon, that's my father, I'm his son,* and he moved forward. The women didn't interrupt their prayer, *I can't go in now*, he stepped back, banging into the door, a whispered *sorry* escaping his lips. Luckily there was no one there except his dead father and the women at prayer, and perhaps God.

Without tears he buried his father. He lowered the coffin into the grave with the hand closest to his heart, trying to remain as invisible as possible as the priest bade farewell to the deceased. Later a few people he didn't know offered him their hands and left without having looked him in the eye. He returned again to his father's house, which smelled of winter, old shoes, and Preference cards. He sat on the sofa, held his face in his hands, and long and slow dragged his fingers down toward his chin. When his middle fingers made it to the jawline, it was all over.

He locked the house and left the keys with a neighbor. The house needed to be sold, but he didn't know how you went about this sort of thing anymore, and didn't actually care about the money. He couldn't go back to Alabama with money in his pocket. If he'd already renounced his former life, he couldn't now return to his new one with earnings from his father's death. Hamid, the neighbor, asked what he was supposed to be guarding the house from, and until when. Osman said he didn't know, Hamid shrugged his shoulders. There was nothing much to be said or debated; silence is probably best when you don't know what more to say.

Passing by the stadium Osman heard the voices from the bingo hall. There was a time when the Zenica bingo hall was the biggest in Yugoslavia. Every first of the month the miners and railway workers would come and burn through their pay packets in a matter of hours. Osman went in and bought three cards: one for him, one for the redhead, and one for fate. He ordered a double rakia, sat at a table, took out a pen, and rolled up the sleeves of his suit jacket. If one of the three cards comes up trumps, he'll tear up his plane ticket, throw his passport in the Bosna, and go back to Sarajevo and find the redhead. He'll never think of his brother and Mary Kentucky again. That's what he decided, convinced it was his human and divine right, that no one could stop him and that he wasn't doing anything wrong because it was all up to chance, and chance is neither good nor evil, chance can't put you in the dock, just like no one can indict a man who accidentally gets in the way of a bullet, leaving behind a widow and three kids.

The fatso caller drew the balls from the barrel and read out the numbers. Osman's own card and the card of fate remained unmarked, but the redhead's numbers kept coming up. Osman felt a booming in his head, the kind of excitement you feel before a final spectacular jump, he was already in love, the redhead wasn't only the most beautiful woman in the airport waiting area, now she was his. He imagined his arrival in Sarajevo, knocking on her door and their embrace, one she would welcome as perfectly normal, because without a word or a memory she would know who he was, why he had come, and what he was meant to be in her life. He'd crossed all the numbers on her card bar one, but the caller didn't call it out. The next one wasn't hers either, nor the one after that, nor the third, fourth, fifth, six, or seventh . . . Osman reconciled himself to his bad luck as fast as he had accepted the good, the excitement disappearing from his stomach, which was already stone cold, like it had been over his father's grave. He waited for someone to finally shout *bingo!*

Bingo! shouted an old man in a beret who looked like Zaim Muzaferija and got up to meet fatso, the caller. *Congratulations Mustafa*, with a hearty swing fatso shook the old man's hand. The old man smiled sheepishly as if his luck had all been a set-up. Osman crumpled the card up and stuffed it in his jacket pocket.

Darkness had already fallen over Zenica. He headed toward the bus station kicking a can in front of him. The can rang hollow on the asphalt, and Osman felt like a fifteen-year-old who still believed it was possible to cheat his own life but couldn't remember how. Maybe a man needs to be careful not to let life cheat him. What would happen, for example, if tomorrow – actually, the day after tomorrow – he turned up at Mary Kentucky's house and caught her in bed with Omer.

If it were possible to believe something like that, if only for a moment, a moment as fleeting as the flap of a hummingbird's wings, Osman would never return to Alabama. But as things stood, his brother's present was going to be a marked card from the Zenica bingo hall with just one number missing, an inconspicuous seven that Osman will remember for just a short time, before it disappears along with the flame that burns and leaves no trace.

Look at me, Anadolka

Vukota remembers his grandma Rina only vaguely, if he indeed remembers her at all and his memories aren't just from his mother's stories. The first image is of Grandma warming herself in front of a grand wood burner, her palms outstretched toward the fire, a glimmering white cap on her head, the kind he had only seen in cartoons, on Olive Oyl's head from the Popeye cartoon when she went to bed. In the second Grandma Rina is holding a candlestick holder, wiping the dust from it, her fingers trembling, flitting about as if each were soon to turn into a sparrow and disappear beneath the high ceiling of the living room. In the third Grandma is furious, her little cap now crooked, and she's yelling, barely audibly, if as someone has muffled her every word with a mountain of feathers. *In my time a man and woman met under a canopy, not under the covers.* That was it, that was the sum of what he knew about his grandma Rina, she had died when he was three, and he had almost never thought of her until the summer of 1992, when the first Jewish convoys left the city, and Vukota remembered that Grandma Rina had been a Jew, and so that made him a Jew too, and under the terms of a new agreement he could leave this war behind.

His mother looked at him, pale and empty, and said *you've got to be kidding, what do you know about all that.* His father, Savo, just shrugged his shoulders, lit one cigarette after the other, and shut up, nothing to say since the first grenades had weaned him off the habit of starting every sentence with "we Serbs." *I don't know anything, but I'm going to Israel,* Vukota replied, his thoughts wandering back to the three images of Grandma Rina, now certain he'd be able to see something, decipher something that had hitherto remained hidden, something that would turn him – who had never been anything – into a Jew.

I am the grandson of Rina Mantova, he said, holding up a yellowed card with his grandma's picture on it. In different circumstances a membership card for La Benevolencija wouldn't have cut it as proof of Vukota's ancestry, but in the mayhem of the present, the people at the Jewish Community offices weren't particularly interested in who was a Jew and who wasn't. They put everyone who registered on their lists. As soon as they got out of the city, people would have to settle questions of their Jewishness on their own, there could be no harm done. They had saved lives, and there's no deception involved there.

When the bus arrived in Makarska, Vukota asked *and how are we going to get to Israel?* Mr. Levi was surprised: *you really want to go to Israel? . . . Well, I don't know where else I'd go.* Vukota didn't want to go to America or Canada; he was afraid of a life among strangers, and if Grandma Rina had been a Jew, then presumably there was something Jewish in him, something that might burgeon and bloom in Israel, magically making a real Jew of him, at home in his own skin among the locals. When you leave home, you have to be something, you need a document and a name on it to protect you. At home you could be Nothing, now you have to become Something. Vukota was worried he lacked the talent for being Something. If alongside his father, Savo, he didn't know how to be a Serb, perhaps he was incapable of being anything except Vukota, and if he was just Vukota, then it was curtains for him.

He arrived in Israel two months later. At the airport a pair in uniform came out to meet him, escorting him to a third uniform who interrogated him and certified he wasn't dangerous. This uniform passed him over to a fourth who gave Vukota a five-minute lecture on the State of Israel, handed him a key, an ID card, and a check to get him through the next month or so. *Welcome, get yourself sorted,* he said, placed his hand on Vukota's shoulder, and sent him out into the world.

I can sing and play a bit of guitar, he told Albert, who on the second day after his arrival had already asked when Vukota intended to get a job. Albert was from Zrenjanin and had been there three months. Vukota had been assigned to him as a roommate and Albert was supposed to assist with his socialization in their free time. *That won't help you none here. You know how to do anything else? . . . Maybe I'd be okay as a waiter . . . Be a waiter then, but get down to it on the double. That's my advice to you. Otherwise it's curtains for you.*

Vukota spent weeks trying to find a job waiting tables, but at the time no one seemed to need staff. Albert grinned, *ha, you Bosnians,* making life even tougher. When Albert was around, Vukota couldn't forget for a minute that he was on the edge of destitution, that little by little the ground was being pulled out from under him, the day not far off when he wouldn't even be able to buy food. He wasn't capable of becoming a waiter, but worse still, he hadn't even become a Jew, or he had never been that for longer than the moment it had first occurred to him that Grandma Rina might save his neck. In any case, Albert's *ha, you Bosnians,* already sounded like a grenade exploding in the distance, and with every new *ha, you Bosnians,* it drew ever closer and louder. One day it would go off right here, beside him, and that *ha, you Bosnians,* would then require an appropriate response. And what might an appropriate response be? Vukota didn't know, except that if there wasn't one, he increasingly had the feeling he'd rather smack Albert's ears than find a million dollars in the street.

This could be something for you, Albert put the newspaper down in front of him. It was open to the Help Wanted page, there was an ad, something about a musical comedy, a film studio looking for young men and women who could sing, preferably from Eastern Europe.

Vukota silently took down the number, making out like he didn't care, while in reality his every muscle was dancing with joy. He hadn't even called and was already imagining himself pulling up in front of the Hilton in a sporty Mercedes, making his way through a cordon of chicks who were passing out all over the place, like young birches felled by Jehovah's breeze. Then he'd come visit Albert in this dank room, take a fat wad of dollar bills from his pocket, slap him on the forehead with it, and say, *ha, we Bosnians.*

The voice at the other end of the line had already picked up, and Vukota hadn't even got around to being surprised with himself because, hell, for the first time in his life he'd become something, and it was because of Albert; in a fleeting flight of fancy he'd become the worst a man anywhere on the face of the earth could be – he'd become a Bosnian, he'd become *we Bosnians.* Luckily he wasn't aware of it, and calmly answered their questions: yes, he's from Eastern Europe, from Bosnia and Herzegovina, you know, a country in Eastern Europe; yes, he was an excellent singer, he used to have his own band, what do you mean where did he have a band? Eastern Europe of course; it was a punk band, but he knows how to sing Bosnian songs too, no problem at all . . .

A few hundred guys and girls were there waiting outside this upholstered green door. Everyone was given a number and got called in according to some system, at first one at a time, and then someone worked it out that the audition would never end, so they started going in five at a time. Listen to those numbers will you, the number 676 surreal to Vukota, all of a sudden everything seemed different from how he had imagined. Instead of hustling his way to becoming a Jew, he had hustled his way to a number.

Fourteen hours later, a fat black-haired secretary squawked in English: *675 to 679, if you don't get in here now, you've missed your chance.* He pushed his way to the door, holding his number victoriously above his head. Three guys went in with Vukota, two of them were Russians, no doubt about it, the other one looked like a Romanian, and then there was a girl who was really tall, blond hair and blue eyes like in that story by Isak Samokovlija. At a table sat three men, the one in the middle looked like the director because he was wearing glasses like Steven Spielberg's, at least that's how it seemed to Vukota. The director pointed to five chairs, they sat down, he looked at them, rolled his eyes, the fat secretary squawked *break time!* Vukota started to stand up, *sit down!* Vukota sat back down. The director and his assistants headed out the back door. The fat secretary followed them.

For half an hour the five of them didn't budge from their chairs. The girl held her hands in her lap, looking at the floor. She didn't move, she almost didn't breathe, she was tense and looked like she was remembering a song she had heard long ago, one she'd start singing the second she remembered it, she'd just start singing, out loud, not concerned with who was around or where she was. The two Russians really were Russians, and motormouth Russians at that; first they whispered stuff to each other, past Vukota who was sitting between them, then they started laughing and talking real loud, one second Vukota was taking spray on the right cheek, the next on the left. He stared straight ahead, as lost as he would ever be in his life, as far from home as anyone had ever been. He thought how perhaps it would've been better if he'd never remembered Grandma Rina, if Grandma Rina had never even existed, and that if it had occurred to him to leave couldn't he at least have done it the way other people did? How did other people leave? He didn't want to think about it, but he was sure they must've left better than he did, because if they'd left like him, no one would have gone anywhere, everyone would've remained in the city waiting for their grenade or bullet.

To keep from bursting into tears at the terror of his fate, Vukota did what was always helpful and healing in these kinds of situations: Out of the corner of his eye he started spying on the girl; you know, the standard drill – I'm a man and I'm looking at a girl. She really was beautiful, one of those ones you didn't have the guts to fall in love with, but you never got the chance anyhow, because you only ever met them in passing and never got to introduce yourself, but you would see them and ache, that real deep-seated ache somewhere in your chest. You try thinking about them and you always think, they can't be someone's girlfriend, because you only see them when they're on their own, and you can't imagine anyone who's deserving of such a girl.

It was like she couldn't hear the Russians; she focused on her spot, trying to remember her song, wound tight as a string on a guitar – not on a guitar! – maybe on some other instrument, one Vukota had never laid his hands on, maybe a string on a zither. Yeah, she was as tight as a string on a zither, and under a spray of Russian spit Vukota tried to work out what country she was from, but God help him it was really like there was no such country in the whole of Eastern Europe. Frankly, there was no such country in all the Europes of this world, eastern, western, whatever. Christ, what kind of country lets a girl like her end up number 678 in some distant Israel.

He stopped thinking about his fate, in fact, he was ashamed his own fate had even crossed his mind. From the get-go he should've been playing the role of the hero, saving this blond beauty – this daughter of Samokovlija's imagination, this one-off blond Jewess – from general servitude, not to mention this audition. He thought how good it would be were he to get up right now, go over to her, take her by the hand, and lead her out, but in his head there was this pathetic little Vukota, a little scared monster, all panicked, telling him for God's sake don't do it, you don't go up to any woman like that, she won't stand up, you don't pull her by the arm like you want to rip it out of her shoulder, like you'd pluck a star from the ceiling of a kid's room that's not your own. Vukota understood what the little monster inside was telling him: You go up to that girl and grab her by the arm – you'll end up in the nuthouse. Crazy, and not even a Jew.

He tried to look away from her. The Russians kept the spray coming and he faced the other direction, hey, the little Romanian, he'd completely forgotten about him. The Romanian had his mouth open like he was a bit retarded, gazing transfixed at the beauty. *Have a good gawk, numb nuts,* said Vukota. His own voice gave him a fright, but no one had heard it. The Romanian definitely hadn't, he was in a daze, zoned out to everything happening around him. Thank God we didn't have that kind of socialism, thought Vukota, and thus comforted, turned back to the girl. Left and right it rained and thundered, the Russians not quitting for a second, but it was like in those songs from after the Second World War, rain or thunder couldn't stop Vukota: He stood there in a drenched raincoat in the middle of a destroyed city, a city of which there was nothing left, the rain just poured down on Brest that day, as it once had, and Vukota wanted to know her name, to speak it right now, and hell, loud! He wanted her to finally turn around, he wanted to know where she was from, and to tell her: *you got it, sweetheart, that's where we're going. I'll tear up my number, you'll tear up yours, and we're off to your whatthehellwasthenameofit country. There in your hometown, we'll meet again as total strangers.*

The fat secretary came in squawking *silence over there!* The Russian precipitation cleared, and the director and assistants took their places. *Number 675,* said the assistant on the left. The little Romanian jumped up and finally closed his mouth. *Where are you from?* the assistant asked. *From Albania,* replied the little Romanian, who, no shit, wasn't even Romanian. *From Albania,* the three of them were surprised, Vukota too. They've got Jews in Albania nowadays? It didn't matter anyhow, the kid didn't know the first thing about singing and ten seconds later the director had cut him off and the secretary showed him the door, soft-soaping him with *we'll call you if we need you.*

It was Vukota's turn. *Bosnia and Herzegovina*, he replied to the assistant on the left. *Take it away*, the secretary squawked. Not thinking too much about it Vukota started singing the first folk song that popped into his head. *Look at me, Anadolka, I offer my heart, with almonds that you may smell so sweet, with sherbet that you may long for me*, he looked in her direction, she looked back, gripping her chair, *oh my, your locks so red aglow, do they fill you with such sorrow so*, she kept watching him, her eyes shining as if someone had mistakenly let the ocean into the room, *were I to suffer such sorrow so, I'd never let you see such woe*, Christ, she knows the song, she's opening her mouth like she's singing, but so that no one else sees her, so they think she's just yawning a bit, it's easy to hide words, every word can be hidden, remain unspoken, but when you sing – that's hard to hide . . . *Oh my, your face so white, is it sorrow or is it fright*, no, it's not possible, he would've seen her, he would've seen her in Sarajevo, but he hadn't seen her, no way, the ocean flowed from her eyes and rushed down her face and over the whole room, it washed over Vukota and everyone else, but they didn't notice, they didn't have the eyes to see, they didn't know what it meant when an ocean gushed over deserts of dust and thick foreign tongues. *Enough*, said the director, Vukota wanted to sit down, *no, you're done, someone will call you tomorrow, you're through*, the fat secretary signaled toward the door. Vukota turned around, wanted to say something, but what could he say now he was on his way?

Hello, he looked at her for the last time. *Hello*, she said quietly in their language, but so that Vukota didn't hear her voice. He wanted to turn around just once more, to tell her *we don't have time to talk, we gotta get out of here right now*, but he didn't turn around, and he didn't say anything, because if a man were so quick as to in every moment do what he knows he must, he would never have left, nor would he have anywhere to return. There were still a dozen or so guys and girls in the waiting room. Vukota leaned against the wall. Russian numbers 677 and 679 were quickly out the door. The fat secretary called the next group in, but the girl didn't appear. Vukota kept waiting anyway; he waited until the last group came out, and then worked it out that for some reason the girl had gone out the back door, the one for the directors and the secretary.

He went back to the apartment, it was hot, definitely way hotter than it could ever have been in Sarajevo. Time dragged by so slowly, much slower than his footsteps. Vukota roamed Tel Aviv like in those pictures where there's no one except a kid rolling a steel wheel between high buildings where nobody lives. Maybe the streets were in fact full of people, and he didn't notice, because she, who he believed was of his tribe and thus his destiny, she'd gone out the wrong door, the one that led out to the other end of the world, out into a reality Vukota would never set foot in.

I want you to go, now

He was nineteen when he came home from soccer one Sunday; his mother put her hand to his forehead, *Nešo, you're sick*, she said. He put his pajamas on and lay down, from the bathroom he heard the gurgle of water; his mother was cleaning his soccer cleats; he closed his eyes, fell asleep, and dreamed hot feverish dreams.

The doctor came the next day, the fever hadn't gone down, he listened to Nešo's heart and looked him long in the eye. *I don't know,* he said, *we're going to have to run some tests.* Later his mother brought him some chicken soup. The soup had the taste of illness; Nešo will remember it, and more than anything else the soup will remind him of 1967, the year he was supposed to have died. Its comforting mild taste will irritate him and sometimes induce rage; how is one to understand healthy people eating chicken soup, eyeing each other empathetically, like they belong to a society of local pedophiles who meet once a week around a pot of dead naked birds, all gleaming white.

The waiting room at the clinic was full. Nešo and his father got the only two free chairs left. It was to be the last stroke of luck for the next six months. Everything that happened next would be a long mute nightmare.

The nurse came by and gathered the health-insurance booklets. Hours went by, Nešo closed his eyes and dozed; every now and then he fell forward in his sleep, his father catching his shoulders. *I'm not in any pain*, he told the doctor, who sat behind a big black desk. *Sit yourself down*, the nurse came over, the bed covered in a green rubber sheet; she set a rubber tape around Nešo's upper arm and tapped him on the veins with two fingers; everything looked like it was made out of rubber, the doctor not getting up from his chair; the jab was unpleasant, dark blood flowed, Nešo took a look and his head began to spin, he thought he was going to tip over onto his back and the needle stay sticking in his veins.

The results weren't ready for another three days. His temperature stayed up around 100.4 degrees. His father went to collect the results and returned ashen-faced. *Everything's fine*, he said to Nešo. That night his father and mother sat in the kitchen, smoking in silence until the morning. The results showed their son had leukemia and only a few months to live.

For days he looked at his ashen father and his mother's swollen eyes.

Am I dying here? he asked the doctor. *You don't die when you're nineteen,* he lied. Once a week the nurse came and took Nešo's blood. Now he would look at the ceiling. He had learned his lesson. Accustomed to his sickness and the muddle in his head lasting the whole day through, his temperature never below 99.5, already he had a score of experience. Nature has seen to it that those suffering from serious illness have no fear of death, he thought, believing that when the moment came he would greet it with serene indifference.

And then, after three months, the fever disappeared. He still felt weak, and his blood count was catastrophic, but his mind had completely cleared, his appetite had returned, and with it all those human fears, not least the fear of death. His father's face retained its ashen hue, but his mother had stopped crying, the red gone from her eyes. To her, that Nešo's temperature had dropped was more important and far stronger than the word leukemia. She thought that sometimes you shouldn't put too much stock in obvious truths, results, and diagnoses, it was better to just outrun them, behave like everything was normal and everyone happy, and then at a given moment everything would indeed be normal again, and besides, happiness comes of its own accord, when no one expects it but everyone is ready to welcome it with open hearts.

When the weakness began to recede from his muscles and bones, Nešo got up out of bed. *Is he allowed to walk*, his father asked the doctor. *He can if he's able.* It was another Sunday, now in the early spring, when

Nešo left the house for the first time. The news about his leukemia had spread all over town, everyone knew he was going to die; friends smiled at him overenthusiastically, their girlfriends hugging him, hugs that made their skin crawl, as if their hugs were comforting death itself. Nešo sat down on a bench and watched the match with the girls. *In a few weeks you'll be playing too*, he heard them say. They were lying, and he felt like a fraud. It was a feeling he would never forget and that would haunt him for the rest of his life. He knew he wasn't going to die, but he couldn't tell anyone. They knew he was going to die, but they couldn't tell him. They could only sit there in silence, smiling at each other, people on different sides of the same wall: them, beauties in a sun-baked city, and him, a dead man walking, whom you hung out with out of a particular sense of social obligation. Not knowing it, they tried to buy their own deaths from Nešo.

At the beginning of summer, sitting again behind the big black desk, the doctor said to his father: *it wasn't leukemia. We don't know what it was. The main thing is that your son is healthy now.* His father ran out of the doctor's office as if he had lost his head, as happy as a man whom they had told nothing else bad would ever happen to him in life. Nešo played soccer again.

Twenty-five years later, on Sunday, March 30, 1992, he invited a couple of friends and their wives over for fish and hot-pepper stew. Outside the war was about to fire up, inside the smell of fish, hot peppers, and tomato filled the air. No one wanted silence that day; let's just talk about everything, except the war; we'll forget about that, pretend it's not here, like patients with a sudden interest in astronomy and linguistics, in everything they ever overlooked in life, now beautiful because it doesn't remind them of their illness. The men laughed, the women planned their summer vacations, nonstop they spoke the names of days and months to come as if doing so would obliterate the war, that the tanks would cease to exist the second their steel ears heard the women's voices, imposing and insistent, giving the order that August is for going to the seaside. Their stories annoyed Nešo, as he was the only one with no need of them. The war hadn't registered in his head or heart; he was going steady with Magda, and this was all that held his interest and was the only reason he had invited guests over for lunch. He was just biding his time to cut loose. *I killed a carp this morning,* he said, *it was no easy thing, I had to really stick it to him. Thank Christ pike and perch are always dead.* The women fell silent and looked down at their plates. They took Nešo's story about dead fish as an insult, as if he were saying to them: Yeah, you're scared of the war, you should be ashamed, you don't want to admit to yourselves that maybe you'll never go to the seaside again, that maybe tomorrow your men will be holding machine guns in some ditch somewhere, pissing their drawers out of blind fear. They didn't like Nešo, and that's why they hadn't worked out that the war hadn't yet reached him, and they didn't like him because Nešo loved playing the he-man, the kind who didn't wash the dishes and didn't iron his shirts because these kinds of chores were invented solely for husbands to humiliate their wives. Magda couldn't care less; she smiled and calmly ate her food. He couldn't stand that; it was for her that he was playing the he-man. Though they'd been married for years, Magda loved him as much as he did her, and admired him to an extent that would have made any husband happy. But Nešo wouldn't quit, whenever someone came around, or as soon as he met someone at the bar, he couldn't overcome this obsessive need to start talking the kind of shit that would make the stomach of any woman within earshot churn; any woman except Magda. She was either completely indifferent or accepted what he said as something definitive, which one needn't pay any mind, much less fight about. Nešo's were just words without substance, and it had never crossed his mind to try and put them into practice.

My wife always cleaned my soccer cleats after a game, she'd clean them and I'd lie down for a snooze. That's the way things should be. He peered over at Magda, happily slurping his stew, flushed from the hot peppers and a kind of internal warmth that washed over him every time Magda sent apologetic glances to the women at the table. Magda didn't give a thought to revealing that she'd never even laid eyes on those damn cleats, because then she'd ruin their game, and the game was more important to her than Nešo's friends and their wives, who were as wild as two lynxes, kicking their husbands under the table. At the door, one of them, Nataša, said *we're never coming here again!* Her husband bit his tongue; showing your anger like this was bad form. Nešo was his friend, and besides, he had a different take on the story about the cleats. It's just what people are like: They court their lovers in all kinds of ways, and Nešo courted his with chauvinistic he-man stories.

But Nataša was right about one thing: They never came over to the apartment again because soon the apartment was no more. It went up in flames in one of the first bombardments of the city. Friendships got caught in the flames too, the remnants rare late-night telephone conversations, unreliable snippets of news traversing seas and oceans, news that contained but one verifiable fact: Everyone who had eaten fish and hot-pepper stew at Nešo's that last Sunday before the war was still alive. Once they had lived within a forty-five-minute tram ride of each other, but today, even the fastest supersonic jet couldn't round them up in that time.

Nešo lived with Magda in Toronto. He worked for an Italian in a little place that made spaghetti and fanatically tried to make new friends. He wanted people whom he could show himself and Magda off to, for someone in the big wide world to notice and say, look, those two are together; he wanted their love recorded the way it was in some of those burned books in their abandoned city. If you've already lost your life, at least you don't have to lose your love, he thought, huddling down under the duvet, gripping Magda's ankles with his feet, and speaking words that he later claimed he couldn't remember because as Nešo would have it, you only uttered true words of love in your sleep. One Sunday he invited three work colleagues and their wives over for fish and hot-pepper stew. They were taken aback by the invitation but accepted it all the same. Having lunch at someone else's place seemed a good way to save some money, and they had the feeling Nešo was inviting them to a kind of exotic ritual from some distant land, a ritual one really had to experience for oneself, like going off on a package tour somewhere.

A pack of deep-frozen fillets didn't exactly amount to fish and hot-pepper stew, but Nešo didn't care. He tried the steaming broth, huffing and puffing, slurping up his noodles, oblivious to Magda clinking her spoon on the edge of her plate in admonishment. She frowned, her heart pounding like crazy; God, just as long as he doesn't start, just as long as he doesn't speak, she thought. The women were eating quietly and smiling broadly, the men chatting away, Nešo lying in wait for his moment. Magda said *Nešo!* . . . *What?* He looked up, she shook her head, *don't!* . . . *What don't?* . . . *Don't, please* . . . *What?* . . . *Don't, just be quiet.* The others fell silent; they didn't understand the language but sensed it didn't bode well.

Nešo put his spoon down, wiped his face and hands, and not taking his eyes off Magda for a second started with the story about his soccer cleats. Completely still, Magda returned his gaze, not paying the guests any mind. They ate, never looking up from their plates. The women raised their eyebrows pointedly, certain they would never be coming back here.

One of us has to go, said Magda. *Why?* . . . *Because this life isn't the same*

310

as the one where you could roll out your soccer-cleats story . . . Why isn't it the same? . . . If you don't know that yourself, I'm not telling you. I want you to go, or else I'll go . . . Where would you go? . . . Nešo, I want you to go, and I want you to go right now . . . Where would I go? . . . I don't know, you're the he-man aren't you?

She shouldn't have said that; he went straight to their room, took a suitcase from the wardrobe, and half an hour later slammed the door behind him without saying goodbye. He didn't think for a second where he was going, or even where he could go in a city in which he had no family, where friendships developed so slowly that there was no hope of a saving grace, of a bed even for just the night. He walked for a time, and then rested his suitcase on the sidewalk and sat down, making like he was waiting for someone. He was angry and hurt; he didn't know what had just happened or where the exit was that might get him out of this story. He felt so awfully betrayed that his joints were going to jump out of their sockets, every bone racing in its own direction. Once he had been afraid of catching Magda with another man or that one day he would come home to a letter on the kitchen table, but those fears paled in significance compared to what had actually happened. Instead of just taking herself from him, Magda had taken everything he had left in his life. The how and why didn't matter, nor the where and when; to him it seemed she had taken everything except the suitcase on which he had parked his rear. There was one thing he was sure of: He would never go back home, he would never knock on Magda's door, and he would never see her again. Maybe Nešo would change his mind by the morning, but how and where to live until the morning? He thought about the friends he'd cheated when he didn't die of leukemia: Sitting here on the suitcase was the price of that distant betrayal.

It was comforting that the news of what had happened to him would reach them, his sitting down on a suitcase in the middle of Toronto and waiting. Nešo couldn't imagine what it might end up sounding like, but it gave him some release and he already felt a little better. He closed his eyes and wished that everything would come to pass as soon as possible and that he would find out from them what had happened.

A Little Joke

After A. P. Chekhov

Brane Konstantinović works in construction for a boss named Zeytinoglu. He hauls bags of cement on his back and sings *two brothers born on the death wall, you wouldn't believe your own eyes*. The bricklayers and laborers, mainly Turks and Germans, think he's a bit of a doofus because he sings while hauling cement, and always the same song, and always in a foreign language, but because he's a hard worker and never complains, they like Brane. They don't know anything about him, except that he's a Bosnian and that he once studied architecture, but not everyone believes that one; there are those who doubt studying could turn so sour you'd end up hauling bags of cement.

Brane doesn't work Sundays. Saturday night he trawls the precinct around the Hauptbahnhof, doing the rounds of the nudie bars, catching a peep show. For five German marks he watches the beautiful Emina who is now called Susanna, and he always meets someone he knows and they go to Serbez's bistro for a beer. At half past one the girls stop by after their shifts, tall blond sex-shop assistants and gloomy Balkan pickpockets with permanently shot nerves. Brane thinks them all good people, and really they are, because at Serbez's they never do anyone any harm, they never fight, they don't even cuss like other people. In the wee hours they try to be like angels to each other, to make Serbez's bistro a place they can transport themselves from the harshness of their lives back to the dreams of their childhoods. Every man and woman on earth can fall asleep like a child, but it's not easy for a whore, or a pimp, to every day become a child.

Everyone needs Brane and a Saturday without him would be too much to bear, because he's the only one who doesn't belong to their world, he comes from someplace far away, from a life they all believe is better, one they all know about, though none have lived. But how can one not believe there is a life where mothers send their children to the store for bread and milk, where days begin with the morning and end with the evening, where postmen bring letters and packages, and where flags everyone believes in flap in the wind, just as one believes in the good fortune of others.

The story Brane tells for the tenth time is set in his former life. It's one they have all already heard but request anyhow, translating it for each other into all the languages of their world: *I'd always loved motorbikes. When I was seven my old man asked me what I wanted to be in life, and I told him a Kawasaki, what do you mean a Kawasaki, kid, his cigarette almost falling out of his mouth, easy, Dad, if there's any way I can be, I'll be a Kawasaki, and if I can't, then I'm going to ride a Kawasaki. The old man said, fine, kid, so long as you're happy and healthy, you can be a donkey for all I care. I bought my first bike in my first year of college, an ancient Bugatti, it didn't last six months before falling apart. Then during the summer break I went to Germany for the first time, as if I knew it would one day have its payoff. I got a job in construction and earned the money for a good bike. It wasn't a Kawasaki but a Honda; I drove it nights from one end of the city to the other, giving it hell, and I thought nothing in life could ever be as great as sheer speed, nor anything ever more beautiful than when you become the wind, no longer a body or a soul, just pure air, like a storm wind on the sea. And there was this girl, Lejla, a wholesome blonde, barely eighteen, a normal kid from a good home, a kid who when she heads out the front door looks to you like a nurse who got lost down a mine and got herself all dirty, but she doesn't see it because she doesn't know anything about any kind of filth. So this Lejla girl says to me: oh, Brane, I'm so scared of motorbikes, I could never do that. I shrug my shoulders, and I'm like, fine, you shouldn't then, who cares, and head on my way. But then she's there again the next day, we talk about some stuff, and I ask her: so, Lejla, how're things at school, and she says: they're good, how else should they be, and I ask her if she's doing her homework, and she says: yeah, of course, and even when I haven't, I just pretend I have, and*

I tell her: lucky for you, Lejla, when I haven't studied enough for an exam, it's as if everything I don't know is written on my forehead, and that's the stuff the professor always asks me. That's because you don't know how to hide it, she says. How would I know when I'm always scared. But you're not scared on a motorbike. No, I'm not, otherwise I wouldn't ride one, I tell her. Then her again: oh, Brane, I'm so scared of motorbikes, I could never do that. And nothing. A week goes by, and there she is again, just after there'd been that earthquake in Montenegro. I say to her, those people jumping out their windows, nothing would have happened to them if they hadn't jumped. I'm not scared of earthquakes, says Lejla. C'mon, how come you're not scared of earthquakes, everyone's scared of earthquakes, everyone normal. I'm not. I wouldn't jump, but when I see you, my heart stops. And again: oh, Brane, I'm so scared of motorbikes, I could never do that. And something clicked in me, that little bad guy who tickles you when a chick is scared of something, so I ask her: you know, Lejla, do you want to go for a little ride, we won't go fast, I'll take good care of you. Jesus, no way, I'd die. Every time when I'd see her after that, I'd say, c'mon, Lejla, just one time, just a lap, and she'd shake her head like a kid when mom tries to get a spoonful of spinach in his mouth. The more she refused, the more I wanted to see her and talk her into it. This went on for I don't know how long, half a year at least, then the spring came and everything was green and sweet-smelling, and girls who back in the winter were still kids hit the streets, one more beautiful than the next, and the most beautiful of them all was little Lejla. I'm sitting on the bike out in front of Café Promenade, and there she is, always one foot in front of the other, she

316

doesn't see me, she doesn't see anyone, she's taking her beauty out for a walk,
conscious of it for the first time in her life, and nothing else matters. I call out
to her: c'mon, Lejla, let's take a ride. She stops, bowing her head a little, like
a kid who's embarrassed. It's hard to know what she is anymore, or who she
is, but I think she's funny, like little girls in bloom often are, in the season
of their lives when just this once they are neither woman nor child. C'mon,
Lejla, don't be like that, I try and persuade her, and she just stares down at
the bike's wheels, then at my shoes, and says: fine, but just one lap. I tell her,
sit close behind me and hold tight. She doesn't want to, she's scared she'll fall
off. Fine, sit in front of me then, and lo and behold, Lejla sits down. We scoot
down Đure Đaković, then off toward Bare, as fast as the bike will go. I can
feel her trembling like a bird, her heart pounding like it's going to stop, and
it's like she's somehow shrinking there in my arms, like she'll soon be a doll.
And when we hit top speed, I whisper to her: I love you, Lejla. We stop, she
looks at me, like she wants to ask me something, she opens her mouth, wants
to say something, but nothing comes out. I think it's funny, I see her all messed
up, not knowing if I really said what I said or if that's just what the fear was
telling her. She's there again the next day and says: c'mon, Brane, just one
more lap, but slowly, please. I know what she wants, she wants to check that
thing from yesterday, and I like that. I sit her on the bike, fire up the Honda
like it's a plane, she trembles and shrinks, I think it's worse than yesterday,
and again when we hit top speed I joke: I love you, Lejla. You know the rest,
we stop, she looks over, like she wants to ask, like she doesn't want to ask, but
nothing happens, we go our own ways. I don't need to tell you what happened

the next day or the one after that, Lejla found me or I'd find her, I'd smile and say nothing because I knew what she's going to say. And we'd do it all again. At top speed I'd tell her: I love you, Lejla. This went on the whole summer long, through the fall too, right up until the winter. A day didn't go by that I didn't take Lejla for a ride and whisper to her that I loved her, and she just trembled every time like it was the first time, her heart pounded, her soul wanting to escape out of blind fear, and when we'd stop, she never knew whether I'd said what I'd said. In February I saw the war was on its way and thought to myself, c'mon, Brane, Germany calls, save your head, show them your back. Your back can haul cement, but your head, hell your head can't take a bullet. So I left, and Lejla stayed. I locked the bike in a garage, an idiot thinking the war would pass and that I'd ride again, but the war didn't pass, and I didn't ride again, and Lejla never asked me for another lap.

Four years went by, and there I was in Sarajevo for the first time. No garage, no bike, my mother and father aged a good twenty years each, no one I know in the city, and no one who knows me. And I think, fine, that's that then, it's all over, you'll be here for a couple of weeks, then back to Germanostan. It was a beautiful spring. I spent the day sitting in those cafés, one minute the sun burning down, the next a cool breeze, I was looking at the façades of the buildings, spotting the bumps in the asphalt, bidding a peaceful farewell to a city still mine, though I'm not hers, when all of a sudden I see someone I know coming from the cathedral, Lejla as beautiful as ever, leading a little girl of about three by the hand, the little one just like her, I'm about to call out to her, I open my mouth, our eyes meet, and she passes by. She doesn't even recognize me. I stay openmouthed like that, an ambulance needed to come close it, Lejla goes by, and here we are, and to this day there's one thing that's not clear to me, and I can't sleep when I think about it, and that is why I was joking when we rode around on the bike. If anyone can answer that question for me, I'll do any job for them. I will, I swear it Emina, if you can tell me why I joked like that, tomorrow I'll be Susanna instead of you.

Nora, like Ibsen's

It was the beginning of January, the year the war ended, and Mahir Kubat found himself at Zagreb's Central Station with no papers and fifty German marks in his pocket. The story of how he got to Zagreb, and why Zagreb and not someplace else, would take too long, it's enough to know that Mahir Kubat had left for good and that he had no particular country in mind, but was pretty set on not hanging around anyplace too close.

A fine snow was falling, you couldn't actually tell whether it was snow or mist, people were waiting for the tram in front of the station, Mahir had a white Adidas bag with his spare sneakers tucked under his arm and was looking at the king on the horse, who appeared to have especially positioned himself to look right in his direction, as if Mahir and the king formed part of a larger whole, having waited for God knows how long to stand here together on an early-winter evening, one across from the other, both with pretty much no show of riding off somewhere, or at least for there to be any point in doing so.

Mahir Kubat wasn't easily panicked; he had these two Clint Eastwood frown lines on his face, and he was well aware of them, it could even be said that he relied on them; a man with these kind of furrows isn't easily rattled, he doesn't surrender to despair, even when as night falls he finds himself in a city without a single number he might dial.

One foot in front of the other, he headed off toward the underground shopping center to the left of the station. Down below the advertising neon blazed, from the sound system the jabbering voice of Oliver Mlakar, kids with shaved heads drank beer in front of the supermarket, and Jehovah's Witnesses sold magazines with apocalyptic headlines. "Find Jesus Before the Catastrophe," that's what it said under the face of some penitent crone. She tried to look Mahir Kubat right in the eye so he might see the face of God in hers. Mahir gave her a wink and a smile. He was on the lookout for a bar where he could have a beer and not piss the whole fifty marks up against the wall. If he were someone else, and not Mahir Kubat, he would have already figured out there's no such bar anywhere in the world.

An Ožujsko if you will, he tried it on like a local, but it came out bearing that excess courtesy characteristic of people who walk the world without papers, bereft of a single document bearing their name and

321

photo, anything to prove their existence. He poured his beer, folded his arms on his chest, stretched out on his stool a little, and just sat there watching the people rushing by the glass window. The melody of a song from the mid-eighties floated around his head, something like *I can't explain the feeling of a slant-eyed girl in the snow*. He'll hang around in here long enough for something to happen. Mahir Kubat thinks it's like he's in a film and that there isn't a film where resolution doesn't come of its own accord. The trick is to not leave the theater before the film ends, because then you just roam the streets like a deaf whore, going from one film to the next, and then finally the panic wears you down.

Around nine there was barely a stool free. Only Mahir sat on his own, surrounded by three of them. Some whiny little homo came over, *may I sit here*, then nothing happened for ages, until a shaven-headed kid and a girl with a mohawk came in, both in leather jackets and high boots painted with British flags. *You're not waiting for someone?* the kid asked, *sit down*, said Kubat through clenched teeth, sharpening those frown lines of his as much as he could.

He held his gaze on the passersby and just waited, not paying the kid and his girl any mind. *Sorry*, the girl took him by the elbow, *do you maybe have a loosey? . . . Do I maybe have a what? . . . A loosey, you got a cigarette? . . . No . . . You're not from Zagreb? . . . Why's that, that bother you? . . . No, it's just you don't sound like it . . . No, I'm not from Zagreb . . . And where are you from, if I may ask, and it won't cause offense*, the girl chuckled sweetly, and Mahir Kubat thought she was okay. The crew-cut kid was okay too. He kept quiet and let the girl do the talking. *I was from Zenica, and now I'm not from anywhere . . . Aha, Mister Nobody . . . No, my name is Kubat, Mahir Kubat*, he said, offering the girl his hand. *Nancy*, she said, crooking her head, *Sid*, said the kid, *aren't you two supposed to be dead?* said Kubat grinning. *Why do you keep looking out the window*, the kid asked. *I'm watching out for someone . . . Someone important? . . . Yeah, he has to come by, 'cause if he doesn't I've got problems . . . If it's not indiscreet, may I ask who that might be?* The girl leaned across the table to catch Mahir's gaze. *No idea, but someone has to come by . . . But you must know why you're waiting for him . . . That I know . . . How long are you going to wait? . . . Until he comes by . . . Do you know anyone in Zagreb? . . . No, but I know maybe a million people who've been in Zagreb, so maybe they'll come by tonight . . . Well, now you know us too*, the kid banged his hand on the table. Mahir Kubat turned away from the window and looked at him, icy as he could, straight in the eye. Sid had these childlike green eyes that turned yellow just before the pupil. *And you, little man, what would you know about all that? . . . Nothing, just what I see . . . What do you see then, wise guy? . . . I see James Bond who doesn't have anywhere to sleep and probably left his checkbook at home, so he's a little anxious . . . I'm not anxious, I am never anxious*, Kubat turned toward the window again and folded his arms. *Whatever, but if you want you can come with us, we've got a place where we all crash.*

The night tram was heading toward Novi Zagreb. Sid was laughing like crazy, Nancy sitting in Mahir Kubat's lap. *You're so cute and grumpy, a real stooge.* At that moment Mahir felt like crying.

They arrived at a tower block in Sopot and took the lift to the eleventh floor. *Whose apartment is it, asked Mahir, Nora's . . . Who's Nora? What's she going to say . . . Nothing, she's probably asleep, and when she wakes up, just tell her my name is Kubat, Mahir Kubat, she'll like that.* The kid took a key out of his pocket, Mahir had no idea what was going on anymore, he took off shoes in the hall, you don't do that here, so what, they're already off, he tiptoed, the two of them were being a bit loud, like no one was asleep, they snuck a glance into the living room where a girl was asleep on the three-seater, *we'll crash here,* said Sid, *you'll have to crash on our sleepodrome,* Nancy took Mahir by the hand, fuck this is like Hansel and Gretel, and led him to a big bedroom where almost the whole floor was taken up by the bed, the biggest bed Mahir Kubat had ever seen in his life. A chick with long blond hair was asleep at one end, and in the middle, almost a meter away, there was another one, the same long blond hair; now Mahir Kubat really had no idea what was going on. There were two and a half meters of empty bed, but it seemed more appropriate for him to go back out in the hall and lie down on the floor. But he can't do that, they've told him it's normal to sleep here, so presumably that's what he needs to do, he must be cold as ice, a man who heads out into the world with fifty marks in his pocket has to be cold as ice, otherwise he's finished at the outset; he thought of Mahatma Gandhi who slept surrounded by women to prove the resolve of his abstinence, or maybe he slept like that for some other reason, it doesn't matter.

He dropped his trousers, took his jersey and shirt off, and in his boxers and a UnisTours T-shirt with the slogan "East and West Kiss Best" on it crept over to the bed. He lay down, the girls didn't flinch. In the darkness he saw the face of the one closest, so still, her lips closed, the face asleep as if dreaming of nothing or maybe she wasn't even there. *She's not there*, thought Mahir Kubat, *I'll never see her again because in the morning I'm gone.* He didn't feel anything in particular for the sleeping girl, but the idea of her and the image saddened him. It was an image far from his reach, in itself of no importance, but nonetheless an image he would never see again, from which he would soon be so far away that he would never know if how it remains etched in his memory is how it really was, or if someday it might just escape him altogether. At that moment, on that bed, Mahir Kubat felt like someone who leaves forever, leaving behind everything his eyes have ever seen, and more than anything else, things he has only seen once and can't even recall anymore.

He turned onto his back and gazed at the ceiling, letting sleep slowly slip up on him, his thoughts imperceptibly sliding away, like the loved ones of a dead man after the janazah. He felt the tears rolling down his cheeks, dripping into his ears, flowing like the Buna and crashing down like the waterfall at Kravice; he was in the seventh grade when they went swimming there on a school trip, he stood beneath the waterfall, the water heavy and strong, and his tears fell, just like they are now, without a sob and without sense, for he knew the water would never again fall from such a height, hitting him straight in the head, in the seventh grade on a school trip to Kravice.

He opened his eyes and it was like someone in a film had drawn broken roller blinds and with a crash and bang introduced a new scene. Maybe he'd slept for just a minute, maybe he'd been asleep for hours. He lay on his side, the girl's wide-open eyes right in front of him. Her face was as it had been while she was asleep, only now her eyes were open. *You are . . .* he whispered, and remembered that he should have started with *I am . . .* but now he didn't know how to swap the words. His lips were stuck on the *m*, clasped shut like an aquarium fish when it catches sight of a soft kitty paw on the other side of the glass. *I'm Nora,* said the girl, *Nora, like Ibsen's Nora.*

He didn't dare move; she thinks she's still asleep, he needs to wait for her to close her eyes and then quietly slip out, he needs to keep quiet and not be from this world. *What do you want to do now?* she said, very, very slowly. *Nothing . . . You want something, you want it, because you wouldn't be here otherwise, that's for sure . . . No, I'm just about on my way . . . Who kisses best? . . . East and West . . . I'm dreaming and I won't remember. Please, you remember, please, please, please . . .* Nora closed her eyes and repeated *please* until her sad face fell back into a deep sleep. Mahir Kubat didn't move a muscle. He waited until he was completely sure Nora was asleep, and he thought that maybe he'd stayed on in her dream, that maybe everything was not yet lost. Nora might dream of him even when he's far away, even when he's gone.

He slid off the bed, crouching he checked if Nora and the girl next to her were asleep, then he grabbed his clothes and tiptoed out into the hall. He closed the bedroom door, a door he'll never open again, and immediately it ceased to exist. He got dressed, took his suitcase, and headed for the front door, and then he stopped, fixed his two Clint Eastwood furrows, scratched his head, and started rummaging through his jacket pockets. He took his keys out and tried to get the key ring off with his fingernails. There was a metal pendant on it, a black-and-red ball with the words "FK Čelik Zenica."

He snuck into the living room, Nancy and Sid were asleep in a hug, her naked, her right leg straddling him; they looked like octopuses in a lover's embrace, their tentacles inseparable. Mahir Kubat went over and put his pendant down beside Nancy's head.

It was freezing outside, the dawn breaking behind four high tower blocks, on the other side the sky still in complete darkness. Mahir Kubat held his suitcase in his right hand, in his left the keys he'd taken off the key ring. He needed to toss them somewhere, but not on the street because someone might find them and think some kid lost them. Mahir Kubat looked for a trash can, but there wasn't one in sight. When he finds one, nothing will stand between his life and his departure.

Death of the president's dog

I.

This is a new start. Like a second honeymoon, said Kosta the day Rajna came back from the hospital. He ripped out the doorstep in the entrance way, leveled out any bumps in the rooms, shifted the wardrobes so the wheelchair could reach every corner of the apartment, even get into the pantry, where once Rajna and her wheelchair were in there you couldn't fit anything or anyone else. She watched him as he worked, and he smiled, holding three nails in his mouth. He waved the hammer here and there, as if it meant something and all the merriment was completely natural, that the goal of every sound and happy marriage was the woman ending up in a wheelchair after three years.

Everything will be okay, he said. *There's so much we can do now that we'd never thought of before.*

At first life continued with a semblance of normalcy. They'd wake every morning at six, he would unfold the wheelchair, lift her out of bed, and say *soon you'll be able to do this by yourself.* She'd wheel herself to the bathroom, him trailing a step behind. He walked with slight pangs of remorse, almost hoping he'd be able to trick her, that Rajna wouldn't notice there was any difference between walking and wheeling. But in the bathroom a ritual began where nothing could be concealed. He removed her underwear, sat her on the toilet seat, and waited.

Wait outside, she told him after a few days. From then on, every morning he smoked his first cigarette of the day slouched down against the closed door. It could be worse, he thought, at least she can control her bodily functions. Ten minutes later, she'd shout *Kosta*, and he'd go in. She had never called him by his name before, she'd said *darling*, or used his surname, Ignjatović, but with things having changed so much, little terms of endearment when summoning the man whose help she needed to perform what she was no longer able to do for herself, well, that just seemed inappropriate.

Their life together reduced to one of home help, she never called him *darling* or Ignjatović again.

After the bathroom they went into the kitchen. Breakfast would bring a kind of calm. She was silent, and he'd talk about his plans for the day. He spoke fast and loud, trying to outrun every silence. It was silence he feared more than anything in those first few months, like a nighttime DJ who knows he can't stop talking, that at the core of every silence slouches the darkness of the abyss.

Stepping out into the street, he would breathe a sigh of relief. At the newsstand in front of the Landesbank he would buy a newspaper and then head off to work. Asked about Rajna he kept his responses brief; his voice cold to the secretary, not hiding that he wished she'd stop talking, and polite to the manager, to whom he gave a good dose of self-pity. *She's brave, she'll get through it all; I don't know about me though.* That's what he'd say. The manager would tap him on the shoulder and walk out.

Kosta would then sit at his desk and begin reading the paper. He read everything, from business and share market updates to the sports section, from the obituaries to the classifieds and inserts; not a scrap of news escaped him, none of it of any relevance. He read and remembered without any obvious sense or purpose, as he had done when his father was dying and he had waited in the park in front of the hospital, so the final word of the day would be one not to cause him pain, a word from the newspaper.

He didn't work a whole lot, generally only toward the end of the day when he'd finished reading the paper and the fear of going home had caught a good hold. He knew what Rajna was going to say, what he'd say in reply, their movements, when they'd head to the kitchen, and when they'd leave the room; he knew everything that was going to happen between now and tomorrow, until the moment he again would shut the door behind him, sigh, and head to the newsstand.

Life's a grind, he said as the closing credits of a Partisan film played on TV. *Life is beautiful*, Rajna replied, her mouth curled up in a cynical smile. He thought of a perch he caught long ago, when he was a kid on the Danube, on a school trip when the teacher showed them how to hook freshwater fish. *Fish are dead creatures, they don't feel anything, they don't know anything, and they're not scared*, that's what the teacher had said with a smile, a perch struggling lazily on the end of his line. The smile seemed to have more to do with the hooking than feeling.

He put Rajna to bed and went into the kitchen, lighting his last cigarette of the day. The water puled in the pipes, the poplars creaked below the window, somewhere in the valley there was the clang of a tram. Kosta sensed that none of it was part of his story anymore. The world, as it does before a journey, had split into two parts: the part left behind, foreign, reduced to sounds that soon would longer be heard, and the part that was opening up before him, predictable and gray, every day the same as the next.

One day you'll leave and never come back, she said to him as he lifted her from the toilet seat into the wheelchair. *Where would I go?* he sighed sulkily. After the first month he was no longer capable of being constantly chipper and polite. *You'll find another woman, and you'll leave me on the toilet . . . Right here on the toilet, huh? . . . Yeah, with a dirty ass.* Stunned and speechless, he looked at Rajna, or rather, at the crown of her head. Her face and eyes were on the other side; like a toy, he only saw her on the side from which he'd set her down. *Words are sometimes uglier than what they mean*, he wanted to sound cold. Rajna had become a talking doll.

There was a note fixed to the front door of their building: "Dear residents! As you know, on the twenty-fifth of August the heart of Osman Megdandžić stopped beating, he was our neighbor and long time president of the homeowners' association. So that our environs, stairwell, laundry room, and attic remain as clean and tidy as they were under the mandate of the sorely missed Osman, a new president needs to be elected. A meeting will be held at half past six this evening. Please show your communal spirit and come along. Signed: Ivan Pehar, retired ensign." Kosta read every word of the message slowly and carefully. Even though they lived next door, he'd never met the sorely missed Osman, he'd never taken a peek in the laundry room, nor had he even been in the attic. But that's okay, sometimes there are things a man doesn't have to know, he thought as he headed to get the paper and went on to work.

There's a homeowners' association meeting at half past six, he told Rajna as soon as he walked in the door. *And you're going of course . . . Yeah, I have to. The president of the homeowners' association has died . . . Interesting. He must have been very young if he was president*, she tried to be ironic. *Well, you know, the building has to be to looked after, no one wants rats breeding and drunks pissing in the stairwell . . . So you'll be leaving me . . . Yes, just for half an hour*, he replied, agitated. Since she'd come back from the hospital he hadn't spent five minutes out of the apartment. Except going to work, but surely there's no way that counts.

Sitting on a wooden school chair, Ensign Pehar was alone in the laundry room at half past six, on his knees a black diary and ancient wooden coloring pencil, the kind where both ends are sharpened, blue at one end and red at the other. After fifteen minutes of waiting Kosta lit a cigarette. He sat on a low three-legged stool. *That's a milking stool*, said Pehar after a long silence. Kosta gave a start and automatically turned toward the door. The ensign raised his index finger: *It's a milking stool! You're sitting on a milking stool.*

They sat there in silence for half an hour. Kosta smoked. Pehar drew blue five-pointed stars on the tabletop. Kosta looked at the clock, Pehar put his pencil and paper down. *It's decided then. There's nothing else for it, you have to be the new president of the homeowners' association. I'm the other candidate, but that won't work – given my delicate past and all*, said Pehar, sweetly stressing the word delicate as if it were a nougat praline and not a word. *So what does the president of the homeowners' association do?* Kosta asked. *Organizes and chairs the meetings. Everything else is up to us*, Pehar replied collecting his notebook and pencil and offering Kosta his hand: *congratulations!*

II.

It was the beginning of September, kids were going back to school, beauties in bright dresses displayed their summer tans for all to see. Kosta was hurrying home from work and for the first time the thought happened upon him that he didn't love her anymore. It terrified him like a wet dream terrifies a bashful monk. We have only one life, and he knew he'd spend his on the route between home and work, moving his wife from the bed to the wheelchair, from the wheelchair to the toilet seat, and from the toilet seat back to the wheelchair . . . That afternoon, for the first time, Kosta sensed his own mortality and that this was how it was going to be until death.

Not knowing what to do, he called a meeting of the homeowners' association.

Ensign Pehar turned up with a bottle of slivovitz and two shot glasses. He poured one for himself, took a little sip, and then poured one for Kosta. They sat in the laundry room until it got dark outside, drank slivovitz, and waited around killing time. They exchanged a few general observations about stairwell hygiene and the security situation in the building. Pehar raised his index finger and said *our strategy has to be* . . . and then let his hand fall dismissively, not knowing how to finish.

My wife's an invalid, said Kosta . . . I didn't know. In that case I wouldn't have saddled you with this . . . It's okay. At least I get to be president of something. A couple of hours here and there . . . You work. She must be on her own all day . . . I can't do anything about that. I don't have anyone to keep her company. Neither a hare nor a hound, as we say. Everyone we used to know around here is either dead or scattered someplace abroad. And then when we were on our own, the accident happened. On a zebra crossing, the light was green, not that it mattered. We made it through the whole of the war and then this, on a zebra crossing . . . I've got something for you, Pehar whispered confidentially. Kosta looked at him, downed his slivovitz, and said he had to go.

The next day the ensign brought the dog over. He was four weeks old, lost his balance when he walked, and whined nonstop. *We'll call him Željko,* said Rajna . . . *But that's a person's name . . . There isn't anyone here to complain. He can be Željko.*

The first few days the dog pissed all over the apartment and took a dump in the most unusual places. Kosta cleaned and wiped up after him, and Rajna thought it was all too funny, like the three of them were in a sitcom where every mishap and misfortune just made people laugh, contented. The first month Željko was a little bigger than a fattish cat, the second he looked like a regular dog with disproportionately huge paws, the third he was already so big that when he tried to sit in Rajna's lap he tipped the wheelchair over. He kept growing even after he looked like an average-size Saint Bernard, and after nine months he looked more like a calf disguised as a dog.

He had a bovine nature too. Hopelessly devoted to Rajna and Kosta, he was scared of everything else: dogs, cats, children, people. He scampered away like they were aliens, aliens who might be stronger than you, or smarter as well, but you weren't sure, and who might turn you into a pumpkin, a mouse, or something even more terrible as an experiment. Kosta took him for long walks in the park and called out after him – hiding in a bush, under a car or a bench – because some little munchkin had scared him to death again, opening his arms to hug him, burbling *doggie, doggie.*

Željko seemed to have completely changed his masters' lives. Kosta stopped reading the paper from cover to cover, he'd leave it on his desk and do other stuff, like flick through dog-food brochures, buy Željko rubber bones, cabbage- or carrot-shaped toys, or a red collar with his name on it. Rajna learned how to arrange things in the house so she could reach Željko's food, and the dog would follow her everywhere she went. She'd wheel around the apartment the whole day, talk to the dog, try to explain things you couldn't say to people, and he looked at her the very way you expect people to look at you, but the way only dogs do: straight in the eye, with endless trust and a hope that nothing is lost and that all is well and that everything will stay the way it is, because time has stopped and days no longer fly by, nothing is evanescent or perishable. With Željko's help Rajna learned how to get from her wheelchair into the armchair and back. He'd sit firm in place, she'd grab a tight hold of his head and perform a maneuver she couldn't explain to Kosta, and which, so she believed, she had learned from the dog – and presto she was in the armchair. The grip didn't work when she tried it using Kosta arms. He offered that she grab hold of his head, but that didn't work either. They laughed until they cried and were happy for the first time. Željko brought the rubber cabbage over and dropped it down in front of them, his contribution to the fun.

III.

My life has completely changed since Željko's been with us, said Kosta raising his glass of slivovitz. *Bless his good mother, we have to look after our president*, said Ensign Pehar clinking glasses with Kosta. *The president has to have his bodyguard . . . Only I don't know who's looking after whom, we him or he us. One day Rajna was telling me about when a cockroach scooted past, and Željko took off under the table!*

They had homeowners' association meetings every Tuesday, fortified by a few short ones and a little cheese. Pehar would methodically put notices up, but no one else ever came, so he and Kosta completely forgot they had any neighbors. Pehar insisted on spending at least five minutes talking about "building infrastructure," a pedantry that amused Kosta no end, but he accepted the game all the same. Later they'd chat about anything and everything, mostly about life, which for both he and Pehar had taken some strange turns. The ensign's wife had died in childbirth in 1958. Seventeen years later, his son, a high-school senior, put a bullet in his temple using Pehar's service pistol. Left on his own, Pehar had spent his life between home and the barracks, until five years ago, as soon as the election results were out, he was pensioned off, or rather, hounded out of the army because he didn't fit within the "new organizational structure."

I don't believe in God, but I'm sure he's been punishing me for some thirty years or more. When Anđa died, I knew that's what he was doing, and I told him, go on then, do your work, and I'll do mine, but I won't believe in you.

And when one day I didn't have a son anymore either, I told him, okay then, now you've taken everything from me, but I'm not giving you anything, you do your work, but you're not getting an empty shell from me. And that's how things stand to this day, he's punishing me because I don't believe in anything to do with him, and I'm alive and I've still never asked myself why I'm alive, said Pehar, completely at ease, as if he was giving his report before taps.

Maybe that's how one manages to live, thought Kosta, reconciled with both his own and Pehar's story.

IV.

Željko was almost two when Rajna suddenly got it into her head that the dog needed to learn something. She tried for days. But when she'd say *shake hands*, he'd try to jump into her lap, four legs and all. When she'd say *bring the ball*, he'd lick her on the nose, and on the command *on your mat*, he'd wag his tail and think he was going to get a biscuit.

The dog doesn't know anything, she said to Pehar that Tuesday when he came by to collect Kosta for their meeting. *Of course he doesn't when no one's taught him,* Pehar replied, clicking his heels, creasing his forehead, and transforming himself into a soldier from a Socialist film journal.

Željko, play dead! he thundered. Željko put his tail between his legs and his head down and began, as if ashamed and not knowing what to do with himself, to turn in a circle in the middle of the room. *Željko, play dead!* he yelled again, pushing the dog to the floor. The dog looked at him confused, and was then even more confused when Pehar gently patted him, turned to Rajna, and in a somewhat more restrained command, as if addressing a sergeant in front of a regular soldier, said: *Rajna, biscuit!* Rajna handed him a dog biscuit in the shape of a bone and Pehar gave it to Željko, who was already beside himself with surprise.

That night they skipped the homeowners' association meeting, but Željko had learned the first thing in his life: to play dead and get a biscuit for it.

Rajna and Kosta repeated the *Željko, play dead!* game over and over.

The dog quickly understood that the game gave his masters incredible pleasure. Later, whenever he sensed Rajna was sad or that Kosta had come home from work a bit uptight, he'd lie down of his accord and play dead. He knew it would cheer them up.

It was a Sunday, a week before Christmas, when Rajna's condition deteriorated. The nausea started in her stomach, spread through her body, and settled in her thoughts and head. *Everything's messed up*, she said just before her head slumped over.

Kosta ran to the telephone, the dog paced around the room, out of sorts and whining. The ambulance was there in ten minutes.

In the morning, Kosta was there standing in front of a hospital room holding a plastic bag full of oranges. They didn't let him see Rajna. *She's sleeping now*, said the nurse. *How long's she been asleep*, Kosta asked. The nurse didn't answer him.

The doctor was tall and blond. Like a German in a Partisan film. Except he had sad eyes, and neither Germans nor doctors have sad eyes.

An aneurysm, he said . . . *She's asleep? . . . No. Your wife's not asleep . . . She's awake?* The doctor shook his head and lowered his gaze. *She's alive? . . . Yes, she's still alive.*

On the way home he didn't know what to do with the oranges. He had to dump them somewhere because he thought someone, some angel, might be betrayed if he should simply carry them in over the threshold. The oranges.

He went into the post office, people were busy filling in their payment forms, he put the bag down on the counter and walked out. He didn't have to run, Kosta was already invisible to them.

V.

He sat in the armchair and smoked. Night fell, and the things in the room disappeared one after the other, but Kosta didn't turn the light on. At the other end of the room sat Željko, watching him. One needs to believe in God, thought Kosta. I'll tell Pehar that tomorrow. He has to believe because he knows God exists. I can't because I don't know that. The cigarette had burned down between his fingers. He tried to pull himself together and decide what to do. To turn on the television, turn on the light, go to the kitchen, to the bathroom, wherever, to give Pehar a call, take Željko to the park, to do something, anything . . . Everything he thought of dissolved before his eyes. He looked at the glow of the cigarette, which had already completely burned down. He stubbed the butt out and started to cry. He knew the telephone would ring any minute now. No one had to tell him that.

Željko came over in near silence, as if every strip of parquet felt the pain of his footsteps, and then at Kosta's feet he collapsed like a dead dog. He looked at his friend out of the corner of his eye, expectantly awaiting a smile. At that moment nothing in the world was more important than his smile.

The second kiss of Gita Danon

I'm going to tell you about Lotar. You don't have to remember the story, there's no life wisdom to be had, it'll be of no use to you, you'll never meet such a man and then know how to handle him, I'm telling you about Lotar because of the woman who loved him, she's real, maybe you'll meet her, her or a woman like her, maybe you'll fall in love with her, maybe she'll stay with you for a lifetime, or maybe you'll just pass by her, see her in the supermarket and say *good morning, Gita, how are you, Gita*, but she won't answer, because Gita doesn't answer, Gita is deaf to every greeting.

In those years Lotar was the strongest man in the city. That's what people said, though no one ever really thought about testing it. He lived alone with his mother, Miss Edita, who had a shop where she pleated skirts. No one knew anything about his father. The story went that he had been a German officer, apparently his name was Otto, and that it had been a great love. He would secretly visit Miss Edita at night and stay until the dawn. No one ever saw him, as their love could only be in the time of the curfew. Otto, so the story goes, didn't want to retreat with the rest of his army in April 1945, so he deserted and hid out in the forests above Sarajevo for two years. Every Saturday and Sunday Miss Edita would go and collect mushrooms, strawberries, raspberries, always returning with an empty basket. *Dear God, you know I only go up there for the fresh air and the scenery*, she told the neighborhood women, but they knew she went because of Otto. Lotar was born in the fall of 1946: *it's a child I wanted, not a husband*, said Miss Edita, and no one ever inquired further. In an exception to the usual ugly custom, the neighborhood kept her secret and no one ever called Lotar a bastard. This was probably because he was an exceptionally placid and quiet child, always bigger and stronger than his classmates, but he never got into fights. It was as if every belligerence in his bloodline had been expended and exhausted before he was born.

One Sunday in the early summer of 1947, Miss Edita took the child into the hills. *He needs to learn from a young age*, she said to old Mrs. Džemidžić, who kissed her and the child: *you just go, sweetie, and hold tight to what you've got while you've got it*. They came back in the early evening. That was the last time Miss Edita went up into the hills, and people said that after that Otto had set off for Austria on foot, and then on to Germany. He'd waited to see his son, and then he'd gone home forever.

Lotar graduated high school and as a star student enrolled to study medicine, and right when you would have thought that everything in his life was going to be like it was in those stories about happy and healthy children, in his third year of college he met Gita Danon, a pharmacist's daughter, two years older than him. Gita studied a little, but spent most of her time hanging out and breaking men's hearts, all over Sarajevo, drunk and wild, as if she were breaking beer bottles until the morning came to clear her head. But the morning never did come for Gita, nor did she ever tire of her strange game. She would draw a man slowly to her, toy with him until the first kiss, and then she'd push him down the street, letting him roll to the end, to his shame and the horror of others who hadn't yet felt Gita's charms but knew their turn would come and that they too wouldn't be able to resist her. The men would get over Gita after a time, wouldn't mention her for a while, but sooner or later lips that had once tasted her kisses would say Gita was a whore. The only one who never got over Gita, who never spoke an ugly word about her, was Lotar, and both she and this reticence would change him and his life.

I'll wait for you, it doesn't matter how long, but I'll wait for you, and you'll come for me when you finally tire, he told her after their kiss, and she laughed, she laughed long strolling down Tito Street and on into the night, she laughed so hard the shop windows trembled and women came to the windows to see why someone was laughing so at this hour and in a world where nothing was that funny, where no one had a belly laugh like Gita, who wasn't from this world in any case, and who not a single woman thought of as competition because she lived a life bestowed with a thousand lovers and a lone kiss, and come tomorrow she might be dead.

Lotar believed Gita would come back to him and that until her return he must defend her honor. In company, if anyone ventured to say something about her, Lotar would always cut in *shut up, I'm here.* And miraculously, everyone did shut up, even though no one really thought Lotar might use his terrifying strength. This is how things went until Gita chewed up Dino Krezo, a hothead and ex-jailbird who had marauded his way around Italy for years, returning to Sarajevo only to show off and spend a bit of money. So anyway, this Krezo was beside himself with rage, and to add insult to injury, someone told him about Lotar, probably warning him in jest about mouthing off about Gita in front of Lotar. Krezo immediately demanded *you're going to show me this guy* and tore over to the medical school. They say he waited two or three hours, which only served to enrage him further, so when Lotar finally came out, Dino Krezo no longer registered the size and kind of man he was talking to but just went up to him, grabbed him by his coat collar, pressing himself up under Lotar's face and saying in the quiet voice of a man who had a pistol tucked in his belt, *fuck you and your fucking Kike whore.*

What happened next is almost not for the telling, but they say Lotar grabbed Krezo by both ears and ripped them off, and the poor bastard collapsed, Lotar smacking his head in as he lay there on the ground. When the police arrived, there was nothing left of Krezo's face. Four cops jumped Lotar, but he tossed them off, walked toward the street, sat down on a low wall, lit a cigarette, and from three or four meters away the cops cocked their pistols, not daring come any closer. *It's all over now*, he said, *I killed a man*. It was then they hurled themselves on him, pounding him viciously with their fists, legs, and the butts of their pistols. Somehow they knew Lotar would never defend himself. Perhaps they had experience with this sort of thing, though I doubt they had ever come across a man like Lotar.

He was sentenced to fifteen years for a "particularly brutal murder." Lotar sat a whole twelve years in the Zenica prison, just long enough for the city to forget him and for a new generation to appear on the streets, one that would never know anything about him or Dino Krezo. But Gita, no one could forget her. Through the years her beauty and laughter had not diminished in the slightest, nor had she quit driving men crazy with her lone kisses. Her lovers were now some fifteen years younger than her, but nothing had changed, and a man was yet to come along who could resist Gita giving him the eye, nor was there anyone in the whole city smart enough to work out that a story repeated for the hundredth time must always end the same way.

That summer when Lotar got out of prison, Miss Edita Burić, the owner of a workshop for pleating skirts, and Mr. Moni Danon, the oldest pharmacist in the city, both died on the same day. Two days later they were buried at the same time in the Bare Cemetery. One procession set off from the Catholic chapel, the other from the Jewish one. Lotar followed behind one coffin, Gita behind the other. The processions marched one beside the other, right up to the fork where the paths leading to the Catholic and Jewish plots veered off. Gita didn't even look at Lotar, but instead of following his mother's coffin, Lotar went after Gita. It was a terrible scandal. The crones in black made the sign of the cross, the priest said extra prayers, the Catholic procession appalled, the Jewish one afraid. Nobody knew what Lotar might do to Gita.

But he didn't do anything to her, just said *hello, Gita*, yet she didn't respond to his greeting, he said *Gita, I'm waiting for you*, and she looked at him as if she was going to smile, he said *Gita, this is forever*, and she took him by the hand and said *sweetheart, that in front of me is forever*, and pointed to the coffin.

After his release from prison Lotar started up his drinking. He drank with discipline and according to a set calendar, every seventh of the month, you could see his father was a Kraut, that's what people in the neighborhood said, and not without respect. This is how it went: Lotar would find some dive and order a liter of rakia, the guests would start making tracks for the door, and Lotar's husky *no* would stop them dead. They'd all fall silent and wait to see what would happen next, you could hear the buzzing of a fly and, every three minutes, the neck of the bottle touch the glass. Lotar needed exactly fifty-five minutes to drink a liter of rakia, not a minute more, not a minute less. Then he'd order another liter, dutifully pay the waiter and then thunder *everyone out!* and they'd leave all right, the owner and the waiters too, without even a word to Lotar. Fifteen minutes later the police would show up, Lotar would rise to his feet, and say *hit me before I fuck you up, you, Tito, and the Party*, and they'd give him a thrashing, he wouldn't defend himself, and afterward they'd take him down to the station, he'd sleep it off in the pen, and wait again for the seventh of the month. For five years Lotar took a beating once a month, and tongues were already talking about how much longer he could survive, how many more sevenths of the month the police might need to kill him.

And then the war began, and one September morning during the first siege Lotar found a note under the door: "If you want to know. I'm in Madrid. Gita." She'd probably been scared of the war and had left Lotar a message, anxious as to whether in Madrid too there would be someone to desire her lone kiss. Gita was already fifty years old, which Sarajevo eyes didn't notice but maybe Spanish eyes would, and Gita wouldn't be Gita without a kiss; she'd never make it alone in a world without her humiliated men.

So now, whether Lotar hoped his waiting was finally over, that Gita had tired and exhausted herself and was waiting for him in Madrid with her love, or he simply couldn't imagine staying on in a city where Gita wasn't, it's hard to say, but from that day on Lotar began planning his escape from the city to Spain. He didn't have any money, nor did he have a passport, and didn't know how he might acquire one or the other either. A giant alone in his own city. He started to skip sevenths of the month, his kidneys and ribs hurt, and with every day that passed following Gita's message, Lotar aged more and more. His hair turned white, his muscles no longer smooth and taut, more and more people would pass him by, blind to his strength. Only one thing remained as monumental as Trebević: his will to go to Madrid, to his Gita, for a second kiss.

Two and a half years after the war started, Lotar vanished from the city. Before leaving he'd tried to borrow money for the journey, but no one wanted to lend it to him; people were sure that there was no returning from such a journey. He tried to get a passport, but they didn't want to give him one of those either, he was still strong enough to fight and his love held no sway with the authorities. No one was surprised that Lotar left in spite of all this. People knew that when it came to getting to her, what existed between he and Gita allowed no obstacle, even when she was as far away as Madrid.

No one ever found out how Lotar made it across Bosnia, how he made it across all the countries that stood in his way, the manner or mode of how he traveled, or how he never encountered a single customs officer or policeman. What is known is that he appeared like a ghost at a police station in suburban Madrid, skinny, barefoot, and covered in scabs. He took the first policeman by the hand and said *Gita Danon, por favor*, the man took fright, Lotar repeated *Gita Danon, por favor*, and the whole of the station gathered, and backup arrived too, as did an ambulance, and Lotar stubbornly repeated *Gita Danon, por favor*; it took the Spaniards half a day to work out that he didn't know a word of Spanish, so they tried in different languages, in German, Italian, English, and French, one even tried to address him in Hungarian; Lotar shook his head, clasped his hands in prayer, or took people's hands in his and repeated *Gita Danon, por favor*.

A man in a white hospital coat took him by the arm and led him out of the police station, *Gita Danon, por favor*, Lotar gazed out the window of the ambulance, the man held his hand, and he glided through Madrid as if in a film, as if in someone else's life, Lotar hunted the faces of passersby, hoping he'd see Gita; instead he spotted a billboard for a charity event, on it a photograph of Sarajevo's razed National Library. *Sarajevo*, said Lotar, *Sarajevo?* the man in the white coat gave a start, *Sarajevo*, Lotar confirmed, *Gita Danon, por favor*, and clasped his hands.

Lotar lay in a hospital bed. His heels poked out through the bars. So frail and with his bushy beard he looked like the long-dead branch of a magnificent tree. A kindly older gentleman approached his bed, behind him followed a policeman and a doctor, the man sat down next to Lotar, Lotar opened his eyes, *Gita Danon, por favor*, the gentleman put his hand on Lotar's shoulder and said to him in their language *are you from Sarajevo? . . . I am . . . When did you get here? . . . Yesterday . . . From where? . . . From Sarajevo*. The gentleman's eyes began to glisten the way the eyes of Bosnians who've lived for twenty years someplace far away glisten when a dying man says that he has just arrived from Sarajevo. *I'm looking for Gita Danon*, Lotar tried to sit up, *she's from Sarajevo, and now she's in Madrid, I have to find Gita Danon, she's waiting for me, and I've been waiting twenty years and some for her.* The gentleman nodded his head, *we'll turn Madrid upside down if we have to,* Lotar didn't believe him, but he was too tired to move.

That night in Madrid the strongest man of our city lay dying. This you have to know because you'll never meet such a man again anywhere. There isn't one anywhere in the whole world, not where you live, and not in Sarajevo were you to go looking for him. Yes, Lotar lay dying, the one and only Lotar, the Lotar who had ripped Dino Krezo's ears off and beat him to a pulp on the cobblestones in front of the medical school, as well he should have, when it was for Gita's honor.

In the morning he never regained consciousness. He didn't even wake when the gentleman from the day before came in, nor when Gita Danon came in after him, crouched next to his bed, and placed her hands on Lotar's enormous elbow, he didn't even wake when she said *my darling Lotar, I wore myself out, you don't need to wait for me anymore, I've come to you,* he didn't even wake when she kissed him long on his gray lips. But listen well to what I'm telling you now, only Gita Danon knows whether Lotar's lips moved back then, only she knows whether it was too late for love or whether it had remained forever. If you meet her, don't ask her anything because she won't say, she won't say hello, Gita doesn't respond to greetings, because she broke a thousand hearts for a single Lotar.